MAYDAY!

"We've got a SAM tracking us!" Kruger shouted. "Break hard left!"

The Phantom made a hard break and Vince fought to look down and back, the great pressures pinning him to his seat.

The SAM was breaking through the clouds and arching over to follow his break. Vince rolled the jet over on its back and tore several panels off the wings in an attempt to outtwist the SAM.

But he never got into the dive that would have eluded the Soviet missile. The impact wasn't violent. It sounded like the tap of a nickel on a tabletop, and only made the F-4 lurch slightly.

But every panel light in front of him turned bright red—and suddenly the inside of the cockpit glowed like a Christmas tree. . . .

ACTION ADVENTURE

FLIGHT OF THE PHANTOM

BY RICHARD PARQUE

ZEBRA BOOKS
KENSINGTON PUBLISHING CORP.

ZEBRA BOOKS

are published by

Kensington Publishing Corp.
475 Park Avenue South
New York, NY 10016

First printing: July 1987

Printed in the United States of America

Chapter 1

A fork of lightning split the low-hanging clouds and thunder boomed through the hills, rumbling across the villages ringing Da Nang.

The air was hot, cooking the tropical rain—the drops large and coming down hard on Colonel Dasher's clean, bald head. Cleanhead, the troops called him. Every morning he carefully shaved his pate smooth and curried his red handlebar mustache before dressing in the starched utilities laid out fresh on his bunk by his personal hooch maid.

Cleanhead scanned the sky with his gunmetal-gray eyes, rock jaw jutting into the rain, his wet cigar smoking between clenched mule teeth. The lightning fork quivered, then faded, leaving a phantom image where it had cracked the sky. The rain fell steadily, streaking Dasher's head with rivulets of water that ran down his neck and into the collar of his starched utilities. He remained unmoved, bullet eyes frozen on the sky, humming the "Marine Corps Hymn" as he always did when he was thinking about his men. The silver eagles on his shoulders seemed agitated: they wanted to fly, but the weather had grounded them.

Colonel Cleanhead Dasher sensed danger out there in the clouds. He cocked his ear to the north, up the unfinished 5000-foot-long runway and toward the jade sea, listening during the breaks of thunder; he paced back and forth in front of the jeep, waiting out the long painful wait that he never got used to.

"Should be hearing them soon—that right, Sergeant?"

"Right, Colonel—they should be over Da Nang TACAN right about now."

"Who led this one?—Blackjack again?"

"Yes, sir—Major Bamburger took them in—should be a good strike."

"Bamburger's a good man—one of the best." Dasher's eyes stretched to see through the soup; he paced faster and bit down harder on his shredded cigar, hands clasped behind the small of his back. His craggy, weathered face showed the strain of many years of war. "Is Lieutenant Battaglia flying Blackjack's wing?"

The sergeant gave Dasher a glance out of the corner of his eye and turned back to the paperback he was reading under the protection of the jeep's canopy. "Affirmative, Colonel."

"Good—that's where I want him in case there's any trouble."

"There's always trouble, sir."

Cleanhead hadn't heard the sergeant—he was walking out closer to the flight line, his spit-shined boots splashing over the tarmac, uniform soaked through and a thin veil of steam rising from his shoulders. He laid a big hand over his eyes to shield them from the rain and looked up, moving his eyes over one patch of sky to the north.

Far out on the perimeter a 105 howitzer barked, and a few seconds later the round exploded ten miles away on the crest of the hills ringing the western approach to the base. Behind the clouds Huey gunships raked the forest with their door guns, flying crisscross patterns over a pinned-down patrol and firing red smoke for the med-evac choppers coming in close behind. In twenty minutes

6

the assault would be over—the wounded on the operating tables in ten.

Dasher's back was to the hills, he was facing north and east in the direction the F-4s would come. During the last few minutes he waited he closed down, like he always did, drawing into himself, stilling the voice of the little man perched on his shoulder; he fought the memory, not allowing it into his brain, strangling the little man on his shoulder before the words came out of his mouth.

The wet, hot wind blew down the runway and slashed into Dasher's face. He didn't even blink. "Have you picked them up yet?" he shouted to the sergeant.

The sergeant dropped the paperback onto the seat next to him and adjusted the squelch knob. "I've got the lead elements, Colonel. They're feet-wet, approaching the coast." There was a pause: "Joy Ride reports one of the ships in trouble."

Dasher was leaning against the dripping roof canvas on the jeep, his face etched with anxiety. His words were spaced and clearly enunciated, purposely controlled: "Who is it, Sergeant?"

He looked up at the colonel, pain in his eyes. "Victor-Whisky-Five: it's Lieutenant Battaglia."

Dasher turned his head up into the rain. "Keep me apprised of his condition."

The sergeant nodded and went back to his paperback. Lightning flashed over the field and there was a loud clap of thunder, causing him to recoil against the backrest; the book flew out of his hands and splashed onto the tarmac. The colonel stood steady as a rock, statue-still, head slightly tilted back looking thirty degrees above the horizon, out to sea, the rain pounding on his skin head.

Cleanhead loved the Marine Corps, he loved his jets, and he loved to command. Most of all he loved his men; his affection was imbedded deep. He understood them because he was one of them, and he marveled at their

7

courage to repeatedly climb into confined, lonely cockpits and fly north into the most awesome assortment of hellish weaponry ever created. He wondered if their resolute bravery could sustain them at Ban Dau.

The pilots and troops complained a great deal about his tyrannical, hard-ass methods of command and they cracked jokes about his skinned scalp; but to them Cleanhead was a great Marine, the last of the old corps, a patriot and career grunt who went to any length for his men, rank be damned.

The troops in his command had a great respect for his record and taught each new man who came aboard the wing that the colonel was a man to be reckoned with. They tangibly demonstrated an affection for their commanding officer by building him a private shower that never ran out of hot water, by providing him with a steady diet of pretty hooch maids smuggled in from Da Nang City and Chu Lai, and by making sure that he was never without iced Thai beer, his favorite.

"How's that pilot doing, Sergeant? I told you to keep me posted on his condition," he said through clenched teeth, cigar held tightly at the corner of his mouth.

"The radio is pretty garbled, sir—he's still coming though, approaching the coastline. Joy Ride says he's low on fuel and may have to punch out. Hydraulic pressure is falling too."

The klaxon went off—a long-and-a-short, a long-and-a-short—and pilots and their RIOs sprang from the hot pad, sprinting for their aircraft parked at the end of the runway. The klaxon blared the incessant cry over the field and the ground crews were up and readying the jets for their commanders. By the time the pilots and backseaters reached the planes and put their boots into the footholds and clambered up into the open cockpits, a corporal was waiting on top, knee on the cockpit rail, ready to help strap the pilot into the confined seat and assist him with the preflight checks.

Five howitzers were firing now and the puffs of smoke on the top of the hills were mixing together to form a spreading pall that drifted eastward over a company of North Vietnamese Army regulars that had slipped from their redoubt in the mountains and encircled a Marine recon unit patrolling outside the base's perimeter guard. The patrol called for air support and thus the hot pad was activated. In less than five minutes the two loaded F-4 Phantoms would be launched to give the troops relief so they could safely remove from their tenuous position. The helicopter gunships had expended their ordnance and were withdrawing behind the med-evac choppers, making way for the jets to make a napalm drop on the NVA force.

The whine of jet turbines sounded across the tarmac and Colonel Dasher turned his head away from the sea and toward the end of the runway where the two Phantoms were ready to roll with full racks of napalm and rockets. The canopies came down over the pilots' gold helmets and snapped shut as the ground crews pulled the wheel chocks and the crew chiefs signaled the pilots onto the runway.

Cleanhead smiled into the rain and stood with his arms folded over his chest, feet planted squarely on the edge of the runway; the Phantoms taxied past him. His back stiffened and he returned the salutes of the pilots rolling into their turn for engine run-up and takeoff.

"Plaster them, boys," Dasher shouted into the rain. The pitch of idling engines rose until the twin J79s screamed at full power. The exhaust blast vaporized the rain behind the aircraft and the air turned hot, swirling around Dasher who thrust his head forward breathing the fumes deeply into his lungs. "The perfume of the gods," he said.

The aircraft commanders released their brakes and,

9

wingtip to wingtip, the jets accelerated full-throttle down the runway, tires rooster-tailing water behind the tail fins until they reached 120 knots and the pilots rotated into the air, immediately heeling the heavily armed planes over into the hills.

Before the F-4s disappeared into the clouds, Dasher had turned back to the sea to continue his vigil of the strike force returning from its bombing mission in North Vietnam. "Sergeant!" he bellowed. "What's Battaglia's condition?"

"No change, sir."

A jet-fighter pilot himself, Dasher had flown two hundred missions from Da Nang and from carriers steaming off the coast before turning over the stick to the younger toads. As a young lieutenant in World War II he flew F-4U Corsairs against the Japanese, downing ten Zeros in the battle of the Coral Sea. In Korea he flew the first Marine jets—Banshees—from the U.S.S. *Hornet*, supporting Marines fighting their way back from the Chosen Reservoir while twenty divisions of Chinese swarmed across the Yalu. By the time the war was over he had flown more than six hundred missions off the *Hornet*'s deck and shot down six Migs.

So now, in Vietnam, commanding the Marine air wing, he knew what Battaglia was feeling as he nursed his shot-up jet over the South China Sea, fighting the controls to bring the plane into Da Nang. He understood the slippery feeling in the pilot's stomach, knowing that the man would soon have to decide if he was going to punch out or try to bring the plane in. He knew the terrible fear that haunted Battaglia when flying north—the fear of being shot down and captured, having to endure the humility and torture of becoming a prisoner of the North Vietnamese and paraded in the streets and before the television cameras as a sideshow freak and bloodthirsty monster that lusted in murdering innocents. And he

10

knew the bitter taste in Battaglia's mouth—the taste that comes when you don't know if you have enough fuel to get home and the tankers can't refuel your aircraft because your probe won't separate.

Colonel Dasher's line of sight traveled out beyond the base and over the flat countryside that was rich with alluviul soil from the hills and far mountains of the northern highlands. It was there in the mountains that mud Marines slugged it out with the tough Viet Cong and NVA, spending their thirteen-month tour laid up in red-dirt fighting holes, living with rats and jungle rot, isolated in heavily defended enclaves with romantic-sounding names like Fire Base Zebra and Murphy's Bar East. To keep them alive, Dasher's jets would fly as many as ten missions a day, sometimes more, dropping ordnance into the mountains and the valleys, keeping the elusive communists at bay; for it was now a defensive war the Americans were fighting, pulled back into their outposts and perimeters.

He sent his boys into North Vietnam too, into Ho Chi Minh's front yard to hit the rail yards and bridges, barracks and storage areas, and into Laos to bomb the truck yards and staging routes, and the Ho Chi Minh Trail, that bur-under-the-collar that brought a continual flow of enemy supplies from North Vietnam into South Vietnam.

Never in the history of warfare were the odds so great against a fighting man. An aviator flying the route packages north couldn't avoid advertising his flight path, and the North Vietnamese were always ready for him with a well-coordinated defense of antiaircraft guns, surface-to-air missiles, and Migs. Dasher's men had to learn tactics of surrival that were never dreamed of in flight school, never mentioned in the manuals, tactics that were successful in the face of terrible odds. It was a crazy war, regulated by dumb restrictions, like the rule

11

from Washington that wouldn't allow a pilot to attack a Mig while it was taking off or landing at its base.

As frustrating and confusing as the war was, the pilots flew professionally, and Dasher couldn't have been prouder. He knew their difficulties and he fought for aircraft design improvements, the lifting of target restrictions, and for small comforts that would make the air crews' tour of duty more tolerable.

While his eyes searched the skies for his returning ships, one of which was in big trouble and might not make it back, Colonel Dasher thought for a moment of the other Vietnam that lay at the end of the runway and that stretched along the fertile coast south to Nha Trang and Cam Ranh and Vung Tau, and north to the ancient capital of Hue and the DMZ. The verdant countryside was alive with waist-high rice growing in wide fields sectioned off by crisscross patterns of earthen dikes. These green checkerboard paddies were the life of the people and it had been so for hundreds of years. Not only did the rice bring sustenance, but it provided the roots of a people, the spiritual comfort and mental strength that comes with knowing that the land is there and that as long as it is there the people will be there too, growing the rice, raising families, marrying, dying and going back to the land.

The only hope these people had for the future was in the land. Take the land away from them and they were through, for they had no faith in governments. Cleanhead had studied Vietnam not only as a military commander but also as a philosopher, and he was amazed at the stupidity with which the war was being managed. No one in Washington had taken the time to learn the culture or what it was that motivated the common Vietnamese; therefore, the Americans were blundering from engagement to engagement, winning the battles but losing the war, stymied by the political and economic problems that directed the course of the conflict. No one concerned themselves with the people's land.

The klaxon came alive again, this time announcing the arrival of crippled jets returning from the strike over the north: "All personnel, now hear this: several flights of Fox-Fours will be landing in five minutes. At least one aircraft will be coming in with battle damage. All emergency equipment to the flight line." The loudspeaker repeated the message several times, but it was unnecessary, for crash trucks and ambulances with sirens screaming were already racing from parking spaces on the apron to their emergency positions on the line.

The rain was falling steadily and the ground crews and maintenance personnel taking shelter from the storm squatted under the wings and fuselages of parked aircraft and watched the emergency vehicles tear past them on their way to the flight line. Others with more immediate duties wheeled bomb racks into position under planes and loaded 500-pounders without regard to the downpour. The war went on despite the inconvenience of dirty weather.

"Battaglia is bringing his aircraft in, Colonel," the sergeant said. "He thinks he can make it; he's coming straight in low on fuel; hydraulic power is fluctuating badly and he's fighting the controls."

Dasher stiffened. "The kid's got balls—he's going to get a DFC for this."

In Battaglia, Cleanhead had more than the usual concern he showed for pilots. Dasher had lost an only son over the north and Vince Battaglia resembled the young man in a most remarkable way. He had the same quick, alert ways, flashing smile, powerful build, and dark features. Like the colonel's son, Battaglia was an exceptional pilot with an intense, competitive personality and drive to excel. Also, Vince was twenty-seven years old, the same age the colonel's son would have been if

13

his F-4 hadn't been blown apart by 100mm guns when bombing Ban Karai.

But unlike Dasher's son, Battaglia was not a Marine lifer and had no intention of making the corps his career. He enjoyed civilian life too much and Vietnam was his great bitterness. He resented the Marines for calling him up from his reserve unit and putting him on active duty to fly combat missions while the rest of his friends back in the States continued to progress in their professions, leading normal, uninterrupted lives.

Battaglia in Victor-Whisky-Five looked down at the hole in the floor between his legs and watched the South China Sea drop behind him. The coastline and the green checkerboard pattern of rice paddies slipped into view underneath the dangling wires and pieces of torn metal flapping in the wound made by the SAM. He scanned the gauges for the hundredth time since the SA-2 had exploded into the belly of his Phantom, and noted that he was dropping faster now, 500 feet a minute, and he was down to 6000 feet. His air speed had dropped off to 150 knots and the field at Da Nang was still miles away.

"Still think you can make it, Vince?" Blackjack said, flying next to him.

"Roger, Dash One—got it knocked." He grimaced in pain behind his oxygen mask and his hand involuntarily went to his bleeding leg.

"You still have time to punch out."

"Negative, Dash One; I'm bringing it in," Vince said. "Drop down and look me over again."

"You're still losing fuel and hydraulic fluid." Blackjack brought his plane up the other side. "You can drive a truck through the hole in your fuselage. SAM sure did a number on you."

With his left engine shot out and flying on reduced

14

power, and the controls ready to freeze up on him any minute, Battaglia's position was precarious. He could attempt a bailout but his instruments showed an ejection-system malfunction and his chances of survival were about 1 in 4; he figured his odds were better staying with the jet.

The other option, ditching at sea, was discarded because the F-4 was a proven tomb in a crash landing. The main fuel cells directly behind the cockpit would be torn apart by the heavy engines breaking loose from their mounts and driving forward. He would be crushed in the weakly structured cockpit, and a fire would immediately erupt. The intelligent choice was to try for the base and a wheels-down landing—that is, if the gear functioned properly, the hydraulic system didn't fail, and the fuel lasted.

"Better go through your final checks," Blackjack said. "You don't want to get caught short if she quits on you."

"Roger, Dash One."

While he went through the checks with his radar operator in the backseat, he glanced at the clock, noting the time difference between Da Nang and Wichita. He thought of his friends and relatives back home living out their normal lives. Hank, his partner in a successful consulting business, would be dining with a client; Ruthie, his fiancée who had broken their engagement when he got orders to 'Nam, would be watching the Friday night movie on channel nine with her mother and sister, if she didn't have a date; and his father would be cleaning his shotgun like he always did on the eve of opening day of the pheasant season. Mom would be reading her favorite poet, Whittier.

And here he was on a bleak rainy morning in Southeast Asia, fighting to keep a Marine Corps jet in the air, his life riding the razor edge of decision. *Why me? Why did it have to be me?*

Blackjack eased his Phantom up next to Vince and the two men looked at each other across the fifty feet of airspace. Vince knew that Blackjack had never liked him much; they didn't have a lot in common and spoke to each other only when necessary and then only in the briefest terms.

Blackjack had a way of giving orders that Vince found offensive, and being a civilian at heart, Vince didn't hide his impatience with Blackjack's show of military authority. Though Blackjack Bamburger was a good officer and flyer, Battaglia resented being under the major's command. The two men were both from the same cut of cloth: aggressive and highly competitive perfectionists, each felt the need to be out in front. Friction was naturally created between the two men and there wasn't room in the same corral for both of them.

Bamburger had trouble accepting Vince's relationship with Colonel Dasher. Cleanhead had called Battaglia out from the rest of the airmen, and though the colonel was diplomatic about his favoritism, Blackjack resented the competition. More importantly, as a professional he knew the effect this could have on his own career if he was unable to influence his superior's good favor.

On top of all this, Battaglia was a reserve pilot brought into active duty and couldn't care less about a Marine Corps career. Privately, Blackjack referred to Vince as *the civilian*.

To conserve fuel, Vince throttled back and the jet grew nose-heavy, dropping too fast. When he brought the nose up to increase the glide path so he wouldn't run out of altitude short of the base, the Phantom shuddered along its airframe, signaling a stall. He held it there, playing with the edge of the envelope, gaining as much distance as possible before dropping the nose again and increasing the angle of attack. It was a dangerous game he was playing, trading elevation for fuel, for with each

16

porpoising manuever the jet dropped several more hundred feet in precious altitude.

The Phantom had developed a left yaw and he had to keep applying rudder to stay on course, further cutting his airspeed. In the dense air at the lower altitude he was flying, together with his reduced airspeed and a crippled hydraulic system, the F-4's control surfaces were heavy and he had to exert all his strength on the stick to manuever the ship and keep it on the flight path.

In the back of his mind was the final question: Would the landing gear come down and lock? This was something he wouldn't know until the long runway at Da Nang came into view and he was on final approach, a bet that he wouldn't be giving any odds on if there was someone around to take it.

The probability that he would even come in sight of the base before augering into the ground was slim, let alone getting the landing gear down. The bitterness swelled up in his throat like a trapped animal that, hating its captors but unable to reach them, struggles with the trap, its anger ineffectual and misdirected.

He focused his sharp pain on the airplane as he fought inside the cockpit to keep the F-4 flying, draining off his bile by muscling the stick and keeping busy reading the gauges and making constant mental calculations of the condition of the aircraft's systems and figuring the probability of whether or not his fuel and altitude were enough to make it to Da Nang.

The acerbity he felt for the Marines was equaled only by the pain he'd experienced when Ruthie returned his engagement ring the morning he boarded the C-141 at El Toro Marine Air Station in California. "Vince," she said, "I've come all the way from Wichita to see you off and it's been a great week together. You're a good man and I think I will always love you, but I'm not going to sacrifice the next few years of my life waiting for you to come

17

home from some stupid war that nobody cares about."
She slipped the diamond off her finger, unbuttoned the
pocket on his khaki shirt, and dropped in the ring. While
he looked at her in astonishment, she carefully
rebuttoned the pocket, patted it with the palm of her
hand, and kissed him on the cheek. "I wouldn't give it a
second thought if you walked away from this airplane,
got in my car, and drove straight to Canada." She held
the keys out to him. He stared at the keys for a painfully
long time, and if it hadn't been for the dispatching
officer calling his name from the manifest, and the cough
of the engines starting up on the transport, he would
have taken the keys and ran. "Will you write to me?" he
said. "No way, José. There's no sense in keeping something alive just to watch it suffer. Why prolong the pain?"
She stepped back and he saw the tear wiggle out from the
corner of her eye and curl down her cheek. She turned
and ran through the gate, leaving him looking after her
with a terrible emptiness in the pit of his stomach.

The depression had stayed with him all the way across
the Pacific to Okinawa, where he had laid over for a week
before getting final orders to Da Nang. It wasn't until he
met his fellow pilots and got into the business of flying
and getting shot at that he finally snapped out of his
melancholy.

"Dash Two—you're losing too much altitude—apply
some power. Keep your nose up."

Vince looked over at Bamburger. *I swear if I get back in
one piece I'm going to punch out his lights. He's only happy
when he's giving orders.* He balled his hand into a fist.
"Roger, Dash One—bringing the nose up." He pulled
back on the stick and pushed the throttle forward.

The air tore through the hole between his legs, making
a sound similar to that of a gale-force wind, and whistled
around inside the cockpit, buffeting him even though he
was tightly strapped into the armored seat. The shredded

metal and broken wire bundles and tubing reminded him of the exposed entrails of a large, wounded animal that had the misfortune of being gut-shot by a hunter's high-powered rifle.

The severed wires violently being whipped about in the damaged fuselage by the airstream sparked and flashed, creating the additional danger of igniting any escaping fuel. Battaglia watched the sparking, helpless to do anything but pull a few circuit breakers that did nothing to eliminate the problem; the thought of the Phantom becoming his funeral pyre was very real to him.

The minutes dragged on, and he called Joy Ride to get a new heading and came around five degrees, putting him on a deadhead course, straight into the Da Nang strip.

"Victor-Whisky-Five, I've got you on one-eight-five at angels three-point-five; keep coming, you're looking good."

"Roger, Home Plate," he said to Da Nang control, taking over from Joy Ride. "Get the reception committee out—I'm coming straight in."

"What's your fuel?"

"Less than one thousand pounds and it's going fast."

"Come around to one-eight-four."

"Hang tough, Dash Two," Blackjack said. "We'll get you home."

Hero for the day—Major Blackjack Bamburger. Vince set his teeth.

"Your approach looks good, Victor-Whisky-Five," the calm voice said, "but you're going to need more altitude."

"Negative, Home Plate. No can do—on reduced power already."

"Need altitude," came the calm voice.

"Negative—no can do."

There was a pause and Vince envisioned a conference taking place.

"Victor-Whisky-Five, you have permission to bail out. Jolly Green will be dispatched on command, ETA five-point-zero. Your position mark."

"Dash Two"—it was Blackjack—"you still have enough altitude for a good chute. You should have separation in thirty seconds."

Spare me, Major.

The F-4 began a new series of violent shakes and Vince held to the stick like it was the saddle pommel on a bucking bronco. *I hope Julie is enjoying her movie.*

"Do you read me, Victor-Whisky-Five? When are you going to bail out?"

"Negative, Home Plate—have ejection-system malfunction. Will stick with the bird." He closed his eyes and saw himself and his father walking the corn rows together on opening day of pheasant season. "Looks like you guys are going to have to shovel me out of the rice paddies," he said to the calm voice.

And that was that—there was nothing else to do but hold tight and wait. The cockpit conversation dropped away to the bare essentials and the Phantom kept dropping and the fuel got down to just a few hundred pounds. He rode the bucking jet all the way into Da Nang, beneath the ragged bottoms of the monsoon clouds. When he caught sight of the runway through the rain, he was flying the treetops and he could clearly see children riding water buffalos in the paddies and the muddy water around the rice stalks glinted into the plexiglass canopy.

He looked at the fuel gauge the moment the remaining engine quit, and the deadness that followed was like the windy stillness he'd once experienced sitting on a granite outcrop on the glaciated slope of Mt. Whitney. He had run out of fuel, he had run out of altitude, and he had run out of time. He caught a glimpse of Blackjack's plane rolling starboard and climbing away to avoid the crash.

Battaglia waited until the last minute to make the final

decision: he reached forward and banged the landing-gear lever. There was a settling *thump* underneath him and a panel light came on indicating that the proximity switches had been activated and the wheels were down and the struts locked in place. A shiver of relief went through him. If the added drag didn't cut his altitude by more than a few feet he still had a chance of making the runway; but if he had misjudged and the F-4 fell short into the paddies, there was absolutely no chance of survival with a wheels-down landing. The Phantom would instantly break apart in a fiery crash.

The heavy jet fell like a stone the last few feet and he watched the muddy rice fields whisk underneath him at 120 knots. Then hard concrete and the Phantom slammed onto the very end of the runway, wheels touching down with only three feet to spare.

Although he was down on the ground and splashing along the runway, there was still a lot of work left to be done to secure a safe landing. He quickly cut the switches he had forgotten and popped the drag chute. The Phantom had come in too hot and he had to bleed off energy fast, down to the speed he could safely apply the brakes. He was fearful that the tires would blow out, an additional problem he hadn't considered until now.

"You've got a streamer, Victor-Whisky-Five."

In the mirrors he could see the long white trail of the parachute and its tangled shrouds flapping unblossomed in the rain.

Cutting in at an angle to the runway and racing along beside him was the ambulance with a big red cross painted on the olive-drab side, which struck him as being oddly exaggerated for such a small vehicle.

The rain water sprayed up through the torn bottom of the fuselage and soaked his legs, the raw shattered wires, tubing, and hoses dead and sad, dangling uselessly from the wound. The crash trucks chased him.

He flashed by the revetments and idle equipment parked on the side of the runway and caught the wet sheen of a head bald as an egg sitting on top of a set of thick shoulders. A hand was raised high in the air, a stiff thumb pointing skyward.

The F-4 had slowed enough so Vince could tap the brakes: *once . . . twice . . . again . . . now steady pressure . . . the end of the runway coming up fast . . . veering off to the left . . . slowing . . . slowing . . .* The worn-out airplane sighed to a stop. For a few seconds there was no sound except the sound of rain beating on the plexiglass, and he remembered what it was like when he was a child, safe and secure bundled up in his bed, listening to the soft rains pattering on the roof, the sound of familiar voices coming through the walls.

Chapter 2

The hospital bay was uncomfortably hot and Vince wondered if the air conditioning had been turned off, or if there even was any air conditioning. His mouth tasted obscene from the anesthesia and his tongue felt bigger than his mouth. A curtain of sleep folded down over his eyes again and he dropped away into the puffy clouds, only to rise again into the stuffiness of the hospital room.

This continued for about an hour, dropping in and out of sleep as the anesthesia wore off, and he eventually found himself able to focus on the drab wall in front of his cot for longer lengths of time. A frightening feeling seized him and he threw back the covers and looked down at his leg: it was heavily bandaged, but still whole and intact. The breath that he released made a low pantherlike sound, and his eyes lost their nervous darting. He could wiggle his toes.

His leg looked to him like the swollen mummy that slept in the glass case in the main lobby of the County Museum of Natural History back home. When he was eleven years old, he and Wayne Plog would race each other from the bus stop every Saturday morning during football season to be the first one in line when the tall cadaverous guard opened the museum doors. He and Wayne would stand in front of the polished glass, looking down at the yellowed wrappings with the black toes sticking out the bottom and the peeling scalp visible through the top of the partially decayed mask, pondering the great thing that lay before them only a few inches below the glass. The glass was the barrier to fully satisfying their curiosity. They wanted to touch the mummy.

Nor would it have surprised them very much if the wrapped loaf had risen out of the case and walked away like Bela Lugosi did in the movie *Curse of the Mummy*, which they went back to see ten times at the neighborhood theater, sometimes hiding under the seats at the end of the movie so they could see it again without having to pay. From the edges of the glass, if they put their noses close enough, they could smell the faint odor of decomposed flesh.

When it was time to leave to pick up their newspapers and begin selling to the stadium crowd, Vince would always turn to Wayne and ask the question: "I wonder how old it is?" And Wayne would say: "A hundred-million-million years."

Flat on his back in the hospital bed, Battaglia felt as old as the mummy. He felt that his life had slipped away from him and that what he was living was nothing more than the musty leavings of a decayed past, the mummified remains of a shriveled-up hope. Everything he loved, all his dreams, all that he had looked forward to, was twelve thousand miles away back in the States. He was trapped in this pesthole to count the days when he would return to the real world to try to pick up his life once more.

The double doors at the far end of the bay swung open wide with a bang, and Colonel Dasher stepped inside; his deepset eyes that resembled shell casings settled in turn on each bed and the wounded Marine in it until they found Battaglia. He walked down the aisle, slowly, back rod straight, slapping a polished mahogany swagger stick (with brass tips) against his thigh, stopping at each bed to give a word of encouragement or to crack a joke.

When the colonel reached his bed, Vince was sitting up and toying with a piece of SA-2 that the doctors had taken out of his leg. For all of his macho, there was a twitch in Dasher's tight lips and a softness in his eyes as he looked down at the young lieutenant.

"How's the boy?" Dasher said.

"Sir, the Marine Corps will be happy to hear that I'll be flak bait again in two weeks." His face was without expression.

"Still bitter, Lieutenant?"

"Yes, sir—I won't ever be able to shake it."

The colonel sighed and sat on the edge of the bed, feeling tired and more like a father than a wing commander; he wanted to help Battaglia overcome his difficulties with the corps, but understood the limits of what he could say as Vince's commanding officer. However, there were things that needed to be said and he decided to take the risk: "I don't agree with everything that's going on in this war, son, but it's created an opportunity for many of us, including you. You're a fine pilot and officer, and I'd like to see you stay on as a career Marine. We need you."

"Not me, sir—I've got too much resentment inside. Sometimes I get so mad I want to go AWOL—disappear to Thailand, or just screw up so bad I'll be taken off flying status."

"So what's preventing you?"

Vince studied him, and Cleanhead liked the arrogance he saw in Battaglia.

"Once I step into the cockpit and strap in and the canopy snaps shut, the job becomes more important than anything else," Vince said. "When I'm up there with the rest of the guys everything changes."

Dasher's head was nodding slowly in agreement.

"But when I come back from a mission and I wind

25

down, the bitterness crawls back up into the back of my throat and I say: 'Why me?' It's a stinking war that nobody cares about; the others stayed home but I had to go. Why did my life have to be thrown out of whack while the draft-card burners and college boys and demonstrators kick back and draw unemployment and welfare and curse me for being in Vietnam? Even regular Marine pilots remained Stateside, and a guy like me, a reserve, was sent over. That's injustice."

Dasher slid his hand over his shaved head and he looked amused. "After you've been in three wars like I have, you'll understand that what's happened to you isn't unique—everything about war is injustice. You see, Lieutenant, wars are always fought by men like you who have been uprooted from their private lives and selfishly set upon by their countrymen who stay home at their cushy jobs, screwing the troops' wives, far away from the shooting and pain, enjoying the security and safety provided them."

"Why did we have to get mixed up with Vietnam, sir? No one understands why we're over here. We're not being allowed to win." Vince looked down at his heavily bandaged leg. "It's the wrong war."

"Every war is the wrong war. The few carry the many. Even the battles are wrong: today who would think of fighting another Fredericksburg, Chapultepec, Belleau Wood, Iwo, Chosen Reservoir, or Ashau Valley?"

"Colonel, a minute ago I told you that the reason why I don't go over the hill or mess up so badly that I'd get grounded is because of the job being more important than anything else once I'm in the air. There's more to it than that."

Dasher nodded and whacked his leg with the swagger stick, knowing what was on the young man's mind. "Go ahead, say it."

"No disrespect intended, but I don't care much for all

26

that patriotic stuff that you and the corps cherish. The glory of Guadalcanal, Saipan, and Inchon—the esprit de corps—doesn't impress me. I'm not fighting for the flag, or Mom and apple pie, or to preserve democracy. The reason I do my job is because the guys in the trenches and fighting holes are depending on my skill and judgment to come out alive. If it wasn't for them I'd be dropping my napalm and bombs in the South China Sea." Vince looked nervously at Colonel Dasher, not yet ready to cut off the vitriolic flow that had broken through the dam. "And there's another reason why I keep flying and swallow my bitterness," Vince said, realizing that he had stepped across the boundary. "I've got feelings about the men I fly with and it's important to me that I have their respect. If I let them down I couldn't live with myself."

Cleanhead raised himself from the edge of the bed and stood with his feet planted firmly on the floor, looking down at Battaglia, his face set sternly, yet with compassion in his voice: "Listen, Lieutenant. Those are the same reasons we all stick in there. I suggest you get your head screwed on right and stop feeling sorry for yourself, or one of these times you go up you'll be wallowing in self-pity and forget to check your six-o'clock and some hotshot Mig driver is going to flame your young ass; no soft hospital bed for you in Da Nang, only a coffin of stones on Karst Ridge." He liked Vince's straight-ahead way of expressing himself, but he was irritated that the young lieutenant didn't have a firm hold on his emotions.

"I might have a better attitude if our own countrymen would back us up."

"Stop being so pious. Given the political temperature back home, do you think you would be any different if you weren't in uniform? The truth is that you're here and they're there, and you will continue to do your job well because of the reasons you made so clear: it's the right thing to do while you're here, and you couldn't live with yourself otherwise. That's why you'll take out the guns at Ban Dau."

The aviator looked up from his bed at the mention of Ban Dau and stared at the grizzled veteran. The hospital ward became silent, the kind of silence that comes from knowing that something unmentionable has been spoken, the silence that covers fear.

Dasher read Battaglia's thoughts. He remembered his own reaction when years ago in Korea he had quietly set his beer glass down in the O-club when someone let the name *Inchon* slip and there was total silence for a full minute before he got up with Weed Ketchum and walked to the fantail and let the icy wind coming down from Manchuria numb his fear.

Against the Japanese, pilots stopped talking too at the mention of Wake, The Slot, Bungo Straits, and The Canal, names that stopped men in their tracks and hit them hard down deep where the nerves were sharp and the terror quick.

To this list would be added Ban Dau, a North Vietnamese redoubt protected by a forest of antiaircraft guns and missile sites imbedded deep in the slopes of a Pleistocene granite pass used by ancient Chinese armies to invade the land of Annam. Ban Dau was a vital staging area—the most important target of the war—the jump-off point for supplying the Viet Cong and NVA regulars fighting in the south. Here was the main link in the chain of roads, footpaths, and jungle passages that made up the thousand-mile-long Communist spinal cord called the Ho Chi Minh Trail without which the north could not sustain the war.

"The cost to take out Ban Dau is going to be high." Battaglia's lips tightened.

"We have no choice but to take it out." The colonel could feel the tension growing and knew that Vince was thinking that the decision coming down from Washington to strike Ban Dau was just another of a long series of ill-conceived plans developed by know-nothing bureaucrats. "Yes, the cost is going to be high, but if we show our resolve by attacking the enemy's heaviest-defended target and we successfully shatter his lifeline, we will destroy not only the means for supporting the troops, but also his morale, which in the final analysis is why he will lose the war." He smacked his thigh with the swagger stick. "There is no alternative—Ban Dau has to be wiped out. I'm convinced that when it is obliterated from the face of the earth, the North Vietnamese will come to terms and the people back home will understand why we had to fight here, and the war will come to a close."

"No offense intended, Colonel, but I don't agree."

Dasher wasn't sure he liked Vince's directness. However, he had to admire Battaglia for not being as afraid of him as were the other men in his command. He lifted his chin a few degrees and studied the young man's face. Vince had the same flashing, intense eyes and determined jaw of his son. The colonel's voice was even: "Be specific—what is it that you take exception to?"

"No matter what we do here, the people back home are not going to agree to the war, though they may eventually understand our military and political purpose—and that's the problem—our purpose; it has no credibility. America's mood has changed—it changed in Korea."

Colonel Dasher was impressed with Battaglia's answer and in one sense agreed with him. Yet Vince was a Marine officer and it was his duty to protect the traditions of the corps and its capacity to defeat an enemy. Battaglia might not agree with the war, but by damn he would understand what it meant to be a Marine. Cleanhead leveled his bullet eyes on the young man lying in the hospital bed: "Listen up. The patriotic, hellbent-for-victory attitude that was commonplace in World War Two may be gone today from the homefront, but that doesn't mean the change is right for the country nor does it mean that the American fighting man is going to step aside and let communism enslave the world. When you fly against Ban Dau remember that the masses don't know how to live, they've never known how to live, and it takes a few dedicated, hard-nosed elitists like ourselves to straighten them out." His eyes snapped at Battaglia. "Those gold-brickers back home owe you something, boy. That piece of SA-2 the doctors took out of your leg requires payment."

Vince's scalp edged back at hearing the mention of Ban Dau again. The tips of his fingers were tingling. "Destroying Ban Dau won't stop the North Vietnamese. Believe me, Colonel, those people are a different breed of cat. They won't give up no matter how much punishment they take or how long they have to fight. They don't have our values—they don't think the way we do."

Dasher noticed that Vince was trembling slightly. The conversation had excited him too much and in his weakened condition the effects had quickly reached the surface. He decided to shift gears and calm him down. Their talk had gone farther than he intended and it was time for him to withdraw. The young man needed to rest. He looked at his watch. "The North Vietnamese are not so greatly different from us—they hurt too; and when we take out Ban Dau they'll quit." He looked at his watch again. "Have to meet General Diggs, but there is one last thing. I came here to tell you to take your time getting well. I think it's best you get some leave away from your duties, so as soon as you're on your feet I'm ordering you to take ten days of R and R to think this thing through and get your head clear. Catch a hop to Bangkok or Singapore or Guam or Okie or wherever you want. Raise hell or just stare at a blank wall the whole time; and when you return be sure your head is screwed on fore and aft, 'cause you're going against the guns."

A nurse carrying a tray with a hypodermic needle and syringe stopped at the bed. "I'm going to have to ask you to leave now, Colonel. I have some business with Lieutenant Battaglia." She pointed at the syringe.

Vince looked at her dully. "I've got ten days of R and R from the colonel, honey. Can you get away?"

"When do we leave?"

"As soon as you get me walking again."

"Well, let's see what we can do about that." She rolled him over on his side and pulled down the blue cotton pajamas, exposing his bottom.

"Drop by again, Colonel," Vince said.

Cleanhead smiled. "I'll bring a box of chocolates next time, or would you prefer a bottle of *nuoc mam?*"

"How about my discharge papers?" he said. "No disrespect intended."

The nurse rubbed alcohol to a spot on his buttocks and picked up the needle from the tray. "Hold still, Lieutenant."

"Break it off in him," Cleanhead shouted from the door.

"*Owwww!*"

Chapter 3

Though the doors and windows of the hot-pad trailer were open, it was sweltering inside and the perspiration showed through the shirts of the pilots sitting at the gaming table. Two F-4s, bomb racks empty, circled the base and slid into their approach, wheels down, flaps down, noses angled up and flared.

"Twenty-one," Blackjack said with a big smile. "Pay me."

Vince rested his foot on the packed seabag on the floor beside him. He eyed Bamburger suspiciously. "That's three straight."

"How do you think he got his name," another pilot said. He passed the deal to the next man. "Disgusting."

Blackjack smiled and raked in his winnings. Without looking at Vince he said, "When's your hop leaving?"

Battaglia glanced at his watch. He was dressed in his class "A" uniform, the others were in flight suits. "I've got time for another hand."

The cards were dealt by the new dealer.

"Can't figure why you're going to Saigon for your R and R," Blackjack said; he motioned for another card from the dealer. "I spent mine in Bangkok; now there's a place to forget the war."

The other pilots playing at the table nodded in agreement.

"I've got a more important reason for going to Saigon."

Everyone stopped playing and looked up at him, particularly Blackjack. "A more important reason?" he said.

"I'm going to Saigon to get a question answered," he said. "Give me another card."

The dealer slipped a card across the table to him. The room was quiet—no one was talking. The seconds ticked by.

Vince looked up from his cards. "Saigon is where I can get to know these people I'm risking my life for. I want to know if Ban Dau is going to be worth it."

Bamburger was reaching for a card. His hand stopped in midair when Vince said Ban Dau. The others laid their cards quietly on the table and looked at each other. The F-4s hit the runway, their tires burning into the tarmac, and with a roar the engines reversed thrust.

Vince neatly folded his cards and tossed them to the dealer. "I fold," he said and raised up, pushed the chair back with the heel of his shoe, and slung the seabag over his broad shoulder.

He took a few steps away from the table and paused in the doorway to watch the C-130 Hercules that would take him south to Saigon taxi up to the ramp. No one spoke inside the trailer.

It was all so strange to him—the circumstances that led up to his being in this war, and the forces that were dividing his loyalties—and he wanted to get a handle on the whole swirling mess and stop it long enough so that he could see what was happening to him. Why were men like Colonel Dasher and Blackjack Bamburger capable of breaking the war down to its simplest terms and he wasn't? and why were they comfortable with their roles as participants whereas he had to struggle every day to justify climbing into the cockpit of his Phantom and flying north to drop his load on people he knew nothing about and who had never done him any harm? Maybe he would find answers in Saigon, where he could talk with the people and see the real Vietnam. And maybe in this way he could find a way to assuage his growing fear of the guns he must face at Ban Dau.

He looked back at the pilots. They were all staring at him, their eyes questioning and their faces drawn. Vince understood what they were thinking: whether or not he would come back to fly against the guns. If they had asked him he wouldn't have been able to give an answer.

Because the men were looking at him with such seriousness he felt obliged to soften their concern, so he smiled and said, "See you in ten days," and quickly walked away to the C-130 loading passengers and equipment, its turboprops continuing to turn for the short time it was to remain on the ground.

Once in the air, Vince experienced a slow release of mental tension that had held him tight ever since Ruthie had left him feeling confused and abandoned standing on the tarmac at El Toro. There was an assurance of change in his spirit—for better or worse, he didn't know which yet, but change there would be.

The hum of the turboprops and the moan of the vibrating structural members of the transport were like sleeping music to his tired brain and he began to doze off in the jumpseat. There was nowhere to rest his head, and his chin would bounce off his chest, snapping him back awake, each time he started to nod off.

After a few attempts to place his head in a more comfortable posture, and finding that there was no position conducive to napping, he gave up the effort, unbuckled the seatbelt from the jumpseat, and walked forward through the cavernous bowels to the flight deck.

The pilot and copilot, seeing Vince come through the hatch, smiled in a friendly enough way to encourage him to come all the way inside the crew station.

"How's it going?" Battaglia said.

"We're doing all right," the copilot said, glancing at the pilot's wings pinned above the pocket on Vince's tropicals. "Getting bored back there?"

"Yeh—I'm not a very good passenger—too used to a cockpit."

"I could use a cup of coffee and a stretch," the copilot said. "Want to take it for a while?"

"Thanks—wouldn't mind it a bit." Vince slid into the right seat and looked over at the pilot. "Battaglia's the name."

The major nodded. "I'm Haggerty." He released the control. "She's all yours, Lieutenant."

Settling his hands on the controls of the multi-engine plane and feeling its throbbing energy pass through into his arms, Vince smiled with a deep sense of satisfaction that came to him only when he was in command of an airplane, when his life was fused with that of the power of aircraft engines and the efficient operation of hydraulic lines, avionics equipment, and miles of electrical cables and tubing, bell cranks, push rods, and a beautiful assortment of gauges, switches, and levers, feeling the aluminum skin, spars, and longerons all working together with him at the controls to breathe life into the individual components and systems to produce the miracle of flight. He breathed deep with a great sense of satisfaction that spread all across his face in a broad healthy smile and a sparkle in his dark brown eyes.

Haggerty noticed Vince's contentment. "Transports seem to agree with you."

"They're a refreshing change from F-4s." He gripped the yoke tightly in his hands, enjoying the different feel from that of the Phantom's control stick. "There's a lot

35

of airplane here—a whole lot of airplane," he said as he scanned the spacious flight deck and its instrument panels. He looked out the side windows at the high long wings extending over the top of the chubby fuselage and at the four turboprop powerplants churning out their rhythm slung under the wings, and he felt a oneness with the big Hercules. Lord, he felt good!

"It's a beautiful day," Haggerty said. "Take her through the clouds and let's see what we've got up there."

Battaglia slowly pulled on the yoke and the sound of the engines immediately changed to a more strenuous pitch as they worked against the force of gravity created by the Hercules' new angle of attack.

Up they reached, Vince pointing the blunt nose of the C-130 into the mass of towering white pillars, freestanding vertical supports holding up the pristine blue sky.

And when on top—the domain of Zeus—the crisp, clean elastic air that only the gods (and pilots) breathed stretched up . . . up . . . up to the purple fringe of space and beyond into the ebony of deep space.

Below the Hercules (still climbing) were the endless reaches of a white hilly plain so dense that it seemed to be held together with impenetrable fibers. The Hercules and its passengers were destined to wander forever on these ethereal fields above the clouds, never to see land again.

"Makes a guy want to stay up here forever," Vince said.

"Sure does."

"In this kind of beauty you wonder if there really is a war on—or maybe it's all a dumb dream that we're going to wake from."

Haggerty grunted and looked out the window. Vince decided that the major was not of his ilk and that it was a waste of words to discuss the philosophical side of the war with him.

The forces driving this war were mysterious to Vince

36

and he considered it not only a personal tragedy to him to be caught up in it in such an inextricable and complicated way, but he also judged the war to be an American tragedy, an entanglement of terrible consequences that was tearing the country apart.

He looked over at Haggerty in the left seat, occupied with recording data on a clipboard. It was obvious that he was a career grunt (old for a major) and had come up the hard way, through the ranks. To Vince he represented the heartbreak of America, crushed dreams and a hope gone sour, swimming hard to stay even with the competition, slowly, insidiously, without notice, slipping behind to feed off past glories that no one cared about any longer.

"Had enough to get you through until we land?" The copilot was standing behind him with a coffee cup in his hand.

Vince looked over his left shoulder at the copilot and gave him his most ingratiating smile. "Hey, thanks for the chance to fly this bird; she handles well, though much slower in response than the F-4 . . . like my girl."

They all laughed at his not-too-successful attempt at a joke. He laid a hand on the pilot's shoulder and thanked him, then walked through the hatch, bending down so as not to bump his head, and found his way back through the fuselage and strapped-down equipment to his jumpseat.

"No need to strap in yet, Lieutenant," a crewman said. "We won't be landing for a while."

"Force of habit," Battaglia said, snugging the seatbelt over his waist. His chin quickly began bouncing against his chest, but he didn't wake this time until the Hercules touched down at Tan Son Nhut Air Base and taxied up to the ramp.

*   *   *

When the engines shut down and Vince unbuckled and stepped out of the C-130 onto the tarmac, the first significant impression of Saigon to hit him was the smell, an offensive concoction that he regarded as the signature of all cities in Southeast Asia, composed of a stiff mixture of motorcycle exhaust, decaying garbage, and urine.

He found the base officers' club with little difficulty, and after a few attitude adjustments he walked out to the main gate to wait for the bus to take him into downtown Saigon.

It would have been easy enough for him and much more convenient to take one of the many Renault taxi-cabs lined up outside the gate. However, he had come to Saigon to find out who these little brown people were that he was supposed to be defending—and what better way to start than by riding with a busload of them across town?

While standing with a group of chattering Vietnamese waiting for the bus and being entertained by a policeman directing traffic whose hand signals were being ignored, Vince noticed a striking young woman about his own age, possibly two or three years younger, standing alone a few feet away from the others, indifferent to her surroundings and eating tiny dried shrimp from a cellophane bag.

Needing directions, and thinking that broaching the subject with the young lady might lead to interesting developments, Vince casually walked up to her and set his seabag down. He unbuttoned the breast pocket of his uniform and took out a drink napkin on which, thirty minutes earlier, a fellow officer had written the name and address of a well-known hotel catering to Americans.

The girl either didn't notice him standing next to her or was purposely ignoring him, for she gave him no sign of encouragement whatsoever, though he had been standing beside her for some time.

"Miss," he began, "would you please tell me how to get

to the Caravelle Hotel on Nguyen Hue Street. This is my first day in Saigon and I have no idea how to get there." He held out the napkin to her, hoping that she could read, or at least speak, English.

She slowly turned her head to him, cocked it up at an angle, and gave him such an unpleasant look that his first impression was to walk away without saying another word. However, since he had already taken the first steps to opening a conversation and because he really had no knowledge of how to get to get to the hotel, he held the napkin closer to her face instead of being discouraged as the girl intended him to be, and said, "Please, I would appreciate it very much." He smiled, hoping to disarm her.

At first she said nothing, just stared up at him with very long and narrow eyes that were filled with a kind of brooding mystery that transported him back a thousand years to high-walled courtyards and provincial warlords and palatial rooms filled with Annamite concubines.

"No talk-talk to American Marine," she said, and picked a tiny shrimp from the cellophane bag with her long fingernails that looked lethal in their coat of blood-red paint, and placed the tidbit between her front teeth.

Battaglia, undaunted by the girl's rebuff, arrogantly looked her up and down; and to his delight she watched him through the tails of her eyes while he took his time studying her physical attributes. She was wearing a black miniskirt that revealed a pair of attractive honey-colored legs (she wore no stockings). The skirt fit tightly to her compact doll-like figure. Her hair, black and heavy bodied, hanging ruler-straight down to her small waist, was parted in the middle so that threads of silk fell easily along the sides of her unpainted cheeks to frame a small bridgeless nose and full, pouting lips rich in their natural color. An inch below the outer corner of her eye, a small, half-inch crescent scar was etched into the cheekbone, the only blemish to her face.

"No look me like that," she said turning away from him. "I no like." She chewed her little shrimp and kept her back to him.

"What's the matter?" he said as pleasantly as he could though his anger was rising. "Don't you like Marines or are you just nasty to everyone?"

"I no understand that word . . . nas . . . ty." She glared over her shoulder at him. The scar on her cheek increased her look of hostility. "What it means?"

"It means not being nice."

She turned the back of her head to him, raising her chin into the air. She picked at another shrimp. "I no nice any Marine. They think they bigshot—big tough mans. I no talk-talk to Marine. I no talk-talk no mans. My family no like . . . get mad. My family very rich . . . no want me talk mans . . . no like Americans. I good girl—come from good family." Keeping her back to him she looked over her shoulder and smiled coldly, and said, "Sorry—no talk-talk no more. Mother, father, uncles, aunts, cousins, grandmother, grandfather—all get angry I talk to bigshot Marine. No talk-talk no more." She quickly turned her face from him and her thick hair swung in a graceful curve across her back. She then proceeded to give the name of each relative who would disapprove of him.

Not at all satisfied with how his first contact with a Vietnamese woman had turned out and feeling the sting of such an open rebuke, he decided to try to recover some of the ground he had lost without further offending her; and he didn't want to create a street scene which he realized could easily develop with this volatile woman.

"I hope you don't mind if I continue to talk with you even though you don't want to talk to me." He waited for a response but she remained taciturn, chewing her dried shrimp. "I'm sorry that you don't like Marines; we're not

40

such bad guys when you get to know us."

"Ha!" she said, not turning her head. "That what you say."

Encouraged by her response, though it was tinged with a characteristic bitterness that he was getting used to, he boldly said, "Let's be friends."

Silence.

"You're very pretty."

This hit a nerve. She turned around. "You like the way I look?"

"I do."

Her long narrow eyes studied him for a moment, then she abruptly swung her back to him again, her hair sweeping over her expensive white brocaded blouse. "I know Marine mans. They take ad . . . van . . . tage (she was not sure of the word) of nice Vietnamese girl—treat her very bad. I good girl, come from—"

"I know, I know," he said impatiently, "you come from a good family."

"Very rich . . ."

"Yes, very rich."

"Family angry I talk American mans. Father, mother, uncles, aunts—"

"Cousins, grandmother, grandfather . . ."

". . . all get angry I talk—"

"—to bigshot Marine," he finished for her.

There was a noisy rumble and a squeal of brakes, and a bus bursting with people stopped to take on more passengers, though there didn't seem to be an inch of space left inside. The girl rushed past him on her high heels and pushed against the wall of riders along with the other boarders, and made an opening for herself. The doors closed behind her and the bus roared off in a cloud of black smoke, leaving Battaglia standing alone on the street and looking abandoned with his seabag laying at his feet.

41

The swaying bus turned the corner in front of the policeman directing traffic, and through the veil of exhaust smoke, Vince caught a last glimpse of the girl pressed against the door glass, her pouting red lips and long narrow eyes surrounded by a cloud of black hair.

Well, you can't win them all. Discouraged by his experience he walked back to the base gate and got into a cab after giving the driver the name of the hotel. The driver handed the napkin back to Vince without saying anything and started the motor.

"Do you speak English?" Battaglia said. He caught the scornful look the driver shot at him in the mirror.

"Of course—and French and Chinese if you choose to converse in those languages."

Vince slumped down into his seat and didn't say another word.

Saigon was a monstrous traffic jam sealed over by a smelly cloud of exhaust gases from thousands of Japanese motorcycles. Jangling bicycle bells competed with the loud buzzing of small 75cc Yamaha and Honda engines and the blare of horns from French Renaults and military jeeps. Stone-faced mama-sans rode stiffly in mechanized richshaws called cyclos, and people of all ages walked rapidly between the vehicles, carrying boxes, baskets, or bundles on their heads and backs, some loaded on the ends of bamboo poles.

Hawkers sat on reed mats on the sides of the streets, surrounded by piles of mangos, tamarind fruit, ginger root, papaya, rau, and heaps of coconuts and bananas of various sizes from finger length to foot-long plantains. Live chickens and ducks were crowded into small bamboo cages.

A covey of clean-scrubbed schoolgirls, their solid white ao dais flaring at the side splits as they ran through a break in the traffic, chattered and laughed back and forth to each other, their slippered feet skipping slightly over the pavement. Once on the opposite side of the street, they bunched closely around a street vendor's cart, bending their slim young bodies—tender as bamboo shoots—over the array of sesame candy, crystalized ginger, cups of yellow bean pudding, monkey sweets, and sugared coconut. One delicate creature, about fifteen years of age, who had a pretty round face with high cheekbones framed by a bobbed Chinese pageboy haircut, unfolded several piaster notes from the waist-band of her ao dai and pointed to different samples of goodies which she distributed to her friends. There was much bowing, clapping of hands, and laughter, after which the vendor was paid and the girls ran off across the plaza and past the war memorial and disappeared into the pulsing throng of pedestrians.

"So this is Saigon," Vince said to the cab driver. "Lots of pretty girls, ripe smells, mobs of people and traffic, and French colonial buildings." His eyes were busy taking in the mosaic rush of life around him.

"This must be your first time in our capital city," the cab driver said.

"It is—I'm stationed in Da Nang. I've come to Saigon to get a question answered." He rested his arm in the open window to get the full benefit of the moving air. From the corner of his eye he noticed a bicycle rider overtaking the cab on his side.

The cab driver looked oddly at Vince through the rearview mirror. "You've come to get a question answered?"

Before Battaglia could say anything in return, the bicycle rider pedaled up to the open window, reached inside and tore the gold Seiko watch from his wrist, and rode ahead through the congested traffic, quickly outdistancing the cab. Vince, startled by the lightning snatch, sat dumbfounded in the back seat of the cab, staring at the thief escaping into the noise and smoke.

The robber weaved between the slow-moving Hondas and Vespas, and forced the other bicycles to part for him as he deftly pedaled away, soon to disappear entirely.

Though it took a while to build to the flashpoint, Vince's anger exploded and he jumped from the cab and chased after the thief, not at all careful about who he knocked out of the way in his sprint down the street.

All thought of the cab and his seabag in the backseat left his mind and he became gripped by a force, the same power that took over his controls when he flew into combat, driving him after the man with his watch.

Vince had closed the distance to forty yards between himself and the thief, who was in the middle of a gaggle of bicyclists and looking over his shoulder at him coming on hard. Running, running, running; the street pavement pounded hard against his shoes.

The heat from the sun and cars and motorcycles motors, the strangeness of the surroundings, the noxious smells, and the shouts of people looking at him as if he were an escaped lunatic created a state of unreality for him, as if he were experiencing something mystical and illusory.

The thief could see that Vince was gaining rapidly and that if he stayed with the bicycle he would be overtaken in a short time. He jumped from the bike, letting it crash to the pavement, and ran at right angles to the traffic, into a narrow side street.

Battaglia, seeing the thief's intention, cut through the crowd and onto the sidewalk, shortening the distance between them even more. He blindly turned the corner and crashed head-on into a pile of sugar cane stacked in front of a row of shops. The cane shattered over the sidewalk and street. People coming out of the shops and those on the street stopped to stare at him while he picked himself up off the pavement and once more started after the robber, the shopkeeper yelling at him to come back and clean up the mess he'd made.

Chest heaving, lungs bursting, shirttail flying behind him, he pounded after the man, not so much caring about the watch anymore, but possessed with one focused thought: inflict pain.

Feeling Battaglia's burning breath on the back of his neck, the man shouted a string of Vietnamese, and went down hard under Vince's weight, bouncing off a vendor's street cart and rolling into the garbage-filled gutter.

"You skinny creep," Vince yelled, "I'll teach you to steal my watch." With his right hand he held the Viet tight in a punishing wristlock and forced his knee into the small of his back, keeping him pinned to the street. With his free left hand, Vince shoveled garbage from the gutter into the man's open, screaming mouth, half the sour cabbage leaves and putrefying bean sprouts and animal offal getting packed down his throat, the other half being spread in a paste over his cheeks, nose, and eyes.

Unknown to Vince, the thug had picked this particular side street as his avenue of hoped for escape because it led directly into Cho-Chan, a district of cutthroats, prostitutes, and dope pushers, his private turf and sanctuary from the police. In fact, he had reached the edge of Cho-Chan when he was tackled by Vince.

Three cheap hoods, on their way to a favorite noodle shop to extort a few piasters, stepped out of a damp alley and onto the side street where they saw one of their own being hammered by an American Marine. They stopped short and a few words were passed between them. Their approach was cautious (for they had respect for a Marine's fighting skill); two men snuck behind Battaglia while the other challenged him from the front.

Incubating in Vince's brain was the thought that he was in a strange foreign city, far from help, and had, because of his quick temper, made an error in judgment. He could easily be killed here. He looked up from his armlock on the thief and saw that a hostile crowd had ringed him. Coming through the circle (the mob closing behind him), one of the hoods, a bolo chain hanging from a sinewy arm, walked straight for Vince, not in a hurry, but with slow precision, the bolo chain held with a firm hand and swinging with a natural rhythm to the man's steps. There was a shuffle of feet and Vince turned to see a tall, thin Viet and another man, a fat ethnic Chinese, take up positions behind him on the inside of the ring, their arms folded, easy smiles on their sweating faces. They said nothing and waited. The crowd became silent.

Battaglia took his time getting to his feet and faced the man with the bolo chain. The unconscious thief lay stretched out on the street, his face resting in the gutter garbage. A trickle of gray water flowed down the gutter and dammed up at his head.

"Okay, let's get it on," Vince said. He circled to his left so he could see all three men at the same time. *I found my answer sooner than I expected. Like Cleanhead said, it's a stinking war. What are you doing today, Ruthie?*

The man smiled and showed two missing front teeth. His slight crouch at the shoulders and the easy way he held the bolo chain told Vince that the thug was used to fighting in the streets and no doubt had killed before. He was a small man with pig eyes, a fast-moving tough who Battaglia knew was more dangerous than a much larger man.

"Your last breath will be on this street, Marine," the hood said, circling with Vince.

"We'll see."

"You're going home in a body bag stuffed in a metal box."

Battaglia said nothing, thinking that the man was probably right and that he would much rather be shot down over Hanoi and avoid the embarrassment of being murdered by a slum punk in the alleys of Saigon. *The cost for Ban Dau was too high.*

In the front row of the ring of spectators was a crippled boy leaning on a crutch shaped from a heavy and knotted branch of jungle teakwood. The stump of his leg hung through cutoff trousers and he leaned heavily on the crutch, intently watching Vince. It was obvious that he wasn't getting enough to eat (his ribs showed through his skin and he had a bulging malnourished belly). He was an orphan of the streets, and from his wretched physical condition and sorrowful countenance it could be discerned that the boy lived under the most miserable conditions and that his values were limited to the most practical of matters. In short, he was a survivalist; and even though having lived only a few years he clearly understood Battaglia's predicament: everything about the scenario being played out on this dirty street reminded him of his own fight for survival and was repugnant to him. Therefore, his action, though surprising to the mob, not least of all to the thugs, was in perfect agreement with the hatred he had for the evil in which he had been trapped for most of his eleven years. "Hey, Marine," he shouted.

Keeping his eyes on the man with the bolo chain, Vince circled counterclockwise a few degrees until his peripheral vision made contact with the boy. The bolo chain was doing fancy dances in the air and it made a sound not entirely unlike that of helicopter blades turning slow when the engine is on idle.

"What do you want, kid?" Battaglia said.

There was the sound of strong wood hitting the cobblestone street. "For you," the boy said and he disappeared into the crowd, hopping away on his one good leg.

Vince took a step backward and picked up the crutch. It was heavy and smooth with much use, and felt good in his hands. "Thanks, kid."

He moved in on the Viet whose face had turned a strange hue of gray and whose eyes were snapping nervously as he began retreating a step at a time in the face of Vince's new aggressiveness. The bolo chain no longer whipped the air with authority—rather, it circled slowly, more like a child's toy than like a deadly weapon.

"You don't look so good, riceball," Vince said. "What's the matter—losing interest now that the odds are more even?"

The two men behind Battaglia lost their smiles, unfolded their arms, and moved in, while their partner, being pressed by Vince, continued to back up a step at a time until he had reached the inner row of the circle of people.

Vince didn't have to turn around to know that the tall Viet and the fat Chinaman had made their move. He knew that he had but a few seconds before they would be on him and that he must move fast if he was to eliminate the man who faced him with the chain.

The punk stopped backpedaling; his body became rigid and he waited. The chain came up and began twirling. Battaglia struck. He thrust the crutch forward, catching the chain with one end and tangling it. The other end he spun down in a half-circle and clubbed the Viet square on top of the head. The heavy teakwood knocked him senseless and he was out like a light before he hit the ground. The attack occurred so fast that the crowd failed to comprehend what had happened. For Vince, the quick, automatic response of the crutch in his hands was clear enough. He had spent many hours training with the pugil stick at Marine Corps School, Quantico, Virginia.

Before the man had fallen to the cobblestones, Vince was turned around facing the remaining two hoods. He unraveled the bolo chain, and without giving the men a chance to adjust to the swiftness of his attack he bore in on them with the chain swinging in his right hand and the crutch flailing with his left.

Battaglia swung the chain in a wide arc and lunged forward, catching the fat Chinaman around the neck. Vince jerked hard and dragged him to the ground, hard, then beat him into unconsciousness with the crutch.

The third man, completely unhinged by the swiftness and ferocity of Battaglia's defense, clawed his way through the crowd and ran back up the alley whence he came, to disappear within the dankness of Cho-Chan.

The crowd moved uneasily—not knowing how to react to this young American who had just extracted victory from sure death. Vince stood in the middle of the ring (it had expanded when the fight had started), the two thugs out cold and bleeding in the street. The first man, the thief who had stolen Vince's watch, remained in the gutter with the dam of sewage water building up behind his head and shoulder.

The mob was growing restless and the people began to jabber among themselves. It was apparent that they were in an ugly mood and not going to break up until they had decided what to do about Vince, who was watching them closely, the chain in one hand and the crippled boy's teakwood crutch in the other.

"Go home, long-nose," a woman with pustules on her arms and face shouted.

Someone spit at him.

A rotten banana from the gutter flew into the ring and hit him in the chest.

"We don't want Americans in our country."

"Marines are dog meat."

The crowd was growing bolder and the circle contracted.

"Scatter his bones in the hills and let the vultures pick them clean."

"Disembowel the foreigner and feed his entrails to the river fish."

49

Battaglia rotated the chain in a wide circle over his head. "Get back." He probed the ring for weaknesses, moving up close to the edge and clipping heads, then dropping back to try again at another spot, always ready to move fast if he found a breakout point.

The situation was quickly deteriorating, his efforts only serving to further agitate the mob, and he was about to take his chances in a headlong rush into the center of the circle when there came a commotion at the end of the street. Tires squealing, horns blaring, two jeeps filled with U.S. Army Military Police plowed through the throng of Vietnamese, the MPs firing M-16s into the air. Seated up front in the center of the lead jeep was the crippled kid, his stump resting on the gearshift.

Chapter 4

The jeeps forced their way through the crowd, scattering the angry people to the right and left, and cut an opening to Battaglia. The MPs jumped out of the jeeps, shouting and swinging their riot clubs.

"Break it up—break it up."

"Get moving."

"Out of here, everybody; back to your shops; into your holes."

The crowd, overpowered by the MPs, milled around with resentment in their faces then split into twos and threes and walked away, leaving only a few hangers-on to lean against the walls, their arms folded while they stared at Battaglia and the MPs.

A scowling sergeant whose jaw was set like a brick holstered his .45 and strode over to the three hoods beginning to stir. He motioned to his Vietnamese counterpart. "Better get the cuffs on these guys and put them in the jeeps. See what information you can get out of them while I talk to the lieutenant."

The interpreter and MPs handcuffed the half-conscious men and carried them to the jeep with the dispersed crowd looking on in angry silence.

"Want to tell me what happened here, sir?" the sergeant said to Battaglia. The pantlegs of his combat greens were perfectly bloused over the tops of spit-shined boots and the bottom of a healthy beer-gut hung over his web belt. "Seems to me that you're lucky to be alive." He pointed to the thugs and sullen people, not yet clear as to what had taken place and wondering who were the real victims, Vince or the bloodied men. His voice was controlled suspicion: "Where did you get those?" He pointed to the weapons in Vince's hands.

"The bolo chain I took from one of the creeps; the crutch came from the one-legged kid in your jeep. I take it he's responsible for you being here."

"Lucky we were patrolling nearby." He pointed over his shoulder with his thumb to the main street several blocks away. "He was jumping up and down in the middle of the street, flushing like a toilet on that one leg of his, trying to get someone's attention when we came by. At first I thought it was some kind of ruse and he was leading us into a trap—you never can tell about these people—but he finally convinced me that there was a 'Marine officer in boo-coo trouble' so we whipped up here to check it out."

"Good for me you listened to him."

"Seems like you took care of the situation okay." He looked at the mangled thugs heaped together in one of the jeeps.

"The crowd was getting nasty. I couldn't have held them off much longer."

The boy used his arms to help himself out of the jeep, and hopped over to where Battaglia and the MP sergeant talked. Standing on his one leg, waiting, he looked like the lost street urchin that he was, dirty, hungry, and struggling to hold onto his false bravado.

"Hey, Marine—don't forget this." He held up Vince's gold Seiko, a toothy smile spread over his face.

Battaglia walked up to him and set the crutch in place under his arm. He placed his hand on the boy's small shoulder. "Looks like I owe you a double thanks." He twisted the watchband onto his wrist.

"Say, Lieutenant," the sergeant interrupted. "If you will come over here to the jeep we can get this paperwork out of the way in a few minutes so I can make my report and you can be on your way."

"Sure, Sarge." He bent down to the boy. "Wait here, kid. Don't go away."

The sun had crossed to its high point and the street and shops were awash in light. Life had returned to normal and people walked by without giving much more than a glance to Vince and the MPs. A medical bag was open on the hood of a jeep and an MP was giving first-aid treatment to the thugs. The pool of sewage that had collected behind the thief's unconscious body had drained and the gray water again flowed down the gutter.

"What do you think about the kid?" Vince said to the sergeant.

"I don't think anything about him," he said gruffly, setting a clipboard on the jeep's hood and taking a pen from his breast pocket.

"What's going to happen to him?"

The sergeant looked up from the form he was writing on. "He'll go back to panhandling and scrounging in the streets."

"Isn't there something that can be done for him?"

"Your first time in Saigon, sir?"

Battaglia nodded. "Just got in."

"Kerosene burner from Da Nang, I take it."

"Been up there for ten months."

The sergeant rubbed his nose and lifted the clipboard from the hood of the jeep, looking impatient with Vince. "I've been working the streets of Saigon for two years and I've seen a lot of sorry sights, the sorriest being these street kids. They have no home, the few orphanages that exist are overcrowded and with minimal resources and the older kids run away within days of being placed there.

There's nothing you can do for them—it's part of the screwed-up war." He bent over the hood and began filling out the forms attached to the clipboard.

"Is it worth it Sarge?"

"What's that?"

"The screwed-up war."

"Beats the hell out of me. What's your name and serial number, sir?"

The cabby had been honest, and much to Vince's surprise his seabag was waiting for him at the Caravelle Hotel. The kid had disappeared and when Battaglia left Cho-Chan with the MPs he did so reluctantly, not at all comfortable with being unable to do something for the boy.

He examined the contents of the seabag and found everything intact. The lobby was filled with people in a hurry, Caucasian, European, and U.S. journalists for the most part, along with contract employees from the large construction firms that used the hotel as their base of operations when in Saigon. The mix was completed by military personnel and members of the foreign office and diplomatic corps. The usual camp followers—handsome Vietnamese women looking for their opportunity— lounged about in small groups or singly, appearing relaxed and at home, everyone quite comfortable with their presence.

One of these courtesans standing near the entrance to the dining room, her back to Battaglia and talking to a tall good-looking chap in diplomatic attire, caught his eye. She was wearing a black miniskirt and high-heeled black pumps that set off her attractive legs. There was something about how she tossed her head and swept her long hair in a wide arc across her back that seemed familiar.

A second young woman, wearing a solid pink ao dai and her hair cut short, and escorted by an older man wearing a mint green tropical suit, stopped by the girl in the miniskirt and talked to her in a confidential manner, bending her ear close to her lips. They both giggled while the two men tried to ignore each other.

The group was on the opposite side of the lobby from where Vince stood feeling alone and out of place with his seabag. The girl's head was turned slightly to listen to her friend, and her face was hidden from Vince by the sweep of her thick hair. She pulled back and tossed her head in laughter; her hair fell away from her face and he saw pink pouting lips and long narrow eyes. She put her hand through the tall man's arm and her back was to Vince again. She walked away laughing.

The girl at the bus stop, Vince thought to himself, admiring the honey-colored legs and doll figure. He stopped a porter walking by. "What's that girl's name— the one going into the restaurant with the tall fella?"

The porter looked for a moment. He smiled. "That's Nghia; very special girl." He winked at Vince and walked away with two suitcases in his hands.

This couldn't be the same girl—no way. He remembered that the girl at the bus stop had made sure he understood that she was from a good family and that nice girls like her were not seen fraternizing with men. He could hear her voice: "I come from good family . . . they very rich. I no like talk mans, no like bigshot Marine . . . mother . . . father . . . grandmother, they get angry I talk with mans." *This isn't the same girl—though the resemblance is close.*

He thought of following her into the restaurant to get a closer look, but he decided against it. He didn't feel comfortable going through the back door to find out about people—it wasn't his style. There were more important matters on his mind at the moment, particularly the one-legged street orphan whose memory haunted him. He would have to go back to Cho-Chan and find the boy regardless of how dangerous it was to his health.

"Would you like me to carry your bag to your room, Lieutenant?" It was the porter. He hefted the bag to his shoulder without waiting for an answer. "May I have your room key, sir?" he said in excellent English.

Battaglia followed him to the elevators. "These unattached women that you have decorating the lobby, are they what I think they are?"

"You mean our *tiger girls?*" He smiled and adjusted the wide strap of the seabag over his shoulder, his bandy legs buckling under the heavy weight. "If you are interested I will be more than happy to make an introduction for you. After that you and the young lady can easily work out the details of the arrangement for yourselves. It is quite painless and discreet."

"What do you get out of it?"

"Naturally I would expect a healthy tip." His lips parted in a tight smile. "It is difficult to make an arrangement without a proper introduction. The ladies— and our culture—insist upon certain pretenses." The insincere smile remained.

"The competition looks heavy." Vince looked at the abundance of women. "Is there enough business to go around?"

"As a matter of fact, the tiger girls do little business here. The focus of their activity is in hotels located in the less reputable sections of Saigon." He pushed the button for the elevator and rested the seabag on the floor.

"Are they just showing off their wares—but no touchy?"

"Not really. You see, the initial contact is made through a proper introduction at the Caravelle or similar establishment. The actual arrangement is carried out—

56

or, shall we say, consummated—at a hotel of lesser visibility which makes it its business to cater to clandestine meetings of a promiscuous nature. In other words, it's safer for the men to play in secret. Once a lady has acquired a regular client, that is to say, repeat business, she will entertain her gentlemen friend exclusively in her rooms at the smaller hotel of which she has made special arrangements with the proprietor."

"Where are these smaller hotels located?"

"Most of them are found in the humbler areas of our fair city."

"In the slums?"

"If you wish to call them that." He smiled and hoisted the seabag into the elevator. "The hotels are quite comfortable and the interiors do not reflect the poorness of their exterior environments. And they are safe."

On the elevator and all the way down the hall and into Vince's voom, the talkative little Viet, sensing that he had an enthusiastic customer in the young flyer, continued to expound on the benefits of an efficient system of prostitution catered by the loveliest women in the world.

Vince threw himself down on the queen-size double bed and stretched out with his hands folded behind his head, looking up at the ceiling.

"Well, Lieutenant," the porter said. He placed the seabag on the floor and rubbed where the shoulder strap had bitten into his skin.

"Well what?"

He looked at Vince, an embarrassed grin playing around the edges of his mouth, confident that Battaglia would spring for an *arrangement*. "Would sometime this evening be soon enough for me to introduce you to a nice young lady, informally in the lounge, say . . . at about eight or so?"

Battaglia shifted his concentration from the ceiling to

the Viet. He was quiet for a while, then said, "I've never paid for it in my life and I'm not going to start now. Thanks for the education though."

"You don't know what you're missing . . ."

"Spare me." He gave the man a five-piaster note and ushered him to the door.

"Your leave will be boring without entertainment; how can you ignore the pleasures of the Orient that await you? Just give me a call and I will find a lotus blossom of your most scrutinizing taste who will make you forget the war and drown you in her sensual delights."

"I've not come to Saigon for sensual delights," he said, giving the porter a gentle push out the door.

"What, then?"

Vince closed the door in his face and sat on the edge of the bed and started unbuttoning his shirt. "This won't do at all—it's not what I had in mind." He looked around at the sterile plushness of the hotel room and he felt confused and very alone.

The last button was loose and he slipped an arm out of his shirt with the intention of taking a shower, but he got no farther in undressing. He rolled over onto his side and fell asleep.

Looming up through his sleep stood the heavily fortified pass called Ban Dau and he flew his Phantom down through the steep canyon thick with flak from the guns he feared. The dream replayed the bomb run several times, and each time at the end of the run, the boy with the one leg would be standing in the middle of the narrow pass, looking up at him with pleading eyes, and he would say, "Is it worth it, Lieutenant?" His thumb would reach for the bomb release on the control stick, but someone would pull his hand away before he could ripple the load. The cockpit would turn misty and he would smell jasmine flowers, the kind he'd smelled when standing beside the girl at the bus stop. The mist slowly cleared and was replaced by large teardrops falling from inside the plexiglass canopy. They were not clear like normal teardrops, but blood-red; and the cockpit quickly filled with them dripping—dripping—dripping from the plexiglass and running down the inside of the windshield until they collected in a red pool around his feet. Ruthie's laughing face came up on the radar screen, mocking him. Over her shoulder, Vince could see his father walking the corn rows, a shotgun in his hands and two dead Chinese ringneck pheasants hanging by their necks from his belt.

He woke in a sweat, looking through a red haze, his uniform soaked down to his socks. The room with its impeccable Western furnishings and clean and orderly appearance left him with a feeling of emptiness and boredom and death, and he had to get out right away to where there was life. To him everything in the room and in the hotel was lifeless and without character. The chairs, dresser, bed—still and formless. The ceiling facade and wall molding—decorative fakes. In the lobby downstairs—filled with pretention, superficiality, and falsity—assembled the pleasure seekers, men and women wrapped up in themselves and with time only for their selfish motives, deceptive in appearance and meaning (like the furnishings). It was here that he should drop his bombs—on the hotel—not on Ban Dau. Wipe out the deceit and hypocrisy . . . end the war in Saigon!

He sat on the edge of the bed and hung his head in his hands. *Got to get hold of myself—it was only a dream. Take a cold shower and shake it off.* He threw his wet clothes into the corner and took a long shower, shaved, and for the first time in months splashed down with cologne and bath powder. After putting on a sport shirt and slacks he hurried down to the lobby and headed for the exit without looking at anything but the door in front of him.

Out on the street, his nerves, which had grown through the skin and lay raw and exposed from months of combat flying, stopped jangling and he felt his body relax in the warm lather of the life of the common Saigonese rushing about him. He stopped for a mango and cut it open with his pocketknife. "How much?" he said to the vendor. He placed a slice of the mango on his tongue and let the slippery fruit slide down his throat.

The old woman smiled, showing black, betel-stained teeth, and without batting an eye said, "One hundred American dollar." She held out a weathered hand and the smile became larger.

"One hundred dollars, did you say?" He smiled back.

"One hundred dollar," the woman repeated, her smile growing wider.

Vince ran a hand through his dark brown hair, puzzled. "You don't really mean that, do you?"

The woman nodded her head vigorously, her hand held straight out, palm up.

"If you don't want to pay her a hundred dollars she'll settle for one piaster," a girl of about thirteen, sitting on a box, said. She was wearing a long-sleeved white cotton blouse and black pajama bottoms, and her face was small and round and invited you to cup it in your hands. One bare foot rested easily on the other, her small brown toes wiggling as if they wanted to crawl off somewhere on their own, and she looked at Vince with old eyes hurting with the pain of centuries of uninterrupted war.

While her eyes remained leveled at him, she pulled self-consciously at a sleeve to hide the long scar branded into her arm by searing napalm. "One hundred dollars shouldn't be too much for a rich American like you to pay for a mango."

"That's ridiculous."

"Then give my grandmother a piaster."

"Why doesn't she speak for herself?"

"She doesn't speak English. She can only say 'one hundred dollars.'"

He cut a generous slice of mango and impaled it on the tip of the pocketknife, the orange-yellow juice running down the length of the blade. He held it out to the youngster and she took it between her fingers, which were long and slender. After looking up at him for a few seconds, she placed the slice of fruit between her small lips and took a dainty bite. Her eyes lingered on him.

"What's your name, young one?" he asked.

"Autumn Dove."

The name struck him as being so absolutely beautiful that he stopped cutting the mango and let the words float through his mind, picking up memories of the fall flights of mourning doves migrating across the open fields back home. "That's a lovely name."

The old woman's hand came closer to Vince. The girl looked at him and laughed. The woman laughed also, but her hand remained outstretched.

Vince looked down at the creased and dirty hand. "Will she take one piaster for the mango?" he asked the girl.

"She will put up a fuss and maybe call the police, but she will take it in the end—after she calls you a lot of dirty names." She tugged at the bill of the U.S. Army fatigue cap on her head. "You can just walk away if you want, like some do."

"I don't want to do that."

"It's not a good idea. She'll follow you, screaming all the way down the street, inviting others to join her; it could be embarrassing."

"What do you think I should do?"

"Pay her the hundred dollars."

"That's absurd."

She shrugged her shoulders. "Can you cut me another piece of mango?"

"I'm not going to pay her a hundred dollars for a mango." He shook his head at the grandmother's open

61

hand under his nose. "I don't believe this conversation."

"The police will come and put you in jail, so you better give my grandmother the hundred dollars. Next time you'll know better than to cut into a mango before agreeing on the price."

"This is crazy."

"No it's not—it's business."

The woman's wrinkled hand pushed impatiently under his nose. The powerful smell of fish sauce stung his nose and he recoiled back onto his heels, away from her palm, turning his head.

The girl played with a coconut, tossing it up in the air and catching it like a ball.

"Listen, kid," he said to Autumn Dove, "I'll make a deal with you."

She looked at him suspiciously. "What kind of deal?"

"If you get me off the hook with your grandmother I'll take you to a movie."

She tossed the coconut high in the air. "What you mean 'off the hook'? I don't understand that."

"Square it with her—I mean fix it so I can leave quietly without a big argument over the price of the mango."

"Will you take me to a real restaurant after the movie? The kind that the nice ladies go to with their boyfriends, that have big cloths on the tables and a man in a black and white suit brings your food after you have looked in a book he gives you to read, and the chopsticks are clean and white, and the rice bowls and dishes are not cracked or chipped."

"Yeh, sure—I'll take you to a place like that."

"And we can listen to a singer and watch people dance?" She was smiling now and her eyes were bright and she became animated. "We can pretend there is no war and that I live in a beautiful villa and drive a new Honda motorcycle and . . ." her eyes dropped, "I have a

62

real bed to sleep in and don't have to sleep on the dirt anymore, and I have a dress and new pajamas to wear."

Vince became quiet and looked away. He licked his lips and coughed. "We can do all that. Sure, why not; it won't hurt a thing."

She turned to the old lady and a long string of Vietnamese shot out of her mouth. Vince was amazed at how fast and long she spoke without taking a breath. When she finally stopped, the woman withdrew her hand and looked sullen.

"What did you tell her?" he said.

"I said that you told me you would dig up her husband's bones from the graveyard and scatter them on the hills for the wild dogs to eat if she didn't accept one piaster for the mango."

Vince quickly gave the woman five piasters and grabbed the thirteen-year-old by the hand. "Come on, let's get out of here before she changes her mind and gets nasty."

Autumn Dove knew exactly where she wanted to go to see a movie and how to get there. Battaglia had the taxicab door open and was about to step in when she pulled him back. "The taxi will cost you too much. We will take the cyclo to the movie. It is more fun to ride than a taxi." She pointed to a tricycle-like contraption built with a double seat between the two rear wheels. It had a bamboo roof for protection from the sun and rain, and the driver sat over the front wheel and pedaled. Some cyclos were reversed so that the driver was seated behind the passengers instead of in the front.

"Come." She pushed him into the seat and bounced in beside him. After giving directions to the driver, she turned to Vince, her legs tucked under her bottom, the camouflaged fatigue cap tilted at a jaunty angle on her head, and said: "We will go see a kung-fu movie in Cho-Chan."

The look of shock on Battaglia's face at the mention of Cho-Chan surprised her. "What is the matter?" she said.

"I was in Cho-Chan earlier today and I didn't like it."

"The best kung-fu movies are in Cho-Chan, so we will go there," she said with finality.

There was a jerk, and the cyclo driver heaving on the pedals maneuvered the modern rickshaw into traffic. He cut off a small taxicab, wheeled through the corner onto Tu Do Street, and settled back into a steady pumping rhythm that put the cyclo at just the right speed to flow along at an even pace with the other vehicles sharing the wide thoroughfare.

Half listening to Autumn Dove's description of the last kung-fu movie she'd seen (her only passion was martial arts), Vince watched the bicycles, motorcycles, taxicabs, French Renaults, and cyclos racing alongside of him, each one forced tight into its special groove by the others surrounding it.

In the cyclo next to him, the more advanced model with the driver pedaling behind the passenger, an old man wearing a black silk ao dai and tight-fitting skullcap stared out at him from his seat. In his lap the man was holding a reed basket from which a squirrel-like animal poked its head. The man's small eyes darted back and forth between Battaglia and the girl; he stroked his ragged thin beard and sat back in the seat, a disgusted look on his face.

Autumn Dove prattled on about Bruce Lee and her other favorite kung-fu movie stars and picked at her teeth with a forefinger. On the opposite side of the old man leering at Vince from his cyclo were two young office girls riding tandem on a Vespa motor scooter. They were dressed in European-style skirts and blouses and looked back over their shoulders at Vince from their position about three feet ahead. Their hair was blowing behind them in long rills and he could smell their perfume coming back to him in a slipstream of air. Their faces expressed deep curiosity and they each took a long, generous look at Vince and the girl before turning their eyes back to the road ahead.

The streets narrowed and the tall new buildings were replaced by the small shops and crowded living common to the sinks of corruption in Southeast Asia; the people took on the more typical bent postures and plain dress of rice farmers and country peasants.

"Where are we?" Battaglia said, the words dry in his mouth; he watched the scenery change and he felt unsettled.

"Why, are you nervous?" She shot a foot out in front of her: "Kaaa!" she shouted. "That is how Bruce Lee does it—Kaaa!" She thrust again.

"I'm not nervous."

"Yes you are. Kaaa!" The army cap fell from her head and she caught it just before it tumbled out of the cyclo. "We are coming to the theater."

"Autumn, can I ask you a serious question?"

She looked a little frightened and stopped playing kung-fu fighter; she crooked the little finger of her right hand into the corner of her mouth. "I think so."

The air had turned thick with a smell of street garbage, and a man urinated up against a wall, the yellow pee soaking through an army recruiting poster and trickling down the whitewash.

A gang of draft-age young men dressed in hippie garb of the U.S. and France idled on a street corner, the people hustling by giving them scant attention except to get out of their way.

"What did you want to ask me?" she said. The fatigue hat was fixed firm on her head and she sat up straighter to give the impression that she was attentive.

"Does anyone take this war seriously?"

She thought for a moment while she pulled at the corner of her mouth with her little finger. "I think the Viet Cong and North Vietnamese do, and maybe President Thieu and Vice President Ky."

He smiled at her honesty. "How about you?"

"I don't think about it much—not many people do. I just want to be left alone. It doesn't matter much, does it, if the Americans and South Vietnamese win the war?"

"Maybe you're right," he said. "Have you heard of a place called Ban Dau?"

"Where is that?"

"In the north."

"That's too far away."

Chapter 5

Battaglia fumbled awkwardly for the piasters in his pocket, and looked around with nervous eyes while he stood in front of the Cho-Chan kung-fu movie theater with the young Saigonese girl. The idea of coming here was absurd.

"There you are, fella," he said to the cyclo driver. He handed him a fistful of inflated piaster notes without counting them. "Take your girl out for a whirl of Cho-Chan."

The young man nodded and took the money without smiling, and pedaled away from the sidewalk into an alley, slowing disappearing into the dark environs without looking back. Vince found himself wondering what the cyclo driver's life was like, where the alley would take him, and whether or not the man had heard of Ban Dau.

Being back in this dangerous section of the city was not the smartest move he had ever made, and the fact that he was here to placate a child street vendor made his position difficult to accept.

"We go in now," Autumn Dove said, tugging at his arm.

"What's the hurry?"

"I am too excited—I can't wait." She stopped briefly at the colorful billboard showing kung-fu fighters in

67

action. Her leg flashed out in a stiff kick. "Kaaa!"

Battaglia shook his head and bought two tickets from the sexy girl in the booth. Her painted lips stretched into a critical smile and she said something in Vietnamese to Autumn Dove that sounded arrogant. Autumn stuck her nose in the air and pulled Vince to the door without answering the girl.

"What was that all about?"

She looked back at the ticket girl who was staring at both of them. "She said I was too young to have a boyfriend."

Vince started back to the ticket booth to give the girl a piece of his mind when he noticed a familiar figure, thin and small, hobbling toward him on a hand-hewn teakwood crutch. The waif was sticking close to the shadows, looking along the street for refuse that might be edible.

Autumn followed Vince into the street and began pulling on his arm again. "I want to go in and see the movie now. What are you doing in the street?" She tugged hard and her hand slipped from his arm and she fell flat on her bottom. Her eyes looked down the street in the direction that Battaglia was facing and saw the boy. "Why are you staring at him?"

Vince didn't answer. He reached down and lifted her up with his hand. *Tap . . . tap . . . tap*, the street urchin's crutch sounded on the pavement; he didn't look up, his eyes working the gutters.

The boy had tapped his way to within a few feet of Vince when Autumn said: "Why are you so interested in him?"

The waif looked up, startled out of his preoccupation with the daily chore of scavenging the street.

"Hello again," Battaglia said.

There was a moment's silence while the boy's eyes shifted between Vince and the girl. Recognition expanded

68

on his dirty face. "Hey, Marine; what you doing back in Cho-Chan? You look for more trouble?"

Battaglia, amused with the boy's not-so-good try at sounding tough, smiled down and hooked his thumbs into the waistband of his pants, behind the belt. "I'm not too smart, right?" He patted the kid on the shoulder. "But if you hadn't run off this morning, I wouldn't have had to come back looking for you."

"You come back to find me?" he said with Oriental eyes suddenly grown round.

"Sure I did—and to see a kung-fu movie, isn't that right, Autumn?" He turned back to the boy. "Come in with us, kid."

Autumn Dove was staring at the street urchin with a frown on her face, feeling jealous that someone else was going to share what she thought was her exclusive privilege. Her lips tightened. "I thought we were going to be alone."

She said something in Vietnamese to the waif and he raised the crutch over his head to crack her with it.

"Take it easy," Vince said. "What's the trouble?"

"He's dirty and smells bad and I don't want him to come to the movies with us. I don't like him." A string of Vietnamese flew from her mouth again and the boy raised his crutch.

"Hold it!" Battaglia raised his hands. "You two are going to have to work something out or no one is going to the movies."

"I don't want to go if she's coming," the boy said.

"Look," Vince said, "I know you two can be friends if you give it a try. You both want to go to the movie and it would be a shame if you didn't get to see it just because you can't get along with each other." He looked at both of them, sternly. "Now what do you say? Try to be friends, and let's go inside and see the film." He took them both by the hand.

They eyed each other apprehensively, but didn't resist Vince.

"What's your name, kid? You never gave it to me."

"I'm called Ly-boy."

"All right, Ly-boy, this here is Autumn Dove; Autumn Dove this is Ly-boy."

The two children nodded to each other without smiling.

Vince bought another ticket from the sexy girl in the booth and glanced across the street. Two draft-age young men turned their eyes away from him when he looked their way. One fellow, unable to control his nervousness, fidgeted with a newspaper-covered object tied down on his bicycle rack. He pulled his hands away and tucked them into his pants pockets in an attempt to look casual. The other lad picked at a pimple on his chin and stared down the street, his bony body stiff. A chicken walked out a narrow alley, scratched at a banana peel, started across the street, then changed its mind and ran back into the alley.

Ly-boy was also looking across the street at the two youths, his face shadowed in circumspection. He frowned and turned to follow Battaglia into the theater, stopping at the door before entering to once more look at the youths.

Inside, the theater was very dark, the only light coming from the screen. Vince, holding to Autumn Dove's hand, let her pull him down the aisle to the front seats.

Pulling in the opposite direction back toward the door, Ly-boy whispered, "I want to sit in the back." He tugged hard on Vince's hand, but was unable to exert much force because most of his weight rested on the crutch.

Feeling resistance in Battaglia's arm, Autumn Dove became impatient. "Hurry . . . hurry," she said, pulling harder on his hand.

"Ly-boy wants to sit in the back," Vince said.

"No—we must sit in the first row where we can see everything," she said.

"I want to sit in the back," Ly-boy said, loud.

Offended voices rose in the audience, scolding the two children, but Autumn Dove and Ly-boy paid no attention to them. They had reverted to their own language and the Vietnamese flowed hot and fast.

"*Toi muon ngoi phia sau!*" I want to sit in the back! Ly-boy shouted.

"*Truoc,*" in the front, Autumn said.

"*Phia sau,*" back.

"*Khong!*" no.

"*Phai!*" yes.

"Stop it," Vince said. Since they were closer to the entrance than to the screen, he hauled them, punching each other, up the aisle to the last row of seats and forced them to sit, Ly-boy on the aisle, next to Battaglia, and Autumn Dove on the other side of Vince.

They both sulked for a while (Autumn more than Ly-boy) before the swift and violent kung-fu action on the screen diverted their attention and they became totally absorbed in the film.

"That beautiful girl is the king's daughter, but her stepmother the queen hates her, and she has hired those bad men to kill her so her own daughter, the ugly one, will inherit the throne," Autumn explained to Battaglia.

In the next scene the queen's henchmen were seated in a pagoda situated along a roadside that led from the royal palace. "They are planning her murder," Autumn Dove whispered as she dug her fingers into the back of Vince's hand lying on the armrest. The other hand lifted to her mouth: "Oh—they are going to rape her first." Her fingers dug in harder.

The Chinese king's beautiful daughter left the palace gates and was on her way to visit her uncle, a reigning

71

chieftain in a nearby town, when she found herself surrounded by the band of thugs.

"This is it," Autumn said. She jammed all the fingers of one hand into her mouth and sat bent over in her seat, her legs pulled up under her chin in a squatting posture.

Meanwhile, on the opposite side of Battaglia, Ly-boy sat without saying a word, not watching the screen, but cautiously looking around the theater. Vince watched the uneasiness growing in his face.

The bad guys circled the girl and closed in. She stood her ground, legs slightly spread apart, arms hanging easily at her sides. She was dressed in gorgeous red-and-pink silk pajamas, and her hair was piled high on her head and decorated with bangles and bright-colored beads. Her small lips were painted crimson and pagoda-shaped earrings hung from her earlobes.

A big chap wearing a blue headband tied about his forehead and twirling a bolo chain in front of him stepped forward in attack posture, body bent forward at the hips, legs bent slightly at the knees, an arrogant, confident smile giving the impression that he could already taste the virginal pleasures of the sweet young flower standing defenseless before him.

The other men, equally as brutal in appearance, faces smeared with red and white chalk and glistening with sweat, stood in the background with folded arms, waiting their turn to violate the king's daughter, their smiles and lascivious jokes mocking the lovely creature.

Moans were coming from Autumn Dove's throat, attenuated by her small fist that was jammed into her mouth in fright. She took her hand from her mouth long enough to blurt out to Vince that the gang rape was about to commence and that the poor thing, after the queen's thugs had their fill of her, would be beheaded and her decapitated body sent to the royal palace in a sealed box with a forged message from the leader of the hill bandits

72

(who terrorized the surrounding villages) claiming the murder.

The big fellow with the blue headband, deciding that the bolo chain would get in his way and that the hapless girl could be easily taken with his hands alone, dropped the weapon and lunged for her without giving a second thought to defending himself, so confident was he that she was totally harmless and of no threat whatsoever.

It was not difficult to see that the girl's end was imminent and that the queen's henchmen would kill with impunity. Standing in the center of these men, beautiful, but looking small and frail, it was evident that the princess was going to suffer a violent and most unfortunate death.

"I can't stand it," Autumn Dove cried.

"Be quiet . . . it's only a movie," Ly-boy said.

"Oh, this is terrible—they are all going to do it to her."

"You are so dumb."

"Shut up and watch the movie," she said.

"How can I when you are making so much noise?"

"Isn't she beautiful? So young . . . so pretty." She pushed the fingers of both hands into her mouth and bit down.

Quite unexpectedly Vince's nose detected an unusual not-wholly-unpleasant odor that revived memories of his childhood days fishing for smallmouth bass from a boat on Lake Arapahoe. Between his legs, on the floor of the boat, was a pile of bass that was his and his father's morning catch and whose smell represented all the pleasantness of many hours on the water enjoying the great outdoors. A thin breeze was blowing from the shore close to which the boat drifted, carrying with it the fragrance of spring wildflowers blooming in the meadows. This odd combination of fish and wildflowers Vince now smelled in the theater, and he was astonished when he realized that it was coming from Autumn Dove.

Not sure that he was correct in assuming that the fish and wildflowers were attributable to his young friend, he leaned closer to her and sniffed.

She caught his movement in the darkened theater and took her eyes off the movie, looking oddly at him. "What are you doing?"

"Do you smell something?" he said, feeling uncomfortable that she had caught him.

She screwed up her nose in a way that made him wonder if she was indignant at his insinuation or was sampling the air for herself. "I don't smell anything," she said, and returned to the film and became thoroughly overwhelmed once more by her fantasy.

The strange smell noticeably increased or decreased, Vince concluded after closely observing Autumn Dove's behavior, proportionately with the rise and fall of the girl's excitement. The redolence reached its greatest strength during the love and fight scenes, and completely disappeared when the camera was panning the countryside or during long stretches of dialogue.

With the film starting to build to the rape scene, there was a sudden rise in the smell of fish and wildflowers. Battaglia looked over at Autumn Dove. She was sitting on the edge of her seat, hands tightly holding to the back of the seat in front of her, and her face (camouflaged fatigue cap pulled down over her head) thrust forward between the two people seated in the next row.

One of the Chinese thugs, who had apparently won the right to assault the king's daughter first, was just at the point of grabbing the girl when she came to life in a flashing display of precision kung-fu. A well-placed high kick followed by two quick slashes to the man's throat dropped him like a sack of rice. He lay unconscious on the ground—the other men gaped at each other with open mouths. Autumn screeched her delight.

Behind the princess, looming up out of the rice fields

and spanning a steep gorge in the cleft of the mountains, was a massive stone bridge supported by thick pillars. Not the girl, but the bridge, drew Battaglia's attention. Its heavy construction and permanence represented to him the indestructability of Asia and the ages of unproductive warring between Oriental empires and family dynasties.

Though the cameras and Autumn Dove's squeals were focused on the wild kung-fu action taking place in the foreground around the pagoda, Vince's mind was centered on the bridge in the background. His vision was fixed on the heavy span, and the screen became blurred around the edges, giving him the impression of looking into a lighted tunnel filled with moving mist through which could be seen the hazy image of the bridge.

He first became aware of being transported into a different dimension when he felt the perspiration trickling down the inside of his thighs, and then when he heard the distant sound of 100mm guns echoing in the tunnel. Then came the voice transmissions and he was suddenly careening down the narrow tunnel at combat velocity, the bridge calling to him at the end of the pipe:

"Go to button orange, Dash Two. Ban Dau dead ahead."

"Roger, boss. Tracking target at thirty degrees."

"Bring it around and keep thundering."

"Do you see the smoke?"

"Got it, Dash One . . . beginning one-eighty roll."

Ram the stick over to the knee and kick hard left rudder. Count off . . . one . . . two . . . controls centered . . . now up and over, HARD.

"Dash One in."

"Where's Dash Three?"

"Keep thundering."

"I've got guns at four o'clock."

"Guns at twelve—here come the goofballs."

"Triple A locking on."

75

"Dash Two in."

"My ECM is going bananas. I've got guns to six o'clock and at two. Where are you, Dash One?"

"Dash One off."

"Break right, Dash Two, *now!*"

"Okay, I'm set up for one hundred ninety mils at five hundred. Give me a thirty-second advance and then come in behind me if you see the red. Go to discreet channel and drop away to Tango when you see Dash Three's smoke."

"Roger."

"Dash Two off."

"Dash Three in."

"Geez I'm hit!"

"Who's hit?"

"Dash Two."

"It's Battaglia—he's a sheet of flame."

"Vince is going in—the guns got him."

"Kaa! Kaa! Kaa!" Autumn Dove cried while she stood on the seat, kicking, swinging, and jabbing, her small face bright with excitement, living the action on the screen. The people seated in the next two rows turned around and stared indignantly at her jumping in the seat with her arms and legs flailing. Vince shrunk down, chilled by the sweat soaking him through.

After dispatching the first gangster in a warming-up exercise, the princess proceeded to destroy the remaining men in rapid order until she stood alone in front of the roadside pagoda, her enemies strewn about her in bleeding, moaning piles. Not a hair on her beautifully constructed coiffure was out of place.

Autumn Dove, overjoyed with the success of her heroine, clapped her hands and cried, *"Tot qua! Tot qua!"* Good! Good!

At first the tugging at his shirt didn't register with Battaglia, who was preoccupied with Autumn Dove's antics and the angry people in front of her. The pulling became more urgent and he turned to Ly-boy, who was pointing to two young men who had entered the theater and were taking seats opposite him across the aisle. They were the two youths from across the street and one of them carried the paper-wrapped package under his arm.

Ly-boy straightened himself so he could whisper in Vince's ear, "I have been watching for them."

Vince looked surprised. "Trouble?"

"I think big trouble."

"What kind?" Battaglia said.

"The thing in the paper . . . under his arm."

"What do you think it is?"

"Maybe a *bomb*."

Vince looked into Ly-boy's face to see if he was pretending. The boy wasn't joking—his face was a block of ice.

"Kaa . . . kaa." Autumn Dove slashed at the air, ignoring the other customers. The army utility cap had slipped over her eyes and she had to tilt her head back to see the screen.

"Judging by the size of that thing, it could take out most of the people in the theater—that is, if it is a bomb," Battaglia said.

"It's a bomb."

"You're sure?"

"I'm sure," Ly-boy said.

"How can you be sure?"

"I know bombs." He pointed to his missing leg.

The minutes dragged by with neither Battaglia nor Ly-boy saying anything more. There was a lull in the film action and the king had arrived at the pagoda with his guard to take custody of the thugs and to question them. The queen loitered in the background, being consoled by her female attendants and fellow conspirators.

"Please, may I get some squid?" Autumn Dove said

to Vince.

"Good lord, what do you want with squid?" Battaglia's face involuntarily screwed up in a look of disgust.

"I'm hungry."

"We're going to have dinner after the movie," he said, imagining Autumn sitting beside him with a handful of slimy little sea monsters stinking up the theater.

"It is not so bad," Ly-boy said, discerning Vince's repugnance at the girl's request. "The squid are cut up in thin slices and dried and salted, and they are sold in small packages out front."

"You think you are so smart," Autumn said, still in a combatant mood. "You just want to show off."

Ly-boy returned to his vigilance of the youths across the aisle and didn't bother to answer her. She had hurt him with her corrosive words and there were tears in his eyes.

"Here," Vince said, handing Autumn Dove some money. "Get yourself what you want and bring me and Ly-boy a Coke."

"I would rather have a can of sugar-cane drink," he said. "Can I have ginger candy too?" He rubbed his eyes to dry the tears.

"Bring him what he wants," Vince said to Autumn Dove.

She climbed over Vince into the aisle and made a face at Ly-boy before disappearing through the curtains into the small, shabby lobby.

After thinking for a few minutes, Vince said, "The three of us are going to have a meeting when Autumn gets back."

Ly-boy looked up at him and nodded.

"I have a plan and I'm going to need your help. We will know soon enough if that thing wrapped in the newspaper is a bomb."

"It is a bomb," Ly-boy said simply.

"You may be convinced, but I'm not. I figure if the two fellows leave without the package, then we have a problem."

In the dim light of the theater, Vince and Ly-boy watched the two youths move to another row of seats. A customer came in and sat down close to them. The suspicious package went also, tucked under the taller boy's arm, in the samun position as it was when they had first come into the theater. However, Battaglia got a better look at it this time, and he noticed that the object was round and not square or rectangular as he'd first suspected.

Battaglia whispered to Ly-boy, "Do the Viet Cong ever use land mines to bomb public buildings?"

"Land mines are what they usually use—more effective than plastic. They like the claymore best." He looked at Vince for a moment then turned his attention back to the young men. "And the VC only bomb buildings where Americans are found, like movie theaters."

There was a shriek behind them in the aisle: "Oh, I can't stand it," Autumn Dove cried.

"What's the matter," Vince said, looking around to locate what it was that was troubling the girl and afraid that some life-threatening situation had befallen her.

"The queen is going to kill the princess," she said, unconcerned that she was disturbing the patrons and again getting cross looks. "She is hiding a knife in her robe—I saw it!" She clutched to her breast the food and drinks she had bought and stood in the middle of the aisle with her mouth making an O.

Battaglia pulled her gently into the row and put her in a seat. "Shhh—not so loud." He gave Ly-boy the sugar-cane drink and ginger candy. After popping open his can of warm Coke and taking a swig, he leaned over to Autumn Dove (who already had torn open the cellophane

79

package and was gnawing at the stringy squid), and said, "Don't be frightened, but I think there might be some trouble. Come close so we can talk without anyone hearing us."

With Ly-boy and Autumn Dove crowded close to him, their small heads pressed close to his, Vince explained his plan: "If those two fellows over there—"

"What two fellows?" Autumn said.

"The two sitting on the right side of the aisle a few rows up."

"Oh, I see them; they look mean."

"If they leave without the package—"

"What package?" she said.

"The one they came in with."

"What's in the package?" She was studying the youths.

"I don't know for sure, but it could be a bomb."

"*A bomb!*" she screamed before Battaglia could clamp a hand over her mouth.

There was no panic at first because only a few people in the theater understood English; but as the word was translated and passed along in whispers, the rustle of uneasiness grew to screams and shouts of "*Chat no! Chat no!*" Explosive! Explosive! and people clawed their way for the exits, completely out of control and blind with fear.

Vince's first thought was to prevent the two VC from leaving the theater, for they were sure not to detonate the bomb while they were still in the building.

The surge of people toward the back doors knocked him to the floor. He fought to his feet and struggled forward like a salmon swimming upstream. "Get the police," he shouted to the children.

It was a wild melee and he had to beat his way against the tide of people sweeping its way out of the theater. Vince had never heard such a noise; it was the sound of a dozen freight trains rumbling through a tunnel or an avalanche of snow crashing down a mountain.

He could see one of the youths in the middle of the seats, standing alone like an island in a surging sea. Battaglia used his arms like oars to propel himself forward through the ocean of bodies.

It appeared that the young man was puzzled and unable to decide what to do. His partner was already fighting his way to the closest exit.

Vince had no doubt as to what course of action to take; he homed in on the youth with the package.

The boy's face was horror-stricken with surprise when Vince grabbed him by the hair and twisted him around into a punishing headlock and drove him down between the seats. "You stupid VC jerk," he said. "How many people are you willing to kill to get one American?"

The boy tried to say something, but the headlock had his mouth pressed shut against Battaglia's hip. A kind of loose gravely sound came from the back of his throat.

"You creeps are crazy with hate, aren't you?"

Again the gravely sound.

"Or are you just plain dumb, willing to follow anyone who promises you a few crumbs?"

The youth struggled against the headlock, but Vince tucked it tighter against his hip.

"Ever heard of Ban Dau, creep?"

The adrenaline was racing through Vince's veins and a good bit of it had hit his vocal cords. He had become voluble, the words flowing in a steady staccato rhythm, hammering into the youth's ear like machine-gun bullets.

"You haven't heard of Ban Dau? Well, let me tell you about it. It's a long, steep gorge and your creepy friends are hiding in every crack with their guns and there's only one way in and one way out." He ground harder into the boy's head. "Your buddies will know exactly in what

81

direction I will be coming from and they will know exactly in what direction I will be leaving."

The young man's head had turned purple and he groaned.

"I don't have to fly into Ban Dau—I can stay right here in Cho-Chan . . . become a creep like you, a deserter; quite a few have done it, Americans and Viets. Maybe you can give me a few pointers, huh, kid?"

The gravely sound in the Viet's throat had become a gurgle and long strings of saliva hung like ribbons from his mouth and nose. The theater was nearly empty except for a few stunned people wandering around or lying on the floor. Amazingly, the movie was still running and the bad queen was riding away in her carriage, defended by her loyal guards; and the beautiful princess lay in the king's arms, a jewel-handled dagger sticking in her chest.

"Talk me out of going against Ban Dau, creep. Go ahead—talk me out of it. I'm listening." He laughed, loud. "I hear tell an American turncoat can live pretty well if he makes the right connections. Will you connect me up, creep? Help me get lost in the streets of Saigon, maybe help me to get to Hanoi? Then to the Kremlin— might as well go whole hog, wouldn't you say?"

Outside, sirens were heard in the distance, getting closer.

Vince hadn't noticed that the Viet locked in the vice grip was no longer struggling and hung loose in his arms. He rambled on: "Back home the great American citizenry has turned off the war. No one cares what we are doing over here—they want us to go away, stay away—not contaminate the home shores with our defiled bodies. Baby killer, they call me. War whore."

The sirens stopped outside the theater.

"My girl thinks I'm dirt."

He dropped the Viet to the floor as if he were a bag of dirty laundry. "My partner has taken over my business."

Shouts of Vietnamese came through the doors, and English.

"Why shouldn't I walk away from it . . . go with Ly-boy and Autumn Dove . . . disappear into the streets until I can sort things out . . . in a few months make my way to Thailand or Japan . . . or just lay low here until the stinking war is over. Why not?" He looked down at the Viet. "You creeps are going to get me at Ban Dau anyway."

"American, where bomb?" someone was saying.

A flashlight was pointed his way.

"Over here," he said. "The bomb's over here."

Then he heard Ly-boy's voice. "Marine, come out now."

"Who's there with you?"

"The police."

"Bring them down here. The VC didn't have time to set the fuse on the bomb."

The Vietnamese chattered nervously among themselves while they tried to decide who to send to check out the explosive. There were no volunteers, so the sergeant in command picked one man out of the squad and ordered him to investigate.

Meanwhile, Autumn Dove had snuck back into the back row of the theater and was watching the conclusion of the film while she chewed on the rubbery squid. She had decided that all the commotion was stupid.

Cautiously, one step at a time, the policeman worked his way down the aisle with a flashlight and Ly-boy limping behind him on his homemade crutch.

From the rear of the theater could be heard Autumn Dove's sniffling. "Oh, I can't stand it," she whimpered. "She's dead . . . the beautiful Chinese princess is dead and the queen got away." She carried on in this manner for a while, then there was a fresh outcry: "Oh, great god in heaven! The king has stabbed himself."

83

No one paid any attention to her, least of all the projectionist, who had been the first to flee the theater. The buiding was empty except for the police, Battaglia, the children, and the few who were trampled during the panic and who lay injured in the aisles, moaning.

The nervous policeman shined the flashlight into the youth's face.

"He doesn't look so good," Ly-boy said.

The cop pressed his fingers to the boy's neck, feeling for a pulse. He turned the flashlight on the open eyes. "Dead," he said.

Vince ran a hand through his hair. "I didn't think I was hurting him that bad."

"Where explosive?" the policeman said.

Battaglia pointed to the wrapped object lying a few feet from the body. The newspaper had been partially torn away during the struggle, exposing the insides.

The beam of the flashlight fell on the package and the policeman looked at Vince, his face stony and expressionless. He reached down and picked up the package, tore away the paper, and held up for Vince's inspection a round load of freshly baked French bread. He broke it apart to be sure there was nothing inside.

Chapter 6

"You sure get around, Lieutenant," the MP sergeant said, stepping back to let the Saigon policeman swing the cell door open. "You've only been in town a few hours and you've already managed to kill one Viet and stampeded a theater full of others peacefully enjoying a neighborhood movie; not to mention that gang of fun-lovers you put in the hospital only minutes after stepping off your plane at Tan Son Nhut."

"Cut it out, Sergeant, and just tell me where I go from here. I'm in no mood for wisecracks."

The big MP tipped the helmet back on his head with the end of his baton and smiled without looking cheered. "No, I don't suppose you are, sir."

"What's the verdict?"

"The Vietnamese say you're free—"

"*What?*"

"—in my custody."

"You're kidding."

"It's routine in matters like this. While the Vietnamese are investigating the so-called *incident* at the Cho-Chan theater you are released into the custody of the U.S. Army, who in turn releases you on your own recognizance and that of the Marine Corps. Your commanding officer, Colonel Dasher, has been notified."

"That a fact?" Vince said, not at all impressed with

what the Army had done on his behalf. He had hoped that the Viets would keep him locked up.

"We know where we can find you," the sergeant said, turning to leave.

"Yeh, Ban Dau."

"What's that, sir?"

"A little place up north I plan to visit to rest up after my vacation in Saigon." He chuckled to himself after thinking for a moment. "Don't put that down in the little notebook you keep in your breast pocket. I haven't decided whether or not I'm really going."

The MP scratched his head and walked out to his jeep.

Doubts and confusion about himself, and the contemptuous stares he got from the Viet policemen surrounding him, clouded Battaglia's thinking and it was with a great deal of anxiety that he left the police station. He wondered what kind of justice system the Vietnamese had, and if he would get a fair trial.

"Hi, kids," he said, coming down the steps to the sidewalk. "What are you doing here?"

Autumn Dove and Ly-boy looked down at their feet, not sure of what to say, nervous and looking forlorn.

"Hey, what's the matter?"

"We were worried about you," Autumn Dove said.

"Yes . . . we didn't know what the police were going to do to you. We wanted to help but there was nothing we could do because we are only kids."

Vince kneeled down and put his arms around them. "It looked like I killed a man by mistake, and I'm going to need some time to think that through. I'm not going to be very good company and it would be better for you if you go home."

"I don't have a home," Autumn Dove replied.

"Don't you live with your grandmother, that woman who wanted a hundred dollars for the mango?"

"She's not my grandmother—I don't know where my

86

family is. I live on the streets."

He looked at Ly-boy.

"I live on the streets too."

Vince sighed and glanced down the street at the small sidewalk shops bustling with activity. "Hungry?" he said.

They both nodded, too embarrassed to look up.

"I shouldn't have killed that boy; there was no need to kill him. I should have checked to be sure what was wrapped in the package he was carrying before attacking him."

"You thought it was a bomb—so did I," Ly-boy said. "You had to do something."

"It wasn't a bomb—and he's dead."

"He was a Viet Cong," Autumn Dove said with no emotion. "It's good that he's dead."

Vince frowned at her. "You don't know if he was a VC."

"He could have been. Just tell yourself he was and forget about it."

"Is that how it is?" he said.

"That's how it is."

Silence.

More silence.

Finally Vince said, "Get us a cyclo, Autumn, and we will find that restaurant I promised you."

"The one with the cloths covering the tables and that have men in suits that give you a book to read so you can choose what you want to eat?"

Ly-boy looked at the rags covering his frail body. "They won't let me in a nice restaurant like that."

"You're not coming with us," Autumn Dove said.

"Autumn!" Vince said sternly. "That's enough of that kind of talk."

"You promised to take *me*. I don't want him to come with us."

"From now on, wherever we go Ly-boy comes with us."

Ly-boy brushed the beginning of a tear from his eye.

Another moment of nervous silence passed between them and Autumn's toes wiggled rapidly as if they wanted to crawl into the pavement. She walked into the middle of the street, sullen and looking unpleasant, where she stood with arms folded until she saw a cyclo and than began waving wildly to get the driver's attention.

"The driver wants to know where to take us," she said. "He doesn't speak English."

"Tell him to take us back to Cho-Chan," Vince said with a touch of humor in his voice and stepping into the cyclo. "It suits my mood and I'm beginning to believe it's where I belong. At least I've grown accustomed to the place." He crossed his legs and leaned back in the seat. "And it may become my permanent home," he added under his breath.

"There are no restaurants in Cho-Chan with cloths on the tables," Autumn Dove said.

"I know where one is," Ly-boy quickly said.

Autumn made a vulgar sign with her fingers which Vince surmised was meant to insult Ly-boy. She folded her arms and put on her unpleasant face. "I don't want to eat in Cho-Chan," she said.

"And why not?" Vince asked with irritation. "Just because Ly-boy suggested it?"

"Maybe," she said with a haughty air. "He thinks he knows everything."

"It is a nice restaurant and you will like it, Autumn," Ly-boy said in a friendly tone. "It is in a nice hotel too," he added.

"I won't like it."

"Don't be difficult," Vince said. "Instruct the driver on how to get there, Ly-boy, and let's all try to get along, shall we?" He gave Autumn a firm look.

Battaglia couldn't fully comprehend the significance of all that had happened to him in the few hours he had been in Saigon; there had been a physical and sensory overload. He had learned more about Vietnam and its people then he could have if he had spent months in reading and study. He had suddenly been hit with a kaleidoscope of events with such intensity that his senses were overwhelmed and he felt much like a person waking from a dream filled with symbols and unfamiliar objects that defied interpretation. He required time and rest to mull over the events in order to understand the fullness of his experience. He wouldn't get the time or the rest.

It was with a good feeling in his belly that he stepped out of the cyclo in front of a clean and unpretentious hotel somewhere deep in the bowels of mysterious Cho-Chan. He anticipated that here he would find the rest that he needed to sort out what had happened to him during his wild few hours in the capital city.

And the question of Ban Dau was still stuck in his craw, demanding attention, giving him no peace.

"Here we are," Ly-boy said, his face bright with expectation. It was obvious that this was a great event in his impoverished life.

Beyond the small walled courtyard and arched gate guarded by two lions with dragon heads, Vince could see a curtained window behind which were tables covered with white tablecloths.

"Looks comfortable—not too fancy—but nice, kind of cozy, a quaint watering hole for the denizens of Cho-Chan," Battaglia said, studying the architecture. "This building could have been moved straight from old Peking."

They walked past the two dragon-head lions and into the courtyard, stopping for a few minutes to admire the fountain and its pool filled with gold and white and red carp swimming among the lotus plants.

Autumn Dove fell into the pool trying to catch a fish with her hands, and with his crutch Ly-boy knocked down one of the many hanging lanterns lining the walk.

"Do you like it, Autumn?" Ly-boy said, attempting to placate her.

"It's all right. They better have books with the food written in them or I won't like it."

Ly-boy fingered the rags hanging on his body and examined his reflection in the pool. Autumn saw him and became self-conscious of her own appearance, straightening and brushing her hair with a small hand; she smoothed her wet clothes.

If the restaurant had been uptown in a more class-conscious part of Saigon, Vince and the children would have created a disturbance, but as it was, no one in the Cho-Chan hotel paid much attention to the shabby children and their American benefactor.

The headwaiter gave Autumn and Ly-boy a quick glance, smiled at Battaglia, and showed the humble trio to a pleasant table near the moon gate that led to a small garden filled with red peonies and purple larkspur.

Vince closely watched the children, enjoying what was turning out to be a fun experience for all three of them. At first Autumn and Ly-boy sat quietly and wood stiff, moving only their eyes, which took in everything. Eventually they began to cautiously explore the table.

Autumn Dove slowly brought a hand up from her lap and fingered the tablecloth. "Nice," she said.

"Don't touch it," Ly-boy said.

"I can if I want."

The waiter brought the menus, and with a bit of ceremony opened one for each of the children and placed it before them.

"Ah, they have the food books," Autumn Dove said, pleased.

Vince figured that neither of the children could read the French but were pretending they could by contorting their faces and working their eyebrows to show that they were deciding what to choose.

"I can help you decide what to order, if you wish," Battaglia said.

Autumn Dove looked up from the oversized menu into which her head was buried. Cocked at a rakish angle, the army cap made her look like a young warrior just in from a field operation; it also looked incongruous against the fasionable attire worn by the customers seated at the other tables.

"I can choose for myself," she said indignantly. She returned to the menu.

"Well, I only thought . . ."

"I will have the crepes and frog legs." She pointed to the correct entry in the menu and added, "You should order a bottle of red Bordeaux with our dinner. Ly-boy and I will have a taste and you can drink the rest if you wish."

Vince smiled. "You are marvelous. Where did you learn French?"

"At the school in the Catholic orphanage. The nuns also taught me English and math and other things before I ran away." She smiled sweetly at Battaglia. "Ly-boy was there too. I didn't like him then either."

"She doesn't like anybody," Ly-boy said.

"Where are your parents?" Vince asked Autumn.

"Dead, I think. That's what the nuns told me."

He looked at Ly-boy.

"My father was killed in the war," he said. "There were too many children in the family for my mother to take care of so she gave me to my grandmother. She was always drunk on rice wine and she beat me a lot. She was too old to take care of me, so I ran away."

Vince gave their orders to the waiter and showed the children how to place the napkin on their laps, how to use the knife, fork, and spoon (in place of chopsticks), and the proper way to drink from a glass.

"Some day I will marry a rich Frenchman and live in Paris in a big villa on top of a hill," Autumn Dove said.

"Ha!" Ly-boy laughed. "You will marry a cyclo driver and live in Cho-Chan in a room above a laundry."

She gave him the vulgar sign with her fingers.

Though Battaglia was listening to Autumn's and Ly-boy's patter, his attention had turned to the restaurant's entrance where a long-eyed girl with honey legs stood with a man dressed in a European-cut tropical suit.

Her pouting lips puckered in response to something the man said while she surveyed the tables and waited to be seated. The headwaiter was busy with other customers, and it was apparent by the impatience on her face that she was used to prompter attention. One hand was lightly resting on a cocked hip that rocked to the rhythm of its own tune and she tapped her toe on the wooden floor.

The pouting lips puckered again when her sloe eyes caught sight of Vince. She quickly changed focus to the table next to his and then out through the moon gate to the peonies and larkspur. From the smiles of other men seated at the tables, Vince gathered that she was well known in Cho-Chan.

"Why are you watching that woman?" Autumn Dove said.

"I think I've seen her before." Vince ate an olive from the relish tray and looked back at the girl, who ignored him as if he weren't there.

Autumn contemplated Battaglia. "You're staring at her."

He passed her the relish tray. "Have an olive, and mind

your own business."

"Her name is Nghia," Ly-boy said.

Vince stopped chewing and eyed him. "How do you know here name?"

"She has a room here, and sometimes she gives me food to eat from the kitchen, when she can. And sometimes when I stand near the gate she makes the men she brings here give money to me and the other children. She's nice. The other girls don't give me anything."

On closer inspection of the room Vince saw that most of the tables were occupied by young Vietnamese women with Caucasian men. He remembered what the hotel bellboy at the Caravelle had told him. "Are these all tiger girls in here?"

Ly-boy surveyed the room. "All of them."

Autumn Dove, jiggling around on her chair and bursting with curiosity, said to Vince, "Where have you seen her—is she your girl friend?"

"I can't be sure if it's the same girl I talked to at the bus stop. She wasn't wearing makeup and her hair wasn't fixed this way; and she was simply dressed."

"She's very good-looking."

"Could be the same girl," Vince said. "It's hard to tell from here."

"Want me to ask?" Ly-boy offered.

"No—it doesn't matter; she didn't like me. In fact, she was downright nasty to me." He ate another olive and smiled to himself. "I'm probably mistaken. The girl at the bus stop wasn't at all inclined toward men and this kind of work; she came from a rich family."

The men at the other tables, to the consternation of the women they were with, made no pretense at admiring Nghia's unusual good looks; and many of the men, the evidence being in their smiles and nods in her direction, had more than a casual acquaintance with her.

The headwaiter apologized to her for the delay and

smiled to the anxious-looking man with her. He quickly turned his attention back to Nghia and apologized several more times before leading her to a table that looked out to the small garden and its splashing fountain. Her client trailed dutifully behind, not knowing how to act exactly (his hands made the journey from his pockets to his belt, up to his tie, then to his chin and hair, and back to his pockets during the short walk to the table).

Passing through the tables, Nghia acknowledged the greetings given her:

"Hello, Nghia."

"Good to see you, Nghia."

"*Chao co.*"

"I'll call you next week."

"*Manh gioi.*"

As she passed by his table, Vince glanced up and looked into the same eyes that had hypnotized him at the bus stop. No other eyes he had ever seen had shadows in the corners and a touch of powder blue in the whites around the black pupils. Phoenix eyes the Chinese called them— and he was convinced there were no two sets like them. She gave her tight rump an exaggerated twist and bumped Vince's arm.

"She did that on purpose," Autumn said and stared at Nghia's behind. "She so pretty, prettier than the king's daughter."

Ly-boy gave her a vacant look.

"The movie, stupid; the princess in the kung-fu movie," she said.

The food was served, and the two children forgot their etiquette lesson and ate like starved puppies. Vince picked at his eggs Benedict and watched Nghia seated two tables away. Once she looked up from her menu and he thought she would see him, but her eyes went through his face in that mysterious way they had at the bus stop, and she placed the back of a finely molded hand to her lips

94

to stifle a yawn. It was apparent that she was bored.

"Why aren't you eating?" Autumn Dove said, her mouth stuffed with frog legs and crepes.

"You don't miss a thing, do you?"

"Aren't you hungry?"

He began eating more earnestly. "I've been thinking."

"About her?" she said.

Vince smiled. "Yes, but also about us."

Ly-boy peeked up from his plate. "Us?"

"I figure we ought to stick together. I can kind of look after you two and you can kind of look after me." He looked through the double French doors into the unpretentious lobby of the hotel and then to the pleasant little garden. "I like it here. What do you say if I check out of the stuffy Caravelle and move in here? I can get a room big enough for all three of us and you can stay with me?"

Ly-boy and Autumn smiled through the rest of the meal.

Battaglia called the Caravelle and left instructions at the desk that a little girl wearing a U.S. Army fatigue cap would arrive shortly to pay his bill and that she should be given his seabag.

Putting Autumn Dove in a cab, he told the driver, "Be sure to wait for her. When you bring her back I'll pay you." Then he said to Autumn, "If you have any trouble just call me."

"I know what to do." She regarded him with wide eyes.

"Be sure you get everything out of the drawers and don't forget to check the bathroom."

"I said I know what to do."

"Okay, okay—don't get arrogant. Here's the money to pay the bill."

She took the piasters from his hand and stuffed the money inside her underpants. Readjusting the pajamas around her waist, she tapped the driver on the shoulder and the cab drove off without her giving a backward glance.

Vince stood on the sidewalk scratching his head and watched the cab disappear around the corner, the camouflaged fatigue cap cocked on Autumn's head visible through the rear window.

"She's different," Ly-boy said.

Vince looked up and down the street, and then at Ly-boy. "Listen, kid," he said. "We've got a few things to do before Autumn gets back. Let's start by getting some new clothes for the two of you—take me to a shop."

The look on Ly-boy's face as he stood on his one good leg made Vince swallow hard.

"New clothes?" His chin was quivering and his eyes grew big and filled with tears. "You mean you are going to buy new clothes for me and Autumn."

"Come on, tough guy—don't get soft on me." Vince ruffled the boy's hair. "Let's find a store."

Rather than take Vince to the larger, more expensive shops near the hotel where he was apt to get fleeced, Ly-boy led him through a maze of narrow streets and alleys until they entered a series of passageways that wound downward into dark cellars where bean sprouts and mushroom farms were laid out alongside dimly lit stalls that sold everything from M-16 ammunition to twenty-ounce bars of smuggled gold. Peeking into a makeshift room constructed from discarded crates and cardboard boxes, Battaglia watched men and women with sickly yellow-hued faces, lying so close to each other there wasn't room to step between them, suck on long-stemmed opium pipes. Two middle-aged men wearing nothing but dirty undershorts sat in a corner playing Mah-Jongg.

Squatting in the stall next to the opium den, a woman roasted the haunch of a small animal over a brazier filled with burning charcoal. The smell of the cooking meat

96

mixed with the sickly odor of opium was so bad that Vince had to cover his nose with a handkerchief.

"What's that she's cooking?" Vince said. "It smells awful."

"Dog." Ly-boy limped along on his crutch and exchanged words with the denizens of Cho-Chan.

A girl of about twenty-one with the sallow complexion of the opium addict sat on a pile of sugar-cane stalks, fondling a small monkey. Her long hair was matted together in knots and was heavily streaked with gray. It struck Vince that though this young woman was suffering from a number of serious problems, the saddest was that her hair was turning white at such a young age. Brushing past the monkey he looked down at the top of her head and saw that what he had thought were white hairs actually were strands of hair thickly coated with clusters of white lice eggs.

Everywhere he looked he saw life seeping out of bodies. The disease, poverty, and debauchery, made worse by the stench of feces and rotting garbage, was insidious. Vacant eyes stared out at Vince from holes in faces that showed no expression. The *drip-drip-drip* from the ancient stones walls covered with a thick green slime echoed in the corridors of time, sending the message that little had changed in Cochin China since the days of the Manchus.

Fighting on top of torn sacks of moldy rice, a dozen rats squeaked and bit each other to the complete unconcern of those walking past. A U.S. Army deserter strung out on heroin lay on his back next to the sacks, an old mama-san holding his hand.

"Let's get out of here," Battaglia said.

"What's the matter, Marine, don't you like my home?" Ly-boy had a sardonic smile. "Come along around the corner here and I'll show you more of what the war has done to us."

97

"The war hasn't done this . . . you've done it to yourselves."

Up on top, Vince blinked at the sunlight and breathed deep, thankful to be out of the crypt and its evil sights and smells. "That's as close to hell as anyone can get here on earth."

"You get used to it," Ly-boy said.

"I can't believe that."

Four blocks away they found a clean shop selling ready-made children's clothing made in Malaysia and Thailand. Ly-boy was reluctant to choose anything for himself, spending more time helping Vince make selections for Autumn Dove. The shopkeeper tried to sell the whole stock to Battaglia, making no distinction between sizes or style. However, Ly-boy, cast in a new role and enjoying every minute of it, took his time and carefully examined all the garments and shoes brought out, holding each piece up to the light to be sure there were no flaws, and sizing the dresses, pants, and blouses by holding them next to his body to compare with Autumn Dove's height.

"We can't be sure these will fit her," he said. "Wait here; I won't be long." He stumped away on his crutch.

Battaglia, amused by the boy's concern for Autumn Dove, smiled to himself. He became occupied with choosing shirts, shoes, and several pairs of pants for Ly-boy, and holding a sign-language conversation with the shopkeeper.

Ly-boy was back in ten minutes, pulling behind him a skinny girl about the same age as Autumn Dove. "She's about the right size," he said, looking her up and down.

While the girl stood still, obedient to Ly-boy's instructions, he placed each piece of clothing against her body, now and then slipping a blouse or dress over her head and standing back to survey the fit. He handed his choices (neatly folded) to Vince.

Carrying two large paper-wrapped bundles by their strings and holding two additional packages under his arms, Battaglia left the shop with Ly-boy limping along beside him. The little model, wearing the new pantaloons and blouse Vince had bought for her, walked proudly along a few paces behind, looking pleased. Without a word she broke off and disappeared back into the labyrinth of interconnecting passages and alleys whence she had come.

"Won't Autumn be surprised?" Ly-boy squeezed one of the packages with his free hand.

"Oh, she'll be surprised all right." He glanced at Ly-boy leaning heavily on his crutch as he struggled to keep up the pace. "How about you?"

"Me?"

"Yeh—what do you think of your new clothes?"

Ly-boy looked down at the pavement stones and smiled, trying not to appear self-conscious. "I like them."

"There's one more thing we should do before we go back to the hotel." He slowed his pace so that Ly-boy, having trouble with his crutch on the uneven cobblestones, wouldn't have to work so hard. "We're not going to be eating in that hotel restaurant much—too expensive—and not our style, right?"

"Right, boss."

"So we're going to need someone to cook us meals that we can bring up to the room, right?"

He leaned on his crutch, thoughtful.

"Know of anyone?" Vince asked.

"You want French, Chinese, Vietnamese, or American food?"

"A little of everything."

"Turn this corner here and we'll go down to the end of the alley."

"The food has got to be clean, Ly-boy."

"Don't worry—this food is cleaner and tastier than

99

you can get anywhere in Saigon, I promise you."

Fifty feet before the alley emptied into the next street, a small restaurant with only four tables stood sandwiched between two rooming houses. An indolent, ill-tempered woman on the second floor of one of the houses, her breasts hanging over the balcony rail, shouted down at Battaglia: "You go home, American. No want stinking American here Vietnam." Her mouth was big and full of bean sprouts and pork from the wooden bowl she held in her hand. Much of the food fell out of her mouth while she shouted poorly pronounced obscenities at Vince. Each obscenity was accented with a stabbing thrust of her chopsticks.

As a final punctuation in her string of insults, the woman worked her mouth in a sucking, twisting motion, reared back on her heels, then quickly shot the upper part of her body forward and emptied a trail of sputum aimed at his head.

Vince stepped aside in time to avoid the stringy mass and ducked inside the restaurant before another salvo could be launched at him. A small Japanese woman, wearing a clean white apron and her hair twisted neatly into a knot on the back of her head, stepped through the hanging beads that separated the kitchen from the tables, and smiled at Battaglia.

Vince smiled back and pointed upstairs to the pugnacious woman. "Who is that character?" he said.

The Japanese woman said something in Viet and placed an index finger on her head.

"She says not to worry about that woman—she's crazy," Ly-boy interpreted.

Vince looked at the scrubbed tile floor and white walls and clean windows. The tables were covered with spotless white tablecloths. Bottles of small green peppers, fish sauce, and soy sauce sat in the center of each table, among drinking glasses filled with chopsticks and soup spoons, a box of toothpicks, and a jar of plum sauce and bean paste that had a tiny glass spoon protruding from the crescent-shaped opening in the jar's top. There were no napkins or forks or knives.

Through the beaded curtain, he could see clouds of steam bubbling out of kettles taken from an army field kitchen. Ly-boy said something to the woman and she parted the beads to allow Vince to inspect her food. She went to a counter and began rolling out dough on a floured board, a task in which she had evidently been engaged before being interrupted.

"What's she making?" Vince asked.

"Won ton."

Battaglia looked in the oven. "Croissants," he said, surprised.

The woman left her won ton and poured a measure of peanut oil into a wok. The heated oil quickly vaporized in to a transparent fog and she dropped in handfuls of broccoli and bok choy, stirring the vegetables very fast with a wooden spatula.

"Cho-cho-san," a customer called from the tables.

She turned and called back, then spoke to Ly-boy.

"Cho-cho-san says that the man at the table comes in every day at this time for his bowl of pho."

"Pho?" Battaglia looked inside the kettles, attempting to identify the pho.

Cho-cho-san ladled out the pho noodle soup into a large bowl and cut in a few slices of pork and beef. She set the bowl on a tray and placed a dish of raw leafy vegetables, bean sprouts, and a slice of lime next to it. The soup was taken out to the man pounding the table with his spoon.

Ly-boy looked at Vince. "Food okay?"

"Looks fine, kid—I think you brought me to the right place. We can't go wrong with Cho-cho-san."

Ly-boy laughed happily and turned to Cho-cho-san

coming through the beads. He said a few words and she too laughed.

"Everyone thinks something is funny," Vince said.

"I told her that you were an American Marine that needed the best food in Vietnam so you could go back strong to Da Nang to kill lots of Viet cong and North Vietnamese. She thought that was funny."

The smiling cook and Ly-boy jabbered together for a few minutes before Vince motioned to the door. They said good-bye with the agreement that either Ly-boy or Autumn Dove would be coming daily for the food to take back to the hotel, and that Cho-cho-san would provide a variety of meals, including fresh scrambled eggs and other American dishes that she vowed were tastier than what he could get in Wichita.

For his part, Battaglia promised to pay her a bonus if her cooking came up to the standard she promised and included at least one apple pie and a coconut cake. An additional bonus of a dozen kisses and hugs was to be given if the coffee was always fresh and hot. This set Cho-cho-san off into a fit of giggles that Vince left her with as he and Ly-boy departed for the hotel a block away to wait for Autumn Dove to return with his seabag.

Passing through the garden gate, Ly-boy patted a lion on the head and stopped at the pool to watch the happily colored carp swimming in and out of the lotus. Night was coming on in Cho-Chan, and the Chinese hanging lanterns were already lit. The last shades of a magenta sunset were disappearing into the Southeast Asian dusk and the rooftops glistened with the ending light of day.

Battaglia stood in the courtyard in a sort of dream state, feeling the centuries-old ground pressing against his feet. He didn't have to think too hard to get the musty feeling of old Cathy. He thought back to the Ching dynasty and the conquering army that took the land of Annam for its own, mingling its blood with what was to become the Indochina of today.

The sunset had turned to a raspberry pink so vivid that Vince could taste its sweet flavor. Ly-boy dangled his crutch in the pool and the curious carp swarmed around it to investigate the intrusion.

"It doesn't take a great deal of imagination to be transported back a few centuries," Battaglia said while he admired one of the hand-painted paper lanterns. In his mind's eye he saw a concubine of a wealthy mandarin walking among the peonies, stooping here and there to smell their fragrance. "Autumn isn't back yet," he said to Ly-boy. "I wonder if everything is all right with her."

Ly-boy looked worried too. "It's getting dark. Maybe you should go look for her."

"Let's check at the desk—maybe she left a message."

The lobby of the Khach-san Bong was painted the same color as the ripe persimmon fruit growing in the courtyard. Soft and delicate in tone, the lobby with its carved panels in the ceiling, and its hardwood chairs and kangs void of any upholstering, was pleasant and inviting; yet it reserved for itself a subtle feeling of austerity, retaining a bit of the past's severity and bare, simple ways.

The wood-on-wood sound of Ly-boy's crutch tapping across the lobby floor turned a few heads, but for the most part the tiger girls paid no attention to the waif. Several, however, inspected Vince with more than idle curiosity.

"Room *four-ten*," Battaglia said to the desk clerk.

Vince was handed a heavy-linked, six-inch-long chain with a bronze medallion attached at one end and an ancient skeleton key measuring the same length as the chain attached to the other end. The room number was stamped into the bronze.

"Any messages?" he asked.

The taciturn clerk shook his head and returned to the

103

abacus he was using to balance the hotel's books.

"I'm worried about Autumn," Vince said to Ly-boy, who had his back to him.

"She might be in there," Ly-boy said.

"You kidding—in the bar?"

"You don't know Autumn. She does crazy things."

They walked over to the doorway and looked in. A pair of honey legs as smooth as butter were crossed at the table nearest the door. Vince's eyes followed them up to the firm thighs where the legs ended at the hem of the miniskirt. His inspection continued up to the expensive brocaded blouse and settled on the high cheekbones with the small scar beneath the eye. A pair of long Manchu eyes, brooding and mysterious, burned into him from the half-light of the bar, and the full pouting lips twitched with irritation.

For a moment, Nghia's eyes riveted him to the floor; then came that stare that seemed to be focusing on the back of his brain without noticing his face; a thousand-yard stare.

"She's not in here," Ly-boy said.

"Who?"

Ly-boy looked at him strangely. "Autumn."

"Oh, yeh, Autumn," he said, watching the girl wind her way through the tables to the dance floor and fold her body into the nervous man.

Laying her head down on her date's shoulder, she watched Vince without a hint of expression in her face until the man wheeled her into the center of the dance floor where she was lost among the other dancers.

"Come on, Ly-boy, let's get out of here."

"Are we going to find Autumn?"

"We'll go up to the room and talk it over." He hitched up the packages to get a firmer hold and headed for the elevator. The Khach-san Bong had only one bellhop, and he was busy feeding the pool carp that would later find

104

themselves on the menu.

The elevator, a cagelike affair, was old, one of the first installed in Indochina before World War II, and made groaning and clanking sounds, and gave other indications that it would soon gasp its last.

The elevator operator, an energetic-looking young man from Burmese stock, smiled at Vince with his big white teeth. "What floor please?" he said in stilted English.

"Fourth . . . the top floor."

The elevator door clanged open on its mechanical rollers, and Vince stepped out onto the landing. The door clanged shut and the elevator chugged down to the lobby, groaning on its main pulley and cable.

Vince stood on the landing, struck by the very real feeling that he had been carried back in time to Cochin China before the turn of the century, when only a handful of Westerners had penetrated the mysteries of Annam.

Leading away from the landing was a wide hallway illuminated by one low-watt bulb hanging on a long cord from the ceiling. The light bulb was naked. The floor was uncarpeted teakwood, dark like the raw wood walls and grooved with years of use. A small window at the end of the hall was caked with a thick coating of dirt that had been accumulating since the Boxer Rebellion. Heavy plain doors, fitted with brass latch affairs rather than doorknobs, opened inward from the hall. Room 410 was located at the end.

As Battaglia walked slowly down the musty-smelling corridor, all was quiet behind the doors except for an occasional restrained laugh. A lone mouse crawled out of a hole in the wall and scurried along the high baseboard. It stopped in a corner and quietly watched Vince before disappearing back into the hole. Down below in the lobby the elevator clanged.

In room 409, across the hall from Battaglia's room, a quarrel was in progress. By the time Vince reached his door it was in full swing, and there was a crash of bodies followed by a metallic noise that sounded like a bedpan wobbling on the floor. A scream and the door flew open. A sloe-eyed seductress wrapped in a bedsheet and cursing in broken English jumped out into the hall, followed by a half-dressed GI with a short-cropped haircut and wearing glasses over his long nose. The dog tags around his neck jangled against his bare chest and he too was shouting obscenities.

The girl, surprised to see Vince in the hall, threw herself into his arms and began crying for help in words that he didn't understand. The GI, out of his mind with rage, pulled up short in front of Vince and demanded that he step aside.

"Now wait a minute," Battaglia said. "I don't know what's happened between you two, but I'm not about to stand by and watch you beat this girl."

"It's none of your affair," the GI said, pulling nervously at his dog tags. "Get out of the way or I'll break your neck too—makes no difference to me," he said in a Texas drawl.

By now the doors were open to the other rooms and the occupants were looking out. Several people had come all the way into the hall and had formed small groups of two and threes, asking each other what the trouble was about and who was at fault, and why there were two men and only one woman, though no one was really concerned except out of curiosity, being more interested in what was going to happen next.

It was generally agreed among the tiger girls that there was going to be big trouble and that they should get their clients out of the hotel before the police and MPs arrived to ask embarrassing question. The men resisted the pleas of the girls to hurry and get dressed, thinking that this

106

was nothing more than a small quarrel that would soon be worked out. The girls, however, knowing better, tugged and cajoled the men, explaining that this was not what it appeared, a variation on the eternal triangle, but a more serious matter that could have dreadful consequences.

"Help me, help me," the girl begged, holding tight to Vince. "He kill me sure."

"You're right about that, you bitch." The GI got hold of her long hair and yanked her screaming from Battaglia's arms and kicked her square in the stomach.

Battaglia's fist crashed into the man's face, shattering his glasses and dropping him to the boards.

The tiger girl, made of strong stuff, got up from the floor, holding her stomach and gasping for air. The bedsheet fell away and her hand, clutching a ten-inch Ka-Bar knife, plunged down on the GI rolling on the floor.

"She's a Viet Cong, man," the half-conscious soldier said.

Battaglia caught the girl's wrist in midair and twisted the Ka-Bar to the floor. It hit hard, making a heavy *thud* on the wood. The girl grabbed for it, but Vince kicked it away and stepped on the girl's neck, pinning her to the floor. A siren wailed across Cho-Chan, in the distance, getting closer.

"She's a pig-sucking VC," the GI said. He held his head in his two hands. "I found this in her purse." He held out a photograph.

Vince examined the picture. The girl on the floor was standing in the middle of the photo. She was dressed in black pajamas and an AK-47 was slung over her left shoulder. Raised high in her right hand was the decapitated head of an American Army corporal, his uniformed torso laying at her feet. Three other Viet Cong were standing around her with big smiles.

"Not me, not me," the girl shouted.

Vince looked close at the photo, then back down at the

girl under his foot.

"Not me," she cried.

The elevator chugged up to the landing and after a second the door slid open. Vince glanced up from the photo and saw Nghia step out of the elevator and walk through the crowd.

The girl on the floor struggled under Vince's foot, but Battaglia was little concerned, his attention concentrated on the mysterious Nghia whose eyes were sleepily wandering over him.

Trying to shake off the effects of Vince's punch, the soldier sat on the floor and shook his head, only half-conscious and fighting to remain upright.

The crowd parted and Nghia took a few steps forward, her hand loosely resting on her hip (a characteristic trademark of the girl—one of several), and stared hard at Battaglia. He felt his bones go soft and later, when questioned what had happened, had no recollection of the Viet Cong slipping her neck out from under his foot.

The siren was much closer, but Vince paid no attention to it, neither did the men standing with the girls, their eyes glued to Nghia.

"Police come! Police come!"

There was a great deal of screaming, clothing being gathered up, doors slamming (opening again), and men running for the stairs. Nghia stood motionless in the middle of the chaos, hand on hip, eyes on Battaglia.

In the midst of the confusion, no one saw the VC girl crawl quickly to the Ka-Bar and plunge the long blade into the GI's neck. Vince turned at the sound of the man's cry of pain in time to see him pitch forward on his face, the Ka-Bar sticking straight out three inches below his ear.

When he looked back, Nghia was gone, and so was the Viet Cong girl.

Chapter 7

"Looks like you're having a busy day, Lieutenant."
The MP sergeant was expressionless while he sat at the
worn-out desk and wrote on a clipboard. "I'm going to
have to send back to Quantico for more forms the way
you're making me use them up." He went on writing
without looking at Vince. "Excuse me for asking, sir, but
are you expecting to get back to Da Nang to fly your
kerosene burner or do you have some sort of cockamamie
wish to spend the rest of the war in a tiger cage on Con
Son Island?—because that's exactly where you're
headed."

"He hasn't done anything wrong."

The sergeant cocked an eye at Ly-boy. "Still hanging
around with the lieutenant?"

"A Viet Cong woman stuck the GI. Let Marine go."

"No way—not this time—not until we get this mess
cleaned up, and that looks like it is going to take a few
years."

Vince sat in a chair that was as worn out as the desk,
looking at the sergeant. "I've got ten days' R and R."

"Looks like you're going to spend them behind bars.
There's nothing I can do this time—it's out of my
control." He motioned to a guard who unlocked the
handcuffs on Battaglia.

"I'm innocent," Vince said.

The guard opened the door of the cell.

"Probably," the sergeant said.

"Then why are you locking me up?"

"Politics, sir." He put his pen down and leaned back in the chair. "You stumbled into a rat's nest this time. The Khach-san Bong has a high-powered clientele, people who control what's happening in Saigon: officials from President Thieu's government, ARVN officers, American and European diplomats, and *Viet Cong cadre.*" He blew air. "Get the picture, sir?"

"Yeh, I get it. Someone has to take the rap and it's not going to be the VC girl, right?"

"You got it. That girl is some big cheese's favorite lay and she's not about to go to jail."

The jail door slammed shut.

"What are you going to do?" Ly-boy said, his head pressed between the bars and his two small hands gripping the iron.

"Not much we can do, kid—unless you can think of something. I'm fresh out of ideas."

"There must be something we can do." His knuckles turned white on the jail bars and he looked like he was going to cry.

Although Vince wasn't tired, he lay down on the bunk; there didn't seem like anything else to do. Rolling over onto his side he faced the wall that was covered with peace signs, lines from Ginsberg's poems, antiwar slogans, and porno drawings. A particularly talented artist had illustrated his conception of Vietnam: a Viet woman, holding an infant with the words *All Humankind* written on its blanket, lay on her back, being raped by an American soldier. Overhead, a rain of napalm from U.S. jets showered down on her and her infant. With his fingernail, Battaglia scratched *Ban Dau* under the art work.

"Looks like I won't have to worry about the mission

now, Ly-boy."

The kid looked puzzled.

"Never mind . . . it wouldn't interest you. Just more bombs killing more people . . . more of the same garbage people dream up to make each other miserable."

Ly-boy's puzzled look deepened.

"I don't think they expected me to come back. I know Blackjack didn't. I think Cleanhead was testing me—I don't think he knew which way I would spring. Maybe he wanted to do me a favor—let me work it out for myself."

"Marine, you're talking crazy."

Vince smiled at Ly-boy, curled his hands behind his head, and stared at the ceiling. Ly-boy leaned on his crutch and frowned.

"I guess it wasn't in the cards for me," Vince said. "I wonder if the guys will think I've let them down? Planned this whole thing so I wouldn't have to fly against the guns." Anxiety twisted his stomach. He got up from the bunk and stood in front of Ly-boy. "I've got to get out of here, kid. There's something up north I've got to do. After that it doesn't matter. Maybe nothing will matter after that."

The kid looked helplessly at him. He closed his eyes tightly and his brow wrinkled in thought.

The frown deepened on Ly-boy's face and his closed eyes tweaked sharply at the corners. His head leaned heavily forward on the jail bars as if in prayer. He remained in this posture for a full minute, then slowly raised his head to Vince, a big smile on his face and his eyes bright in revelation. "Autumn will know," he said simply, and hobbled out the door into the early night.

When Ly-boy reached the Khach-san Bong the dining room and bar were full, and the tiger girls sat about on the kangs in the lobby with their customers, saying little, listening a lot, and looking beautiful. The Viet Cong girl, her face freshly painted, her hair combed, and wearing

111

a new white ao dai, walked near the moon gate with an official-looking Vietnamese man impeccably dressed in a mint-green tropical suit. They smiled together.

The energetic-looking elevator operator greeted Ly-boy, mentioned nothing about the murder of the American GI, and chugged up to the fourth floor where he left the waif, looking relieved that Ly-boy had asked no questions.

A bit shaken by the return to the scene of violence, Ly-boy recovered his composure and limped down the spacious hall, his crutch bumping against the moldy boards.

Before opening the door to the room, he stopped and looked down at the floor near the mouse hole. Someone had scrubbed the wood in an attempt to clean away the GI's blood, but hadn't done a very good job. A damp crimson smear marked the spot where the soldier had lain. Ly-boy could feel the soldier's hurt.

The door was unlocked and Ly-boy pushed it open with his shoulder. Autumn Dove was sitting in the middle of one of the beds surrounded with clothes and crumpled paper wrapping. She paid no attention to Ly-boy.

"Where have you been?—we've been worried," he said in Vietnamese.

She had sorted all her new clothes and laid them out on the bed. "Which one do you like the best?" she said, stroking a dress like it was a pet. "This one, or this one, or this . . . ?"

"I like them all."

She stripped off her old tattered pants and blouse, and threw them in a corner. She wore no bra, and her breasts, just forming, were small and pointed rigidly upward. Ly-boy watched her, unimpressed and irritated at her immodesty. She behaved as if she were alone in the room.

"Don't you have any decency?"

"You don't have to look." She chose the yellow dress

112

with the black belt and wiggled into it. The white patent-leather shoes fit perfectly. "How do I look?"

Ly-boy scrutinized her for a few seconds and asked her to turn around. She did a slow pirouette and paraded up and down the room, swinging her skinny bottom; all the time the fatigue cap sat cocked on her head.

"You look fine," he said.

"*Fine?*—is that all you can say?"

"Okay . . . you look pretty. Is that better?"

She glared at him and tossed her fatigue cap to the floor, hard. "I don't like the way you said that."

"You know, Autumn, you're a spoiled brat. You always have to have your way and you need more attention than anyone I've ever seen."

"Shut up. You don't know what you're talking about."

"I think I do—you just don't want to admit it. Anyway, there's no sense in us arguing about how you look, because it doesn't make any difference one way or the other. You're still a skinny poor girl from the streets, and you don't have a mother or father or any family to go to—just like me."

Autumn Dove puckered her lips and looked down at the floor. "I suppose you're right. I'm just a street girl, and nothing good is going to happen to me even if I do have a few pretty things to wear."

"I think you look good though, just like I said, and maybe someday you will meet someone that will take you off the streets and give you a home."

She looked up and her eyes showed appreciation. "You think so?"

"Yes, I think so. You're kind of mean now and then, but most of the time you're all right."

"Are the clothes from Mr. Vince?" she said, ignoring the comment. She pushed Ly-boy's packages over to him and looked sheepishly into his sad eyes. "He bought you clothes too."

"I came back here looking for you because Vince is in trouble—big trouble."

She put her hand to her mouth and gave him a long, hard look. "Go on . . . tell me the rest."

"I thought you might know what to do."

"How can I know what to do if I don't know what happened? Tell me what happened, dummy."

"I will . . . I will. Give me time . . . it was awful." He sat down on the edge of the bed and propped up the crutch. He didn't say anything for a long time.

Autumn Dove stood impatiently in front of him, hands on her skinny hips.

He looked up and rubbed his eye. "There was a murder right outside the door." He went on to describe what had happened from the time Vince had put her in the cab to when they had returned to the hotel from shopping and the Viet Cong girl had stabbed the GI. "The MPs have Vince locked up and the sergeant said they can't let him go because of the big shots in Saigon. I don't understand what's going on except that the tiger girl, not Vince, killed the soldier—I saw her do it. Vince was standing next to me when it happened."

Autumn Dove was thinking hard. She rubbed her brow, took the cap off her head and put it back on several times, and picked her ear. "Come on," she said to Ly-boy and grabbed him by the hand, opening the door. She went back to the bed and put on a bonnet, placing the fatigue cap on the bed and looking at it like she was leaving an old friend. "Okay—let's go see the beautiful lady." She took his hand again.

"Who's the beautiful lady?" he said, thumping alongside her to the elevator.

"The king's daughter . . . . Princess Nghia."

The downstairs of the Khach-san Bong was crowded

114

with the tiger girls and their dates. The bar and dining room were full, and the garden had several couples walking hand-in-hand through the peonies and feeding the carp in the pond.

The two waifs stood by the potted palms in the crowded lobby, looking around for a clue that might tell them where to find Nghia.

"What are you going to do?" Ly-boy asked.

"I won't know until I get my thinking straight."

Ly-boy looked at Autumn Dove as if she was losing her mind. "What do you mean?—sometimes I can't understand a thing you're saying."

"I mean that it's going to take me a while to decide if I should try and find Nghia in this mess of people or go to the jail and talk with Mr. Vince."

"I don't think it would do any good to talk to Vince. The MP made it clear that he has to stay in jail."

Autumn thought about that for a second. "Let's ask the elevator boy where Nghia is—he seemed helpful before."

Before they got to the elevator, Ly-boy spotted the Viet in the mint-green suit. The Cong girl came out of the powder room to join him.

"That's her," Ly-boy said, "the tiger girl that murdered the GI."

"She looks like the bad queen's maid in the kung-fu movie, the one who helped plot the beautiful princess' murder. Look at her eyes." She elbowed Ly-boy.

"I'm looking," he said.

"Can you see the eyes of a dragon?"

He really couldn't but he said he could anyway. The elevator squealed to a stop and the door rolled open, discharging a tiger girl and her customer.

"Do you know Nghia?" Autumn said to the elevator boy, "the prettiest of the tiger girls?"

"I didn't know that was her name."

"She has eyes that look like a Siamese cat's and her

115

hair hangs down past her waist to her bottom. She's the most beautiful woman in Saigon, in all Vietnam, in all the world, and she's a king's daughter." Autumn adjusted the bonnet on her head and licked her lips, trying to look sexy, like she'd seen Western movie stars do.

Ly-boy gave her a disgusted look.

"Why do you want to talk to her?" the elevator boy said, looking at Ly-boy suspiciously.

"We have to see her because she's—"

"None of your business," Autumn said, stepping on Ly-boy's foot.

"I don't know where she is," the elevator boy snapped. "I have work to do." He started to roll the door closed.

Autumn pushed him hard and stuck her new shoe in the door to prevent it from closing. "If you don't tell me where she is, I'll tell the American MPs that you know who killed the GI on the fourth floor and I'll also tell the VC tiger girl that you're going to tell them."

The color drained from the elevator boy's face and his eyes couldn't leave Autumn Dove. Like most people in Cho-Chan he lived in deadly fear of being singled out by the authorities or the communists. "You wouldn't do that."

"She would," Ly-boy said, in a sinister tone. "She's awfully mean."

"I'd be killed and my bones scattered in the forest to be picked clean by the wild dogs. The VC have no hearts."

"Tell me where Nghia is."

"She's busy right now; maybe later you can—"

"Tell me now or I'll go to the man over there in the mint-green suit and say that you are going to inform on the tiger girl."

The elevator boy let out a noise between his teeth that sounded like a snake hissing. "You can't do that—he's a Viet Cong cadre leader and he'll have my throat slit." He was holding tight to the door-pull to hide his trembling hand.

She lifted her shoe away from the door and turned toward the man.

"No." the elevator boy blurted. "The woman you want is in room three hundred."

Autumn Dove and Ly-boy stepped into the elevator. "Take us there," she said.

The elevator chugged ot the third floor and Autumn Dove walked directly to room 300. She stood in front of the door, thinking.

"Well?" Ly-boy said.

"Don't rush me."

"We can't stand here all night."

She squinted at him through eyes half closed. "I have to be sure I say the right thing."

"Do you hear anything inside?"

"It is quiet," she said.

"Put your ear to the door."

"That wouldn't be right—it's like spying."

"Since when are you so particular about spying?" he said."

"This is different—she's a princess."

"If you don't knock, I will." He lifted his crutch.

Autumn Dove took a deep breath and tapped lightly on the door. It opened right away and Nghia stood in front of her looking irritated. She was wearing a blue flowered ao dai and her hair was piled on top of her head and held in place by two large combs. Long pagoda earrings dangled from her ears and two strings of pearls were wrapped around her hair, the ends hanging down to her shoulders.

Little Autumn Dove was paralyzed by Nghia's beauty. Her mouth dropped open and her normally narrow eyes were as round as teacups. *She looks just like the king's daughter—exactly like the princess.*

117

"Well, what is it?" Nghia said in her fluid Saigonese. She stared down at Autumn Dove and the irritation lifted from her face; her eyes became amused at the child's nervousness. "That's a pretty dress and hat you have on."

Autumn Dove gulped. Her lips moved, but there was no intelligible sound.

"What's the matter, girl—can't you talk?"

"You . . . you . . . are even prettier . . . up close . . . prettier than . . . than . . . the king's daughter."

Nghia looked at Ly-boy, recognizing him. "What are you doing up here alone? What happened to your friend the Marine?" she said. She looked back at Autumn Dove. "Aren't you the little girl that was having lunch with the Marine and this boy?" She stood back and studied her. "Yes, you are—what happened to your poor clothes—how is it you're dressed so nicely?"

"Mr. Vince is in trouble, real big trouble," Autumn said, regaining control of her voice, "and you are the only one who can help him."

"I take it Vince is the man you had lunch with?"

"Yes, and he is in love with you and needs your help and there isn't anyone in all Vietnam or the world who can help him except you." She stopped for breath.

Nghia's eyebrows lifted. "Slow down. What are you talking about?" She took a backward look into the room. "Wait here—I'll be right back."

A minute or two passed (the door being left open) with the sound of muffled voices and whispers coming from inside the room. Nghia came out with a Vietnamese man who wore a black patch over his right eye and had a grim look about him. He was ruggedly handsome and about forty years old. He glanced down at the two children like they were pieces of furniture.

"I am so sorry," Nghia said to him. "Please excuse this small interruption." She kissed him on the cheek. "I will

118

meet you downstairs later. It shouldn't be very long."

The man nodded once and said nothing. His leather heels clicked down the hall to the elevator.

"Come in, you two, and let me hear this story." Nghia ushered them in and closed the door quietly, then leaned back against it and scrutinized the kids. "What makes you think I can help your friend, or even want to help him? And what's this about him being in love with me?"

Autumn Dove looked embarrassed. "He sounded like he was in love with you from the first time he saw you. He told us about seeing you this morning at the bus stop at Tan Son Nhut when he first got here from Da Nang; and the way he looked at you in the dining room . . ."

"So he's stationed in Da Nang, is he? What makes him think I'm the same girl? I couldn't be, you know, I haven't been to Tan Son Nhut in months. No—he's mistaken—I have never seen him until a few hours ago in the hotel with you two. He is of no interest to me."

"If you never saw him before a few hours ago, how then do you know he's a Marine?" Ly-boy said. "He's not wearing his uniform."

Nghia smiled at the boy and laid a finger on his nose. "I can tell. It's the way he carries himself, his *lifer* look, the haircut and . . . he has an anchor, eagle, and globe tattooed into his forearm."

"You have taken an interest in him, haven't you," Autumn Dove said, biting her forefinger and smiling. "You've noticed many details. What color eyes does he have?"

"Don't be ridiculous." Nghia walked to the dresser and arranged the pearls in her hair. "For a twelve- and thirteen-year-old you are very alert"—she turned from the mirror and studied Autumn—"and inquisitive, I should add." She turned back to the mirror and freshened the back of her neck with a squeeze of perfume from an atomizer. "In what sort of trouble is this man

119

Vince? Not that I care."

The room was quiet for a few seconds, and Ly-boy looked at Autumn, then to Nghia, who had her back to him. "He's in jail for murdering the GI who was in the room across the hall."

"That doesn't surprise me—someone has to be blamed for it and I suppose he's a good choice." Nghia went on primping in front of the mirror, though she no longer seemed as enthusiastic.

"But he's innocent," Ly-boy cried.

Nghia turned on him and shouted, "Well, what do you expect? He was convenient—he was standing right there—they had words and there was a scuffle. Who else would be the logical choice?"

"The tiger girl, she—"

"Don't be a fool . . . no one would admit they saw her do it."

Ly-boy stood in front of Nghia, devastated and unable to say another word.

"It is the way of things," Nghia said. "Just accept it."

The room became quiet once more and then came Autumn's soft whimpering. Teardrops fell from her closed eyes and dripped down the front of her new dress. The whimpering grew into loud sobs and she pressed at her eyes with balled fists.

"There's no sense in crying; there's nothing that can be done," Nghia said.

"But I thought you would help us—there is no one else that we can talk to. Please . . . isn't there something you can do for Mr. Vince? Please, please."

Beside her, Ly-boy leaned forward on his crutch, his face twisted with anxiety. "You are our only hope."

"You must love him very much." Nghia looked down on the two waifs and put her hands on their shoulders.

"He has been good to us; he took us to the movies and fed us good food and bought us clothes and gave us a

120

place to live in the hotel," Autumn said.

"And I think he needs us," Ly-boy said. "He seems kind of mixed up about something—I think it's the war—and he's sort of lonely."

"Please . . . kung-fu princess . . ." Autumn Dove pressed her fists into her eyes and cried louder.

Nghia gave a long sigh and let her hands slide from the children's shoulders. She closed her eyes and thought for a moment, then said, "It will be difficult, but I will do what I can."

"Oh, thank you, golden lady," Autumn Dove said. "Heaven will give you long life and good fortune for helping us." She took Nghia's hand in her own and pressed it to her cheek.

"Understand, children," Nghia explained, "that what I must do is going to create displeasure with some people in high places, and it could be dangerous for all of us, including your friend, Mr. Vince. But I never have liked that Viet Cong girl and it is time that she pay for the evil she has done to others." She tapped the dresser top with a red fingernail. "I have never liked to see innocent people pay the price of the guilty, and your Marine friend seems a good man."

"What will you do?" Ly-boy asked.

"That need not concern you. I have friends, important friends, that owe me favors. I will talk to them and see what can be done about getting your Marine released from jail so that you can have him for a few more days and so he can go back to Da Nang and do whatever he was doing before he came to Saigon." She poured them each a cup of tea and gave them a small cake of sweet rice to munch, then dried Autumn Dove's tears with the end of a silk handkerchief she drew from the sleeve of her robe.

It was a few minutes before midnight by the wind-up

clock on the wall. The MP sergeant looked up from the scarred, worn-out desk and looked curiously at the starched and pressed Viet standing in front of him with two envelopes in his hand.

"Yes—what can I do for you?" the MP said carefully.

"Do you have a U.S. Marine first lieutenant named Vince Battaglia jailed here? He is being held for a murder committed tonight at the Khach-san Bong hotel."

"He's here." The sergeant leaned back in the chair and appraised the man, who was obviously an envoy from someone in a high-ranking post. "What do you want with him?"

Standing in the shadows of the yellow floodlight outside the barbed-wire gate of the military police compound, Nghia wrapped the silk robe around her shoulders and watched the envoy from President Thieu's palace hand the envelopes to the MP sergeant. One envelope had the national seal of Vietnam pressed into it, the other was from the U.S. Embassy. Her pouting cherry-red lips squeezed in thought and she paced slowly in front of the twisted wire. *I may live to regret what I have done.* A chill from the damp night ran through her and she pulled the robe close. She knew that she had stepped across the invisible boundary that had always kept her safe. She looked back one more time before getting into the cyclo, and saw the MP sergeant carefully fold the letters and replace them in the envelope. He made a phone call, then unlocked the door of the jail cell and the Marine walked out.

"Now we will see," Nghia whispered to herself, and rode away in the cyclo.

Chapter 8

Through the slightly ajar door, Battaglia could see Autumn Dove fast asleep on the top of the bedcovers and still dressed in her new clothes, the bonnet held tightly in one hand and dangling over the edge of the bed above Lyboy, who sprawled face-up on the floor, his snores filling the room with each fall of his chest.

Propped against the bedpost, the teak crutch resembled a third child, one who slept standing up and guarded the other two. The soft blinking glow of neon signs from the shops below drifted across the balcony, entered through the open French doors, and spread a blanket of rose beams over the children.

Standing in the doorway in the weak light, Vince looked down on the sleeping children, feeling more akin to them than to anything else in the world, and wished that Ban Dau was a million light-years away in another universe.

Not wanting to wake the kids, he softly closed the door behind him and walked across the floor to the balcony without making the boards creak underfoot. The unopened seabag rested at the foot of the bed and he smiled at the thought of Autumn Dove dragging it through the hotel to the room.

The lights of Cho-Chan and the outlying regions of Saigon sparkled in the clear night, and flares dropped from gunships patrolling the sky illuminated the rooftops and spread an uncanny glow over the city. Battaglia watched with curiosity, sitting in a comfortable rattan chair, his feet resting on the wrought iron railing of the balcony.

A 105mm battery at Ton Son Nhut pounded the hills along the river and Battaglia hung his head against his chest and listened to Ly-boy's snoring coming to him from inside the room. The deep throaty throbbing of a .50 caliber machine gun carried across the roofs from a mile away and AH-1 Cobra pivoted into the riverbank and fired a pod of rockets . . .

"Dash Two in hot."

"Roger, Dash Two—get the big guns, the seventy-fives and one-hundreds on the reverse slope of the ridge," Blackjack said.

"No sweat—I can see the Bronco's smoke."

"Battaglia's in. He'll be our FAC coming off the target."

The strike force orbited over Ban Dau with their 500- and 1000-pounders, waiting for Vince to make his run on the guns, opening the way for them to level the bridge span and destroy the tons of supplies waiting to be transported to the Viet Cong and NVA fighting below the DMZ.

Vince armed the Zuni rockets and selected CLUSTER on the panel. "I'm forty seconds from target." He set the sights fifteen degrees and gave the Phantom right rudder, bringing the aircraft around in a hard turn at 500 knots, nose low.

The sky in front of him suddenly erupted with black flowers and the air sizzled hot with shrapnel around the F-4's canopy. A flash of silver appeared on the ridge and a Marine Corp OV-10 broke away from the exploding Willy-Peter.

"Strike my smoke, Dash Two," the Bronco pilot said.

Vince could easily see the white phosphorus marking the hidden gun emplacements. "Roger—I'm on your Willy-Peter. Am pulling at two-three-zero. Will salvo all my five-inchers on first run."

"Get in and out quick," Blackjack said.

Don't worry, Major, I'm not sticking around for the cookies and punch; after the first dance you'll have to do without me.

An artillery round exploded on the port side of Battaglia's aircraft and the ship rocked violently, throwing it off the target run. Vince corrected and flew on, straight into the wall of flak exploding in front of him.

He fought hard to keep the Phantom tracking to the target. Bouncing and shaking inside the cockpit, he turned the aircraft to bring the Willy-Peter back into the gunsight while he fought his nerves not to break off the attack.

Long lines of hot shrapnel twisted through the air and reached out for him like arms of lightning zigzagging in an electrical storm. The air popped and crackled, and it was all he could do to keep his eyes open against the rain of fire spitting at him from every direction. *What are you doing right now, Ruthie? Listening to a Joan Baez album with your new boyfriend, lying beside the pool, soaking up the rays and snacking on nachos and those greasy hamburgers from Tommy's you like so much while sipping lime rickeys?*

"Thirty seconds to go," Vince said.

"There's too much flak," someone said. "He's not going to make it."

"No one can get through that flak."

"Break it off, Dash Two. The gunners have your number."

"Keep off the air—maintain strict radio discipline," Blackjack snapped.

"Twenty seconds," Battaglia said.

There was a bright flash and out of the corner of his eye Vince saw the OV-10 lose its left wing and engine. Flames swept back over the length of the fuselage and the spotter plane flat-spinned into the ridge, exploding on impact.

"Damn."

"See any chutes, Dash Three?"

"They were too low—no time."

"Damn."

"Ten seconds," Vince said.

"Dash Four, you're in."

"Roger, boss."

Though Vince was certain that the flak couldn't get any worse, the guns intensified their barrage when he swung into the last few seconds of his run. The space between the two ridges he had to fly was narrow and allowed no room for maneuvering. The canyon was filled with the black smoke of bursting antiaircraft shells, creating near-zero visibility that forced him to fly on instincts.

Unable to see the target, he counted off the seconds before he was to fire the Zuni rockets. The lightning slashes of exploding shrapnel splintered the air and he shrank down, way down, deep into the seat, knowing that it was only by a miracle that he had penetrated this far to the guns.

At the last second the smoke cleared and the battery of big guns was in front of him, filling the gunsight, the Willy-Peter floating across their barrels like a white veil that reminded him of the lace Ruthie had bought for her wedding dress.

"Anyone see Battaglia?"

"We lost him in the flak."

"Jeez, I'd hate to be down there."

"Stay off the air."

"Dash Three in."

126

Vince's thumb was only a nanosecond from settling on the rocket release button when there was a blinding burst of light in the cockpit and he thought how happy he had been walking the corn rows alongside his father with the smell of husks in his nose, the pheasant running ahead, and the air as still as ice. His mouth opened wide but the sound of his voice was obliterated by the explosion . . .

"Mr. Vince, Mr. Vince—wake up, you're screaming." Autumn Dove stood in front of Battaglia and shook him by the collar, shouting in his face. "Everyone in the hotel can hear you."

Vince opened his eyes and stared up at the girl. "All right—I'm all right. Let go—I'm awake." He blinked the sweat from his eyes and sat up in the chair. "Did I frighten you kids?"

"Yeh . . . sort of," Ly-boy said, not sure of what had happened, rubbing the sleep from his eyes. "You were screaming awfully loud."

"Sorry."

The three of them said nothing while they watched the green and red flares burst on the horizon, illuminating the rooftops in a phantom light. A full two minutes passed in silence before Battaglia said anything.

"Ly-boy, how difficult would it be for a person to disappear into Cho-Chan?"

"I'm not sure what you mean." He looked at Vince oddly.

"I think you do."

Ly-boy thought for a second. "If you mean for someone to hide and not be found, I would say that it is very easy. Lips are sealed in Cho-Chan and most everything that happens here never reaches the outside."

Rising from the rattan chair, Vince looked out over the rooftops and neon glow of Saigon. His thoughts were confused and he had a mind to confide in these kids he felt akin to—something he knew could only lead to more entanglement. A soft rap on the door came before he could say anything.

Vince glanced at his watch. "Are we expecting anyone?"

The children looked at each other. "No," they said together.

A moment of hesitation came and went, and Battaglia opened the door. Nghia was wearing her silk robe with the long puffy sleeves, over her ao dai. She had let her hair down and it hung loosely twisted over one shoulder. Brushing past Vince she entered the room without looking at him, inspected everything in an appraising manner without disclosing her thoughts by her facial expressions, and walked out to the balcony to Autumn Dove and Ly-boy where she stood next to the ornamental rail, back to him, surveying the reaches of Saigon and smoothing her hair.

"What do you want?" Vince said with some irritation.

Nghia ignored him and addressed the children: "You two need good bath," she said purposely in English. "This man no know how take care children."

"Now wait just a minute—I'm responsible for these kids and I don't need you interfering."

She pushed Autumn Dove into the bathroom and handed her a pair of new pajamas she was carrying in a paper sack. "You first." She filled the tub and helped Autumn (who was awe-struck by the attention she was getting) undress; she closed the door and said to Ly-boy, "You next." She looked inside his ears, frowned, and handed him his new pajamas.

"I see you're still as bossy and arrogant as you were this morning at the bus stop," he said, and looked at his watch. "Correction—yesterday morning."

She said nothing, only folded her arms over her small,

well-formed breasts, tilted her head in the air, and stared out through the French doors as if she were the only one in the room.

"So you haven't changed your mind about Marines— we're all dog shit, right? Your rich father and mother would get very upset if you talked to me; you come from a strict home and the family keeps a close eye on you, don't they?"

Without turning to look at him she said, "I no talk to dog shit." Her chin tilted higher in the air and her folded arms tightened around her breasts, giving her an air of chastity.

"Dog shit, huh? Well, tell me, Miss High-and-Mighty, just what do you think you are, doing what you're doing in this high-priced whorehouse, and pretending that—"

She turned on him with a vengeance, ready to scratch his eyes out. "I come from very good family, my mother and father very rich, I no have to work here—I do for fun. You dog shit—me ginger cookie. I can have you killed like that." She snapped her fingers loudly. "And I never see you before you come Khach-san Bong. This first time—Never see you Tan Son Nhut."

"Aha! I never mentioned Tan Son Nhut. I only said we talked at the bus stop. If you're not pretending, how did you know it was the Tan Son Nhut bus stop?"

"Children tell me. They afraid for you in jail . . . tell me everything. Tell me about girl at bus stop Tan Son Nhut . . . say you love her." Her features softened and she turned her back to him again, the familiar swing of her hair brushing across his face, and he caught the heady smell of jasmine.

Vince grew pensive and there was a long silence between them. He walked around in front of her and looked down into her long eyes, the same mysterious eyes that had held him in such intense fascination the first time they measured him. "Did you have anything to do with getting me out of jail?"

Her eyes swept up at him and her focus tightened around his pupils, and he could feel his bones going soft in his legs and he wanted to sit down.

"I'm finished, Princess," Autumn said, standing in the open door while the water dripped from her thin body and puddled around her feet.

"Call me Nghia." She pulled Autumn Dove back into the bathroom and closed the door with a *bang*, irritated that Autumn had thought nothing of appearing before Vince and Ly-boy with nothing on. "What is the matter with you?" she said in Vietnamese, "don't you have any respect for yourself?"

"I'm practicing to be a tiger girl," she said honestly.

The sound of Nghia's palm hitting Autumn Dove's cheek was like the sound of a wet towel hitting a wall. The tears burst immediately from the child's eyes and her hands went to her face. She stared at Nghia in stunned silence while she was toweled dry and the new underwear and pajamas were fastidiously placed on her.

Nghia led Autumn out and sat her on a chair next to a small lamp. "Do her hair," she said to Battaglia, placing a comb and small bottle in his hand with a look that meant that he had better do a good job.

He looked at the Chinese writing on the label and frowned. "What's this?"

Nghia turned the bottle over and pointed to the picture of the lice on the back label. Pouring a little of the green liquid in her hands, she rubbed it into Autumn Dove's hair and scalp, then used the fine-tooth comb to comb out the white eggs attached to the hair strands. The girl sat stiffly in the chair with her hand held to the red mark on her cheek, saying nothing, looking at the black overhead fan in the ceiling that rotated slowly and circulated the air in the humid room to make the temperature in the confined space at least tolerable.

130

"You do." Nghia shoved the bottle and comb into Vince's hand and walked into the bathroom with Ly-boy.

He reluctantly rubbed some of the medicine into Autumn Dove's hair the way he had watched Nghia do. "She's getting under my skin," he mumbled to the girl. "I'm going to throw her out in a minute."

"You can't do that," Autumn Dove said, holding her cheek. "She went to a lot of trouble to get you out of jail and we should be nice to her; and she's a kung-fu princess too, don't forget that."

Battaglia became thoughtful. "Hmmm . . . I wonder what her motives are—could be a Viet Cong agent."

"She's not up to anything—she just wanted to help us. She's a nice lady even though she did slap me."

A commotion broke out in the bathroom and heated words between Nghia and Ly-boy were shouted back and forth.

"What are they saying?" Vince asked.

"Ly-boy doesn't want to take a bath."

More words flew between them.

"What now?"

"Nghia convinced Ly-boy to take a bath, but he doesn't want to undress in front of her."

The sound of running water came out from under the bathroom door and Ly-boy's crutch hit the floor. Nghia's voice reached a high pitch and the words rushed together in a torrent.

"What did she say?"

"She said that she is going to beat him if he doesn't stop acting silly and get in the bathtub."

"Well, that's enough of this. Who does she think she is, coming into our room uninvited to give orders and push us around like she's something special, even if she did pull some strings to get me cleared of those murder charges." He was angry, and stomped toward the bathroom door.

131

The door swung open, away from Vince's hand that was reaching for the doorknob, and Nghia walked out holding Ly-boy's rags between her thumb and forefinger. Ly-boy was sitting in the hot water, his stump looking lonely against his whole leg, a big smile on his face, scrubbing himself down with a washcloth and bar of soap.

Vince changed his mind about saying anything to Nghia when he saw Ly-boy enjoying the first bath he'd had in many months. He thoughtfully watched Nghia while she dropped Ly-boy's rags into the trash and inspected Autumn Dove's hair, uncertain how he should deal with her. She was certainly doing a good job with the kids and there was no doubt that they were taken with her, particularly Autumn Dove, who sat quietly in the chair by the lamplight, her face scrubbed and shiny, looking up with a big smile at Nghia combing her hair and cracking the lice eggs between her fingernails.

The splashing of Ly-boy playing in the bathtub reminded him of his own Saturday-night baths when he was a child growing up on the farm in Kansas. The strict Methodist teaching of those tender years came flooding back and he reprimanded himself for the feelings that were growing inside of him for this woman who offered herself for sexual hire.

Nghia caught him regarding her and he turned away to fumble with the watchband on his wrist, embarrassed. He walked out on the balcony to contemplate the night sky with its dreamy glow from the flares and the black curtain behind studded with stars. He stood there for a long time, the confused emotions banging around in his head, his eyes focused on the Saigon night but all the time seeing the ridges that fortified Ban Dau. There was no escape for him from this all-consuming thought that sat on the back-burner of his mind simmering its insidious brew of evil impressions.

How long he stood there, he had no idea. The wind

132

chimes played a tune in the night breeze and he became aware of the delectable scent of jasmine next to him and the guns faded away into the night, their barrels red-hot and smoking.

"Why you no like me?" Nghia said.

"You haven't given me much reason to like you."

"Other mans like me—they think I number-one ginger cookie."

"That's their problem."

Her eyes narrowed at him in disgust.

Hearing the door open, Vince turned to see the elevator boy walk into the room without bothering to knock. He saw Nghia on the balcony and motioned for her, his hand gestures indicating that it was urgent. He whispered a few words in her ear and gave her a message written on a piece of expensive stationary. While she read the note, her pouting lips worked up and down and the scar on her high cheekbone twitched. She said nothing to Vince or the kids when she left, only crumbled the message in her hand and dropped it into the bamboo wastebasket. The elevator boy followed behind her and left the door open.

Ly-boy walked out of the bathroom clean and dry and looking like a different kid with the crust of dirt removed. He buttoned the front of his new pajama tops and glanced around the room. "Where is Nghia?" He looked disappointed.

"She just left with the elevator boy," Vince said, handing him the crumpled note written in Vietnamese. "What's it say?"

Ly-boy wrinkled his nose and quickly read the message:

Nghia—our friend is waiting for you. Be good to him. Are you happy now that the Marine is free?

Kai

"I'm going downstairs," Vince said. "You kids be all right alone?"

"Of course," Autumn Dove said. "Where are you going?"

"I need a drink." He slammed the door and his feet thumped against the boards as he headed for the elevator.

"He's upset," Ly-boy said.

"Jealous," Autumn corrected.

Battaglia had only just gotten comfortable in the bar and ordered a drink when a tiger girl named Chi sat down beside him. He failed to notice the girl, preoccupied with his thoughts and looking glumly down into his glass.

"I'll have what he's drinking," the girl said to the waitress.

Vince looked up.

"He's drinking ice water," the waitress said.

"Yeh—ice water." Vince looked pugnaciously at the tiger girl and turned back to his water.

"My name is Chi," she said.

"So?"

The waitress went away.

"You're the Marine that Nghia got out of jail, aren't you?"

"You seem to know a lot."

"I worked for DAO. They sent me to the Army Intelligence School at Ford Ord in California. My old man is a major."

Vince looked passively at her. "What does he say about you working in the Khach-san Bong?"

"He doesn't know that I do."

"How do you keep it from him? Seems to me something like that is hard to hide."

"There are ways." She licked her lips.

"I suppose." Battaglia turned back to his ice water.

134

"Do you know for a fact that Nghia was responsible for getting me out of jail?"

Chi smiled and played with her lower lip. "It's common knowledge among the girls, and she did it at a great expense."

"How so?" The way she played with her lip irritated him.

"No one gets something for nothing in Saigon—she's obligated to several important people for what she did for you."

"Sexual favors?" he said with distaste.

"How else would a girl like Nghia repay her debts? She has trouble enough keeping her belly full of rice."

"I thought she came from a rich family with a great deal of political influence in Saigon."

Chi laughed and waved around the bar with a loose hand at the other tiger girls. "We all have our dreams and lie about our backgrounds. The truth is that we are ashamed of who we are and for one reason or another continue to work the Khach-san Bong and places like it until we are no longer pretty enough to attract men. In that respect Nghia is no different than the rest of us; and she's much like those kids you've taken in. She has no friends, was abandoned by her family and sold into prostitution, cries a lot when she's alone, and tells big stories to cover up her poverty."

"Sounds like you don't have much affection for her."

"Nghia?" she said. "We get along all right—though we've never been as friendly as we were before she took a regular customer away from me." She stopped and thought for a second while she pulled at her lower lip. "All of the girls' regular customers make a try for her at one time or another, but she's real choosy and doesn't take to very many men. In fact, I think she hates men. I've never known her to be particular about anyone. The man she falls for, if she ever does, will be quite special."

135

She toyed with her lip. "The girls are wondering why she took an interest in you."

"For the kids," he said quickly. "Autumn Dove talked her into it—the jail thing—from what I understand."

"That so?" She said it with surprise. "The children must think a great deal of you, but I can't believe Nghia would do it just for them."

"Frankly, I find it difficult to care much what Nghia's reasons were for springing me." He took a long drink of water and ordered a gin and tonic. "I couldn't care less what makes her tick."

"Are you planning to get drunk?" She watched the bartender mix the gin and tonic and place it on the bar for the waitress.

"Soused," he said. "Enthusiastically soused. Pickling drunk."

"I didn't realize she had become that important to you."

He looked at her with a troubled eye. "What the devil do you mean?" He plucked the drink off the waitress's tray and drank half of it before the girl had turned to walk away.

Chi took the drink from his hand. "I want you with all your strength." She placed the glass back on the tray and smiled pleasantly. "Come on, Marine, let's go up to my room." She stood and smoothed the tight-fitting ao dai over her slim hips.

Vince appraised her doll-like body. "I'm not buying."

"And I'm not selling." The pleasant smile grew more pleasant. "My payment will be the look on Nghia's face when she finds out."

It had been nearly a year in Vietnam for Vince, and during that time he had seen nothing of women except for the snaggle-toothed hags selling dope outside the perimeter fence at Da Nang. He was not surprised to find himself easily rising to his feet at the tug of Chi's hand in

136

his and being led upstairs by a talented professional who knew beforehand exactly what his response would be.

In a way he was disgusted with himself for being so easily persuaded, yet he remembered the many times that he had fantasized that something like this would happen, without the remotest hope that it could be possible.

In her room, Chi became the seductive siren displaying her professional charms, patient and alluring, pouring him hot tea she brewed herself and feeding him tidbits of sweet rice, using her fingers.

The room was spartanly furnished and gave Battaglia the feel of being inside a Chinese restaurant, bare of everything except the absolute essentials. The wooden floor, lightly varnished, was completely exposed to view and without the usual appropriate coverings. The walls too were undisguised and resigned to their blank stares. A small knee-high serving table and two hardback chairs (in which Vince and Chi sat) guarded the only window, next to the vanity.

The focal point of the room was the iron bed, old and in need of paint, covered by the only adornment in the room, a yellow and white Korean comforter, thick and decorated with a green peacock embroidered in the center.

"Pretty," Vince said.

"My grandmother made the comforter—she was born in Pusan." She slipped out of her shoes and turned the comforter back, exposing green silk sheets, freshly laundered and perfumed with sandlewood. "My grandmother was a beautiful lady," she said, and sat down in the middle of the bed, her legs drawn up under her chin. "I inherited her beauty."

Battaglia nodded his agreement, though he thought her face a bit too round and flat, watching her through the mist rising from the teacup from which he sipped, wondering about the men who had lain between the green sheets, and wondering more about the man who was right now lying between Nghia's sheets.

"Do you find me as attractive as Nghia?" Chi patted the pillow and rolled over onto her side, the flared leg of her white pantaloons drawing up above her knee, revealing a well-shaped calf muscle.

Vince placed the teacup on the table and went to the bed. Chi pulled him down beside her and unbuttoned his shirt, her long slim fingers taking their time, and all the while her sloe eyes roving back and forth over his face. Behind her, on the wall, the guns of Ban Dau flashed and Vince closed his eyes. *Not now*, he thought to himself.

Chi had Vince's shirt lying on the floor and was massaging his shoulders and chest when the door burst open and Nghia walked in. Legs spread apart, hands on her hips, and the scar on her cheek twitching menacingly, she looked straight at Chi with ice-dead eyes, forcing the girl to pull the Korean comforter up around her chest and recoil against the wall.

"*Dung lam dau tao*," don't hurt me, Chi said.

"*Tao se cot may vo giuong va don ot vo cho kin cua may cho den khi may van tao*," I will tie you to the bed and stuff your privates with red peppers until you beg me to kill you.

"*Dung lam dau tao*," don't hurt me, she repeated, holding tightly to the comforter.

"*Roi tao se don cut heo vo mieng may de xem voi ria mat dep cua may*," then I will fill your mouth and ears with pig dung and watch the maggots eat away your pretty face.

Vince didn't say a word, staggered by Nghia's sudden and intimidating entry and by the brutal sound of her voice; and she was gorgeous, absolutely the best looking woman he'd seen in his life. Seen in this new light of fiery temper, hair flying and hips swinging, she'd become even more vivacious and his mind was sparking with the

138

fullness and intensity of her presence.

Shirtless and stricken dumb, he lay on Chi's bed, looking up at Nghia, his mouth partly open and wanting to say something intelligent that would exonerate Chi and himself, yet overwhelmed by the thought that he was terribly stupid for feeling the need to apologize for being here.

So he stayed where he was, silent and feeling foolish.

"And you!" She turned on Vince and pointed a long fingernail at him that looked, from the gleam of it, as thought it had been freshly sharpened and would cut out his heart. "You leave children alone while you play with new toy. You bad mans—no care about children—I take children away you and take care them, you no good bum."

Battaglia was dumbfounded and angry, shaking his head, unable to comprehend why she had singled out Chi and himself to unload her hate. This was a wild unbridled woman capable of vengeful retribution who didn't think twice about the consequences of her act.

Finger pointed at his heart, the words poured from her mouth in hot vituperation: "You sleep this girl you get bad sick. One week you look like this . . ." She curled her fingers stiffly and twisted her mouth into a grotesque shape. "Your tongue turn green and skin fall from your bones and you smell so bad no hospital take you."

At these words Chi overcame her fear of Nghia and struck back. She addressed Vince slowly and flaunted her superior English: "Nghia treats a sack of rice better than she treats the men who stay with her. You will be no better than a garbage dog to her, but if you become my boyfriend I will stay with no other men and make such good love to you that your eyes will pop out of your head."

"Pah—what I care he be your boyfriend?" She made the vulgar sign with her fingers that Vince had seen

Autumn Dove make, then crossed her arms and turned her back to both of them and stared at the ceiling with her full, pouting lips working expressively. "You both stupid, dirty people, belong each other. I come good family, very rich, good to me, give me much love. Pah—who want stupid Marine?"

Vince sat up and tried to think of something sensible to say, but everything that he thought of was muddled and lacked conviction. Then the words just boiled up, uncontrolled and angry: "You're nothing but a common street whore and will sleep with anything that comes along to get a few piasters. When I first saw you at the bus stop at Tan Son Nhut I thought you were something special and I sincerely wanted to know you better. But no more—you're conceited and spoiled by men who fall all over themselves for you and I wouldn't as much as give you a second look now that I know what kind of a woman you are."

Her shoulders straightened and she took in a long breath, then turned and walked the short distance to the door, her feet soft on the wood floor. She paused for a moment at the open door, her hand on the latch, and Vince saw the wet tears on her high cheekbones. The door closed softly, and a few seconds later the elevator clanked three times and everything was quiet once again.

Chapter 9

Colonel Dasher's bullet head leaned over the large relief map of North Vietnam and his eyes fixed hard on the long high ridges that marked the communist redoubt called Ban Dau. Many times he had come alone to the map room and studied the model the planners had made from the aerial reconnaissance photos.

The recce flights had been of limited value, unfortunately, bringing back pictures that were of poor resolution and failed to identify key fortifications and the big gun batteries; nor had the well-camouflaged missile sites, truck parks, and supply dumps been located. The true disposition of military forces in the area was still a major question, as was the enemy's reaction time. Much remained concealed in the rocks and under the jungle canopy.

High-flying, high-speed photo recon flights were safe and produced good results for open or nonspecific targets that required minimum identification for the attack planes. Ban Dau, however, was well concealed, a hidden, natural fortress defended by an assortment of weapons that necessitated clear identification to ensure the success of the mission, and whose location and kind could only be determined by close, on-the-deck photo runs.

The door opened and a hot gust of air blew through the

quonset hut, followed by quick footsteps across the floor.

"What do you think, Blackjack?" Cleanhead said without looking up from the map. "One section of F-4s or two?"

"I'd be more confident with two—we'd be assured of better coverage—and there would be less chance of having to go back a second time."

The colonel rubbed his egg dome in thought and his stone jaw moved up and down with a forceful, determined motion. "We'll bring the first section down the slot from the upper end here"—he pointed to the funnel-shaped entry to Ban Dau—"and the second section will swing around to the underbelly and shoot up the nipple a half minute after the first section completes its run. No one is to fly higher than the ridges—I want to see rice straw and paddy mud clinging to the intake nacelles when the planes land."

Blackjack regarded the colonel out of the corner of his eye.

Dasher unwrapped a fresh cigar and ran it under his nose, a nose that looked more like an eagle's beak than anything human and, according to the men, that he used to buck rivets in his Phantoms when he lent the maintenance crews a hand. "What are the men saying about the mission?" he asked.

Bamburger blew air through his nose and smoothed his hair back. "They're not saying much, but I can tell that the waiting is getting to them, not knowing when the strike will be launched. They can fly a hundred missions against the usual targets, but down in their bellies they're waiting for the big one."

"It's not easy."

"No, sir . . . but you won't have to worry about them . . . they'll do their job."

"They always do—they're my boys." He looked at the freshly unwrapped cigar for a long time, delaying what he had to say so that his words would carry the force he intended. The cigar slowly came up to his mouth and he wet its length, first one end and then the other. "I want Battaglia to lead one of the sections on the recce." He fired the cigar and peered down its length through the cloud of smoke at Blackjack.

The uneasiness that filled the room could be cut with a knife, and as Cleanhead had expected, he had to wait for Blackjack's response. The major was in line for a promotion and Dasher was unsure that he was ready for greater responsibilities. The wing's executive officer had completed his tour and was rotating back to El Toro in California, and Blackjack was the logical choice to fill the vacancy. Additionally, Marine Corps Headquarters in Washington wanted Dasher to recommend a combat-experienced pilot to take over training command at MCAS Cherry Point. Both jobs required ability to act without superior authority.

For weeks, the colonel had been thinking seriously about Blackjack Bamburger as the man to fill either of these demanding, highly visible billets. He was a fine pilot, as experienced and well trained as could be hoped for. There were certain questions, however, pertaining to the man's leadership ability for which Cleanhead had not yet gotten satisfactory answers.

Particularly troublesome was the rivalry between the major and Battaglia, a thorn in Dasher's side ever since Vince had come aboard the wing. Though the friction between the two had reached flashpoint on several occasions, the colonel insisted that Battaglia fly Bamburger's wing, where the young lieutenant would have the benefit of the older man's experience and instruction. It wasn't altogether clear how this was working out, given the clashes in personalities and differences in philosophies, though Dasher felt that the difficulties between the two aviators were offset by Battaglia's growing competency in the air and the fact that the major kept Vince so occupied with his job that he complained less about his disenchantment with the corps.

"Well . . ." Cleanhead said, impatient with Blackjack's delay in answering him. "Do you think Battaglia is up to leading a section?"

"I don't know," the major equivocated. "I just don't know."

"Come on, Major, he's been flying your wing for months—you should have a well-substantiated opinion of him by now."

This isn't a good sign, Dasher thought to himself. *The man is hedging. He's more concerned about his fitness report than he is about his personal convictions; not the right response for the kind of leadership responsibility I had in mind for him.*

"He's a good pilot . . ."

Damn it, man, if you don't think he's right for the job, say it. Command decision, Major. Cleanhead looked at him with irritation and Bamburger wilted. The colonel turned away disgusted and silently cursed the mothers of the world who made all the decisions for their sons and the fathers who never taught them to face up to the harsh realities of taking charge of their own lives.

Blackjack weighed Colonel Dasher's fondness for Battaglia against his own feelings, unwilling and afraid that if he spoke his mind he would be passed up for the promotion. He had misgivings about Vince leading a section of F-4s on the recce, valid misgivings that he was convinced were honest and free from personal prejudice, that under normal circumstances would be accepted as a valuable contribution. These were not normal circumstances, however, and the major held back, knowing in the better part of him that he was making a mistake in not speaking what he felt and at the same time cornerd by his survival instincts, so he said: "Everything taken into consideration, Colonel, I think Battaglia is the best choice. He'll do a fine job leading a section."

"Thanks, Major," Dasher said without enthusiasm. "That will be all."

Dasher watched Bamburger walk across the hut and he shook his head in disappointment. *He's not the man for the job; I'll have to find someone else.*

That night, Dasher begged off dinner with the general and spent the lingering hours sipping Thai beer and fondling his eighteen-year-old hooch maid, Nhan, imported from Chu Lai, a complex of rice hamlets south of Da Nang well known for its pretty farm nymphs. The girl thought Cleanhead marvelous and there wasn't a thing she wouldn't do for him, going to great lengths to make his stressful life as comfortable as she could, though she had a childish penchant for stealing his money that kept him busy finding new hiding places for it. She was also prone to tantrums.

Between glasses of beer (he had long ago stopped complaining about her offensive habit of floating ice in the beer) he pontificated to her and the wall about command decision, the old corps, and why the desk jocks in Washington should be drafted and taught to kill gooks. On occasion, before she cut off his beer ration for the night and he became drunk, he would rip off his fatigues and tear about the hooch, burning off his anger and frustration until he dropped from exhaustion and lay on the floor and fell asleep. In the morning he would always find himself in bed, washed and clean, and wondering how a girl that weighed less than a hundred pounds could lift a two-hundred-pound man into bed.

Tonight, Cleanhead was in a morose mood and sat silent in his favorite chair (made of bamboo and palm), looking down at the ice floating in the beer glass held in his two hands. He looked mentally retarded.

"Why you be sad?" Nhan said. She stuck a finger into

145

his beer glass and played with the ice, making tinkling bell sounds, then sucked her finger dry between her unpainted lips.

He came out of his stupor. "I'm worried."

"You worry about Lieutenant Battaglia all time." She wrinkled her face, her small flat nose curling up so that it looked like a squirrel's, and she sighed. "I get jealous."

"Oh, be quiet, Nhan. Tonight is not the time to get testy."

"No use word I no understand. What *testy?*"

He ignored her.

"You still love me?" she said.

"Yes—of course."

"You want I rub your back?"

He didn't answer her, his gaze fixed on the beer. She walked around behind the bamboo-and-palm chair and placed her hands on the back of his neck, massaging deep with the strength of a man.

"That feels great. I've got another of those blasted headaches."

"I take away for you."

"Maybe it's the food."

"No—worry make. I feel hard place in neck where worry make home." She placed her thumbs just below the base of his skull and pressed hard, twisting, sustaining the pressure.

Dasher bent his head forward and his face furrowed in pain. "That hurts good. A little more to the left."

"No think Lieutenant Battaglia—think Nhan."

"My son would have been the same age as him."

"You tell me many time."

"He'd have a fine career ahead of him if he would get his head screwed on right. I could help him, but he won't let me, arrogant pup. He has to learn himself—stubborn and won't listen to reason."

"You not his father. You his colonel."

146

"You're right—I should remain distant, like I do with the other men. I think I do most of the time—but it's hard not to give him my advice."

"He still fight with major?"

"Not so much anymore. He keeps his anger to himself now—but he's burning inside. I'm worried that it's going to cause him to make a mistake that he'll be sorry for."

"Who be sorry—he or you?"

He pulled her hand away from his reddening neck and ensconced her on his lap. "If you weren't so sassy I might think about taking you home with me when this crazy war is over. I might even put shoes on your feet and buy you a real dress."

She bit his lip, hard.

"Ow!" He released her and grabbed his lip.

Jumping from his lap she began twirling and dancing excitedly in front of him. "When you go back America you no have young girl play with—ha, ha, ha," she mocked. "No have pretty young girl love you—ha, ha, ha." She kicked her legs high into the air and spun several times, her ao dai twisting around her waist.

Upset at being taunted, he tried to catch her, but she easily eluded his clumsy attempts by dancing lightly away from him, though a few times she allowed him to get within arm's length. Predictably—for this antic of hers had occurred on more than one occasion—Cleanhead's confusion turned to frustration, then to anger . . . and finally to lust.

"You be sorry you leave me. You go America you only get ugly old woman." She made a horrid face by pulling her lips wide apart and sticking her tongue out. "No find young girl like me let you touch her soft skin, who sing nice song you and wash your fat old body. You leave me here Vietnam you soon be sad GI."

Powerful hormones raced through Cleanhead's veins and he wanted Nhan more than he ever had—and she

147

knew so, playing his need against her revenge, enjoying it.

Dasher, finally needing to stop and rest, leaned against the wall, panting, and watched with heated eyes while Nhan took off her pantaloons and waved them at him. The effect was like waving a red cape in front of a wounded bull. The colonel raised his head, pushed out his jaw, and tore after the half-nude girl who squealed with delight at her conquest.

A group of Marine airmen returning to their hooches from the base O-club, stopped on the gravel walk outside the colonel's quarters and listened. Confined to his four walls and not caring what existed outside of them, Cleanhead chased his hooch maid and shouted obscenities, knocking over furniture, and roaring like a bull elephant.

"He's at it again," a pilot said.

"Never gets enough."

"Let's take him back to the O-club with us."

"You want to get your neck broken?"

They walked off in the direction of their hooches, stopping once or twice to listen to the combat of passion and to envy the colonel.

After ravishing Nhan for the third time and putting out the stub of a Russian cigar (a CIA operative gave him a case in exchange for a Viet Cong ear), he brushed back the mosquito netting, passed gas, and said, "Battaglia's not coming back. I made a mistake in ordering him to take R and R—the timing was wrong. I can see now what I couldn't see then: the boy has an entirely different outlook. Here on the base there was enough pressure and esprit de corps to keep him flying right side up and straight and level, but in Saigon . . . away from the men . . . I'm afraid he's going to lose the edge. He's not coming back, Nhan—he's going to desert, I can feel it in my left gonad, crash and burn." He turned over on his

148

side. "I'd give anything to prevent that from happening."

"He need good woman so he no crash and burn; maybe he find in Saigon."

He smelled her face all over. "I hope you're right," he said, and ravished her young body again before falling asleep.

Regardless of Chi's ministrations, Battaglia no longer could sustain his ardor for her after Nghia's incursion into their intimate adventure, however short. He sat at the bar downstairs and nursed a cold ginger ale until the pink, red, and white peony flowers were discernible in the dawn that crept with slow patience into the Khach-san Bong.

Walking through the empty lobby (except for the desk clerk leaning on his elbow, snoring) his only thought was of finding his bed and letting the fatigue that was overpowering him have its way. He shook the elevator boy awake and the two of them chugged up with a sleepy-eyed tiger girl who had slipped in just before the door closed shut on its squeaky rollers.

The girl leaned against the cage wire and her eyes fell closed in sleep for the short trip up. Somewhere she had lost a shoe and her toe stuck through the rupture in her stocking. Her ao dai was stained in the front with a brown liquid that was yet wet on the material and she smelled heavily of fish sauce.

Vince, though he could barely keep his own eyes open, watched the sleeping girl, fascinated by her quivering chin and rough condition (obviously she had had an interesting night).

Quite unexpectedly her eyes popped open and froze Battaglia in place. "Why are you staring at me?"

That's all she said. Her lids drooped and flickered once or twice, then sealed shut and the small chin began

149

quivering again.

The brief incident brought him wide awake, and when he reached his floor he was feeling hungry and thought it might be a good idea to go back downstairs and order some breakfast. "Is the dining room open?" he said to the elevator boy.

The girl with the brown stain and one shoe cocked an eye open at him. The elevator boy was dozing on the door handle.

"The dining room is closed," she said. The cocked eye slid shut.

Vince pulled the bar, opening the door for himself, and stepped out onto the landing, experiencing once again the musty smell from the old wood that carried him back in time to the days of the empress dowager, bound feet, and gunboat diplomacy.

From down the hall he could hear hard slapping sounds coming from his room where at this time of the morning he expected Ly-boy and Autumn Dove to be fast asleep. He became alarmed. Reaching the room he flung the door open (his muscles strung tight) and looked down into the faces of the children playing Mah-Jongg on the floor, Ly-boy bringing one of the plastic tiles down in midflight. He banged hard on the board in typical Mah-Jongg style.

"Why aren't you two asleep?"

"We were waiting for you to come back," Autumn Dove said. "You were gone a long time and we were worried and wanted to go look for you, but Nghia brought us the Mah-Jongg game so we decided to stay in the room and play; and anyway, Nghia said that you were being well taken care of, whatever that meant?"

"Nghia?" he said, surprised.

Autumn Dove pointed to the balcony.

Walking to the French doors, Vince looked out to the corner of the balcony. Nghia sat with her back to him,

150

surrounded by potted peonies and looking out over the city that was still an hour away from sunrise and had taken on the slate color of paddy mud. Her hair hanging over the back of the chair reached almost to the floor and the pagoda earrings on her earlobes could be seen dangling through strands of black velvet.

"What are you doing here?" he said with obvious irritation. He stood at the open French doors, studying her profile.

She turned to him and he could see the wet tears smeared on her cheeks.

"You have fun with that dirty girl?"

"No more than you had with your friend." He threw her the crumpled note signed by the man named Kai. "It's none of my business."

"That my job."

"I don't see how that makes a difference."

She tossed her head around and away from him and her heavy hair swung in a wide arc along the back of the chair. He had embarrassed her by going with her rival, Chi, and it would be all over the hotel by the time the tiger girls had finished their breakfast of pho noodles in the dining room. It was particularly degrading that the man she had gone to great lengths to get out of jail had rejected her in favor of another girl.

"You her boyfriend now; leave children and go away her room. Go back Da Nang—no come back."

"I didn't stay with her."

There was a long silence.

"What you say?"

"She begged me to stay after you left only because she wanted to get even with you. I lost interest in her and went down to the bar until just a few minutes ago."

She looked at him incredulously. "You lie."

"Ask the bartender."

The slapping of Mah-Jongg tiles had stopped and

151

Battaglia took the opportunity to take pressure off the conversation. "You kids get to bed and get some sleep."

"We want to listen to you argue with Nghia," Ly-boy said.

"In the streets we slept when we wanted." Autumn was being her usual contentious self.

"You aren't living in the streets now, you're living with me, so get yourselves into bed and I don't want to hear a peep from you until I wake you up."

They grumbled and put the Mah-Jongg game into its case and Vince watched them while he wondered what more he should say to Nghia.

"I get this bed," Autumn said.

"I want it—I told you that before," Ly-boy said.

"You can't have it." Autumn hit him in the stump with her fist and bit his ear.

Ly-boy retaliated by pulling her hair and dragging her off the bed onto the floor. She jumped onto the bed and screamed, holding the pillow to her. Ly-boy piled on top of her.

"Break it up," Vince shouted, separating them. "I'm going to make you both sleep in the same bed if you don't behave."

Hearing this Autumn Dove ran for the other bed and crawled under the sheet, her face pale and her eyes wide. With the sheet pulled up under her chin, her eyes darted back and forth between Vince and Ly-boy.

While Vince had a good laugh over his stroke of good luck stumbling on the single most effective threat that would move Autumn Dove to mind him, Nghia soothed the frightened girl by smoothing her hair and talking to her in soft tones that finally put her nerves to rest.

Though Nghia had developed special feelings for Autumn Dove, her attention toward the waif was exaggerated in order to make Vince uncomfortable and to regain some of the lost ground she had suffered during her embarrassment in Chi's room. Battaglia, on the other hand, regarded Nghia's behavior as childish and unnecessary, and he resented her intrusion into his private world with the children.

The tears, only just dried on Nghia's cheeks, welled up in her eyes once again and spilled over to run down her face when Vince, in his insensitive manner, said, "Why don't you leave the three of us alone and go back to work. You must have a line of men from your room all the way down to the street."

It alarmed Nghia, who regarded herself as being a strong determined girl and not prone to shedding tears, that Vince's blunt manner and sharpness of attack found the most vulnerable point in her spirit, broke her feeble defenses, and put her to rout. She had never been talked to like this and it was beyond her control to cope with it, regardless of her conviction that she was an honorable woman and that what she was doing for a living was justifiable in view of the hopeless future that faced her.

For the first time in her life she was being made to look at herself with the sting of cold reality and she didn't like what she saw. The hurt and anger was made more severe by the fact that she had violated her most closely held principle, that of never getting into a position where a man could shame her. Additionally, because she was well aware of the insincerity and selfishness of the men with whom she came in contact, she vowed not to allow herself the slightest bit of affection for any man, particularly any of the arrogant Americans who had turned her country into a cesspool of debauchery under the pretense of saving it from the evils of communism. Yet she had jeopardized her personal safety and welfare in showing interest in the U.S. Marine who had attracted her during an innocent moment of conversation while waiting for a bus, an American who seemed sincere in wanting to get to know her better as a person and not as something to be

153

ravished in order to sate his animal appetites.

She turned her head from Vince in time to hide the flood of tears.

The sun, rising in the morning sky, sent its warm rays across the Saigon rooftops and spread over the Khach-san Bong. On the balcony, the peonies lifted their faces to the warmth and looked down into the street where the people of Cho-Chan hurried to meet the day.

Already the streets were choked with cyclos, bicycles, and the ubiquitious pedestrians and Japanese motorcycles, all moving rapidly like lines of busy ants that rushed at each other from different directions and, by some unseen power, avoided collisions.

Awakened by the sunlight shining over the balcony and through the open French doors into her eyes, Autumn Dove kicked off the sheet and yawned, twisting her lithe developing body (betwixt child and woman) into a delicious bone-cracking stretch. "I'm hungry," she said and threw the pillow at Ly-boy, catching him in the head. She sat up, the army fatigue hat angled over her brow.

Battaglia rolled on his side. "Go back to sleep," he said, pulling the sheet over his head, grouchy and not yet fully rested from the strain of his first day in Saigon.

Autumn Dove piled into bed with Vince and Ly-boy, wide awake and eager to play. She straddled Battaglia with her legs and pulled his hair, riding him like a horse.

"Knock it off, I'm tired and want to catch a few more winks."

She wouldn't leave him alone and Ly-boy, excited by her display of energy, wanted to play too and so jumped on Vince with her and whooped it up. Ly-boy spurred him with his stump and tickled him while Autumn pulled his hair like the reins on a horse and rode him hard.

Finally overpowered and catching onto the spirit of

their play, Vince wrestled around on the bed with them. He nuzzled Autumn Dove in the ribs and under the chin and in her armpits until she thrashed about and squealed uncontrollably with laughter and fell off the bed and lay there giggling and exhausted where Ly-boy joined her in the same condition.

Vince wasn't through with them. "I'll fix you for not letting me sleep."

He continued to tickle them without mercy until they begged him to stop.

"No more—please!"

"I can't stand it."

"Will you leave me alone and let me sleep?" he said.

"Yes, yes, yes," they cried.

"Promise?" He tickled them in a last frenzy.

"*We promise!*" they screamed.

When he let them go and got into bed, they jumped on top of him again and pounded his back and pulled his hair and shouted, "Hurry, horse—run—run—run; the Viet Cong are after us and they will catch us unless you carry us to safety. Run—run—run."

They repeated this over and over, enjoying themselves and having great fun while Vince lay in the bed, groaning.

Finally bored with Battaglia, the two children got off him and amused themselves by punching each other and throwing their clothes and shoes around the room; and they discovered great sport in collecting pebbles from the peony pots and dropping the missiles on the people in the street below: five points for a direct hit and three points for a near miss.

With sleep completely wrenched from him, Battaglia dressed and went in to the bathroom to revive himself. After taking a long soaking bath he lathered his beard and stood before the mirror, staring at his sleep-starved face. It dawned on him that the room had grown suspiciously quiet. In the mirror he watched the bathroom door slowly open (there was no lock on it) and two peanut heads peek through, eyes popped wide in amazement at Vince paring away his beard with a straight razor. Giving no indication that he had seen Autumn and Ly-boy, he methodically shaved away the beard, exaggerating the cutting motions and putting on a performance for the kids.

"What does it feel like?" Autumn Dove said, fascinated.

"Want to try?" He rinsed his face and handed her the shaving mug and brush.

She looked at Ly-boy.

"Go ahead," he said.

Taking the mug in one hand, she churned the brush in the shaving soap and timidly lathered her face, her eyes fixed on Vince.

"Do me," Ly-boy said and stuck his face out to her.

She soaped him up too, covering his mouth and ears in the process.

"Stay still," Battaglia said, holding Autumn's chin between his thumb and forefinger, the long razor poised above her head.

He expected her to have second thoughts about a shave, but she never bolted; she stood still and closed her eyes while Ly-boy, face lathered, stood beside her and watched bug-eyed.

"Go ahead," she said, her tightly closed eyes wrinkling her forehead.

Vince turned the blade over so that the blunt edge took the place of the cutting edge and carefully "shaved" her face, smiling at the grimaces that she made. Finished, he rinsed away the remaining patches of shaving soap and rubbed a few drops of bay rum between his palms and applied the aftershave lotion to her baby face. He repeated the whole ceremony for Ly-boy.

"Let's eat now . . . I'm hungry," Ly-boy said. "So is Autumn."

"You have to brush your teeth first." He gave them each a new toothbrush and a tube of toothpaste.

They looked increduously at the things in their hands.

"What do we do with these?" Autumn said.

"Use them to clean your teeth." He closed the bathroom door and started to make the beds but changed his mind, deciding that it would be a good idea if he left the beds for the kids as a part of their training.

When the knock came he was bending over picking up the children's new clothes strewn across the floor. He had given up the idea that his R & R would be spent, as he had originally intended, in quiet contemplation. The long line of interruptions in his plans seemed endless. He dropped the clothes and went to the door.

Standing outside in the hall the Burmese elevator boy smiled and bowed, making a big show of his courtesy and asked if it would be all right if "Number One tiger girl could visit with the children?"

Vince looked at Nghia standing taciturn behind the boy, her eyes diverted, her pouting lips pursed with indignation, and looking as beautiful as ever.

He thought for a moment about the wisdom of letting her in, knowing that there would be another argument if he consented, but feeling a little bit sorry for her. It must have taken a great effort for her to come back after the way he had insulted her.

"I suppose it will be all right," he said to the elevator boy.

Continuing with the decorum that he obviously was enjoying, the boy turned to Nghia and bowed with arms folded across his chest in the style of the ancient mandarins. "Number One Marine says Number One tiger girl can come in."

He stepped aside, bowed, and smiled at Vince with his ivory-white teeth as Nghia walked into the room, her flowered ao dai twisted about her legs concealed underneath the flared white silk pantaloons. Vince looked

157

hard at the outline of Nghia's legs pressing against the silk visible through the split in her ao dai. For a brief second he was back at the Tan Son Nhut bus stop, all of his attention focused on a pair of perfectly sculptured, stockingless, butter-honey legs growing out from under the shortest miniskirt he had ever seen.

"Fantastic," he whispered.

"Sir?" the elevator boy said.

He gave the Burmese a tip and closed the door, the old hand-hammered latch making a hard *click* as it seated.

Nghia stood in the middle of the room, studying the mess of unmade beds and tossed-about clothing and overturned chairs. An especially disdainful look was reserved for Vince's seabag that lay open in a corner, its contents spilling out of the top. Glancing about for signs of the children, she noticed the closed bathroom door, picked her way through the debris, and tapped on the door.

It opened a crack.

Nghia peered inside and quickly pushed the door open. *"Choi oi!"* Good heavens! she cried and put a hand over her mouth.

"There you go again," Battaglia said to her. "It seems that whenever you come in you've got to start complaining about something."

"Look—look." She pointed inside, her arm rigid and her face perplexed.

He looked over her shoulder at the walls and floor smeared with blue toothpaste. Ly-boy's hair was sticky with the stuff and Autumn Dove had it twisted in coils over her face. Both of them had the tubes of toothpaste in their fists and were squeezing them at each other, the goo squirting out in long streams.

Nghia pushed Vince out of the bathroom—a look on her face that made it clear he knew nothing about caring for children—closed the door in his nose, and could be heard yammering away at Ly-boy and Autumn Dove while she cleaned them and washed the toothpaste off the walls and floor.

What the devil's going on in my life? He walked around the room not knowing what to do with himself. *Here I am tied in with two wild street kids and a prostitute. It doesn't make sense . . . none of it.*

He began picking up clothes. Nghia came out of the bathroom, holding each of the kids by a hand, and gave them stern instructions to clean up the room. The dresses she took out of Battaglia's hands she hung in the closet and in quick order the beds were made, the floor picked clean, and everything put in its proper place. Autumn swept the floor, Ly-boy stumped on his crutch out to the balcony and watered the peonies, and finally Nghia marched them back into the bathroom where they received instruction on how to properly use toothpaste and a toothbrush.

She wouldn't directly address Vince. *"Chung toi an com,"* we will eat now, she said to the children.

"Tell her to speak English," Vince said.

"She won't do it," Autumn said.

"Tell her anyway."

"She won't."

"Tell her."

Autumn shrugged and said to Nghia, *"Anh muon chi noi tieng Anh."*

"Khong," no, she said, folding a set of pajamas.

"I told you," Autumn said to Vince.

"What's her problem?"

"I don't know," she said and sat down on the bed with Ly-boy. "When are we going to eat?"

"Ly-boy," Vince said, "take Autumn with you to the Japanese cook that we made arrangements with yesterday and bring some breakfast back to the room. Be sure there's a pot of hot coffee . . . and take Nghia with you."

Ly-boy took Nghia's hand, but she shooed him and

Autumn Dove out the door alone. She turned back to folding the pajamas as though she were the only person in the room. She eyed the seabag several times and started over to it, but thought better about the idea and passed it by, going into the bathroom to clean the sink and bathtub.

Vince sat in the chair waiting for her to say something to him, though he knew he would have a long wait. He wondered why she remained behind while the kids went for the food, it never dawning on him that he might be attractive to her and in her stubborn way she was trying to show it.

The knock came this time while Vince was leaning over the balcony railing, watching the street traffic four floors below. He didn't go to the door, figuring Nghia would answer the knock.

The street was narrow and it surprised him that so many people could jam themselves into so small a space. Ly-boy on his crutch and Autumn Dove wearing her fatigue hat walked out of the hotel gate and turned up the street for the restaurant. Battaglia smiled and watched the two get swallowed up by the traffic and disappear around the corner.

Over the sound of running water the knocking persisted. He left and balcony and as he passed by the open bathroom door he saw Nghia bent over the bathtub. Her silk pantaloons had caught on the plumbing and were pulled up above the knees, revealing her legs. He stood there for a long time, his mouth dry, shaking his head and marveling at the smooth skin, the fine muscle tone, and exquisite color.

Chapter 10

"Have message for Number One tiger girl." The Burmese's big teeth protruded from his lips in an exaggerated overbite that gave him the appearance of having fake teeth in his large mouth, the kind kids find in Cracker Jack boxes.

It took Vince a while before he could take his attention away from the elevator boy's mouth and decide if he wanted to call Nghia to the door or send the messenger to her.

The boy watched Vince looking at his teeth without a hint of understanding what Battaglia was doing. He stared back at him with the same blank smile that he always wore.

"She's in the bathroom." Vince walked away leaving the door open.

The Burmese said a few words to Nghia. She shook her head in response and went back to drying her hands on the bath towel. The boy became animated and his voice rose, all the while maintaining the same respectful, dull smile.

Nghia shook her head again, this time more vigorously. "*Khong*," no, she said.

The elevator boy's arms were spread wide, palms up in a gesture of perplexity. Not once did Nghia look at him. She turned her back and shook her head. "*Khong*."

161

Battaglia watched the whole scenario and was puzzled. The boy continued to be insistent, even pleading, but Nghia was adamant and refused to comply with the request that was being made. Vince gathered that the elevator boy had been sent to Nghia by someone who had insisted on an immediate and positive response.

"What was that all about?" Vince said to the boy walking out shaking his head.

"Customer," he said.

Vince walked over to the bathroom door and watched Nghia finishing up the cleaning. "You're very tidy aren't you?—and not afraid of work."

She straightened the towel on the rack and stood in front of the mirror, twisting her hair into a double roll and pinning the thick pile on top of her head with a large Chinese comb. She removed the dangling pagoda earrings and cleaned her pierced earlobes with a solution from a small bottle she took from her purse.

"There's something I don't understand about you," he said.

Her look went through him, out the back of his head, as though she heard his voice but couldn't see him. The earrings went back on and she gave them a flick with her finger that made them twirl.

"You're an intelligent good-looking girl and could do any number of things if you put your mind to it."

She screwed the cap back on the bottle and returned it to her purse. "You want know why I choose be tiger girl?" She relaxed her tense look and the hint of a smile began to curl at the corner of her lip, just enough to tell Vince that she was willing to soften a bit to him if he treated her civilly.

Her walk across the now neat and cleaned room to the French doors was pure poetry and Battaglia's diaphragm contracted involuntarily and he sucked in his breath. Her hand, small and leaflike, reached up and rested lightly on the edge of the windowed door; at the same time her head turned and she settled her chin on her shoulder, the long Manchu eyes beholding him in their firm, penetrating gaze that made his stomach do a couple of somersaults. A little breeze from the balcony blew across her shoulders and spun the pagoda earrings.

"When I young virgin girl," she began, "maybe fourteen, fifteen years old, I be sold to old mama-san. My family very poor, not rich like I tell you. Mama-san pay maybe two hundred dollar your money, make maybe one thousand dollar sell me one time to rich Vietnamese man."

"Uh—look, you don't have to tell me all this if you don't want to," he said, embarrassed. "It's none of my business."

"I run away after first time," she continued as if not hearing him, "but mama-san find me and lock me in room her house for one year. Many mans come my room; I be sold many time after mama-san die. One man own me now." She stopped and looked at him boldly. "He make much money from me and kill me I run away."

"Kai?" Vince said.

The long eyes widened momentarily, then settled back to their see-through introspection.

"So you've become indentured to a man who uses you as a money-making machine; and to those people he owes favors, you pay the debt."

She walked up to him, slim hips rocking in their natural even motion that reminded him of the quiet swells of the South China Sea, progenitor of the Orient.

"Now you know why I stay prostitute," she said. "Maybe now you no say bad things to me."

"I'm sorry, Nghia—I'm honestly sorry."

She put a hand on his shoulder and it settled leaf-light, causing his stomach to flip over.

"At bus stop yesterday" (she thought back—yesterday seemed like weeks ago) "I think you like me because you no know I whore, but if you know I tiger girl you hate me . . . so I pretend I rich girl come from good family." Her hand slid along his shoulder to the soft hairs on his neck. "You look at me with your heart, not with long thing between your legs, and I know you kind mans and I no want go bus, I want stay you and be friend you and we talk and war go away and no more dirty mans come my room and—"

His kiss was soft and tender, like that of a friend, not a lover, on her cheek at the corner of her lips, catching her in midsentence. She started and a little sigh escaped her lips. He reached around and pulled the comb from her hair that loosed the black waterfall to cascade down her back. A tiny tear curved around the crescent scar under her eye and left a wet trail down the side of her face.

"I want be your friend. You good mans . . . I see you take care childrens, buy them clothes . . . you no stay with Chi . . ." The hardness went out of her face and she began to tremble. "Please be my friend."

They didn't make love. He held her hand and looked into her wet eyes and she stopped trembling and he was sure the hardness in her face was all gone. They sat on the floor, in the open doors facing the balcony, saying nothing and listening to the putter of Japanese motorcycles, the jingle of bicycle bells, and the hawking of street vendors outside. She returned Vince's grip tightly and he rememberd Chi's words: . . . *she has no friends, was abandoned by her family and sold into prostitution, cries a lot when she's alone, and tells big stories to cover up her poverty* . . .

Sitting on the bare planked floor, silk pantaloons pulled up and exposing her crossed honey legs, Nghia had withdrawn into her secret world, that hard third shell deep inside that would never crack and was out of reach of others. A smile was on her face and her eyes were fixed on the peonies. "I want talk more." The pressure on his hand increased.

"Go ahead—I'll listen."

"I want you talk too. I talk first."

"Sure."

"When Autumn Dove tell me you in jail I want get you out, but no have money to pay for favor. Big mans in government say I be his girl friend, pay that way. I remember your kind eyes so I say yes . . . I pay that way." She squeezed his hand. "I stand at MP gate and see you come out, then I go to him be his girl friend."

Vince was humbled by her confession and wanted to say something to express his gratitude, but this was not the time. He let her go on.

"He want me again this morning."

"The message from the elevator boy?"

"Yes, but I remember bad things you say about me in Chi's room and bad things you say when I wait you here with children. I think you right, so I say no. In my heart I want be your girl friend but I afraid ask you."

Vince felt his bones go soft and his stomach filled with butterflies.

"I think I in big trouble now. Government mans angry I no repay favor. He tell Kai and maybe I be killed."

"You're kidding—killed?"

"They very mean mans. I think Kai have me killed now."

"But you're his meal ticket—he'd be cutting his own throat. You're too valuable to him to lose."

She smiled cynically. "You no understand. Kai must, what you call, save face. Must make government mans happy or government mans have Kai killed. He knows Kai own me. I want be your girl friend, belong nobody else, no more work Kai." She looked up at him. "What you think?" she said, ready to accept his decision, her eyes boldly fixed on him.

"Well, it's pretty obvious if you become my girl friend Kai loses both ways . . . he loses to the government man and he loses to me . . . and I think you're right, he isn't going to stand for it. He'll probably try to kill us both."

She looked away and some of the hardness came back into her face. "You no want me be your girl friend?"

"I didn't say that—I just need some time to think. We have a couple of options that might work out . . ."

"I no care about op . . . tion . . . s; I think too long; my head go 'round and 'round and I feel like fall down."

The door opened and Autumn Dove walked in carrying a typical stack of bamboo hot-food containers used by Cho-Chan restaurants for take-out orders. There were four of them nested together, one on top of the other; and behind Autumn Dove, Ly-boy limped in on his crutch, his free hand holding onto the handle of a basket that contained more food, napkins, bowls, chopsticks, and an assortment of other necessities to complete their breakfast.

"That didn't take long," Vince said and took the nested containers from Autumn. "Did you remember the coffee?"

Ly-boy lifted a ceramic pot from the basket. "Very hot."

Outside on the balcony, Nghia arranged four chairs around a small table, spreading a tablecloth and setting places with bowls, spoons, chopsticks, and napkins. There was a plate and knife and fork for Vince for his bacon and eggs, and the bowls, spoons, and chopsticks were for the standard Vietnamese breakfast of pho noodle soup.

They all sat down among the potted peonies in a setting that was quite pleasant with its view of the busy street; and in full sight, the Saigon River with its ships and sampans and docks full of crated goods and munitions was at its peak of activity before the hot sun drove people

166

to seek shelter.

With an American breakfast in front of Vince and bowls of steaming pho before the others, Nghia ceremoniously poured coffee and tea and smiled pleasantly. She bumped her teacup against Battaglia's coffee cup in a silent toast and they both drank, wondering what the future held for them now that the barriers were down and trust had replaced suspicion.

Autumn Dove reached into her bowl with her fingers and extracted a long noodle, hanging it above her mouth and letting it drop into her mouth. She reached for another and Nghia slapped her hand.

"Use chopsticks—learn be gentle girl," Nghia said.

"Don't slurp your soup," Vince said to Ly-boy.

Vince and Nghia looked at each other, surprised at what they had said, and laughed.

"You would think that we were their mother and father." Battaglia shook a little salt and pepper onto his eggs, chuckling to himself.

"You want taste pho?" Nghia held a bowl out to him.

He ate the last bit of egg in his plate and took the bowl from her. "Smells good."

Nghia spooned a bit of plum sauce for him and added a few leaves of mint and sweet basil, fresh and aromatic.

The kids stopped eating and waited.

He tasted it suspiciously. "Not bad," he said, swallowing a second spoonful. "A bit strong for my taste but not bad at all."

The kids clapped and laughed.

The four of them ate enthusiastically, laughed a lot and talked, and Vince or Nghia occasionally gave Ly-boy and Autumn Dove instructions in table manners. This tranquil domestic picture would have made a visitor believe that a family was breakfasting together.

Nghia was in the middle of telling a funny story about two rice farmers who devised a plan to get rich by cornering the market on buffalo dung when she noticed that Vince was no longer listening, his attention diverted to a flight of jet fighters banking into their final approach to Tan Son Nhut Air Base.

His look is troubled—his eyes have gone inside and they are dull with fear, she noted. *See how he follows the planes; he is up there with them, and he senses danger.*

The children had noticed too and they were watching him.

Nghia finished the story, but Battaglia didn't hear the end. He watched each aircraft disappear into the waves of heat rising above the earth, then stared at the place where they vanished, not speaking, his eyes blinking at the beads of sweat that broke out on his forehead and ran down to blur his vision.

"What is wrong with him?" Ly-boy whispered.

"He looks strange." Autumn Dove bit her index finger.

Nghia collected the breakfast things and began placing them in the basket. "Do not bother him," she said in Vietnamese.

Battaglia had removed himself from the table and was standing at the rail. Nghia noticed that his knuckles had turned white gripping the rail.

"We'll take the basket back to the restaurant," Ly-boy said to Nghia.

"Can we go see the kung-fu movie?" Autumn Dove begged.

"We saw it yesterday."

"I want to see it again."

Nghia turned from Battaglia and pointed to her purse; Autumn brought it to her. Without speaking she gave the children the movie money.

After Autumn Dove and Ly-boy left to return the basket to the restaurant and to spend a few hours at the movies, Nghia waited for Vince's mind to come back from

168

wherever it had gone. She sat down and manicured her nails while she hummed a popular country ballad about a young woman who left her lover to fight with the Viet Cong.

A few minutes passed and Vince looked around as if he was waking from a dream, and saw Nghia sitting calmly at the table, doing her nails and quietly singing. His face was pale and he reached for a handkerchief to mop his brow.

Seeing that he couldn't find his handkerchief, Nghia took a tissue from her purse and patted the perspiration away from his face. Not satisfied with this, she brought a damp washcloth from the bathroom and cleaned his face.

"I've never had a woman do this . . . it feels real good."

Her smile was matter-of-fact. "Where you been?"

He shook his head. "I don't understand."

"You go someplace with jets out there." She pointed into the sky with a freshly polished fingernail. "I think maybe you no come back."

He turned away and looked west. "Let's go to Thailand, Nghia. We'll take Ly-boy and Autumn with us. Kai and your past won't follow you there and we can set up a new life together, and my . . ." He stopped short.

She walked up beside him. "Your what? Why you stop?"

"How long have we known each other?" He ran a finger along her forehead and down to her eyes and nose and chin.

"Not long."

"It seems like years but it's been only hours. Do you realize that?—we've only known each other for a few hours."

"Yesterday we know," she said. "Seem much longer time."

"It has been much longer . . . I've known you all my life."

169

"You make joke."

"I'm not joking—someday I'll tell you what I mean."

Nghia looked awkwardly at Vince. She wanted to have total confidence in him, but she held back, unable to let go of her past doubts about men. He was right—they had only known each other for a short time, and the past told her that she could not allow him the liberties that she wanted so much to give him.

Her heart was another matter. All of her soul cried out for this man who could bring peace to her tangled mind and in whom she recognized the love and security that she desperately needed. "When I tell you I no want to prostitute no more and want run away Kai, I speak truth," she said to Vince. "I go anywhere you go. You want take me Thailand with children I go; I no care how long I know you—one hour—one day—I still go you."

"Listen," he said, "before the children interrupted us you said you didn't think I wanted you to be my girl friend."

"And you say you need time think. How much time you need think? Nghia no have much time . . ."

He put his hands on her shoulders. "You deserve to know the truth. I sense that you are willing to put your life into my hands—and that's a pretty big order for me; and then there are the kids who are part of the deal. I can't abandon them now that they depend on me."

She nodded her agreement and her smooth brow wrinkled.

"I told you that we had a couple of choices and I think the best one is to go to Thailand. With your connections it shouldn't be difficult."

"What we do in Thailand?"

"We can figure that out when we get there. The first thing is to get away from Kai and the . . ."

She was staring at him again, that bold long stare, waiting for him to go on, but he didn't. His face lost color

170

and his eyes became dull.

"Why you stop like before—why you no go on?"

"It's nothing."

"You say you want me know truth." She searched his face. "You afraid something. You afraid airplane—afraid go back Da Nang, afraid fly North Vietnam?"

He took his hands from her shoulders and breathed hard. "I'm not going to lie to you—yes, you're right—I am afraid, I never thought it would happen to me, but I've lost the edge. I despised other pilots who turned coward and quit, and now I'm the one that's quitting."

Starting to turn away, his head down, she grabbed him by the shirt and pulled him back to face her. "Finish," she demanded.

"All right, I'll give you the whole story, but I don't see what good it will do."

She released her hand from his shirt and stood with her arms folded over her breasts. "It do much good. Talk."

"I came to Saigon on Rest and Recuperation, R and R," he explained, "to think about this crazy war and what I'm doing here and whether or not you people are worth all the killing and dying. I've been here less than twenty-four hours and I've already seen enough corruption, debauchery, and hate for Americans than I dreamed possible. I've got my answer and I've decided to leave Vietnam, on my own. My involvement in this war is over; I refuse to throw away my life, to waste it on something I never believed in. This trip to Saigon reinforces my conviction." He drew in a breath. "You can come with me to Thailand or you can stay here. I hope you choose to come with me, because I've grown fond of you and I think we can have a good life together." He paused and his face tightened. "I may not be able to make it without you—it's going to be rough—it will be lonely. It's been lonely."

171

He turned to walk away, but she grabbed his shirt at the front once more and pulled him back. "Okay . . . forget Vietnam . . . maybe it no worth you die for, but how about you? How much you worth?"

"I don't get it—what are you saying?" He looked down into her Manchu eyes and they sparked with excitement.

"You run away—you no find peace. Find trouble—be sad, hate yourself."

"It's important to you that I don't go to Thailand?"

"You go Thailand—I go you; but we no be happy. You always think about flyboys, your friends—many be killed, but you run away, live. Always feel gui—guil-ty."

"Guilty?" he said, helping her with the pronunciation.

"Yes, that word."

"I've thought of that."

Her active and alert mind perceived that there was more to his story. She stooped and picked a peony flower. Standing up she twirled the blossom in her fingers and smoothed her black tresses over a shoulder. "You fly many times bomb communists—no afraid. Why you say you afraid now?"

He paused and folded a stick of Blackjack Gum into his mouth, wondering if he could tell her, this high-priced Cho-Chan whore who he had become attached to . . . maybe fallen in love with. "It's the guns," he said.

"Tell me about guns." She pulled him down into a chair beside her and waited, elbows on the table and her chin resting on folded hands.

He began simply. "We will fly down a long narrow canyon, straight, unable to maneuver. They know we will be coming and they will be waiting; their guns, more than we've ever seen before, will be pointed down the slot where we will come slow and heavy with bombs." He tapped the top of the table with his fingers, nervous.

She waited.

"I will be the point aircraft. It is my job to draw fire, to

172

locate the guns and put them out of action so the attack planes can have a clear run on the target." He stopped tapping and looked up. "That's Ban Dau."

The silence was long, but not uncomfortable. Her full pouting lips puckered in thought and she leaned back off her elbows and crossed her legs. The morning sun had climbed higher and the veranda roof, made from bamboo and painted green, cast a shadow across her face, hiding the lines of concentration in her forehead. The ends of her hair moved slowly in the warm breeze from the river.

"Best you go back Da Nang. No go Thailand."

"Da Nang?" He spoke the word like he had never heard of the place.

"You face guns. After, you still feel same-same, come back Khach-san Bong and I go Thailand you."

"If I'm still alive."

"You be alive."

"How do you know?"

"I know."

"How about Autumn Dove and Ly-boy?"

"I take care."

Both of them knew what the next question had to be; neither wanted to be the first one to bring it up. Nghia uncrossed her legs and sat up a little straighter like she remembered doing when in school and the teacher was about to ask her a question dealing with the colonization of Indochina by the French.

"How about Kai?" he said.

She shrugged. "I go back be same-same before you come. Be ginger cookie again."

"And you will be the government official's girl friend?"

"That my job."

Battaglia was frustrated. He walked back and forth like a caged leopard and kicked the peony pots. There wasn't much of a choice open to him. He reasoned that Nghia

173

could take care of herself, her future was no concern of his and whether or not she and the children made it in Cho-Chan was in the hands of God—or someone else—possibly the pimp named Kai.

In the minutes that went by as he alternately fumed at himself, the Marines, and all of Southeast Asia, it began to imprint on his mind that Nghia and the children had in such an extraordinarily short time become important to him, and the thought of being separated from them or possibly never seeing them again was painful and unacceptable.

"Nghia," he said and sat down at the table with her, "I don't think it's right that you go back to Kai, it just doesn't sit well with me. Nor does running to Thailand or anywhere else. You're right—I should go back to my unit and fly the mission; I could never live with myself if I didn't; I've known that all along—it just took you to get me to admit that what I was planning to do was wrong and wouldn't work out in the end."

The more Vince and Nghia talked, the more they realized their growing attachment to each other and the need to find a solution to the dilemma confronting them. For the most part, Nghia remained quiet and let Battaglia do the talking, though she was sure that she had the perfect answer and felt that Vince would agree to it if she could steer him around to realizing that he needed her and that she could help him meet the danger that waited at Ban Dau.

"Maybe you already have Vietnamese girl—no want Nghia," she probed.

He laughed quietly. "Being confined to the base I had never seen a 'Nam woman worth looking at until I saw you standing outside the gate at Tan Son Nhut. Looking at you was like drinking a cup of cool water after crossing the Mojave Desert, and I'll honestly tell you, on the chance that you'll get so puffed up I won't be able

174

to talk to you, that I thought you were the finest thing I'd ever hoped to see."

"You have girl friend back home America?" she adroitly said, maneuvering him into position with her questions.

"I did—maybe I still do, though she made it clear when I left for Vietnam that she didn't at all agree with what I was doing. I kind of got the impression that she left the door open a crack instead of slamming it completely shut on our relationship."

"She have blond hair, blue eyes?"

"Yes she does."

"Pretty?"

He nodded.

"You miss her?"

"Yeh, I miss her . . . so what?" he said, a little angry at her exposing his weakness for Ruthie.

Leaning to him she took his hand in hers and looked him square in the eye and his brain turned to Cream of Wheat and he saw her sulking lips that invited him to kiss her and he did and forgot all about Ruthie and Ban Dau and all the rest of it and floated away on a magic carpet with a Manchu princess who had eyes that turned his head to mush.

She unbuttoned his shirt and rubbed his chest with her two hands, fascinated by the carpet of hair, the dog tags clinking on the beaded metal chain hanging around his neck. "You love me, don't you, Vincent Joseph Battaglia, USMC, 1802327?" She kissed him, hard, pulling her hair forward and covering his head with the black silky cloud. "I make you forget blond hair, blue eyes." She pulled back a few inches from his face, her half-lidded eyes paralyzing him, and her hair, covering the two of them, created a cozy burrow in which she held his head cupped in her hands. "After today you always want black hair, black eyes."

175

The knock at the door broke the spell and Vince mumbled an unwholesome epithet and started to get up, but Nghia's hand restrained him.

"For me," she cautioned.

He looked worried, but her smile assured him that she would be right back and that she would pick up where she had left off with him, and that he need not be disappointed by the interruption.

Her walk to the door was as graceful and sure as the ebb and flow of the sea lapping at the sand, and he watched with an appreciative and skilled eye that recalled all the walks of the woman he had known, none of which could approach the pure aesthetic pleasure evoked by Nghia's natural movements.

The old hand-hammered latch clicked and the door opened on hinges that creaked from years of neglect and Vince could see the elevator boy standing in the hallway, the perpetual fixed smile absent from his face.

Nghia was speaking to the boy, and by the tone and inflection of her voice, Vince could tell that she was repeating her earlier refusal. An evil-looking Viet pushed the Burmese aside and Nghia was grabbed by the arm and pulled into the hall.

The time it took for Battaglia to cover the distance from his chair on the balcony to the hall could be measured in nanoseconds. Nghia was being dragged to the elevator by the man and he had a hand clasped over her mouth. He was big for a Viet, and the eyes that squinted at Battaglia were dead and unfeeling, like a shark's.

Another man, smaller but with an equally wicked look, and more dangerous because he held a U.S. Army Colt .45 in Battaglia's nose, spoke perfect English and told Vince not to intrude or he would have to paint the hotel's walls with his brains.

Vince, who didn't have to be convinced that the man

176

meant what he said—for this was the inglorious Kai—
froze with one foot outside the door, cursing his
helplessness and the odius pimp in front of him.

With the impatience of a wild dog that hasn't had a
meal in days, Kai pushed Battaglia into the room and
stretched his gums back over his yellow teeth in what
could be imagined as a smile. From the ruckus kicked up
at the end of the hall it sounded like Nghia was putting up
a devil of a fight.

"None of this need concern you, Marine—it's just a
small matter between two business partners that will be
worked out in short order." Kai shoved the .45 closer to
Vince's face.

"At whose expense?" Vince studied Kai for an
advantage, any weakness that would give him the
slightest chance to get the gun from him.

The Viet was a professional, however, and it was clear
that he knew exactly what he was doing. He had a great
deal of experience at the control end of a gun.

"Might as well calm down," he said, inspecting Vince's
heaving chest, "because you are not going anywhere, at
least not until Nghia is out of the hotel and on her way to
a place where you will never see her again."

"Going to lock her up like the mama-san did when she
was a kid, Kai?"

"It may be necessary to apply a bit of friendly
persuasion. Now and then these tiger girls get independent ideas and the stronger-willed ones like Nghia require
more forceful methods to purge their minds of disobe-
dient thoughts." The gums spread wider over the stained
teeth and the laugh was deep in his throat.

Just outside the door, rooted to the floor, the elevator
boy shifted his nervous attention back and forth between
Vince being held inside the room and Nghia down the hall
kicking and scratching at her assailant stuffing her
into the elevator. The young man was concerned for his

177

own safety and at the same time frustrated in that he was unable to help Nghia and Vince. The confusion showed in his face.

"Don't look so hostile, Mr. Battaglia." Kai spoke with affected politeness. "This nasty business will be over within a few minutes and you can return to the rest and recuperation, I believe you call it R and R, that I wouldn't think of begrudging you after spending a long year in the north heroically defending me from the evils of communism." His laugh was loud and mocking.

"You're a funny man, Kai."

"I will even arrange for another of our beautiful ladies to entertain you. How about the lovely Chi, with whom I understand that you are already somewhat acquainted, though unfortunately is not as talented as my Nghia— but what woman is? Right, Lieutenant?"

Battaglia took a step forward and Kai's gun hand tightened around the butt of the .45, a black and ugly-looking weapon loaded with dumdum bullets that flattened on impact and could tear off an arm at the shoulder.

"Steady, young man. We don't want to see the American tax payer's two-hundred-and-fifty-thousand-dollar investment splattered all over a cheap hotel room, do we?"

"You had better kill me, Kai, because if you don't I'm going to root you out of whatever snake hole you hide in and personally tear each of your tiny gonads out of your scrotum and then stuff them down your throat and make you swallow them."

The sneer on Kai's lips began on the left side of his mouth and slowly twisted to the right side. "I have always admired the colorful language of the U.S. Marines; so graphically descriptive and so macho. However, I must disappoint you. As fate would have it, I am a eunuch, the victim of a sweet young thing whose

178

hymen I punctured some years ago when I was young and brash, unheedful of the hidden revenge and insidious thoughts that lurk in womens' breasts. She castrated me in my sleep with my own knife while I dreamt of the hot pleasure and exceeding profits I would reap with this beautiful damsel I had rescued from the Mekong rice fields; never mind that her parents claimed that I had brazenly stolen her from under their noses while the family slept in its hooch." His sneer turned to a smile and he laughed loudly.

"I'll find you," Vince said, "if it takes me the rest of my life, I'll find you. Rats like you give off a stink that can't be hidden and I'll follow your trail wherever you go."

"Come, come, Lieutenant Battaglia. You're upset right now and are saying things that later will seem very foolish to you. You won't waste your time looking for me because in time you will come to realize that a whore like Nghia isn't worth the trouble of saving." He laughed louder and shook all over. "You are an intelligent young man and surely you must know that you aren't the first that Nghia has conned into thinking that she's in love with and that she's worthy of being freed from a life of sexual hire. Why, my good man, the next thing she will have you believing is that her parents sold her into child prostitution and since that day she has been owned by a series of men and women, a prisoner to their private interests; and that I, Kai, am her most recent master in this chain of indenturement, continuing the insidious cycle that will keep her bound for the rest of her life." Again he laughed. "It's the same story she tells all her men. The truth is, sir, that Nghia is a born whore and very good at it; so good that she makes a great deal of money for both herself and for me, more money than any other woman in her line of work in Saigon and possibly in all Southeast Asia. She enjoys her work and entered concubinage voluntarily."

"So why is she out there fighting to get free of your goon?"

"Every now and then she takes a fancy to a young man like yourself and wants to break away for some independent action. It is my responsibility as her guardian and business partner to protect her interests, to protect her from her own foolishness. When she does succeed in eluding me on these rare occasions, she always returns in a few days. The longest she's been gone was two weeks—an Australian sailor who became enamored with her and jumped ship. She called me from Bangkok, broke, and spent of her childish notions, and wanted me to come to get her, which I did, spending another week cleaning her up and getting her back in shape and rested for work."

From deep inside Battaglia a groan surfaced and the starch went out of him. His body sagged and his eyes stared past Kai, vacant and lifeless. "You can put away the gun," he said.

The Viet returned the .45 to a shoulder holster under his light tropical coat and looked at Vince with curiosity. The elevator clanked and the hallway was quiet once more.

"Don't take it so hard, Marine. Chalk it up to experience and don't fall into the same trap again. Someday you may even thank Nghia for opening your eyes to the ways of Asian women. Was she not mysterious and much more penetrating than your Western women?"

Vince's eyes came back into focus and widened at what Kai had said.

"I take it she was your first Oriental?" He nodded his head at Vince's silence and patted his shoulder, fatherly. "I can understand how you feel, but you must realize that our women, the ones like Nghia who make a living of men, have developed their art to such a point of

180

refinement that it is difficult if not impossible to detect any false appearance or action with the intent to deceive. Nghia, in the strictest sense of Vietnamese society, plays a vital role. At her level we have no prostitutes, only concubines, and Nghia is a deluxe model."

"She made me feel like she was mine alone and willing to go to any length to please me."

"Exactly. This is what men want, and here in Saigon they are willing to pay handsomely for a woman's talents, though they know that it is all pretense."

"But the money—payment for service—breaks the bubble right away and turns the relationship into something sordid," Vince said.

"Did Chi ask you for money?"

"Well, no, she didn't, as a matter of fact." He rubbed his chin and lines in his face deepened.

"Did Nghia?"

"No, of course not."

"There is never a fee. The man, however, derives great pleasure in dressing *his woman* in gifts of expensive jewelry and clothes, providing gifts of cash, and giving special favors that often exceed the gifts in value. This is all understood beforehand and prevents the relationship from becoming *sordid*, as you say."

"And you receive your share . . ."

"From the client for making the arrangement."

"And from Nghia . . ."

"As a token of her gratitude and commitment to our partnership. She fully understands and appreciates my role as her protector," he said, patting the gun, "and, shall we say, as her booking agent."

"Chi said that she wanted to make Nghia jealous, that's why she asked me to her room."

"All part of the subtle deception—makes for an interesting game in an otherwise boring life of a tiger girl. I'm afraid you were naive, Lieutenant, and, of course, the

181

girls were quick to spot it. Did Chi not tell you that she wanted you as her permanent boyfriend and she did not want to see any other men?"

He drew a breath and nodded reluctantly.

"And did not Nghia say the same thing?"

"I suppose I've been stupid, but that didn't give you license to bust into my room and stick a gun in my face while you hauled her away like a wild animal."

"I apologize for my rudeness, but I've been with Nghia a long time and I know how best to handle her. This isn't the first time I've had to act firmly with her, nor, unfortunately, will it be the last. She calms down quickly, she's probably already back in normal, and will thank me for showing her the error of her ways and we will go on from there."

Kai continued talking but Vince wasn't listening any longer; he had heard all he needed to hear and his thoughts were now concentrated on more practical matters. It was clear that he must return to Da Nang right away and get back to the harness before thoughts of deserting recurred. If he hurried he could catch one of the morning hops flying out of Tan Son Nhut and be at the base in time to fly an afternoon ground-support mission.

Then there was the matter of the children.

"Listen, Kai," he said, interrupting the Viet's elucidation on the virtues of the Orient's system of concubinage, "I can't say it was a pleasure meeting you, but you have taken the scales from my eyes and I suppose I should thank you for that. I'm still undecided as to whether or not you and your tiger girls serve the good purpose you claim or if the whole operation is nothing more than a sleazy con game. My experience with it has been less than favorable and obviously I have a prejudiced viewpoint. Be that what it may, I must take care of personal matters before I return to the base, and I'm pushed for time. So if you will excuse me, I'll have to ask you to leave."

Without another word, Kai bowed slightly and backed out the door.

Vince gathered his clothes and toiletries together and stuffed everything into the seabag, taking a last look around at the hotel room that held the memories that he knew would haunt him as long as he lived. The picture of Ly-boy with his crutch and stump, and Autumn Dove with her camouflaged fatigue hat cocked on her funny little head, brought a heartrending sadness that gave him second thoughts about leaving. And Nghia's pouting lips and exquisite beauty that would knock the socks off any man, whether she was seen at Yankee Stadium, in a Paris salon, or eating a bow of noodles at the Khach-san Bong, promised to keep him awake nights for a long time to come.

The short letter he wrote to the kids, expressing his sadness in having to leave without saying good-bye or without explaining the real reasons for his hasty departure, was particularly painful and took several attempts before he was able to complete it. The envelope was sealed with the piasters inside and he slowly and carefully printed the names *Ly-boy and Autumn Dove* on the front and placed it on the table where they would be sure to see it. In the letter he instructed them to return to the Catholic orphanage and not to run away again. He would send money now and then, and write as often as he could. He had signed it, *Your always grateful friend, Vince.*

In the lobby the Viet Cong girl sat with the sophisticated-looking man wearing the mint-green tropical suit and watched Battaglia traverse the length of room without taking her eyes off him. When he reached the potted palms on each side of the doors she threw back her head and laughed loudly. A few of the other tiger girls joined in mocking him.

183

Passing through the moon gate he caught sight of a slender figure and trim legs bending over the fish pond. At first he thought it might be Nghia, but the girl turned and Chi's small seductive face smiled at him; and she nodded in a wise manner, slow and very Asian, blowing him a kiss and twirling a peony flower between her fingers.

Chapter 11

"He's back."

"Who's back?" Cleanhead leaned over the relief map and rubbed his egg dome.

"Battaglia," Blackjack said.

The colonel straightened and sucked in his paunch, a small embarrassment that was becoming noticeable since he'd stopped eating meals at the officer's mess and begun feeding on his hooch maid's sumptuous meals. "Well . . . I'll be an egg-sucking frog. Where is he?"

"Down at operations trying to get scheduled for a sortie this afternoon."

Dasher's grin was big and wide. "And I was worried that he might not come back. It's only been twenty-four hours and he's already got the bit in his teeth and straining to get the harness around his neck. Hot damn?" He pounded a meaty palm with the bunched fist. "That's my boy," he said, smiling and forgetting that Bamburger was standing across from him on the other side of the relief map.

Blackjack frowned and stuffed his hands in his pockets like a schoolboy who had just been rejected by his teacher for giving the wrong answer.

"If Headquarters Marine Corps would give me a squadron of men like Vince Battaglia I would break North Vietnam in a month." Cleanhead unwrapped a fresh cigar and lit up. The smoke shot out his two cavernous nostrils like escaping exhaust from the twin tailpipes of one of his F-4s.

By the time Dasher got to the flight line, Battaglia had drawn a mission and was up in the cockpit with his backseater, going through his checks. The big master sergeant, crew chief of his Phantom, was under the aircraft's belly, plugged in with earphones so he could talk with Vince as they went over the preflight together.

"Nothing else like it," Vince said to the radar intercept officer sitting behind him, tuning his equipment.

"Roger that, Lieutenant," the RIO said over the intercom. "My systems are all up."

The smell of JP4 jet fuel was sweet perfume to Vince. He lifted his nose to the fumes before slipping on the crash helmet and sun visor, and snapped the oxygen mask in place over his mouth and nose.

"All systems go, Lieutenant—you're up and ready to roll," the crew chief announced.

Battaglia signaled for the chocks to be pulled, and he taxied out of the revetment and wheeled the long-nosed jet onto the apron to the arming pad. Rolling past him, the second jet in his element hit a bump in the tarmac and the five-hundred-pound bombs slung under the wings rocked on their racks.

For a brief moment he thought of Nghia, the smoothness of her bronze skin, her honey legs, the picture of her standing at the bus stop when he'd first seen her—ebony hair, thick and lustrous, twisted over her shoulder, then shaken clear with a twist of her queenly head—flashed through his mind and he smiled down deep where the best of memories dwelled.

"Dancer One and Two ready to launch."

The voice of the element leader cut off his thoughts of Nghia and Cho-Chan. Vince wanted to talk to God and he thought that was the weirdest thing right at that time. He imagined his convoluted brain under his cranium and all the past stuff lodged in there, and he marveled at the strangeness of him being in Vietnam and losing Ruthie and finding Nghia; and he wanted to talk to God, but the tower was God right now and wouldn't let him talk except to the element leader, who was asking questions and getting launching instructions, and all the other last minute stuff that prohibited conversations with God.

"Dash Two up?"

"Roger—let's launch." Battaglia took a last minute suck of ice water from the tube leading to the thermos and snapped the oxygen mask back in place.

"Dancer up."

"Cleared for launch," came the tower's reply.

The plexiglass canopies dropped down over the pilots and backseaters and the Phantoms turned onto the runway.

"Saddle up at twenty thousand."

"Roger."

Vince watched Dash One go into his takeoff roll, the F-4's wings flapping with its heavy bomb load, birdlike, struggling to get in the air. The afterburners lit and Dash One launched into the afternoon sky.

"Dancer, this is Home Plate, turn right twenty and climb out to angels ten and hold. Flight of fox-fours approaching at two o'clock."

"Roger, Home Plate . . . I've got 'em."

Vince was right behind Dash One and off to the right, making the turn and climbing into position, afterburners cooking. "Nothing like it, huh, Davey?" he said to the RIO in the backseat, pressing the mike button.

"Yeh—nothing like it," came the bored reply.

The lines around Vince's eyes, above the mask, crinkled in smile. He was relieved to be back, still frightened, but relieved that he hadn't bolted for Thailand or stayed to hide in Cho-Chan. That kind of fear

187

was insidious. Up in the sky he could deal with the fear; down on the ground it gnawed at his innards like a ravenous dog where he couldn't get to it.

Nghia made sense—he liked the way she talked. They could have been good friends, maybe something more, and that was the pain of it; nothing sadder than a might-have-been.

What a set of legs that girl had, he dreamed.

"Fox-fours passing underneath."

"Roger, Dash One." He brought the nose up and gave some right rudder.

"You're drifting out, Dash Two. Get your mind on the job."

Vince wiped the sweat from his face and pulled the sun visor down over his eyes. *Got to forget her.*

By the time the two jets completed their turn and had climbed above the clouds, Battaglia was in position tucked up tight into Dash One's wing.

"Don't overdo it." The element leader looked across the short piece of sky and let his aircraft drift left a few feet.

"Dancer—I'm turning you over to Joy Ride. Plug in at Dong Hoi."

"Roger, Home Plate."

The clouds were building taller north of Quan-Chu and the two planes in their camouflaged battle colors of mottled brown and green climbed higher to stay above the worsening weather. Droplets of rain hit the windscreen and quickly vanished on impact; and high above, standing on the crests of the folded masses of nimbus cumulus, Zeus stood spread-legged, throwing lightning bolts down to earth. Nghia sat on one side of the magestic Zeus, her legs handing over the edge of her cloud throne, dressed in a white robe and wearing the crown of a queen.

The memory of Saigon and all that had happened to

him there seemed light-years away, as did the thought that he had seriously considered vanishing into the underworld of Cho-Chan or deserting to Thailand with Nghia and the children. As soon as he got back he should have stopped to talk to Dasher in order to clear the air about the MP report and the killings and other trouble, there hadn't been time. The only thing that had been on his mind when leaving the Khach-san Bong was to climb into the seat of an F-4 and get in the air. If he had hesitated for any length of time he might have changed his mind and wound up trekking through the jungles of Southeast Asia or operating a brothel in Cho-Chan.

Now that he was back at the business end of a control stick and the old fears were making the familiar noises in his head, he wondered if he had made the right choice; and when Joy Ride told them to abort the mission because the weather had socked in the target so badly that they couldn't find it, he felt a great relief and the stiffenss in his neck suddenly disappeared and the terrain looked lovely and the clouds that had been dark and threatening now became friendly and reassuring.

"Okay, Dash Two, let's go feet-wet and dump our load," the element leader said. "This mission cost the taxpayers a sweet tune, with nothing to show for it."

The two men turned east with their jets and streaked for the South China Sea, two fish in an ocean of air. They jettisoned their bombs into the ocean, each one hitting the water separately and sending up a plume of white against a glass surface of green jade. The splashes took Vince back to one day in the good old days, a hot summer afternoon in Kansas when he was ten years old and his world was filled with new things to learn every day, every minute from the time he woke to feed the chickens to bedding down his pony at night before going to bed, and everyone said the Pledge of Allegiance to the flag in school and no one heard of Vietnam.

189

Ruthie wanted to stop off at the secret hiding place on the way home from school, something he never did because the chores were always waiting for him and Mom never accepted any excuse if the animals weren't fed on time and the vegetable garden went unwatered and if he didn't practice his trumpet lesson. Ruthie called him chicken, and it was hot like only Kansas can get in June and it was the last week of school, so against his better judgment (he knew he'd get a whipping) he went with Ruthie to the secret hiding place for a swim.

Ruthie called him chicken again when he wouldn't skinny-dip, so he obliged her and they stood side by side on the ledge ten feet above the jade-green water and jumped into the cool spring-fed swimming hole and life was good for ten-year-olds on that hot summer afternoon in Kansas.

They jumped off the ledge many times and the green water splashed white from the impact of their growing healthy bodies and neither of them ever thought that there would be a place called Vietnam that would forever change their lives . . .

After Vince landed and taxied to his parking spot in the revetment, he shut down the engines, leaned back in the armored seat, and took a deep breath of relief. The canopy lifted on its actuators, breaking the seal on his microcosm, his special corner of the universe, and opened to the rush of intrusions common to the rest of the world.

"Chalk up another one, Davey. Ready for a cold beer?"

Davey in the backseat wasn't talking at the moment; he was too busy throwing up. His reaction hadn't been fast enough and about half the bellyful spewed over the gauges and switches and floorboard before he got himself hung over the canopy rail and emptied the rest on the crew chief standing on the tarmac below.

"Jeez," Battaglia said, looking back at the mess.

Davey's face was pale and bewildered. "Must have been something I ate."

The sergeant walked away cursing and holding his wet arms out from his body. A crewman climbed up to the cockpit and handed Davey some greasy wiping clothes and a pail of water, and descended again without saying a word.

At debriefing, Battaglia had just sat down at the table when Dasher's orderly spotted him. Vince saw him coming over.

"Do any good, Lieutenant?" the orderly said.

"Milk run."

"The colonel wants to see you on the double."

Battaglia looked across at the debriefing officer.

"I'll catch you after you finish talking with Dasher." the major turned to another pilot sitting down.

Every Marine has a crazy streak running through him, and Colonel Dasher was convinced after reading through the MP report from Saigon that Vince Battaglia was the consummate representative.

"You sent for me, sir?"

Cleanhead studied Vince who still wore his flight gear; a Mae West and survival vest were fitted loosely around his upper torso and his pressure suit was wringing wet with perspiration. It was the way he remembered his son. He drank from the coffee mug held tightly in his fist and sucked on a black cigar.

Vince sat down without being invited, a breach of military etiquette that he may have been aware of but chose to ignore, and which raised the hackles on the back of Cleanhead's neck, though he said nothing.

"Coffee?" Dasher poured a cup without waiting for a reply and handed it to Battaglia.

191

Stretching his legs, Vince glanced at the red-and-gold Marine Corps emblem on the heavy coffee mug and lifted it in toast: "Semper Fi."

Dasher frowned. "How did your sortie go?"

"Target wasn't visible—entire sector and everything north of Dong Hoi was socked in solid. We orbited the area looking for a break in the clouds until our fuel got low and then we dumped our load in the sea and came home. Davey vomited when we landed."

"Davey's been jittery lately," the colonel said. "Reports to sick bay too often—Doc says nothing wrong with him but nerves. My guess is that he's thinking ahead to Ban Dau."

Battaglia back stiffened at the mention of Ban Dau, and the back of his thighs began to tingle.

"I'm going to ground Davey—can't afford to have somebody mess up a mission because he's afraid. I'll have another RIO assigned to you."

Cleanhead watched Vince closely for his reaction, but Vince's expression was unchanged.

"Back from R and R early, aren't you?" He was reading the telexed MP report.

"Uh-huh," he simply said, noncommittal.

"You packed in a lot of action in the twenty-four hours you were there." He waved the three-page telex at Vince.

Battaglia drew in his breath. "I didn't go looking for trouble—it came looking for me. I got some answers to important questions."

"And I suppose there are things that happened to you that aren't mentioned in this report and that are significant by their omission," he said with the perception he was famous for. Dasher drank from the mug and chewed his cigar.

That statement made Vince uneasy, causing a muscle in his jaw to twitch slightly just under the skin, noticeable to someone who might be looking for it as the

192

colonel was.

"It's what's left out of a report like this that interests me most—the details and interconnecting circumstances and particularly the people involved. The reports seldom mention the people—I mean the ones that count—the motivating force behind the incident. They're usually women." He eyed Battaglia at an angle, his look long and penetrating.

"There's nothing more to tell, sir. The MP sergeant seemed like a thoroughgoing chap and I'm sure he covered all the facts in the case. Like I said, I never went looking for trouble, it came looking for me."

Cleanhead's grin was intimidating. "Let's not kid around, Lieutenant . . . there's more here than what's on paper. As far as Saigon and the military is concerned the case is closed, but I don't think we've heard the last of this."

"What makes you say that, sir?"

"Let's just say that over the years of commanding Marines I've become a suspicious old goat that has a well-honed sense of intuition. The murder charges against you were mysteriously dropped and you used only one day of your ten days of R and R. That to me adds up to being peculiar. But I didn't bring you here to chew you out. As far as I'm concerned the matter is over with and you're back at work. More coffee?"

Vince drank the last from his cup and placed it on the table beside him. "No thank you, sir—one cup is fine for me." He waited for Cleanhead to get to the point, anxious to get on with what was coming.

"I told Bamburger that I want you to take a section of F-4s up north for a photo recon."

"Ban Dau?" The words almost didn't get out of his mouth.

Cleanhead nodded. "The only pictures we have of the area are poor and tell us nothing. I don't need to tell you how important it is to the success of the strike that we get clear, identifiable targets."

"The NVA defenses are concealed in the ridges and a pilot is going to have to be close enough to kiss the gunners before any worthwhile photos can be taken."

"Precisely." Colonel Dasher watched closely for any nervousness in Battaglia.

"That means surprise—complete surprise."

"Impossible," Dasher said.

Vince leaned forward, his bulky flight gear hindering his movements. "Colonel, there's only one way to get the pictures you want."

"I'm listening." Dasher smiled, anticipating Battaglia.

"A flight or more of aircraft will telegraph our intention; we'll be picked up miles out and they'll be prepared for us."

"Major Bamburger recommends two sections for maximum coverage and efficiency."

"Major Bamburger is an ass."

Cleanhead raised his rock jaw, irritated at Vince's disrespect. "What do you suggest?"

"One aircraft—one pass—on the deck at Mach one."

Dasher was sitting forward, elbows on the desk, chewing his cigar rapidly. "Go on."

"The pilot should come in high, above thirty thousand, as far as Mua Xuan, then dive to the deck and fly treetops to Song Danh. At Song Danh he should change directions and head into Laos, come back over the border at Bep Chanh, make a final course correction and dash for Ban Dau, coming in under the commie radar."

The colonel leaned back off his elbows and settled in the chair that creaked on its rusty swivel. He looked around his quonset-hut office, taking his time, his gaze settling first on the corregated steel roof that curved down into a half-moon shape to form the walls that met the wooden floor constructed out of one-by-six planks.

The office was spartan and consisted of a few uncomfortable wooden chairs, a table, the colonel's metal desk and filing cabinet, and a bookcase filled with technical manuals and operations manuals. A large map of Vietnam was secured to the wall behind the desk. Close to the wall was a water cooler, as was the table upon which were a hot plate and coffeepot, scattered papers, and stacks of unfiled reports that remained to be read. On the desk a model of an F-4 Phantom in full battle colors and markings stood atop a pedestal, ready to fly, and a box of black Malaysian cigars lay open for quick access.

"I like it—I think you plan has a lot of merit." He drew on the cigar, blew the smoke at the ceiling, and without looking at Vince, and appearing casually unconcerned, he said: "Any ideas about who the pilot should be?"

"Me."

Both men looked at each other for a few seconds, silence between them. Overhead a jet roared into the landing pattern, causing the metal in the quonset hut to vibrate.

Cleanhead reached into the lower desk drawer and set two shot glasses next to the cigar box. From the bottom file cabinet drawer he removed an unopened bottle of amaretto. "This calls for a drink." He ceremoniously opened the bottle and poured the golden liqueur into the glasses.

The answer had come without Vince thinking. Before he knew he had said it, he had committed himself to fulfilling the plan he had concocted and Cleanhead had bought it. He drank the amaretto without tasting it and the colonel's congratulations were lost in the buzzing that filled his head. It was insane. He would have to fly twice into Ban Dau, not just once; he had to be mad.

That night Vince lay awake in his bunk, thinking of

ways he could get out of flying the photo reconnaissance mission; droplets of sweat trickled across his forehead and soaked into the pillowcase. Feeling the perspiration curling down his face, he recalled the seventh chapter of John and how Jesus sweated drops of blood before going to the cross.

Bamburger's eyes had looked like they would fall out of his head when Dasher called him into the quonset hut and told him that Vince was flying the mission solo. His anger was not only due to being passed over in favor of his wingman and a less experienced pilot, but more particularly because his plan had been ignored and he hadn't been consulted with regard to the new plan. The colonel hadn't batted an eye when Blackjack stormed out of the office, looking pale and shaken. He had decided after the discussion a few days previous that the major was expendable.

When the Viet hooch boy came to wake Battaglia, the base was dark and he had slept only in snatches. The strange quiet blanketing the runways gave the morning an introspective quality, something that poets used to create their best works, or composers felt before beginning a magnum opus.

For Vince the silence was more tangible. It meant that the morning flights were not taking off, and the reason could only be that the weather was so bad in the north that all strikes had been cancelled.

He hurried to operations. In the planning room, Cleanhead was bending over the topo map with Bamburger and the planning officer. They looked up when he walked in and their faces told him that he had his reprieve.

"Target's socked in . . . zero-zero," Dasher said.

"Better stand by—could clear later today," the planning officer said to Vince.

"No," Dasher interrupted, "we'll wait twenty-four

196

hours—have to, we're committed to a morning recce; best possible conditions for success exist at that time. Sorry, Battaglia."

Vince tried to look disappointed, but his expression didn't come off right and Blackjack caught it right away. From the living room in Wichita he heard Fats Domino singing "Blueberry Hill" on the hi-fi (or did they have stereo by then?). *I tried to lie about taking Dad's shotgun, but he could tell something was wrong by the way the skin on my face tightened and how I glanced at the record player too often as if Fats was wedged in the cabinet with a microphone. Children don't know how to lie.*

"There are going to have to be some trade-offs," the planning officer said.

"What trade-offs?" Cleanhead growled.

"Depends on how much you want those photos."

"They're indispensable—the entire success of the mission depends on them." Bamburger looked over at Vince and made no effort to hide the fact that he knew Battaglia didn't want to fly the mission.

"Then you're going to have to be more flexible on your time requirement, because this weather may last longer than expected, and you'll have to take advantage of any break in it, regardless of the time of day, or go without the photos."

Colonel Dasher massaged the shiny surface of his head and turned to Vince. "I suppose he's right; we can't put off the raid indefinitely, so you had better go on ready alert at the hot-pad trailer."

Bamburger looked evenly at Vince and the hate between them smoldered; only Dasher's presence prevented it from erupting into a conflagration.

"Yes, sir," Battaglia said to the colonel, feeling an emptiness inside him that he knew would not leave. He walked out into the dawn.

A group of pilots strolled by outside the operations

building. Davey glanced his way, but said nothing, continuing on his walk to the officers' mess for an early breakfast.

"Davey," Vince called.

The man hesitated, walking slower and allowing the others to outdistance him. He finally stopped. "Yeh— what is it, Vince?"

"What are you doing up so early?—all missions have been scrubbed." He noticed that Davey was smiling and he was wearing his class A uniform.

"I'm leaving the 'Nam—going home."

"What?"

"Don't look surprised—it was you that got me grounded."

"Hey, man . . ."

"Don't worry about it . . . you did me a big favor. While I'm in El Toro and surfing at Laguna Beach during my off-duty hours I'll think of you occasionally in between girlies and my trips to TJ." He knocked the ashes off his cigarette and rocked on his heels, obviously pleased with himself. "Thought you were in Saigon on R and R."

"I went there looking for answers, and all I got were more questions."

Davey was looking at the ground under his feet. He looked up abruptly. "There are no answers to this mess over here." He looked back at the ground. "Why don't you turn in your wings, Vince? You don't want to be here. Get reassigned."

"No one wants to be here."

"Dasher does."

"He's different."

"There are others like him—lots. Let them have their war; all it does for me is make me throw up."

"I've noticed."

"It got me what I wanted," Davey said.

198

"Maybe."

"Do you know what you want, Vince?" He turned and walked away without looking back, hurrying to catch up with his buddies.

Vince watched Davey disappear down the gravel walk. At that moment he would have given a lot to change places with Davey.

It rained all day and there was no break in the weather. Vince spent his time playing acey-deucy and twenty-one with the other pilots on alert, and he got so bored that he thought of hopping a ride in a Huey chopper going out in the bush for a combat assault. He liked the look he imagined on Cleanhead's face as he got the news.

Parked outside the door of the hot-pad trailer, his RF-4 equipped with special photo reconnaissance gear looked vulnerable without armament. Battaglia figured that he had made the second biggest blunder of his life talking the colonel into sending only one aircraft (unescorted) with himself in it to photograph the target area. The first biggest blunder of his life had been joining the Marine Corps.

Only a few hours of light remained and it looked like Ban Dau would have to wait at least one more day. A C-130 transport landed and rolled down the runway. Battaglia stood in the door opening, folded a stick of gum into his mouth, and watched the last Air Vietnam flight from Saigon turn into final approach. He looked at his watch. Another hour and he would be at the O-club for a cold one, dinner, and back to his quarters to write a letter to Ruthie (she never wrote), and then lights-out to wait it out all over again in the morning.

The Air Vietnam passenger jet hit the tarmac with a screech of rubber, and a puff of white smoke blossomed from each tire. He watched it slow at the end of the runway and turn for the terminal. The rain had stopped.

Card games never appealed to Vince, but he sat down

at the table to play another hand of acey-deucy to stay occupied and to keep his mind off the dangers that were crowding in on him. The Air Vietnam jet from Saigon throttled up on the taxiway and rolled onto the apron. The engines returned to idle and the plane parked at the base terminal.

The games, like the faces at the table, were all one big blur to Vince. It was his deal and the cards shuffled automatically between his nimble fingers as he took his time, in no hurry to play, anything to delay tomorrow from coming.

"Hurry up, Battaglia—we haven't got all day."

"I have."

"What are you talking about?"

"Forget it." The cards flew from his fingers in practiced and flawless motion.

The little cuckoo clock that Nhan had given him for his fiftieth birthday announced 2400 hours. He thought of how much he hated that clock; Dasher hated everything when he was wakened out of a sound sleep at midnight. He hadn't been able to figure a way to get rid of the clock without hurting Nhan's feelings so he toned down the cuckooing as best he could by covering the sound mechanism with insulating material. The infernal wooden bird irritated him no end.

"Where did you get the cuckoo, Colonel?"

"Came straight from the pit of hell," Dasher said. "What do you want at this hour?"

The master sergeant handed the message to Cleanhead. "From General Waring, sir. Major Bamburger said you would want to see it right away."

"Bamburger, huh?"

Dasher read the message quickly and stared at the clock on the wall as if he was waiting for the cuckoo bird to spring out of its little door and taunt him.

"Is there any return message, sir?"

"Just acknowledge that I have received the order and that it will immediately be put into effect."

The sergeant left and Dasher stood in the doorway looking out over the runways into the night, thinking about the many stupid decisions made in this war and how many more were going to be made. He stood there for a long time tightening and untightening his fist around the message stuffed in the pocket of his robe. *The chuff-chuff-chuff* of a Huey broke the silence and he closed the door.

Nhan's body didn't have a bit of fat anywhere, and when he lay beside her he could feel her heat and nervous energy pass unobstructed into him. She was wide awake and waiting for him to say something. The longer he remained quiet, the greater became the vibration and heat build-up from her body. Cleanhead smiled, knowing how sexually excited she became when in this state. He would get no sleep for the remainder of the night.

"Who that man?"

"My sergeant."

"What he want?"

"He brought me a message."

"What message say?"

"Can't tell you . . . it's classified."

She sat up quickly and the colonel could see her small breasts outlined in the darkness of the room, the small flat nose and dark slashes for eyes facing him, framed in a deeper blackness that was her hair.

"Why you no tell me? I no Viet Cong."

"Maybe . . . maybe not."

That always got her going. Her legs, lying nimbly over his, tensed, and he knew she was going to be exceptional when he took her. He grew enormous under the sheet.

"You think I VC?"

"Like I said, I don't know. It doesn't matter one way or the other . . . I couldn't tell you anyway what was in that message. Marine regulations are quite clear when it comes to classified information. You don't have clearance and you don't have a need to know and you're not a U.S. citizen."

"Why you no trust me?"

"It's not a matter of trust—it's against regulations."

"That for regulations." She made a filthy Western sign.

Dasher knew that no amount of logic would budge Nhan's emotions, though she expected an understanding reaction on his part to her flare-ups. He had learned from past exercises with her that keeping silent was the worst response he could make, and if he kept talking he would eventually drain off her anger, leaving behind the sweet residue of wild passion.

"You no love me." She leaped on top of him, pulling his hair and scratching his chest and shoulders like a frightened panther.

"Damn you, Nhan . . . if you don't calm down I'm going to send you back to Chu Lai and the rice paddies where I found you, and there you'll rot without even your ancestors to take pity on you."

Insensed by his taunts and unable to get at him because he held her arms tightly behind her back while she sat on his stomach, she became wild with frustration and anger, and her body went into spasms and she threw back her head and an animal howl the likes that he had never heard crawled from her bowels and froze the night.

"Shut up, you crazy girl—you'll bring the sentries with all that racket and they'll take you away for good."

She was crying now, her tears wetting his chest and mixing with the blood from the scratches. "You no love me."

The howls turned to low moans of pain and suffering

202

and desire. The rigidness went out of her body and she became limp and collapsed on his chest, whimpering like a child.

"You love me?"

"You poor kid—you're so insecure. Of course I love you."

He could feel her heart bouncing against his, and in the dark the slits for her eyes had widened into a sparkling wetness. She lifted her head from his chest, lips parted, breathing heavily, hair falling forward into his face. The room was thick with her primitive, musk smell.

She fell on his neck and bit him, drawing blood. "Hold my feet and make love to me," she whispered in his ear.

He took her crudely and without sophistication, the way she liked it. Raw.

Later she slept and Dasher sat in his favorite chair, smoking one of his Malayian cigars, legs crossed and wearing nothing. *If Ban Dau is clear this morning I'll send Battaglia.* His fist tightened around General Waring's order. *I won't tell him that President Johnson has called a bombing halt. What a way to run a war.* He bit savagely into the cigar and spit half of it on the floor. *I need those photos.*

Chapter 12

Technically, Battaglia was flying a photo reconnaissance mission and not a strike and, therefore, was not directly in violation of General Waring's orders that all bombing of North Vietnam cease immediately. In sending Vince on the recce, Colonel Dasher was making a judgment call and riding the fine line between what was actually written in the order and what was implied by Waring and President Johnson.

"We need those pictures," Cleanhead said to Bamburger. "The gooners are going to use this friggin' bombing halt to rebuild their defenses and rush supplies south for their big push on the northern highlands. When that dummy in the White House finally figures out that Ho Chi Minh isn't coming to the peace table just because we stopped dumping on him, the suspension will be lifted and we'll be right back where we were—facing Ban Dau, a Ban Dau that will be more formidable than before the bombing halt. I want to be able to hit the gooners within minutes of when we get the green light again, bust them with our best left hook at the opening bell so they're on the ropes for the rest of the fight; and I'm betting that the fight will only go a few more rounds after we mash them at Ban Dau. That's why I need Battaglia's photos."

"You did the right thing in sending him, sir," Blackjack said.

Dasher was sure that Bamburger always sat in the front row at school, where the teacher would notice him, and made statements that were trite and noncontroversial.

"Yes . . . you did the right thing, sir."

From his position hunched over the relief map of North Vietnam, Dasher turned a tired eye to Blackjack and said, "Why, Major, do you think I did the right thing?"

"Well, it seems to me . . . that . . . well . . ." He stumbled, fishing for an impressive answer.

"Did it occur to you that I could get my ass nailed to the wall for what I've done? A photo reconnaissance flight into North Vietnam could easily be interpreted as a violation of orders, particularly when it's in direct support of a bombing mission."

"Yes, I see, sir . . . I see what you're getting at."

"Not only that, I failed to tell Battaglia that the President had ordered a bombing halt, just a minor oversight that I'm sure the general will ignore—right, Major?"

"I hadn't thought of it that way, Colonel."

"You know what your trouble is, Bamburger? You haven't got any imagination. Wars are lost by going strictly by the book. The Japanese in World War Two proved that. The Japanese soldier was the most obedient and most unimaginative foe we had ever met. He never deviated from the book, never changed signals; and when we found out what was in his book, we cleaned his ass. Didn't matter how courageous he was."

"There are a great number of similiarities between the Viet Cong and Japanese soldier," Bamburger said in his inept style.

Cleanhead gave him a pained look that didn't affect Blackjack one way or the other, and said, "The VC is an excellent field quarterback." He left it at that.

205

The first sunrays sprayed across the flooded rice paddies in a broad pattern that transformed the fields into large mirrors that reflected a beautiful collage of shadowed earth tones and light.

Dasher looked at his watch. "Battaglia will be over Vuon Di."

From twenty-nine thousand feet, Vietnam was a carpet of green and brown checkerboards. Off the left wing of Vince's Phantom, the Plain of Jars in Laos, which would become the battleground of one of the most bitter fights of the war, spread its ancient fingers and palm eastward into the interior of still unmapped jungle.

The F-4, light and fast without weapons and external fuel tanks, was responsive to the slightest touch and handled like an unbridled colt. Knifing through the sea of air, the wingtips vaporized the thick, wet air into long whispy trails that clung like ribbons tied to the rivets.

The long nose of the RF-4, with its black radome and painted shark's teeth, sat far ahead of the wings and was pointed a few degrees upward in a shallow climb. On top of the forward fuselage, just behind the radome and slightly ahead of the engine intakes on either side, was the plexiglass-covered cockpit, Battaglia in the front seat, looking out over the nose, and behind him in the backseat sat his new radar intercept officer, a stolid second lieutenant of German extraction by the name of Kruger. Vince's call sign was Dogbone; Kruger's was Kraut. They were flying in Victor-Whisky-Ten.

"Hope the planning people got this fuel figured right, Dogbone; I'm not used to flying without external tanks."

"No sweat, Kraut; with the full bag we picked up from the tanker back at Vuon Di we'll be cool all the way to Ban Dau."

"I'm not sweating the ingress. What bothers me is

getting out."

"If the tanker is where we left it, we'll fly the egress with a thousand pounds to spare."

"That's cutting it might close, Dogbone."

"It's the best I can do. See your local Civil Liberties representative if you have any complaints." He laughed.

The break in the weather that the planning officer promised over the target was not materializing, and heavy clouds were everywhere in front of Vince; they looked ominous. The RF-4, bouncing and shaking in the dense air, required frequent course corrections and Vince was, on one hand, hoping that the planners would be wrong and he would have to abort the mission and, on the other, wishing that he could get it over with and not have to return for the photos another day.

"My radar shows worsening weather ahead," Kruger said. "I don't think we're going to get in."

"We'll have to ride her all the way to the end of the line to find out. There might be a hole we can get through."

The Phantom suddenly dropped a hundred feet, putting Vince and Kruger into a brief negative-g condition, and for a few seconds the aircraft was unresponsive to the controls.

"Lose your stomach, Kraut?"

"I'm cool Dogbone—how's the bird taking this bashing?"

They both scanned their gauges.

Into Laos they flew, taking a left turn at the border and still climbing in search of the top of the storm. The rocking and rolling persisted without any let-up and Vince continued checking the navigation equipment to keep the Phantom on course.

Now and then the cloud cover would break and he could see the familiar checkerboard pattern of rice paddies far below; sometimes the paddies were transected by rivers and fringed by deep blue mountains whose tops rose until cut off by thick gray clouds. The clouds climbed beyond the altitude of the RF-4 and continued growing to merge with the black mass that hung over all of Southeast Asia.

Enclosed in his airtight, self-contained environment, snugly encapsulated by the plexiglass canopy, Vince plotted his course and fed new data into the navigation gear while the Phantom held together and flew with precision through the hostile sky, keeping him and Kruger dry and comfortable and safe. Vince couldn't appreciate this marvel of science, for he had become so jaded by advanced technology that he viewed everything in the military as being commonplace and boring. Only one thought could ignite his enthusiasm: going back home to the real world.

"Coming around to three-five-zero. Give me a time check, Kraut." He had turned north and would fly this leg for a few minutes before turning east again, hoping to confuse communist radar operators who might be tracking him. "Stay alert, Kraut—we're coming into SAM country."

"Roger, Dogbone—the ECM has been strangely quiet."

"Let's hope that our penetration tactics work and it stays strangely quiet all the way in . . . and out."

Victor-Whisky-Ten bumped and shaked through the storm with Vince frequently changing altitude to find a smoother ride through the weather. The gauges and consoles rattled in the rough ride, and the two men were jostled around with the rolling and pitching jet.

"Dogbone, turn to zero-nine-zero."

They were now on a reciprocal heading and would soon cross the border into North Vietnam. It was time to begin the final checks and start the descent for the dash into Ban Dau.

Almost too calmly, Kruger said, "Bogie contact . . . picked them up as we made the turn."

"How many?"

"Two of them, flying a little low at eleven o'clock, range ten miles."

"Thuds from Korat, maybe," Vince said.

"Or Migs."

"What's their course?"

"Bearing zero-five-five."

With a sudden rush, Victor-Whisky-Ten broke into clear blue sky, giant cumulus columns billowing high in the distance. Ahead of the Marines, two shiny silver Mig-21s were in a shallow climbing turn. Surprised by their sudden appearance and held fast by their beauty, Battaglia made no move to avoid the enemy fighters.

"Remember, Dogbone, we're not armed. Let's get out of here."

Entranced by the majesty of the scene and not wanting to take his eyes off the two beautiful fish swimming in the sea of air, Vince changed course to fly the same heading as the North Vietnamese.

"Come on, Dogbone—it's time to make ourselves scarce."

The Migs, flying ahead and below the Phantoms, altered course a few degrees and began to turn into the Marines.

"We're going to get flamed—let's go."

"They don't see us," Vince said.

"They will—let's cool it."

"Ever see anything so graceful and hypnotic?" Vince said. "I'm going to follow them."

"I don't believe we're doing this."

"We can always duck into the clouds."

The Migs were cutting in front of the RF-4, climbing, and Vince had to roll starboard to keep them in view. The two Mig pilots wearing black helmets and goggles were clearly visible. The lead pilot wore a white scarf, like some fighter pilots in WW II had worn, and Battaglia wondered if he had gotten the idea from an old war movie he had seen. Vince reversed his roll and turned in behind the Migs.

"This can't be happening . . ." Kruger said.

"Hang tough, Kraut—we can outrun these guys."

"The mission, Dogbone—remember the mission. We came to get photos, not play hide-and-seek with Migs. It's time to get on with the mission; let the Migs go."

"In a minute—we're on course, and as long as they're going to in the right direction we might as well have some fun. Dumb riceballs . . . I want to see how long it takes for them to spot us. I bet they crap their pants when—"

The lead Mig did a neat wing-over and split-S, breaking away, and his wingman popped the dive brakes and flaps, throttled back, and pulled his nose up, bleeding off energy. Battaglia, caught with his pants down, was unable to compensate and flashed underneath the second Mig.

"What were you saying, Dogbone?"

"Damn!"

Kruger was twisted around, desperately trying to keep the Mig in view.

"What's he doing?" Vince said. He could feel panic setting in and he fought to gain control.

"Just what the book says—gaining energy, nose low and dropping into our six-o'clock."

"There's number one . . . at three o'clock. How did he get there?" Vince said.

"These guys know how to fight, Dogbone. They were wise to us all the time—suckered us in. They've got us right where they wanted us; still think you can outguess a

Mig driver?" Kruger threw his weight to the right side as Vince broke hard left, watching the Mig turn inside of the RF-4. "Don't try to dogfight these guys, Dogbone . . . just get out of here."

"What do you think I'm trying to do?" He reversed the break, coming around hard right.

Battaglia was sweating hard and he sucked large breaths from the oxygen mask. *Got to stay under control—concentrate.* "Where is he?"

"Right on your ass—where do you think?"

"They want us bad, Kraut."

"How can you tell?—*break left!*"

Battaglia reefed the Phantom over and the g-suit tightened hard on his gut and upper legs. An ATOL, rooster-tailing behind him in the turn, bent hard to stay with the U.S. jet, its plume of white smoke from the rocket engine arched high. Vince pulled harder and the cockpit went gray and he felt the g-suit strangling his tissues, preventing the blood from rushing into the extremities. He struggled against the blackout, concentrating on the image of Ly-boy and Autumn Dove dressed in their new clothes while they slapped Mah-Jongg tiles on the hotel room floor. Outside on the balcony the wind chimes played a tune.

"That's good flying, Dogbone," Kruger said as Victor-Whisky-Ten rolled level and the missile went ballistic in a series of wild gyrations, its metal brain confused by the wrong signals.

The chase had taken them down to ten thousand feet and the checkerboard squares filled the windscreen with subtle hues of green. Battaglia unsnapped the oxygen mask and leaned his head back on the headrest, breathing with difficulty. His face was covered with heavy perspiration that rolled from his face in large drops and fell onto his survival vest.

"How you doing, Dogbone?"

211

Vince didn't answer.

"Dogbone—are you all right?"

He drew the palm of his hand across his face and wiped the sweat on the g-suit. "Do you still have the Migs, Kraut?" His voice sounded like a stranger's to him.

"Roger—four o'clock and high."

The two 21s had formed up and floated high up in the clear air like two ocean denizens tracking prey, hungry and waiting above the Americans, confident that if they were patient they would outlast their quarry who would eventually make the wrong move.

"Listen, Kraut, we've got few options. The Migs look like they're willing to wait us out, and that means they have full bags of gas and know that we're getting low on ours and will have to turn for home soon, at which time they'll jump us."

"We can outrun them—we've got more soup in a flat-out race."

"Probably, but they're between us and home and we'd lose a lot of fuel maneuvering . . . like we did a few minutes ago. And we've got Ban Dau in front of us. Any way you cut it we're in a sticky spot."

"You're the boss, Dogbone; that's what you get paid for."

"I'm going into Ban Dau and get the pictures."

"The Migs will be waiting for us when we come out."

"One thing at a time—first we get the photos, then we deal with the Migs. Next time I come back I don't want to be carrying cameras again; I want to be loaded with bombs and rockets."

"That's if we survive today."

"You're a joy to have along, Kraut."

The fear of Ban Dau was still in his belly and it was a greater fear than that of the Migs; the Migs he could see and maneuver against, and his radar would tell him where they were when he couldn't see them hiding in the clouds or coming after him miles away. The guns were sinister and evil and spit invisible stuff at him and they hid in camouflaged holes.

The olive-drab paint was worn clean at the top of the control stick just below the hard plastic grip where his hand fitted, showing gray primer and metal underneath. His grip was firm as he pushed the aircraft over and gained energy for the run into Ban Dau, and in less than a minute Victor-Whisky-Ten was just off the ground, flying the treetops and rice paddies.

Browns and greens that blended together in watercolor smears flashed by both sides of the canopy and defied him to take his concentration off the flight path coming at him through the windscreen. So critical was the need for his full attention to the ground ahead that he couldn't look at the instruments. "What's our speed, Kraut?"

"Coming up on Mach One."

Victor-Whisky-Ten boomed through the valleys and over the rice paddies, cutting across rivers and canals, the force of the exhaust from the twin tailpipes blasting water into the air.

"You get any lower, Dogbone, and we'll be harvesting rice. We're down to fifty feet."

Battaglia's hold on the stick was firm but not tight, computer-sensitive to the RF-4's subtle movements. He snatched a quick look at the airspeed indicator which was only a round blur in the center of green chipped paint.

"What's our airspeed now, Kraut?"

"Mach one point five," came the impassive reply.

The broad valley made a sweeping turn and Battaglia brought Victor-Whisky-Ten around to follow the river that flowed through the center of the lowland between the range of heavily treed hills. The sonic boom following the jet turned the heads of peasants plowing the paddies behind water buffalos and who walked the dikes and roads with mattocks resting on their shoulders. The river

213

spray flew high behind the RF-4, leaving a long trail of troubled water to splash against the banks.

"Where are the Migs?" Vince said.

The sky, filled with stuffed white pillows, revealed no Migs. Kruger continued to twist and turn in the backseat, ready to report the first appearance of the enemy jets that he was certain lurked behind the clouds, waiting their opportunity.

Meanwhile, Vince thundered down the valley, low and under the communist radar, flying the bends in the river and porpoising over the hills, the shout of the Phantom's engines heralding the approach of an iron eagle and the rice stalks bowing to the ground in the hot breath of its passage.

"Mach one point six." Kruger was bent forward into his screen and indicators. "Come around five degrees— four minutes to target. Begin pull-up."

Tension was high in the cockpit.

"Roger, Kraut . . . I have ridges in sight."

Ingressing at a thousand miles per hour, Victor-Whisky-Ten would cover the sixty-two-mile corridor to Ban Dau in four minutes, a short four minutes but time enough to go through the final setup and checks.

The approach into the target was tricky, requiring the pull-up from the deck to clear the mountains that grew abruptly out of the plain, then a rolling right turn that would put Battaglia and Kruger along the high ridges that led to the rocky fortress that was Ban Dau. The last leg was a near-ninety-degree turn into the canyon that Vince would have to twist down to reach the redoubt.

In his mind, he had rehearsed the approach dozens of times. Now that he was minutes away from the real thing, his mouth went dry and the fear in his belly climbed to the back of his tongue, and he wanted to heel the aircraft over, go back to Da Nang, make any excuse to Dasher that he couldn't go in.

214

The sweat trickled down his legs and he felt the urge to urinate.

"Start pull-up . . . now," Kruger said.

The hot pee filled Vince's pants.

"Dogbone, are you okay? Start pull-up or we are going to be part of the North Vietnamese landscape in less than a minute." Kruger's eyes were fixed on the radar screen.

Battaglia heard wind chimes and smelled jasmine flowers. *Other men like me—they think I number-one ginger cookie.*

"Come on, Dogbone . . . the mountains . . . time to wake up."

You haven't given me much reason to like you. The jasmine was delectable and the wind chimes on the balcony tinkled their night music.

The hard plastic grip was real in his hand and he moved it into his belly, the big Phantom's nose coming up with it. "Kraut, what's our heading?"

"Stay right where you are . . . three-four-nine."

"Roger." He looked down at the fuel gauge "We ate boo-coo fuel in the fight with the Mig."

"Fly this heading for one minute and turn right when you come to the ridges. Looks like the weather's holding. I can't believe we're not taking fire—the ECM is quiet."

"We're coming in too low and hot for the gooners—the plan's working."

The Phantom felt good under him and he rode her like a gentle filly, giving her the reins and touching her in the flanks with his spurs when he felt her hesitate.

His fear was still there, but it had crawled down into his belly again and he knew he had caught the NVA asleep at the guns. It would be a good mission and Cleanhead would have his photos.

The high ridge that he was looking for rose over the nose. "Making the turn now, Kraut."

"You're riding the beam, Dogbone . . . won't be long

now . . . look for the entrance on your left. You're on visual from here on in to the target."

"It feels good, Kraut—all systems up and working."

Seconds passed and miles of craggy ridge ripped by.

"There's the canyon! Cameras on . . . film running."

He turned the Phantom into the open maw of Ban Dau and gave Victor-Whisky-Ten full throttle. Lord—how they were thundering. They were here! Down the chute they screamed, cameras rolling, tailfin flicking like a mako shark gaining speed to make its kill.

He saw them and the cameras recorded them—75s, 100s, all the guns hidden down deep in the rocks, their long noses sticking out of lairs invisible to anything looking down from above, concentrated at three sites and looking arrogant and indestructable.

And the SAM ring, located below the guns and in the open, protected by high walls of sandbags and covered with camouflaged netting, stood guard before the entrance to caves and rooms of underground storage that held equipment and supplies being readied for the trip down to the Ho Chi Minh Trail.

A few guns were firing, the bursting shells too high and too far behind to be effective. NVA soldiers were running everywhere.

It only took a few seconds and they were out of the target area, the flak flowers chasing them, the walls of the mountains opening up to blue sky and white clouds.

Neither man spoke for a while, only the dull throb of the engines and the pneumatic sounds of the oxygen regulators breaking the silence.

"We did it, Kraut—Dasher has his pictures."

"Roger, Dogbone—you know the way home, I'm taking a nap."

Battaglia laughed and looked at his fuel. He stopped laughing.

Putting the nose of the Phantom high, he banked up

and away from Ban Dau, climbing into the upper regions where fuel consumption was more efficient. He would rather have stayed close to the ground, hugging the terrain as he had on the ingress, but that was impossible now that fuel was critical.

At thirty thousand feet he leveled out the jet and throttled back to nurse the fuel into the engines. This was SAM country, high and vulnerable where the clouds wouldn't help you, because the SAM could see you through the clouds but you couldn't see the SAM.

The wetness in his pants was an embarrassment and angered him. Losing control at a critical point in a mission was for the new guy on his first hot run—not for someone with nearly a hundred strikes logged in.

"I can feel the tanks sucking dry, Dogbone. We're not going to have enough fuel to make it back."

"Call up Zulu, Kraut, and tell him to be in orbit—we don't have any reserves and will have to come straight into the probe on the first try. Go to button red."

Kruger spoke clearly and slowly to the tanker pilot, wanting him to get the full impact of their critical condition: "Zulu One, Zulu One—Victor-Whisky-Ten."

"Roger, Victor-Whisky-Ten . . . this is great mother cow in the sky . . . go."

"Little calf needs a drink, big mother. We're ten miles south of bull's-eye and flying on fumes. Situation critical."

"Roger, little calf. Tit will be hanging out and waiting. Rendezvous angels fifteen over Vuon Di."

There was a pause.

"Want me to alert RESCAP?"

"Negative, Zulu—we'll keep you posted on our condition."

"Good luck, Victor-Whisky-Ten."

A half minute after the tanker got off the radio and the two Marines were resuming the SAM watch, the Migs

217

showed up again.

"I've got radar contact, Dogbone. Two bogies in front of us, range five miles on a reciprocal heading and high. Looks like our gooner friends."

Less than a minute later the two Mig-21s broke out of the clouds a thousand feet above the RF-4 and began their turn down together to get into a six-o'clock firing position.

"We don't have the fuel to maneuver with the Migs, Kraut . . . I'm going to try to outrun them. They must be getting low on gas too, hanging around up there waiting for us."

As soon as Vince went to afterburner and the airspeed indicator climbed to Mach one, the fuel-quantity gauge began to fall rapidly, draining from the tanks what little fuel was left.

"The gooners are going to lose a lot of energy in their turn and will have to play catch-up," Vince said. "They're not going to be able to close with us, but they may launch a missile on the outside chance it will overtake us, so keep an eye on our tail."

After a couple of minutes, the Migs saw that they had no chance of closing within the effective ATOL range and broke off the attack. The last view Battaglia had of them was a long vapor trail swinging east behind the two silver fish before they disappeared into a towering mass of cumulus.

Vince quickly throttled back and looked at the fuel gauge. "We're on empty, Kraut. Call Zulu and let him know that we're coming in on the glide and he'll have to refuel us using dead-engine procedures."

Approaching Vuon Di, both engines quit within seconds of each other and the heavy Phantom began its descent.

"Zulu One, Victor-Whisky-Ten. I'm over Vuon Di at angels twenty and looking for your gas station."

218

"Victor-Whisky-Ten, Zulu is two miles south of village at angels sixteen."

"There he is," Kruger said, "at ten o'clock low."

"We see you, mother cow. Coming in on dead engines."

Battaglia gave the tanker pilot all the required data he would need for the tricky dead-engine refueling, made more difficut by the weather that had turned foul again.

Dropping down to Zulu One's altitude, he had to glide into the long refueling probe hanging from behind the tanker in such a way that he didn't overshoot, undershoot, or ram, all to be done without power on the RF-4. It had been a long morning; he had survived Ban Dau and the Migs and here he was now with dead engines, empty tanks, and close to losing his aircraft because of an unavoidable miscalculation.

He could see the crewmen in the tail, operating the boom and talking him in.

"Make it good the first time, Zulu. No second chance."

When Vince and the tanker were evened up on the glide path, the boom extended out and the crewman guided the end into the RF-4's refueling receptacle. Coordinated flying between Battaglia and the tanker pilot kept the boom engaged and the Phantom drank thirstily, filling her dry tanks.

"Saved another one, mother cow," Battaglia said, his gauge reading full.

The crewman retracted the boom and saluted Vince off the rigging. "Glad to be of service."

Rolling left, Victor-Whisky-Ten broke off from Zulu One and under full power vectored for Da Nang.

"That's it, Kraut . . . we're home free."

"Good show, Dogbone; we breathe another day."

"Next time we'll be loaded with weapons and I hope we meet those two Migs again."

"Ever tangle with a Twenty-one before?"

219

"First time."

"Learn anything?"

He didn't say anything. He was already thinking about when he would be back; this time there would be no surprise and the guns would be zeroed in.

As usual when Battaglia landed, the pride in completing a successful mission vanished and his bitterness and fear of Ban Dau returned to nag him. The photo reconnaissance only proved to him that the communists had built the most formidable defenses imaginable to protect their supply line to the south, and surviving the mission would be a miracle. Cleanhead was right: destroy Ban Dau and the North Vietnamese would come to the peace table unconditionally; but this wasn't his problem and he shared neither his superior's enthusiasm nor his ambition.

Vince sat in Colonel Dasher's office after a long and tiring debriefing that had taken the better part of two hours and had led to the understanding that there would be another two hours minimum after the film was developed and the planning people had a chance to review the results.

The quonset hut was hot and the single fan oscillating on top of the filing cabinet did nothing to improve the discomfort. Cleanhead sat leaned back on a swivel chair, his feet resting on the green blotter (filled with doodling) that covered his desk, curling and stroking his handlebar mustache and humming the last bars to the "Marine Corps Hymn." A satisfied smile and the glint in the gunmetal eyes said that he was happy with the mission. Vince was scowling.

"I'll be right up front with you, Lieutenant," he began. "It was a good mission, the photo lab said the film is excellent. Also, it was absolutely essential to withhold from you that a bombing halt had been ordered, at least until the mission had been completed. For personal reasons, with which we are both well acquainted, you may not agree with me, but there is no doubt that you understand the strategic and tactical importance behind the decision."

"I just want to get my part of the war over with so I can go home to Wichita and my girl and my consulting business, Colonel. That's all. I'm not here to pass judgment on command decisions. I just carry out orders, regardless of whether or not I agree with them."

Dasher sensed sarcasm in Battaglia's answer and he felt disappointed as he always did when discussing military policy with the young man. The colonel disliked it when others failed to share his own enthusiasm for the Marine Corps.

"I can tell by your attitude that you disagree with me."

Battaglia shrugged. "It was a tactical decision that you had to make."

"Your arrogance is showing, Lieutenant."

"Sorry, sir—but how would you feel if you were me?"

"That has nothing to do with what has happened. What concerns me is that you are close to throwing away a fine career, and if you continue to stew over this, your self-pity is going to get the better of you and you could very well end up doing something you'll regret the rest of your life." He smiled to relieve the growing tension and showed his mule teeth. "I'm not one to question what goes on in a man's personal life—I figure that's his own affair—but I suspect that the answers to the questions that are eating at you are locked up in something you left in Saigon."

Vince's eyes met Cleanhead's and they held tight.

"There's someone here to see you." Dasher pointed to the door at the far end of the quonset hut that led to another office.

Vince looked at the door and back to the colonel. Dasher nodded. Battaglia was halfway across to the door when the colonel stopped him.

"Incidently, Lieutenant"—he picked up a folder and opened it—"that GI at the Khach-san Bong, a Viet cong prostitute he was with is being held for his murder; and the young man whose lights you permanently put out in the kung-fu theater was found to have enough plastic explosive strapped to his body under his clothing to kill everyone in the building." He closed the folder and let it fall to the desk. "Thought you might sleep better if you knew."

Vince had his hand on the doorknob when Dasher stopped him again.

"She must love you a great deal to come all the way to Da Nang to explain to you. Don't screw up, Lieutenant."

Chapter 13

Nghia stood with her back to Vince, the dimples behind her knees deepening when she heard him come in.

"Hello, Nghia."

She was wearing a pink skirt with a pattern of little blue flowers that brought out the lovely golden color of her legs and contrasted well with her black hair that fell ruler-straight to the top of her rounded buttocks.

Against her soft curves and silk, Vince looked crude and offensive in his bulky flight suit covered with survival gear and bulging pockets, the holstered .38 with ammo belt slung across his chest, and helmet and oxygen mask tucked under his arm.

She bent a knee and brought one platform shoe up against the other, and in characteristic style, rested a leaflike hand on her elevated hip.

The pagoda earrings that he never saw her without shifted slightly when she turned her head to look at him out of the tails of her eyes, her heavy hair fanning out over one shoulder.

She quickly took in the paraphernalia of war that he was wearing and said, "You have been over the north." The hand on her pelvis lifted to her neck and the jade bracelets slid against each other and made a ringing sound reminiscent of the wind chimes that had serenaded their conversations at the Khach-san Bong only two days ago. It seemed like two years.

The strap on her shoe had come unsnugged and without thinking, since it seemed the natural thing to do, he kneeled before her and buckled the strap, allowing his eyes to linger on the trim angle of her foot under his fingers. His focus followed the curve of her calf to her dimpled knees thence to the smooth firm thighs. His nose was close to her skin and he could smell the fleshy redolence of her legs which was the smell of sweet shelled lichees.

"Why you do that?"

"You have come a long way and I wanted to do something for you."

He was off his knee and standing in front of her, not too close. Was that redness in her cheeks and neck? A whore blushing?

She could feel the rush of blood into her face and she tried to hide it with her hands. He gently pulled them away.

"I kissed you once."

"Yes," she said.

He watched her pouting lips, red as young cherries, pull at the corners.

"Did you like it?"

She nodded and took a half step to him, her tapered phoenix eyes regarding him with their shadowed corners and touch of powder blue around the black pupils. As he pulled her to him, her eyes faded dreamlike into themselves and he kissed her, gently, like he had the first time in the hotel room, and she seemed to become detached from her physical surroundings, a peaceful cloud passing over her face.

She sighed, deep and long, and her head fell back into the crook of his arm, her hair swinging in short sweeps. "Why you go away?" she whispered.

"Because I was confused and didn't understand—and

maybe scared." `

She took his hand in hers and her eyes were far away. "Please kiss me again. No man kiss me like you kiss me; you make Nghia feel like young girl again—like first time." She touched his cheek with her soft fingers, working them in a circle down to his chin and throat.

He kissed her again and he could feel her strong abdominal muscles tighten against him, and a birdlike cry fluttered from her mouth, causing his lips to vibrate.

"I run away from Kai, bring children with me." She was trying to catch her breath, the fingers of one hand spread across her chest.

"We stay hotel . . . Da Nang City." Her bold eyes searched his face. "I afraid come see you, want send Autumn Dove—I come anyway." She became nervous and was talking rapidly, her eyes looking worried. "I want explain everything to you . . ."

"Take it easy," he said. "There will be plenty of time for explanations, but first I need to decide what to do with you and the kids now that you're in Da Nang. Kai will be looking for you."

"We stay here on base with you."

He smiled. "That's against regulations and quite impossible."

"Girls at hotel tell me colonel have ginger cookie stay him on base."

"That's much different—a special arrangement that officially doesn't exist—and I don't think I could explain to you because I don't thoroughly understand it myself."

She looked disappointed. "Maybe we stay hotel."

"That's not a good idea either . . ." He put his two hands on her shoulders and looked seriously into her eyes. "Nghia, I have to ask you this and I hope you will understand."

Her black eyes moved slowly across his face, and that little worried look he had come to know well made her

225

lips tighten.

"How sincere are you?" he said. "How long do you plan to stay? Kai told me some things about you that—"

"I stay until you no want Nghia no more: one day, one week, one month, or forever. I bring children me, show you I sin . . . sin . . . cere."

His smile was mischievous. "You know you have already complicated my life beyond what I can accept, but now that you're here, I don't want you to go."

"I make you happy man sure . . . you see."

It was the first time he had ever seen her really smile, an open, unrestrained, happy smile. She pulled two handfuls of her hair up over his head and let it fall down his face. She kissed him lightly and her breath smelled like a baby's and he forgot about Ruthie and Wichita and pheasant hunting and his business and going home; and he loved the Marine Corps.

"I don't even want to know who she is," Cleanhead growled, though the gunmetal in his eyes had a glint that wasn't there before. "You've become a different man, and any woman that can improve the morale of my Marines has my respect." He inspected Nghia's figure with an appreciative eye. "Frankly, my first impression was to send her back to Saigon when I heard about the ruckus she kicked up at the main gate, demanding to see you. She didn't behave very well in the brig either, shouting and screaming epithets that would turn a barnacled sailor red; but when she was brought to me, she was a perfect princess and stated her case so eloquently and sincerely that I had no choice but to grant her request."

"Thank you for your kindness, sir," she said and bowed from her waist forward.

Dasher pulled Vince aside and whispered, "She's the

best-looking riceball I've seen in 'Nam and I envy you."
He glanced over at her, a black stogie smoking between
his clenched teeth. "Like I said, I don't care to know
anything more about her; a Marine's private life is his
own affair and I expect him to use discretion in matters
pertaining to his duties, and that includes women,
especially women. Do we understand each other,
Lieutenant?"

"Perfectly, sir."

"Good," he said. "Now with that out of the way, you
get her and those two kids she told me about settled in
somewhere and be back here at seventeen-hundred hours
to go over the photos the lab is developing." He put a
hand on Vince's shoulder. "Listen, boy, I've no doubt
that this girl has special feelings for you and you for her,
but be careful. Don't screw up and forget who you are
and what you're doing over here. Ban Dau is too
important for all of us."

Vince left Nghia at the officers' club with two
waitresses to look after her while he went to the pilots'
locker room to change out of his flight gear and to take a
shower. When he returned to the O-club with a borrowed
motorcycle, Nghia was seated at a table with a Pepsi-Cola
(she never drank alcohol) and surrounded by pilots from
his squadron.

Vince stood back from the table, feeling both pride and
jealousy, listening to the men doing their best to outdo
each other in getting Nghia's attention, although she was
doing nothing to encourage them except to be herself,
which in itself was enough to make men weary of war.

As soon as she noticed Battaglia standing behind the
men, she rose from her chair and walked around the table
(all eyes following her) to stand beside him, waiting for
him to tell her what to do. It was her way of taking the
pressure off him, and, in her wisdom, eliminating a
potentially difficult situation. As a result, no question

was left in the minds of the men with regard to where her faithfulness lay, and she thereby removed any embarrassment for Vince.

With Nghia tucked in behind him on the Yamaha, her arms wrapped around his waist, Battaglia roared away from the O-club. "I liked what you did back there—you shut their mouths right away."

"You not mad?" Her hair waved behind her like a black cape. "I think you be mad come back see mens with me."

"Don't worry about it. It was bound to happen with all those guys in there; they haven't seen a decent-looking woman in months."

From the hotel, Nghia telephoned a cousin who put her in touch with a friend who had a small furnished house to rent in Da Nang City, not too far from the base. After a brief inspection and some haggling about the rent, Nghia decided it was suitable and insisted over Vince's objections that she pay the rent and not he.

"Nghia, I know you can't have much money because Kai took it all from you. Isn't it true that he gave you only enough for you living expenses?"

"I able save some. I pay rent," she asserted.

Meanwhile, Ly-boy and Autumn Dove had explored the backyard and each came into the house with an armload of mangos, bananas, and papayas picked from the trees.

"Where shall we put these?" Ly-boy said, having difficulty maintaining balance on his crutch while holding the fruit.

The fruit were deposited in a bamboo basket that Nghia took from a shelf. Autumn Dove cut one of the larger papayas in half lengthwise and scraped the black seeds out, then squeezed the juice of a lime onto the yellow meat. Ly-boy stood beside her, watching closely and moving his lips in anticipation.

"For you," Autumn Dove said, giving Nghia and Vince each a half of the papaya with a spoon buried in the fruit, and looked at both of them for approval.

Vince took his papaya and patted her cheek. She was wearing her white bonnet and a new pair of jeans that Vince had bought her. The army cap was shoved into the back pocket of the jeans.

"Better cut Ly-boy a piece before he faints," Battaglia said.

"He can get his own." She turned to walk away.

Nghia caught her by the arm. "You take care Ly-boy like brother, and Ly-boy take care you like sister. Cut him papaya." She turned to Vince. "Tomorrow I put them in school."

"Good idea." He spooned out some papaya. "Looks like I've got a ready-made family."

"Will you live here, too?" Ly-boy asked.

Battaglia looked at Nghia and she smiled.

"Yes, Ly-boy, I'll be living here too. Looks like we've come a long way together."

"Kind of like a family, huh?" Ly-boy was smiling too.

"What do you think, Autumn?" Vince glanced at her.

She cut a papaya for Ly-boy and reluctantly handed it to him. "I guess so," she said and added, "it's better than living in the streets."

Anxious to set the house in order, Nghia gave the children instructions to wash the floors, beginning in the kitchen, while she pulled everything out of the drawers and cabinets and cleaned everywhere she looked. Battaglia got the job of washing the pots, woks, dishes, bowls, tea set, chopsticks, everything used in cooking and eating, and when he finished that, Nghia placed the inoperable electric rice cooker in front of him and told him to fix it.

When Autumn Dove refused to pick the gecko lizards off the wall and ceiling, Nghia cut a bamboo switch from

229

stalks growing around the pond and threatened to whip her, upon which Autumn Dove announced that she would run away back to Saigon to live in the streets again where no one told her what to do.

"It's more than four hundred miles to Saigon," Vince said. He had found the problem with the rice cooker and was reconnecting a lead wire.

"Long walk." Nghia had wrapped some cold rice cakes and dried squid and a few finger bananas in a newspaper. She handed it to Autumn Dove. She said something in Vietnamese to the girl and turned back to cooking.

Vince watched Autumn while he worked on the rice cooker. The tears started slowly as a trickle down both dusky cheeks and crawled over her rose-petal lips. She was a pretty girl and beginning to ripen, and she felt the urge to exercise her independence, yet she wasn't confident to the point that she thought she could make such a long journey on her own. She was too proud to say that she was sorry and wanted to stay, so she just stood by the wall and silently cried.

Battaglia pushed the rice cooker aside. "Come here, Autumn."

She stood in front of him, looking at the floor, the tears running over her lips. He took the newspaper with the food from her hand and wiped her nose with his handkerchief.

"Kick her out," Nghia said. "She be big trouble." She didn't turn around but continued to stir-fry the bean sprouts and water chestnuts with a wooden spatula. She measured in a small amount of peanut oil and dropped in a handful of Chinese cabbage leaves.

"You really don't want to go back to Cho-Chan," Vince said.

Autumn remained resolute. She wiped the tears from her lips with a finger, not looking up.

"You want to stay with us, don't you?" He held her

230

hand and lightly rubbed her wrist.

She nodded just enough so he could see her agreement.

"I'll help you throw those creatures out of the house. They're not so terrible to touch and they can't bite if you catch them from behind."

"I'm afraid of them."

"Don't be—they make nice pets; I used to play with lizards all the time when I was a youngster. It was great fun to put them in women's purses and teachers' desks."

Ly-boy laughed loudly and Autumn looked at him, horrified. Nghia stirred her vegetables, listened, and said nothing.

No amount of coaxing could get Autumn Dove to touch a gecko even though Vince had the patience to demonstrate how to catch a few. In the end, Ly-boy hopped around the house on his one leg, knocking the green lizards off the walls and ceiling with his crutch and throwing them outside into the garden.

"You can't blame her," Vince said to Nghia. "The kid's just afraid of the things."

She looked out the tails of her eyes at him and her smile was dry though her eyes sparkled with humor. "You easy be fooled by woman, Lieutenant."

Vince held a serving bowl under the wok and Nghia scooped the stir-fried vegetables in with the wooden spatula. She had added a sprinkling of sesame seeds and slices of pork and chicken that were cooked separately.

"You think she was acting?" he said.

"Young girl want attention just like woman." Nghia smiled at him with affected shyness and pushed him to the table. The amber light clicked off on the rice cooker and she called Autumn Dove to set the table.

A heavy, wet steam rose from the rice pot and its rich aroma spread through the kitchen. Autumn Dove carried the rice pot (a serving spatula protruding through the hole in the lid) to the table. An octagonal ceramic vessel

231

with bamboo plants painted on the sides was filled with hot sour fish soup and was centered on the white tablecloth, four soup bowls stacked beside it.

"Did you wash your hands?" Battaglia said.

"Yes." Autumn Dove showed him her hands.

"I did too," Ly-boy said, holding his hands out to be inspected.

He winked at them. "You kids are learning."

"*Chung ta ngoi,*" everyone be seated, Nghia ordered. She ladled out the fish soup into the bowls and Autumn Dove served. "Vince first," she said.

Autumn set a steaming bowl in front of Battaglia and placed a ceramic spoon on the tablecloth next to the bowl. She looked at Nghia for a favorable word. Nghia smiled and handed her another bowl.

"Ly-boy next." Nghia said.

Autumn frowned, but obeyed.

"Men first. You learn right way."

The teapot was tipped over the small handleless cups and the green, highly aromatic brew bubbled out the spout in a hot, thick stream. Nghia placed the teapot next to her on the table and gave everyone a cup. She raised hers in a toast: "We all have long life together."

Vince, Ly-boy, and Autumn raised their cups to Nghia, no one knowing how tightly enmeshed their four lives would become in the following months.

"*Chung ta an com bay gio,*" we will eat now, Nghia said.

"Who gets the fish head?" Autumn Dove was pointing into the soup vessel. She glanced around the table at each person.

"You three can argue over it," Vince said. He tasted the soup.

"You like food?" From now on, Nghia would always ask the same question at the table. She wouldn't consider her cooking acceptable unless Battaglia was pleased.

"It's different." He tasted another spoonful.

232

She waited patiently, not yet touching her soup.

"The soup is good, Nghia."

She smiled without parting her lips and began eating.

Autumn Dove hadn't taken her eyes off the fish head. "Does anyone want the head?"

Ly-boy would have liked it for himself, but he said nothing.

"*Con an,*" you eat it, Nghia said and ladled the head, eyeballs intact, into Autumn Dove's bowl.

Vince looked at Ly-boy sitting next to him. "Why aren't you eating?"

"At the Catholic orphanage we always prayed before we ate."

Battaglia regarded Nghia. She put her spoon down, looking surprised.

"He wants to pray before we eat. What do you think?"

"What you think?"

"Are you Catholic or Buddhist?" he asked.

There was a loud crack.

"Take the fish head out of your mouth, Autumn . . . we have to decide something before we eat," Vince said. "What religion are you, Nghia?"

"I no religion."

"Would you object to saying grace before we eat?"

"What is grace?"

"To bless the meal—we ask God to bless the food we are going to eat."

"Which God?"

He could see that she was mystified by this. "We will ask *Jesus* to bless the meal."

"Oh, that man; he say he son of God and people kill him on cross. He good man, promise we go heaven. That why he die for us. Yes . . . we pray Jesus . . . he bless meal. Good idea."

Battaglia made a mental note to ask her at a more convenient time how she came to hear the gospel;

233

probably from a French missionary who visited her village when she was a child. Right now he was hungry.

Ly-boy said grace, the way he remembered it from his orphanage days. Autumn Dove folded her hands like everyone else, but her eyes remained wide open staring at Ly-boy.

When Ly-boy had finished the brief prayer, Nghia announced that she liked the prayer and that they would pray before all meals. The meal then began in earnest, the kids finishing the soup and starting into the rice and vegetables before Vince was halfway through his soup.

"I don't want to go to school," Ly-boy said, picking up bean sprouts and chicken with his chopsticks.

"It's best you go to school," said Battaglia. "It's important to your future."

"The other children will make fun of me because I have only one leg," he said to Vince.

Autumn stood on her chair and a leg flashed out. "Kaaa! I'll hurt anyone that makes fun of you. I can kung-fu good."

"*Ngoi xuong, con,*" sit down, child, Nghia said.

"If anyone gives you trouble let me or Nghia know and we'll have a talk with the school authorities. I don't think you'll have any trouble."

After the meal and while Autumn Dove and Ly-boy were washing dishes, Vince and Nghia walked in the small garden and under the fruit trees, talking, and picking flowers. The chrysanthemums were in full bloom, showing off their colors—white, baby blue, yellow, light magenta—and the white-and-red-striped flowers of the tamarind tree covered the path and floated in the pond water with the lotus and lily blooms.

"The home is lovely, Nghia—right out of a child's picture book or a Pearl Buck novel. Nowhere in Vietnam could there be a home as comfortable as this and I want to congratulate you on finding it. The walled courtyard with

234

its reflecting pool, the flower garden, the fruit trees and ornamental shrubs and bamboo, this beautiful tamarind tree, the songbirds and frogs . . . the house with its stone-tiled floor, polished rosewood furniture, carved teak doors, hand-painted ginger pots, rosewood figure sculptures and delicate ricepaper etchings—I could go on, there is so much—are everything I imagined that the Orient could supply in pleasurable domestic living."

Nghia spun a tamarind flower between her thumb and forefinger, and watched a fat bullfrog on a lily pad sunning himself.

"Some years ago I read a wonderful book called *Pavilion of Dreams*, translated from the Chinese and written during the time of the Ching dynasty," he continued. "In it is described the elaborate detail of the home of a well-to-do Canton family ruled by a forty-year-old matriarch who had moved out of her husband's rooms to avoid the embarrassment of becoming pregnant in her old age. Her total abstinence and self-denial . . ."

"I no understand." She smiled pleasantly at him.

"It's not important."

"I think you want say you like way we live. You like quiet life . . . yes?"

"Very much."

"The war . . ." she said.

"It intrudes on everything."

"Here, our home . . . no war. Here I make peace for you." She bowed her head toward him.

He took the tamarind flower from her fingers and placed it over her ear. A small yellow bird, a warbler, only slightly larger than his extended thumb, landed on the rim of the bird feeder and picked at the seeds.

"It won't be any trouble for me to get special permission to live off base with you and the children," he said.

She looked down at the patio bricks under her feet.

"Your colonel, he like me . . . he maybe think I be good for you." She reached up into the tamarind tree and plucked one of the long curved seedpods and handed it to him.

He looked at it and turned it over in his palm, noting the four large seeds bulging underneath the cover, snuggled close together.

"Like us," she said.

Vince drove back to the base on the motorcycle to go over the recon photos with Dasher and the planning people, leaving Nghia to pick tamarind seeds that she promised she would transform into a chewy candy for him to eat when he returned.

She had changed into a plain, solid-colored ao dai, pink with black pantaloons, and sat in the courtyard, her lap filled with tamarind pods.

"I wish you would let me pay the rent for the house," Vince had said to her before leaving.

She refused, of course, aware that her small savings wouldn't last very long, but wanting to do this to show him that she was sincere in her relationship and didn't want to exploit him as she did other men when working for Kai. When the money ran out she would get a job in Da Nang City to pay the rent.

At heart she was a plain girl, simple in her needs, the unnoticed things of the world holding her interest most. She marveled at a drop of morning dew clinging to a blade of grass, was saddened by the calls of nighthawks at dusk, and her heart beat faster at the sight of small children playing in the schoolyard.

Kai would come after her—to take her back to the Khach-san Bong. She had no intention of returning to Cho-Chan and the life that she abhorred, so when Kai found her she would have to find a way to deal with him.

236

She wouldn't tell Vince.

She called Autumn Dove to take the pods into the kitchen and begin preparing the tamarind candy. The mango and papaya trees were heavy with fruit and she walked beneath them, thinking of her future with Battaglia. Later when the children were playing she would go into the kitchen and tie a knife to her calf, under her pantaloons, the way she did in Cho-Chan, just in case there was trouble with Kai.

In the normal sense of things it would seem impossible to wash away the years of debauchery, but she had begun a new life with Vince that had created a new girl, one that was virgin pure, never before touched by a man. She would be born anew, unblemished by past sins, her loins fresh and unstained. When she gave herself to Vince, he would become her first man, and her last; for when he left her she planned to enter a convent in Hue, there to live a life of contemplation and abstinence.

That evening when Vince came home from the base, she had a steaming tub of water waiting for him. She ushered him into their bedroom, unbuttoned his shirt, and rubbed his chest, toying with the forest of hair. As if by sorcery the tension immediately left his shoulders and neck and his body sagged with relief.

"You've got magic hands," he said.

She worked her hands up to his shoulders and massaged deeply. After a minute she said, "Okay I ask you important question?"

Her voice had dropped and taken on an air of concern that caused Battaglia to look troubled.

She saw the look and was glad, because she wanted him to ponder what she was about to say and to respond with his sincerest feelings. The nighthawks expressed their sorrow in the falling night and Nghia felt a deep regret.

"What's wrong?" he said.

She smiled a little and her eyes flickered up at him.

237

"You sorry I be ginger cookie to other mens?"

The question came as no great surprise; he had been thinking about it from the time he had discovered that she was a tiger girl. The idea that she was sleeping with other men did not affect him in the beginning, because he only thought of her the same way most men thought of a prostitute—a faceless woman for temporary use. The fact that she had experienced many men was of no consequence (a necessary condition of her trade) and only a person with a warped sense of reality would give it a second thought.

When Nghia became special to him—and he was not sure at what point that happened, though he suspected that it occurred when she visited his hotel room after the MPs released him and she wanted to take charge of the kids—all that changed and he began to think of her differently. He had even become jealous which was a disturbing development for him; but more difficult to handle were the contradictory love-hate feelings that he suppressed, all of which could be traced to his belief that she could never totally be his, part of her always to be claimed by the men that visited her room at the Khach-san Bong.

He felt that expressing this to Nghia would only do harm, so he lied to her. "You being a ginger cookie to other men doesn't bother me in the least."

A very perceptive young woman, Nghia could always detect insincerity. "You no tell truth," she said, rolling her hands over his deltoid muscles. She smiled her little smile to encourage him to express his true feelings.

"All right," he said reluctantly, "it does bother me."

"Good—that mean you care." She worked her fingers into his temples, causing him to half close his eyes. "I have big surprise for you."

"And what might that be?—I don't think much can

238

surprise me at this point with so much happening so quickly."

"This will." She removed all of his clothes and made him lay face down on a mat that she had spread on the cool stone tile floor. "I virgin girl."

He rolled over on his back and stared up at her with open mouth. "That's your surprise? Who are you trying to kid?"

"It true—I no be with other mens before; you first time for me."

He started to laugh, but something had changed in Nghia's face that stopped him. The hard lines at the corners of her mouth had disappeared and her eyes were deep and clear. A soft, pink light covered her face and she looked fresh and childlike; a sweetness came over her that he had never noticed before.

She pushed him over on his stomach and walked on his back, digging her toes into his skin. Her steps were only an inch apart and she was careful not to put her weight directly on him, rolling her ankles back and forth so that the bottoms of her feet kneaded his flesh rather than hammered it.

"So you're a virgin," he said, beginning to understand. "I never would have suspected."

"I fool you," she laughed. "You will know for sure soon." She giggled, covering her lips with the palm of her hand, and worked her feet fast.

"I guess I'm a pretty lucky guy."

After a thorough deep-muscle massage, she put him in the hot bath and washed every inch of him. She rinsed him off by pouring water from an urn over his body, and then refilled the tub with clean water to let him soak while she brewed tea.

Returning with the tea, she filled two cups and they sipped and talked and the virginal glow deepened in her face and Battaglia could only watch with awe what was happening to her.

A thick towel was used to dry him off, and when he had finished his second cup of tea with Nghia and she had folded him into bed, it was everything he could do to keep his eyes open. Somewhere beyond the pink cloud on which he floated he could hear the distant booming of guns and the far-away scream of jets. And then there was nothing and he slept.

Once during the night he started awake, not knowing where he was and feeling an urgency to go to the base. It took him a while to remember that he was with Nghia and the children and that the bombers would not be going north that day. He was instantly asleep again.

In the dark coolness of the predawn hours Nghia stood beside the bed and undid the ties on her ao dai and dropped it to the floor. She slipped out of the pantaloons (she wore no underwear) and looked down on Vince asleep between the sheets. Her tigress body, sleek and beautifully conditioned, gave off a soft glow from the starlight coming into the bedroom through the uncurtained windows. One golden leg was bent at the knee, a hand lay carelessly on her pelvis, and her head leaned a bit forward, ebony hair falling in a straight line to her shoulders and curving forward over her firm, pointed breasts.

If Vince had been awake and turned his head slightly, his face would be only inches from Nghia's velvety thighs and pubic area that was absent of all hair except for a soft down that was silky to the touch, like that of a young girl.

The crescent scar on her cheek twitched and she placed a knee on the bed, edging in under the sheet and moving in close to Vince so that her breasts rested on his chest and her left leg lay across his thighs.

Stroking his hair and tenderly kissing his eyes and lips, she slowly aroused him from sleep and whispered into his ear, "Young virgin girl want lay with tough Marine. My first time and I scared. You please show me how make love?''

Her body was odorless except for the faint smell of ripe apricots coming from the wetness between her thighs, and she could feel his hardness pushing against her stomach.

"I think you too big for new girl, but I want try. You teach me please?''

"I will be careful and go slow," he said.

"No hurt me."

"A virgin girl must be treated like a new flower—a bloom that has just opened. I promise to be gentle."

Nothing could prepare him for the great outpouring of love that Nghia had waiting for him—a love that had lingered in the fathoms of her heart—like the rapture of the deeps that took control of unsuspecting divers and led them off to risk their lives in unexplored caverns.

"I love you," she whispered.

He wanted to tell her he loved her too, but when he tried, the words were too low for her to hear, so overcome was he by her sensuality; his muscles felt like they had turned to quivering Jell-O.

"Be good to me, Vince oi—I give you something I can never give again."

She was on top of him, covering his face with kisses, and he had never experienced a woman so totally, so intensely, and so sensitively. Her cloud of hair covered their heads and the silky touch of it on his sensitized skin carried him higher onto the crest of the wave that was Nghia, rushing too fast toward the shore where he knew he must crash.

"Is it possible?" he asked.

"Yes," she answered.

"I never in my life thought it could be possible."

"It true."

Nghia's tears wet his chest, his face, his neck. Her

kisses were wet with her weeping. It was truly the girl's first time.

The entire bedroom wall was a double sliding door made of pine wood in the Japanese fashion and opened to the pool courtyard with its chrysanthemums and flowering tamarind tree. Nghia sat on a palm mat facing the open doors, brushing her hair in long sweeping curves, the rising sun warming her face and the yellow warbler trilling in the tamarind, warming her soul.

Beside her on a round black-lacquered tray, green tea brewed in a white porcelain dragon pot from which steam rose out of the spout in a tiny stream. A narrow ray of sun filtered through the lower branches of the tamarind and brightened the hand-painted golden peacock on the tray, bringing it to life.

Nghia smiled to herself and took a deep breath of the cool salt air blowing lightly across the courtyard from the South China Sea. All of her felt alive for the first time that she could remember, and she was sure that if she died she would go to the Christian heaven the French missionaries told her about. She turned to the bed and smiled. "What time you go base?"

Vince was supporting himself on an elbow, absorbed in the beauty of the moment—his first occasion in experiencing the fullness of Oriental womanhood and the tranquility the right woman can bring to a man's life. "I have to be there in an hour."

"Plenty time."

He nodded, thinking that he had never seen anything so graceful as Nghia brushing her hair in the first sunlight of morning. "Tea ready?"

She lifted the lid and her hair spilled forward in a black cloud as she bent to inspect the tea. "Not right color. Soon."

242

The chafing dish on the floor mat began to sizzle with breakfast dumplings and the aroma filling the room caused Vince's stomach to rumble and brought his taste buds to full alert. *I've died and gone to heaven.*

Nghia didn't allow the dumplings to remain on one side too long, continually turning them with chopsticks; and when they had cooked to the color of the bark on the tamarind tree she placed two of the crescent-shaped dumplings on a plate and brought them to Battaglia, her nude body mottled by different shades of light passing through the garden trees. "Hot," she said, holding a dumpling with the chopsticks and bringing it cautiously to his mouth.

He bit into the juicy dumpling and his brain filled with the taste of a dozen teasing spices mixed with pork and crabmeat.

The tea she poured him was dark green and swirled with bits of dried tea leaves. She held the cup to his lips while he sipped down a cupful, and she poured him another, his back resting against three duck-down pillows she had propped against the great bed's rosewood headboard.

She fed him another dumpling. "You like?"

"*Ngon qua*," delicious, he said. "Can I have another?"

"Last one . . . must save room for pho." She pointed to the burner from which the chafing dish had been removed, replaced by the pot of pho.

He ran his index finger around the edge of her pouting lips. "What's happening to us?"

"Good things."

Thick strands of her hair slipped through his fingers and fell limply around her bare shoulders and down her back. "President Johnson ordered us to stop bombing the north."

Her eyes widened for a second or two then returned to the normal long black ellipses, brooding and secretive,

243

that always seemed to lie behind a screen of the unexplained. The impact that they had when they lingered on Vince any length of time, as they did now, was one of quick arousal and a strong sense of déjà vu.

"No more worry Ban Dau?" She stirred the pho with a long-handled wooden spoon, her eyes steady on his.

"Not for a while."

"How long?"

"There's really no way of telling for sure, though Colonel Dasher thinks that the North Vietnamese will show disdain for a peaceful settlement and we'll be going back north real soon. My personal opinion is that the communists will nurse this respite for as long as they can, to strengthen their regular NVA divisions, and then strike hard across the DMZ into the northern highlands, take Hue and Da Nang, and then push south into Saigon to end the war fast."

She fed him the pho and massaged his body when he had finished a last cup of tea. Before she let him get up to shave and put on the freshly laundered and pressed uniform she had set out, she laid a hot towel on his face to soothe his skin and soften the beard. Sitting on the edge of the bed, her legs hanging loose next to his arm, she talked to him about small matters to take his mind off Ban Dau. "Today I take Autumn Dove and Ly-boy to school and I go city to shop for rice and food. I see about job too."

He looked out from under the hot towel. "You're going to look for work?" He felt a pinch of anxiety. "What kind of work?"

"Not know yet. I go talk people . . . look . . . cousin maybe help me. Find something pay good."

Her going back to entertaining men became very real to him and she saw his startled look. Taking the towel from his face she kissed him and said, "No worry, I know what to do; I be careful . . . you no lose me."

244

He saw her legs resting on the edge of the bed (loosely entwined), the small smooth feet and delicate bone structure, the superb muscle tone and honey-nut color of her thighs, all of which raised him to the top of the wave again, and when she let her eyes linger on his face the black ellipses pulled him under at the second he crested and he went tumbling down the breaker, twisting and falling, and the next thing he knew he had Nghia in his arms, ravishing her young beautiful body and wanting nothing more than to feel the reassurance of her honey legs mothering him, pulling him closer, mystifying him with the comfort of their embrace, and, finally, losing himself in them as he came crashing down the curl of the wave, and he washed up on the beach, limp and exhausted.

Chapter 14

In the weeks that followed, the North Vietnamese high command, as Battaglia had portended, appeased Washington in a crafty strategic move designed to buy time to mass its northern divisions for an all-out assault on the highlands, capture Da Nang, and strike south along the coast to link up with attacking forces streaming east out of Cambodia in a final siege of Saigon. By feigning a desire to schedule peace talks, arguing and rejecting of conditions for the meetings, and by use of other delaying tactics, the communists were effective in stockpiling enormous stores of munitions at Ban Dau in preparation for the dash to Saigon. President Johnson, in his blindness, kept the bombers grounded.

The Viet Cong in the south, to assist the NVA in putting over its masquerade, retreated into the jungle and interior villages and fought only minor skirmishes to encourage the U.S. and South Vietnamese commanders to believe that Washington's effort to attract North Vietnam to the peace table were working.

With the war slowed down, the Marine air wing at Da Nang, ordered to stand down and not antagonize the enemy, put few aircraft in the air. Sorties were flown primarily to prevent pilots from getting rusty and to provide what little ground support was necessary.

Battaglia, to keep busy, assigned himself to the

maintenance shops where he rolled up his sleeves and worked alongside the enlisted men repairing the Phantoms he flew. He worked on damaged fuel-transfer pumps, engine-mount struts, wheel-door-closed switches, shutoff valves, nitrogen-relief manifolds, oxygen-fill panels, and other parts needed to keep the aircraft flying. He derived great satisfaction from working with his hands, and took pride in knowing that the men respected him for being able to both fly the warplanes and repair them as well.

During the best parts of the day, when his spirits were high and he allowed himself to think about home, he would entertain thoughts of an armistice and the Ban Dau mission being scrubbed. The picture of fields of waving Kansas wheat was so vivid that he could sometimes smell the harvest while torquing down a locknut.

At home with his family, for that was how he now referred to the Da Nang house and Nghia and the kids, he had become at least partially domesticated and was teaching one-legged Ly-boy, Autumn Dove, and their friends how to play American baseball. He had scrounged enough balls, bats, and gloves from the base to start a three-team league. Interest had grown to the point that parents had cleared a field and erected a backstop, and they brought chairs and food and watched the games. Though most didn't understand what was going on, they all shouted and clapped when someone hit the ball and there was lots of running.

"Strike one," Vince said, and took another bite of spring roll.

The kid turned around and looked at Vince umpiring behind home plate. "That pitch was outside."

"Yeh, yeh—get back in the box and hit."

The kid set his jaw and turned back toward the pitcher. Autumn Dove wound up and threw a fastball in the same place.

"Strike two," Vince hollered.

Stepping out of the batter's box, the barefoot kid fixed his eyes on Battaglia in a wide-eyed gaze, his mouth open. He said nothing, stepped into the box, and pounded the plate with his bat.

Autumn came in with a knuckleball-curve that Vince had taught her to throw. It was a good pitch, but it was a little high and hung a bit too long and the kid connected, lining the ball hard down third. Ly-boy only had time to put his glove up in self-protection and the next instant he was knocked off his crutch and lay sprawled in the dirt. He waved the glove with the ball trapped in the web for everyone to see, more from surprise than pride. The crowd stood and cheered and clapped, and Ly-boy was helped up and given his crutch.

Autumn Dove tossed the fatigue hat into the air and shouted, "We won . . . we won . . ." and hugged Ly-boy until he had to push her away from embarrassment and lack of breath.

The small crowd of spectators gathered around Ly-boy, congratulating him, and he smiled and looked at the ball in the glove and smiled some more.

"Nice catch," Vince said, finishing the spring roll. "Feels great, doesn't it?" He licked his fingers and put his hand on Ly-boy's shoulder, and remembered the elation when the shortstop for Bloomfield had blasted a sure double into left field and he'd made a running catch against the fence to end the game and win the Little League state championship.

"Can I wear one of the hats now?" Ly-boy said.

"You bet," Vince said.

There were only three baseball caps, one for each team. Each time a player made an outstanding play, the

248

team cap was rotated to him. Being awarded the cap was such an important honor that the kid wore it night and day, even to bed.

Nghia poured Vince a cup of tea and he sat under a flame tree talking to her, and watched the children pack up the gear and pick the field clean of trash.

"Enjoy the game?" he said.

"I no understand baseball, but I like watch. Children like much much and many people come see games." She patted his arm sister-like and smiled. "You do good thing bring baseball Da Nang. Soon all children play baseball and all peoples come watch games, and they remember you be man bring baseball Vietnam."

"Better than being rememberd for dropping bombs," he said. He finished the tea and handed her the cup. "I went to Saigon looking to find a reason for fighting in this war and I found you and Autumn Dove and Ly-boy. I was too wrapped up with myself to see the answer right under my nose, until you were standing in front of me in Colonel Dasher's office and I was never so happy to see anyone in all my life, and you told me that the kids were with you and I realized that I had found my reason. That seems like a long time ago and the reason has grown stronger every day." He touched her cheek and smiled.

For a while they watched Ly-boy and Autumn Dove play catch—all the other children had left the ballfield—in no hurry to leave the shade of the flame tree. Nghia poured Battaglia a cup of tea from the pot kept hot in a padded basket and he chewed on another of her tasty spring rolls.

"You know, Nghia," he said, leaning back against the tree trunk and feeling philosophical, "I'm haunted by the ghosts of the past."

She pursed her lips in question, not sure of what he had said, but knowing from the tone and emphasis that he was saying something important—more for himself than for her benefit.

"There are these things that happened to me a long time ago and some not so long ago that I dream about. I didn't understand then what they meant, and I don't understand now except that I can't get through them— they keep me pinned down."

"I hear you talk talk in sleep . . . no understand what you say, but you talk talk sometime all night."

He held the cup tight and his knuckles became white. "There's a woman in one of the dreams and she's staring down at me sick in bed; and she's telling me to get up, that I have no right to be sick and make her feel bad. She starts crying and says that she can't stand it and she runs away to leave me to die in bed."

The ball sailed back and forth between Ly-boy and Autumn Dove, easy-to-catch tosses that matched the listless, slow afternoon.

Unexpectedly, Vince blurted, "Ruthie is an ass."

Nghia sat with her legs pulled up and crossed in front, her dusky bare ankles showing. She looked at him out of the tails of her slanted eyes, her face expressionless.

"I wanted to say that—I don't know why."

"You love your American girl friend?" She wouldn't say her name; she would be recognizing Ruthie as a real person if she did and she couldn't bear that.

"I love her quite a lot." He didn't feel that he should have been so direct, but the words came automatically, like they had to be said. "Does that make you feel bad?"

She shook her head.

"I thought it would."

"What you say no true . . . you no love her . . . so I no feel bad."

"Of course I love her," he said. "It's ridiculous to think otherwise. We've been together too long, planned too much together, been too much a part of each other, for me not to be in love with her."

"You afraid her—no can love her. You afraid she hurt

250

you, leave you forever. She able hurt you too much and you afraid her. No can love woman when you afraid her, when she your se . . . cur—no can say that word."

"Security," he said, knowing exactly what she meant, because it was true.

"You depends her make you happy; that no good. When she say she leave you when you come Vietnam you think you sad because you lose her, but you really sad because you lose se . . . cur . . . ." She turned and looked him full in the face. "That woman—she be your good friend? You can tell her your secrets and no be afraid? You no have worry all time what you say her . . . what you do? You always know she like you? No want hurt you?"

He looked at his hands. "I can't say any of that is true."

"You able talk me like friend, right?"

"I've told you things I could never tell Ruthie, or anyone else."

"You like be around me, talk talk, even I no make love you?"

"Yes—of course; I enjoy being around you." He threw a pebble and watched it bounce into a patch of grass. "You're comfortable to be around."

"You afraid me—afraid I hurt you?"

"Don't be silly."

"I make feel glad you man?"

He smiled and nodded. "Very much."

She stood, brushed off her ao dai, and proclaimed, "You love me—not that woman," and left him alone to watch her walk off down the path, the basket with the teapot in it swinging from her hand, her sugar-sweet walk and the outline of her legs under the white silk pantaloons taunting him.

That night after the table was cleared and the dinner

dishes were done and Nghia stood at the kitchen sink washing soybeans and mashing them into a paste, Battaglia walked up behind her and pulled her hair aside and kissed the back of her neck. "Want to play Mah-Jongg with the kids?"

"I think you want talk me, no want play Mah-Jongg. I watch you at dinner . . . you nervous . . . eat only soup . . . little rice." She dried her hands and tucked her arm in his. "Come, you need talk; we go outside in garden be alone—you talk."

There was a quarter-moon hanging over the courtyard wall, and a breeze carrying the smell of salt blew in from the bay to fill the garden. Frogs in the corner of the pond croaked and chased each other under the lily pads, and a fat red-and-black spotted carp jumped among the lotus and splashed water on the red brick path.

"I've been thinking about what you said today under the flame tree," he said. "I haven't been honest with myself or with you, though I'm sure you have been aware of everything I've been doing and thinking."

Her bold eyes roamed over his face.

"I'm surprised you followed me to Da Nang—decided to rent this house and asked me to stay here with you and the kids; and there are the murder charges against me you got dropped. I've done nothing to deserve any of this, particular when my loyalties have been with a girl twelve thousand miles away and who I hope to marry."

"I do for you because I love you," she said simply.

He looked away, feeling uneasy with the conversation. Trying to find explanations always made him uncomfortable. Nghia sensed his discomfort.

"You no have say anything. I no care about that other woman twelve thousand mile away. She there and I here and I have you now."

She paused and in the moonglow her pouting lips looked more inviting than ever. He was glad she wanted

252

him to talk.

"Today under the tree you said something about friendship that made a lot of sense to me: friendship between a man and a woman." He felt very close to her tonight.

"Mans must be friend with woman—like her much before can love her truly." She looked at him with that characteristic blushing shyness of hers that was such a jarring contradiction in a prostitute and said, "Many mans think they love woman, but no like her . . . can never be friend."

"After listening to what you said at the ballfield I realized that I've never in a true sense really liked Ruthie as a friend; but I think I love her." It was hard for him to admit this.

The quarter-moon threw a soft glow onto the pond and it reflected into Nghia's face to give her features a shadowed, veiled look. She was looking down at the lotus flowers that had closed, not to reopen until morning's light.

"You no love her," she said, "not way mans should really love woman. You think you love her because you need her, no because you want to give to her, help her. You love selfish—take take, no give—not true love: baby love." She smiled at him around the curtain of hair that concealed half her face.

"You are amazing. Where did you learn that? Not from books."

She pointed to her heart. "You forget that before I become virgin with you I tiger girl . . . stay many mans."

"I haven't forgotten," he said.

She pulled the hair back from her face so that he could see the fullness of her smile, and she placed her palm on his cheek. It was soft and warm, like a bird's nest. "Your eyes sad. I no want you worry about other mans." Her finger was on her heart. "This yours, belong no other

253

mans. My love for you not baby love, not selfish . . . I want nothing from you, only want be your friend. Nghia give—no take; trust me."

His arms went around her and she melted into him like warm butter. Nothing had ever felt so good to Vince.

"I pray someday soon you wake beside me and love me way I love you; but first we be good friends."

The Mah-Jongg tiles slapping against the table carried into the garden and a wall panel slid partially open.

Autumn Dove's head looked out and she called to Vince and Nghia, "Ly-boy is cheating and I don't want to play with him anymore. Will you come in and play Mah-Jongg with me?"

Ly-boy's head poked beside Autumn Dove, his mouth full of soybean milk and sweet rice. "I'm not cheating— she's just mad because she can't beat me," he said after swallowing the food in one gulp.

'You kids should get along better," Vince said. "You're always fighting over the most trivial matters."

Autumn Dove purposely shut the door on Ly-boy's hand and he let out a howl. Nghia saw what happened and ran to the house with a bamboo twig she had snatched up from the garden path.

"Don't beat me," Autumn cried, and took off running.

Nghia had her by the hair before she could run five feet and whipped her across the bottom. Autumn fought to get loose, but Nghia jerked her around by the hair and hit her again with the switch, and again and again.

"It hurts! Don't!" Autumn wailed.

Nghia was livid at what the girl had done to Ly-boy and would have beat her until she bled if Vince hadn't stopped her.

"You're going to kill her," he said, twisting the bamboo from her hand.

"Why you stop me?—she need be beat."

"Not that way—enough is enough."

Autumn, seeing her moment and taking advantage of it, ran to Vince and threw her arms around him in a melodramatic display of emotion. "She hates me . . . she hates me . . . she wants to kill me."

"I hope she does," Ly-boy howled, holding his hand.

Vince wisely pulled Autumn Dove into the kitchen, away from the other two, and sat her in a chair.

"Protect me," she said, "Nghia is jealous and wants to hurt me."

"Shut up, Autumn, or I'll take up where Nghia left off. You are an ungrateful little girl and undeserving of what she has done for you."

"What has she done for me?" she said defiantly, intentionally trying to provoke him.

"Taken you with her, out of that pit of hell you were living in, given you a home here in Da Nang and putting you in school—that's what she's done for you, without putting too fine a point on it."

"I'm going to run away and never come back."

Battaglia put his finger under her chin and lifted her face to his. "You are going to do no such thing. You're going to pull yourself together, apologize to Ly-boy and to Nghia, and become a part of this home."

She was quiet and didn't attempt to twist her head away from Vince, her eyes looking directly into his.

Vince could see that he had gotten through to her and that she was thinking about what he had said, her emotion drained away.

"Are we a family?" she said soberly, looking subdued.

"You can say that . . . even though we are not blood-related we are looking after one another, and we care about each other the way a family should."

"And Ly-boy is sort of like my brother and I'm sort of like his sister?"

"That's right."

"And you and Nghia are our parents?"

255

Vince took his hand away from her chin and smiled. "Now you're catching on."

Her eyes brightened and her lips opened to speak, and then they closed while she thought again about what she wanted to say and then they opened and she said, "Maybe you and Nghia will get married and you can adopt me and Ly-boy and we will be a real family and we can live together forever and never be separated." She looked down at her hands that she was wringing together and her rose-petal lips puckered in the pleasantness of the thought. "That's possible, isn't it?"

"All of it is possible, but it's too early to think about us being a legal family, though I think both Nghia and I have thought about it without mentioning the idea to each other."

"Do you really like me enough to want me to be your forever daughter?" Her face lifted up from her wringing hands. "I'm not always a good girl."

He patted her on the cheek. "You've become very important to me, and I'm willing to take the good with the bad just like you must be willing to do the same with me; nobody is perfect."

"Jesus was."

"But he was God."

She looked anxious, as if he might reject her. "I didn't mean that you had to be perfect . . . I only meant—"

"Don't worry about it. Now what do you think about saying you're sorry to Ly-boy? And it wouldn't hurt to apologize to Nghia also—would that be too difficult?"

"Oh, I don't mind," she said. "I felt bad at first, but after you talked to me I feel much better." She started for the living room where Nghia and Ly-boy waited. "Do you mind answering a question?"

"What is it?"

"Do I still call you Vince if you become my legal father or do I call you Dad?"

"Whatever you're most comfortable with."

"Okay, Vince," she said, smiling, and went to apologize to Nghia and Ly-boy.

After the children were in bed for the night (an argument had developed over who would use the bathroom first) and Nghia brought tea and sweet rice cakes to the deck where Vince sat watching the crescent moon rise above the courtyard wall, a quiet settled over the house that brought a refreshing peace to the close of the day.

In her bedroom, Autumn Dove watched the same moon through the latticed window, her pajamas and underwear lying on the floor next to her bed. She rolled on her side and one foot slid up her leg and scratched an itch on her knee. A lizard crawled across the outside of the lattice and peered into the bedroom at her.

"Ly-boy . . . are you awake?"

"What do you want?—I was falling asleep."

"Do you remember your mother?"

"No—I don't remember anything about her."

"Do you think you could find her if you wanted?"

"I don't want to."

"But if you wanted to?"

"She disappeared and no one knows where she is. Someone said she went to live in Cambodia or Laos, that was before my grandmother died. She's never tried to find me."

"You don't have anyone?" she asked.

"No one except Vince and Nghia . . . and you." He sat up in bed and looked sleepily at her. "Why are you asking me all these question?"

"I don't have anyone either and I'm afraid of going back to Cho-Chan. I want to stay with the princess and Vince for the rest of my life, but I'm so bad I don't think they want me, even though Vince talks to me nice."

"You should try to be better," Ly-boy said. He was

watching the lizard on the window lattice.

"Do you remember that mean-looking man that Nghia would talk to in the lobby of the Khach-san Bong; the man you said was her boss?"

"You mean Kai?"

"I saw him today at the baseball field," Autumn said.

Ly-boy sat up straighter, wide awake, and looked across the darkness between their two beds. "You saw Kai—here in Da Nang?" he said with alarm.

"He stood behind the people watching the game, close to the trees where no one could see him, but I saw him."

"We will have to tell Nghia," Ly-boy said.

"I don't think we should—it will only worry her and she would run away and we would have to go back to Cho-Chan. I don't want to go back to Cho-Chan; do you?"

"No, but what will happen to Nghia if Kai knows she's here?"

"Maybe nothing—maybe he just wanted to see that she was all right, or he came to visit friends or relatives and just happened to be at the game by chance. He could be in Da Nang for any number of reasons other than to see Nghia."

"That's possible, but I still think we should tell her."

Autumn got out of bed and sat beside him.

"Put on your pajamas," he said.

"Don't look at me if it bothers you that I'm not wearing anything. Vince says we are like brother and sister, so it shouldn't matter."

"It's not right—you should be more modest."

"If we tell Nghia, that's the end of us; back to the streets, begging and sleeping in alleys. We shouldn't scare her away by telling her something that could turn out to be harmless; and it could cause Vince to get upset when he has enough to worry about flying his airplane and fighting the war."

Ly-boy looked dubious, but decided to go along with

Autumn Dove because the prospect of returning to the slums of Saigon was unthinkable for him. He laid on his back and watched the lizard until it crawled away, and then he fell asleep.

The days passed without event, and Vince surprised Nghia with a brand-new Honda motorcycle fully equipped with all the extras. They immediately went for a ride, Nghia driving and Battaglia holding onto her from behind, her cloud of hair whipping at his face.

"Not so fast, girl—wait until you get the hang of the machine. Aren't there any speed limits in Vietnam?"

"This not fast," she said and laughed happily. "I show you what fast."

Giving the Honda full throttle, the motorcycle leaped forward in a burst of speed and raced down the country road.

"Okay—okay, you've showed me what you can do, now slow down. You'd make a good jet jockey."

She let off on the throttle and returned to normal speed. "Very good motorcycle; thank you, Vince oi."

"You're welcome, but be careful. Lord, you're a wild thing."

They cruised down the road to a river and followed it for a few miles, passed through a hamlet and watched the water buffalo plowing the rice paddies, stopped at a hooch with coconuts piled outside and refreshed themselves with a drink of coconut milk, and ended up back at the house two hours later in time to watch the sun dip below the courtyard wall while they sipped green tea and nibbled at Nghia's homemade tamarind candy.

"I enjoyed the ride—gave me a chance to see the land close up that before I had only seen from the sky in my plane. The scenery was beautiful."

She took off her shoes and dangled her feet in the

pond. The fish swam up and curiously nibbled at her toes and she giggled at the strange sensation.

Sitting on the edge of the pond she looked lovely, and Vince undid her hair from behind and let it fall. Without asking he lifted the comb from her hand, and acting on a sudden impulse began running the comb through her hair in long determined strokes that gave him erotic pleasure.

"You like comb my hair?" she said, enjoying the attention.

"I never combed a woman's hair until I combed yours."

The long tresses freshly shampooed in coconut oil slid through the large comb and gave off a heady fragrance that smelled only of Nghia. Looking at the beautiful natural fall of her hair, the queenly shape of her head and the proud way she held it, the straightness of her back and the artful, smooth curve of her leg resting over the edge of the pool, the skin wet with droplets of water, created in him a strong desire for her that sprang insensibly from his primitive wells. She was pure poetry sitting by the reflecting pool and he had to drink of her pleasures or go mad.

Nghia, however, had other plans, and when he saw her chilly stare that looked through him, the look that combat Marines called the thousand-yard stare, he knew that he would have to wait.

"My cousin very sick . . . must go visit, take care her."

He tried not to look disappointed. "What's her problem?"

"Not know, find out tonight." She left him with his tea and tamarind, and walked to the courtyard gate, her candy walk exaggerated by the tightness of her ao dai. "Autumn Dove cook your dinner; she know what to do for you. I be late, no wait for me."

A callous fear tightened his chest, unexplained and

unjustified, but nevertheless there. "Be careful," he said.

Her arm was on the gate latch and she partly turned, her chin resting on her shoulder; she looked much like she had that day she watched him in the bar at the Khach-san Bong, making him feel like a zoo oddity while she danced with her date. "No worry . . . I be careful." Her smile didn't reassure him.

The whir of the Honda's starter was a lonely plea, and when he heard the cough of the engine and the crush of tires on the loose gravel, he wanted to chase after her and tell her not to go. The Honda accelerated, and with a roar, Nghia was gone.

He sat alone, teacup in one hand, the taste of tamarind on his tongue, and he listened to the drone of the motorcycle melting away in the emptiness of the night, and he felt terribly alone.

"Do you want to eat dinner with Ly-boy and me?" Autumn Dove said. She had been standing beside him and saw the sadness come over his face.

"No—I don't think so. I'm not hungry. You two go ahead and eat without me."

"I'll save something for you and put it on the stove to keep it warm."

"Thanks, Autumn . . . you're a good girl."

"It must hurt to love someone a lot." She walked into the house and looked back at him staring into his tea.

The hours passed and Nghia never returned. He sat down at the kitchen table and tried to eat some of the food that Autumn had left for him, but he had no appetite, the first bite catching in his throat like a ball of cotton.

Thoughts of the Khach-san Bong and the men with whom Nghia went upstairs tortured his mind, and he grew more nervous about her until mental exhaustion overcame him and he fell into a slumber.

In the early morning hours the throaty sound of the

Honda pulling up front woke him from a turbulent sleep. His first sensation was relief, which was soon replaced with suspicion and anger, and he was ashamed of himself.

The sound of her footsteps (light on the courtyard brick) and the dim cast of her shadow on the wall from the moon reminded him of how much he cared for her and that his mistrust and fear were infantile. The bedroom panel slid open and she slipped out of her shoes, careful not to disturb him, and glided across the room to the bed. Within seconds her clothes were on the floor and her warm body was against his, and he didn't care that she smelled of cigarette smoke or where she had been or what she had been doing because now she was home and she was his.

That night he dreamt that he flew his F-4 into the bar at the Khach-san Bong with Chi in the backseat as his RIO. The cockpit canopy lifted and he helped Chi down to the dance floor and he danced a slow number with her, all the while looking over his shoulder at a woman with no eyes who had come in the door riding a flying carpet. On closer inspection he discovered that the flying carpet was actually the woman's hair that hung all the way to the floor and that the white stripes on it were rows of lice eggs. She was eating out of a gallon can of honey made from the nectar of peony flower.

A patch of grass growing in the center of the dance floor seemed to be the right place to have lunch, so Vince brought the picnic basket from the jet and Chi spread the food out on a checkered cloth and they sat down with the woman with no eyes and ate.

While he chewed on a haunch of roasted dog he combed the lice eggs from the woman's hair as she listened to the five-piece band playing a ballad from a large ornate bed hanging from the ceiling. Without warning she flew up to the ceiling on her hair and fornicated with the band, each member taking his turn with her.

The next evening after Vince had come home from the base and was sitting on the courtyard deck drinking a 33 beer, Nghia announced that her cousin was worse and that she would be spending every night with her for a while.

"How long will this last?" he said.

"Doctor say until she get well—take long time. My aunt take care her day, I take care night. Vietnamese way."

And that was final, with no further explanation. Once Nghia made up her mind it was useless to try and persuade her otherwise.

The following days passed with Nghia showing no less affection for Vince but spending considerably less time with him and the kids. She was always waiting with a big meal when he came home from the base and would spend an hour with him over tea before she climbed on the Honda and dissolved from his life until dawn when he would feel her honey-smooth body slip between the sheets and she once again performed her magic and brought him back to life.

Chapter 15

Autumn Dove rolled another cha gio and placed it in the hot peanut oil. "I saw him again," she said and looked through the open door to be sure Vince was out of earshot.

Ly-boy picked up the platter of spring rolls already cooked and carried it to the table. "I saw him too," he said calmly.

Autumn looked up with surprise. "Why didn't you tell me?"

"You didn't tell me either," Ly-boy said.

"I didn't want to get you excited—remember what we agreed to?"

"I remember, but I didn't think it was a good idea."

"Where did you see him?" Autumn Dove said.

"Sitting in a car down the street. Where did you see him?"

"Watching Nghia when we were at the market."

Ly-boy was quiet for a while, then he said, "I want to tell Vince."

"Go ahead and tell him—that will fix us right away. Sounds to me like you're begging to go back to Cho-Chan. We had an agreement, remember?" She turned the cha gio in the wok with a pair of cooking chopsticks, the long kind, and looked out at Vince seated in his usual rattan chair in the courtyard, drinking a 33 beer. "That poor man has enough trouble without giving him another headache to deal with. He worries a lot about Nghia, you know, now that she's gone at night."

"I think he's troubled because he thinks she's gone back to being a tiger girl. It does look suspicious with Kai showing up at the same time Nghia began going out."

"The princess would never be a tiger girl again; she's taking care of her sick cousin like she said."

"Shhh . . . she's coming," Ly-boy said.

Her hair put up high on her head and held in place by two large pearl-inlaid combs, Nghia walked into the kitchen, looking overdressed for a visit to her cousin's sickbed. She asked for Vince and they pointed to the courtyard.

The sun had gone down and a purple-blue light from the South China Sea colored the sky. The evening was warm and Vince sat by himself, wearing a loose cotton shirt that Nghia had bought for him on impulse. They had been walking by a shop in Da Nang City and Battaglia mentioned his proclivity for silk shirts of the style that were displayed in one of the shops; so Nghia, without saying another word, had purchased the most expensive one for him. She was always buying him things and it worried him because he knew that her savings were not large, and with the expense of the house rent they must be close to exhausted by now.

"Very nice tonight," she said to Vince and shook the empty beer bottle. "You want me get you another beer?"

She was standing at his side and a little behind so that he had to turn to see how she was dressed. As usual when she went out these nights, she was wearing one of her better ao dais and her good jade jewelry.

"How's your cousin?"

"Same same," she said and quickly changed the subject to his duties at the base. "You fly today?" she asked.

265

"Just a routine training flight—orientation for a new RIO."

"How your colonel?"

"Cleanhead?—getting in everyone's way and complaining how stupid Washington is for believing Ho Chi Minh is serious about peace talks."

"Communist never quit," she said. "They fight until last soldier fall . . . never talk talk."

The small talk continued for a few minutes, then her eyes locked on him in that bold gaze of hers and he knew that something was on her mind. Her pouting red lips wrinkled and she smoothed a strand of hair back in place on the back of her neck. He liked her hair pulled up like it was tonight, showing off her elegant neck and natural grace.

The bold look in her eyes faded to the thousand-yard stare, and if she planned to reveal something important to him the inclination was now gone. Battaglia felt the loss go through him as if he had just been emptied of a long-waited-for promise.

"I go now—cousin wait."

"Nghia, can't you stay for a few minutes more?" If he could delay her a while she might tell him what it was that was on her mind. "Just a cup of tea together. I miss you a great deal when you're gone."

She picked up his hand and held it to her lips for a long time, something she had never done before. "I go now," she said. "Cousin wait."

Battaglia listened to the lonely sound of Nghia's motorcycle starting, and was waiting for the crunch of the tires on the loose gravel when Ly-boy appeared at the door.

"Vince," he said in a troubled voice.

"Shut up," Autumn Dove said, trying to cover his mouth with her hand.

Vince stood and turned around, sensing danger.

"We have to tell him—it's wrong for us to keep quiet," Ly-boy said as he wrenched free from Autumn.

The bottom of Battaglia's stomach dropped out like he had hit an air pocket. The Honda's engine revved and Nghia was gone down the street.

"Kai is in Da Nang and—"

He didn't get any more out—Autumn Dove hit him square in the back with her doubled-up fist and sent him sprawling out the door, his crutch flying out from under him.

Battaglia picked up Ly-boy in his arms and ran out the courtyard gate, dropped the boy onto the buddy-seat, fired up the Yamaha, and was onto the street in time to see Nghia turning the corner. Accelerating hard he reached the corner and almost went down in the turn, but righted the bike in time and sped after Nghia, staying far enough behind so that she wouldn't recognize him if she turned around. Ly-boy held tight behind Vince.

Once a whore, always a whore, he thought to himself. He braced against the deep pain that cut him like a knife; he couldn't have expected anything less from this girl who all her life had known nothing but moral corruption and who had made her living selling her flesh in one of the vilest cesspools of Asia. He had been quick to believe her and not Kai. How wrong he had been. Sick cousin—ha! *The pig always returns to the sty to roll in the mud.*

He followed her through the streets (she was in the main part of the city now) and wound in and out of the crowded buses, the bicycles and cyclos, and he turned corners, paying no attention where she was leading him and thinking only of what a fool he had been and what pleasure he would take in strangling her.

Why am I following her? . . . The harm has already been done . . . do I want to punish myself? . . . Is that it? Several times he almost turned off and returned with Ly-boy to the house, but a perverted desire to see her

267

debauching herself, to catch a glimpse of her lovers, maybe to see her in the evil act itself, kept him on her trail like a hound panting to tree its quarry.

Up ahead, the Honda slowed and turned into the parking lot of the fashionable, palm-lined Dai Duong Hotel. Battaglia followed her in and parked between several cars that shielded him from view.

He watched Nghia dismount and lock the Honda, straighten her ao dai, and tuck in the loose hair that had blown free in the ride over. She looked at herself in the handlebar mirror on the motorcycle and decided that her lipstick was on straight (she used only a touch) and walked up the hotel steps to the entrance. The doorman recognized her, smiled, and opened the door for her.

As soon as the door closed behind Nghia, Battaglia walked out around the cars and started after her. Abruptly he stopped and ducked behind a car; in front of him a taxi was parked at the curb and Kai was getting out. The pimp followed Nghia inside and a great rage exploded in Vince's head.

He charged up the steps and into the hotel, but both Nghia and Kai had vanished. He and Ly-boy checked the lobby, the dining room, and lounge (he even checked the men's toilet for Kai), but neither of them could be found. *Nghia was gone directly upstairs to meet her customer for the night*, he concluded. *If I hang around downstairs long enough, Kai will eventually show up and I'll force him to reveal the room in which she is entertaining and have a showdown.*

After standing around the fringes of the lobby without Kai showing, Vince decided to wait in the lounge, convinced that Kai would eventually get thirsty. He put Ly-boy on guard in the lobby and took an inconspicuous table located on the opposite side from the entrance, close to the bandstand where he would be able to see Kai when he came in.

"*Ong uong gi?*" What are you drinking? the waitress asked him in a bored voice, her attention on the band setting up and her boyfriend, the guitar player who was plugging in his amplifier.

Vince's eyes were not yet used to the dim light in the bar and he hadn't noticed the waitress come to his table. Hearing her voice he looked up at her. "What was that?"

She quickly turned, surprised at hearing English, "I'm sorry," she said. "I thought you were Vietnamese."

He ordered a lime ricky, not so much because he liked them but because they reminded him of Ruthie, and right now he very much wanted to be reminded of her.

Her curiosity aroused at a lone American being in the hotel, the waitress delayed at his table. "Shall I hold your order until your friend arrives?" she said and pointed to the empty chair across from him.

"I'm alone tonight," he said.

"Oh . . . how sad."

"Yes, isn't it." He smiled and said, "There's a girl in one of your rooms that should be sitting here with me, but she's conducting some prearranged business that will detain her for the rest of the night."

He didn't know if she got the hint, but she didn't look stupid, and when she left to get his drink he thought that she exaggerated her wiggle for his benefit.

The band played its first number, a slow dreamy instrumental, typically sad and Vietnamese, that served only to deepen Vince's melancholy and remind him that something akin to his spleen or liver had been ripped out of him.

From the front the waitress's wiggle wasn't so pronounced and when she put the lime ricky down on the table he noticed that she had long legs like Nghia's, but not nearly as provocative.

"That's the first order I've ever taken for a lime ricky."

269

"It's a romantic drink," he said.

"Remind you of someone back home?" she smiled and sucked her thumb.

"You're only a kid—how would you know about things like that?" he said sarcastically, not in the mood for conversation.

"We have a new singer," she said, trying to be friendly. "She's only been here about a week and she's very good. She's from Saigon."

"Good for her." He drank his lime ricky and looked away.

The girl left and Battaglia saw that she had lost her wiggle; he smiled belligerently to himself and watched the dancers, frequently shifting his look to the lounge's entrance and expecting Kai to walk in at any time.

The band was playing a tango for its next number and a long-haired girl floated by his table, her head lying on her partner's shoulder and her slender body moving expertly to the Latin beat. Vince became absorbed by the thought that he had never taken Nghia dancing, and right then he wanted her in his arms dancing alongside the girl with the slender body.

The waitress walked by his table and saw his empty glass. "Another lime ricky?" she said.

He was absorbed in his thoughts of dancing with Nghia and didn't answer her.

She pushed him on the shoulder and pointed to the glass. "Another?"

"Bring me a beer this time."

"A Thirty-three?"

He nodded and went back to his thoughts, keeping his eyes on the entrance.

Suddenly there was a drumroll, and center stage lit up with a spotlight to the applause of the audience. Vince glanced up, annoyed, then returned to watching the door. The dancers had all returned to their seats and the

270

full house waited expectantly. The tinkle of glasses and shuffling of chairs had ceased, and conversation had dropped to a whisper as the house lights dimmed. The band began softly and then the most remarkable fluid voice that Vince had ever heard, a voice as smooth and sweet as warm honey that penetrated to the quick. The song was a narrative poem of folk origin and consisted of simple stanzas and a recurrent refrain. It was a slow, romantic popular song beautifully performed and the audience showed its appreciation. He looked up at the stage and his heart stopped. Nghia was standing in front of the microphone.

He sat with his hands flat on the table, the beer between his hands, not yet fully accepting that the girl with the rich contralto voice singing on the bandstand was Nghia. She was wearing the same ao dai she wore when leaving the house, but her hair was no longer swept up exposing her neck; it was brushed out and fell heavily on her shoulders and rippled down her back in long tails.

All eyes in the room were focused on her, and by the look on the faces at the tables she had transformed the lounge into a romantic castle of dreams. For the time being he had forgotten his suspicions and listened with everyone else to her hypnotic singing that settled on him like the soft blanket of sleep that comes when overpowered by exhaustion.

Her high Annamese cheekbones were exaggerated by the stage lights and her long elliptical black eyes looked out over the tables to a point in the center of the room, seldom changing focus.

Before Nghia finished her song, Kai appeared and was shown to a seat at a front table. The blood drained from Nghia's face when she saw him and she finished the last bars of her song visibly shaken. She left the stage and didn't reappear until the audience began calling for her, and even then it was apparent to Battaglia that she was

271

struggling for control.

For his part, Kai remained as stoic as a piece of common granite, ordering a garish Singapore sling and insisting on sipping it from a straw.

Nghia finished her numbers and was called back for an encore but did not reappear, to the disappointment of the customers. Battaglia looked at Kai's table. He was gone.

Vince finished his beer, got Ly-boy, and looked for the backstage entrance. Searching for a few minutes he located a hall that led to short stairs that came up to an open door. He entered the door and stood in an area backstage filled with ropes hanging from the ceiling, electrical wall panels, music stands, instrument cases, stacked tables and chairs, and a variety of equipment.

Along the far wall were dressing rooms, one of which had light coming from the partially open door. As Vince and Ly-boy approached the room they heard voices and stopped. Kai and Nghia were talking in Vietnamese. Battaglia asked Ly-boy to interpret.

"*Anh tuong la em da hieu, Nghia,*" I thought I made it clear to you, Nghia.

"*Dieu nay that kho, rat kho, em can thoi gian,*" it is difficult, very difficult; I need time.

"*Anh da cho em thoi gian, hai nguoi khach rat giau, ho khong kien nahan nha,*" I've given you enough time. I have two good paying customers waiting and they have become impatient.

There was a long pause, then Nghia said, "*Em khong the lam,*" I can't do it.

"*Em khong can mang song cua Vince Battaglia ja cac con em,*" apparently you don't value the lives of Vince Battaglia and the children.

"*Hay la em tro lai Cho-Chan,*" maybe if I go back to Cho-Chan.

"*Neu em chiu khach o Cho-Chan thi hoi khac,*" it makes little difference to me if you service my customers in

Cho-Chan or Da Nang.

Nghia began crying. *"Van anh hay de em tu do, day la dip dhy nhat trong doi de em song hanh phuc voi vince va cac con,"* please give me my freedom, I beg you. I have a chance at a new life with Vince and the children.

"Nuoc mat khong mang tien cho em," spare me the tears; there's no money in tears.

"Anh co the hoi quan ly khach san them tien va giu lay cho anh het," maybe if I ask the hotel manager he will pay me more for singing. I'll give you that too.

"Tien hat cua em khong du cho anh xai, neu co them cung chi la mot so it so voi tien em di khach," what you are making now is not enough to pay my bills, and anything additional will be only a pittance compared to what you can make for me as a prostitute.

"Em khong con su lua chon khac phai khong?" I have no other choice?

"Khong," none.

Nghia stopped crying. *"Tem theo anh toi Khach-san Bong. Chung toi co the di ngay bay gio khong?"* I will go back to the Khach-san Bong with you. Can we leave immediately?—I don't wish to go back to the house.

Vince stepped into the room. "You're not going anywhere with this slime, Nghia."

The look on her face when she saw Vince was classic. Her hand went to her open mouth, her chin dropped, and her eyes, naturally long and tear-shaped, became as round as plates. "Why you here?" she cried, struck with sudden wonder.

Kai's hand went to the inside of his jacket, but Vince's hand was quicker and he clamped Kai's wrist in an iron grip. "Not this time." He relieved Kai of his gun and pointed it into his nose.

"It no good you come," Nghia said in anguish.

"Go home with Ly-boy," Vince said. "I'll be along shortly after I take care of Kai."

She pulled at his shirt while Kai stared cross-eyed at the muzzle of his own gun jammed into his face.

"I said go home," Vince ordered and pulled her hand away from his shirt.

"Please—I go back Cho-Chan, take children—no other way. Kai find me again kill us all. It wrong me come Da Nang, look for you; I bring you big trouble. I go back Saigon . . . you go back Marines . . . we forget everything." She was crying again. "No more be together—no good—no good; I just dirty ginger cookie, no good for anything but be dirty ginger cookie.

"All I have to do is pull the trigger and that'll put him out of business; he can't harm us then."

"No good," she pleaded. "He have plenty friends, they find you, find me. No good—no good." She pulled at his arm. "Let him go—let me go. Please, it best way."

"I can't, Nghia . . . you've become too much a part of me," he said, gritting his teeth and breaking out in a sweat. He fought Nghia's hold on his arm.

Kai remained paralyzed and wide-eyed, afraid the gun would go off.

"I love you, always I love you, never forget you, but no good we stay together. I go back live my life, you live your life . . . best you listen me."

"There must be another way. Give me some time—I'll think of something—I just need some time." He slumped into a chair and mumbled, "There must be something we can do."

Kai smiled.

"I bad luck for you, Vince. You forget Nghia, forget children . . . better this way. I no good for you, forget Nghia—please, you forget." She kissed him, tenderly.

The gun hung from his hand, pointed at the floor, and Ly-boy stood in the doorway, crying. Nghia took Ly-boy by the arm and led him away, leaving Battaglia staring at the floor, numb and cold with the loneliness that had become his constant companion.

Vince moved back on base and two days later the North Vietnamese struck in full force as Cleanhead had predicted, racing down the Ho Chi Minh Trail from Ban Dau and crossing over from Laos to hit the Marines in the highlands and streaming in from Cambodia to attack the delta.

Battaglia, upon hearing the news of the communist breakout, retreated into himself to find the reserves that he needed to endure the future; and that is how he saw the coming weeks, as an endurance, a contest to see if he could beat his fear and loneliness.

Now that Nghia had gone back to Saigon, Vince became restless and irritable, shunning companions and companionship, seeking solitude, and being acutely aware of his loneliness. His world had been laid waste with the departure of Nghia and the children, and the gloom of his separation from them brought back thoughts of desertion.

To assuage the bitterness of separation and the creeping, insidious fear that time had run out and he must face the guns, he sought escape in the rawness of warm female flesh.

The close, narrow streets of Da Nang City, smelling of urine and rotting garbage, provided the natural habitation for the social outcasts he was searching for. The sun went down and the women came out of their holes from beneath the roads and stood in the doorways, recesses, and alleys, some to get out of the drizzling rain, others to hide their old sagging faces from the yellow light of the street.

Here the war was fighting off hunger, staying dry, struggling against disease, and finding a place to sleep at night. Many of the women were young and pretty, most

275

were not; all offered fantasy, entertainment, and temporary freedom from unpleasant realities.

The rain was slow and light, only dampening the oily street. A neon sign, twisted into Vietnamese words, shed a diffused glow on a small brown face:

"Hello, mister; what's your name?"

"Vince."

"Want me make you happy, Mr. Vince?"

The face was smooth, unwrinkled, and very young. He walked on.

"Looking for a good time?" came another voice.

"Maybe."

"I make your eyes fall out with pleasure."

The face was drawn back into the brick alcove and the heavy makeup ineffectually concealed falling flesh.

Farther down the street a girl leaned against a wall, her long hair and comely legs reminding him of Nghia, and he thought he would take her and make-believe. The rain came down in fine drops and she said nothing, only arched her torso toward him and spread her lips in what she thought was a smile.

He turned the corner and didn't look back when she questioned the legitimacy of his birth.

Half a block away a bar loomed out of the drizzle, dark and brooding, and he saw the words on the sign and the strange Viet marks connoting the cluster of sounds and tones that meant desire or lust, and he suddenly hated everything Vietnamese, the cheap sloe-eyed women, the strange pho soup and cha gio, the pungent nuoc mam fish sauce smells, the sleazy bars and pits of debauchery like Cho-Chan, the war-torn bodies of beggars, the orphaned and diseased . . .

He stopped in the doorway of a shop that smelled of incense and watched old women and men in conical straw hats, carrying baskets of longan and breadfruit supported by a bamboo pole laid across their backs, trot through the rotting cabbage leaves and gray water in the gutter.

He was weary of Vietnam and mortified by its pain, and he longed for Wichita where everything was familiar and safe, where there was Ruthie with her short curled hair and blue eyes and white skin, and the only sound resembling war was on the Fourth of July or from an occasional backfire from a car.

"Lonely, Marine?"

Her eyes had a lovely tilt, slanting downward.

"I can take away all the shit for you."

Low and alluring, her voice was comforting and he heard the wind in the cottonwoods and he smelled the harvest.

"I will make you forget the war and you can talk to me about home. Where you from, Marine? New York, L.A.?"

"Wichita."

"Sure, I know that place." She pulled a cigarette from between her breasts. "Got a light?"

"I didn't think Viet women smoked."

"My father was French."

"Suit yourself."

"I won't smoke . . . for you."

The incense was strong, so was her perfume. Ruthie always smelled good, like an American girl, light and flowery, the way a blonde was supposed to smell.

The black hair and black eyes dropped the cigarette back between the bosoms and the tilted orbs contemplated his face with a hidden scorn.

The rain ran from the tile roof of the shop and puddled in the street. He heard the cottonwood-lined creek running beside the school path and he saw Ruthie skinny-dipping next to the big rocks at the secret hiding place. The water was clear and he could see the pebbles on the bottom where he would dive and come up with a handful of sand to impress Ruthie. It was there in the secret hiding place, skinny-dipping with Ruthie, that he decided he was going to be a jet fighter pilot.

He had heard the scream of their engines and climbed a cottonwood to see what the noise was. A mock dogfight involving two F-86 Sabrejets was in progress over the wheatfields. They would climb high into the deep blue midwest sky, their contrails tracing their twists and turns, and then fight their way down to treetop level, thundering across the fields right in front of him perched in the cottonwood.

When the dogfight had ended, and the planes joined up and flew away, Vince watched them until they became specks and vanished into a pinhole in the sky; and he knew he had to fly one of those airplanes.

Through the years he nurtured his ambition, and when the Navy pilots came on campus to recruit he signed up in the reserves, and upon graduation from college he was given the choice of Navy or Marine air, and opted for the Marines because his father had been a Marine and Vince had been enthralled by the stories his father told about the Marine pilots that flew at Tarawa and Iwo, who flew so close to the deck that an infantryman lying in his foxhole could reach up and touch the planes' bellies.

Vince received his orders for officer candidate school, Quantico, Virginia. He graduated as a second lieutenant and after a two-week leave home, where Ruthie and his family and friends decided he was the greatest thing since ice cream, he reported to Pensacola for flight training. He won his wings and made jets, completed his active duty and returned to Kansas to become a successful business consultant and to fly as a weekend warrior with a reserve unit. He settled into his comfortable life, was making lots of money, became active in the Jaycees, vacationed in the Bahamas and Cozumel, and was approached by the Republican party to consider running for the state legislature in a few years. He and Ruthie decided to marry. Then came Vietnam and everything changed.

He moved out of the doorway to get away from the cheap perfume and smell of incense, and started across the street for the bar.

"Hey—where you going?"

He ignored the street girl and walked around a bicycle.

She caught up with him and pulled his shirt-sleeve. "Why you brush me off like that?"

He continued to ignore her and went into the bar. She followed him inside and was stopped by a tall Viet who spoke to her roughly and pushed her back into the street.

Something came over Battaglia when he saw the girl being roughed up; maybe he felt like an outcast himself and identified with her. Whatever it was, he angered, and went back to the door.

The Viet bouncer had his hand in the air to slap the girl. Vince caught the hand in midair and twisted the man's arm around behind him and into a half-cobra, slamming his head into the wall. He went down, out cold.

The girl looked in wonder at Battaglia. Her eyebrows were arched high and her jaw had fallen. "Can I come in with you?" she said, amazed.

"Suit yourself."

She followed him in, cautiously, and sat next to him at the bar. "What's your name?" she asked timidly.

He didn't answer her. "I'll have a Thirty-three," he said to the bartender, a small man with glasses.

"Can I have a drink?" she said.

He jerked his thumb at her for the benefit of the bartender. The bartender looked at her impatiently when she spoke to him in English rather than in Vietnamese.

"I'll have a Thirty-three also," she said. "Do I have to pay for my own?" she asked Vince.

He slapped the piasters on the bartop, enough to cover both beers, and turned away.

On a small platform raised a foot off the dance floor, a

girl accompanied by a small combo was singing a poor imitation of Peggy Lee. Her eyes were heavily made-up and her hair hung loose and straight. Her bored look was only exceeded by that of two enlisted Marines on the dance floor who were entwined around bar girls.

The one table that was occupied had a Marine lying with his head in a puddle of spilled beer, and next to him a bar girl sat staring at the wall, her miniskirt wet from the beer draining over the edge of the table.

The men on the dance floor moved their feet a few inches at a time, generally turning in a circle and molded tightly to the girls. The drummer slapped at the snare like he was swatting a fly, and when the foot pedal came down on the base drum, the torn skin gave off a raspy noise like there were seeds rattling around inside.

The bouncer lay on his back unattended, the back of his head and neck jammed against the door, and his chin pressed against his chest. A few feet from him a 33 beer bottled rolled off an empty table and bounced once on the floor without breaking, coming to rest with the mouth of the bottle pointed at a scurrying cockroach.

The inside of the barroom was illuminated by two low-wattage light bulbs painted red and hanging from the ceiling, one over the bar and the other over the bandstand.

The entire scene could be described as a chronic deficiency disease marked by skin eruptions and digestive and nervous disturbances in need of a massive dosage of penicillin to halt a spread of infection.

"Want to dance?" the street girl said.

Battaglia refused to pay attention to her, staring straight ahead at his image in the mirror behind the bar.

She poked a finger into his shoulder blade. "I want to dance."

He drank his beer and disregarded her.

She slipped off the barstool and walked around to the

other side of him where she had more room, and began to rub up against his side like a cat scratching its back.

He gave her a quick look, irritated but feeling her warmth and softness through his clothing, and he remembered how Nghia felt when he held her close.

On the dance floor she was a temptress, and her young firm body, well-trained to the likes of men, moved in the right places and in the right way so that Vince, well-lubricated with beer, began to respond in the way she knew he would once she was allowed to practice her art.

Her tilted black eyes regarded him and they smiled, knowing that this man would be different from the slobbering fools who normally shared her bed, and she would take pleasure in draining the pain and loneliness out of him though she would only have him for a few hours.

His hand was holding to the tail of her hair like it was a life rope and she liked it. He danced stiffly.

"What's your name?" she said.

"Vince."

"I'm Trang."

He danced, holding to her hair, not wanting to know her name.

"I will be good for you." She felt his hand tight on her hair and she knew his loneliness was big. "How much time do we have?"

"Until tomorrow morning."

"Early?" she asked.

"While you sleep I will be flying against the guns."

Ah, she thought, *he is afraid as well as lonely. I will be the best I can be tonight, better than I have been to any man, and he will remember me with a big heart; and many years from now when he is old he will think back to his youth, like the old do, and he will recall how I helped him fly against the guns.*

He danced the way the other dancers did, a few inches

281

at a time, rotating in a circle, slow and moving his body without regard to his feet. The music was unnecessary.

The smell of stale beer and fish sauce was a required part of the total atmosphere and Vince no longer cared about it, for without it the bar would be too clean and his presence objectionable. He welcomed the debauchery, the offensive smells, the hopelessness and the debased people.

The girl didn't matter to him either. He didn't care what she looked like; she was warm and moved and wanted to be his friend. Her perfume was cheap and smelled like bitter melon, and her skin was coarse and oily. Her hair felt dry between his fingers and needed brushing.

Though she was small (the top of her head reached only to his shoulders) and thin, her breasts were large and motherly against him, and her legs firm and pleasing pressed next to his. Her youth showed in her eyes, bright and not yet dulled by the poverty of years, and they looked at him with much the same craving that he had for her.

"I am not very old," she said, wanting to be attractive to him.

He didn't care how old she was. She was here and she fit in with the atmosphere of the bar and suited his mood. That was all that was important about her.

"I went to school and studied English." She wanted to impress him.

He looked down at her upturned face while they shuffled around in their circle, her legs and breasts pushed into him. Her nose was quite flat with no bridge and she had a large blackhead growing in the corner where the skin above the lip meets the nose. He squeezed it with a thumb and forefinger. She winced but said nothing, looking up at him as if something wondrous were happening.

"I need someone to love," she said. "Will you be my regular boyfriend?"

He unexpectedly felt compassion for the girl, and he looked into her misty eyes and saw how very young she really was.

"You're just a baby," he said, really seeing her for the first time.

He pressed harder on the blackhead and it slowly rose out of the skin and snaked onto his fingernail, and all the while the girl blinked at him in astonishment as if a miracle were taking place, her black tilted eyes wet with admiration.

"I have one in my ear too," she said.

"I'll take that out later," he said. He worked his fingertips over her oily face and then took out his handkerchief and wiped her skin dry. "I'll get you some skin ointment at the PX."

"Will you be my regular boyfriend?" she asked again.

"For tonight I will be your boyfriend. In the morning I must fly against the guns and I won't be coming back. You can make-believe that I have been your boyfriend for a long time."

"Will you tell me about the guns when we are in bed so I can fly there with you when you leave me?"

"Maybe."

They stood in one spot, her flat, hard belly quivering against him, both arms wrapped around his waist, hugging him close like he was a sack of rice. The music had stopped and the singer picked her nose, waiting for the combo to start the next tune. Vince and the other dancers paid no attention that the music had stopped. The bodies continued in a dragging, sliding motion over the floor.

"What did you say your name was?"

"Trang."

The band began another sad song and the singer with the heavily painted eyes and white lipstick moaned into the microphone. It didn't matter how well she sang; no one cared. She was part of the atmosphere.

"How long have you been working the streets?"

"Six months."

"What did you do before that?"

"I was in school."

The bouncer had revived and was sitting at the end of the bar with his head buried in his arms. The bartender was holding a bar towel packed with ice on the back of his neck. The Marine at the table raised his head a few inches out of the beer, saw the bar girl sitting beside him, smiled, and fell back into the beer.

Vince noticed that the girl, Trang, lurched to one side while she danced, something he had paid no attention to until now. He looked down at her leg and she tried to hide it behind the other one.

"What's the matter with your leg?" He would not have asked such an insensitive question if she had been someone else.

Her eyes showed shame and he was sorry that he had asked. The shame turned to hate and her face darkened. Unbalanced with her leg held behind her, she toppled and he grabbed her by the arm.

"I don't give a damn about your leg," he said.

She scrutinized him through narrowed eyes, hurt that he had discovered her handicap, and became stubbornly defensive, as social outcasts are prone, at the insinuation that she was less a human being than others. She limped away from him and sat down at a table in the back of the room, in the shadows.

One of the girls went to the bouncer and complained that Trang didn't belong in the bar and that she was taking business away from her and the other bar girls. The bouncer looked at Vince then waved the girl off,

284

moving the ice pack off the back of his neck to his head.

The girl walked through the empty tables to where Trang sat alone, and shouted curses at her and told her to get out. Trang listened to the abuses with arms folded, then reached up to pull the bar girl's hair, but she was frail and much smaller than the bar girl and was slapped and kicked to the floor.

No one became concerned; the combo continued to play, and the singer moaned on, the dancers dragged their feet and rubbed their bodies together, and the Marine slept with his head in the pool of beer. Vince shook his head and went back to the bar.

The street girl picked herself up off the floor and limped to the door, her lip bleeding down her chin. The bar girl followed her to the door, screaming obscenities at her and pulling her hair. She kicked her hard in the butt and sent her sprawling out into the rain.

Vince frowned and turned back to his unfinished beer.

The girl lay in the gutter until her strength returned. She stood for a minute, shaking, and hobbled across the street, a Renault honking at her to get out of the way and swerving to avoid hitting her.

Two Air Force sergeants walked into the bar and stood just inside the door, getting their bearings. Before they could decide to leave, the girl at the table with the passed-out Marine wiggled over in her tight miniskirt and asked them to buy her a drink. They looked her over in the dim light and thought she might be worth it, so followed her to a table. They were joined by the girl who had beat up the street girl.

Finishing his beer, Vince got off the barstool and started for the door. A cockroach jerked across the floor in front of him. He stopped at the end of the bar and put his hand on the bouncer's shoulder. "Sorry about that," he said.

The man nodded without meeting Battaglia's eyes.

Vince squashed the cockroach with his shoe and walked out of the bar, closing the door on the anemic singer making another attempt at a Peggy Lee torch song.

He walked a half-block down the street and found the street girl, Trang, in a dark doorway next to a refuse-strewn alley. She turned away, acting like she hadn't been watching for him. Her cotton pajamas were wet from the rain and she was soaked to the skin. Her lip was still bleeding and he saw that her face was scratched and her forehead bruised where it had hit the street pavement.

He cleaned the blood from her face with his handkerchief, and her tears mingled with the rainwater on her cheeks. She wasn't wearing a bra or underpants and the thin, wet cotton of her pajamas was pasted to her privates, revealing the taut healthy breasts and hairless pubic area.

"Do you have a place here we can go?" he said.

She pointed down the street to the bend where the buildings and shops ended and a loose line of hovels wound down to the bottom lands. He shuddered at the sight and took her hand in the dark.

On the way he stopped at a shop and bought her a candy bar. He also bought an umbrella and some other things that he would need.

They came to the bend and left the paved street that continued on to the sea. The dirt path had become a river of muddy water running down to the bottoms, and along the side of the path, boards and scrap tin had been laid to walk on.

Holding the street girl's hand, Vince negotiated the makeshift walk until he came to a washout. He gave her the umbrella to hold and carried her piggyback to the other side.

On the edge of a banana grove stood a one-room hovel

constructed of discarded cement blocks and stone. The roof was built from corrugated tin and palm thatch. There was no door, only an opening through which the rain was blowing.

She lit an oil lamp hanging from a wire and unrolled a palm mat tied over the door so that it acted as a barrier to the rain.

The only thing of value in the tiny house was the bed, a well-constructed affair made from jungle mahogany and fitted with an American-made mattress and box springs, the tools of her trade. She saw him looking doubtfully at the bed so she pulled back the worn Chinese bedspread to show him the clean, white linen sheets underneath.

She looked at him for approval—her wet pajamas stuck to her skin, her hair hanging down in strings around her shoulders—and smiled weakly. Her lip and scratches were bleeding again and the bruise on her forehead had turned a yellowish blue.

From the bag of things he'd bought at the shop, he took a bar of soap and held back the mat hanging over the door opening. "Come outside for a few minutes."

While she held the umbrella to the rain, he skinned the pajamas from her and soaped her down, washing her thoroughly, giving her orifices proper attention and scrubbing her hair good. She stood before him, uncomplaining at the bath he was giving her, and there was again wonder in her eyes. She did, however, express annoyance when he attempted to wash her crippled leg, and she pushed him away.

He made her stand in the rain until all the soap had been rinsed away and then he brought her inside and toweled her dry. He dressed her in the new pajamas he had bought and sat her on the bed and looked closely at her face. Her lip had puffed and a knot had grown on her forehead. "Not too bad," he said, and squeezed some

287

first-aid cream on his finger and rubbed it over the cuts and bruises.

"Are you going to take the blackhead out of my ear?" she asked. She rolled over on her side, pulled the hair back from her ear, and waited.

"Do you have any hairpins?" He moved the kerosene lantern closer.

"Look inside the box on the table."

Inside the shoe box was a hairbrush, needle and thread, pins, a toothbrush, a small bottle of cheap perfume, and a ballpoint pen that didn't work. A few hairpins were scattered in the bottom of the box with the remaining odds and ends.

The largest blackhead he had ever seen was lodged in a difficult-to-get-at fold in her ear and he used the curved ends of two hairpins to apply pressure since his fingers could not reach it. However, the blackhead had been in her ear so long that the top had oxidized into a tight crust and it wouldn't budge.

Going back to the box he found a needle and used it to separate the edge of the oxidized surface from the skin, loosening the blackhead. Trang lay quiet, eyes closed, like a dog being scratched, while Vince worked on her ear.

The separation of surfaces completed, he pressed down around the encrustation and the blackhead easily came out. It was an eighth of an inch wide and about the same length, and left a large hole in her ear. He showed it to her.

"*Choi oi!*" my goodness! she said.

He looked around the hovel and felt an unusual sense of comfort in the midst of its poverty. The rain pinging on the tin roof had a kind of musical quality, and the flickering kerosene lamp hanging from the ceiling produced soft shadows and a consoling glow that brought the closeness of the room even closer so that the feeling created was that of being encased in a moth's warm cocoon.

She lay on her side in the middle of the bed, her legs pulled up in the fetal position, a finger crooked in her mouth, looking like a baby in a crib. She rubbed her hand over the soft cotton material of her new pajamas and she wanted him to love her.

Chapter 16

"Are you going to tell me about the guns?"

"No," he said. "Not now."

The rain pinging on the corrugated tin roof collected in the folds of the metal and dripped off the edge and made splashing sounds like tiny waterfalls.

Her hairbrush was old and the bristles were worn down to almost nothing, those that remained. The handle was made from wood and the paint had long ago chipped away.

"I'm going to brush your hair now."

He put her on his lap, facing him so he could study her face. At the moment, that was important to him; he didn't know exactly why, but maybe it was because she was the last woman he would see and he wanted to remember what she looked like. Nghia had left him and was in Saigon, her face dim in his memory and far away. The street girl was here and he was in her warm cave and she was real and he could touch her. That was important and there was nothing more to it than that.

He pulled the brush through her hair slowly, his face only a foot away from hers, and he studied her tilted black eyes that looked back at him in that wondering way she had, bewildered by his attention. Her genitals were wet and she was embarrassed.

The pimples were distracting and he became concerned

that she would not get the acne medicine that he had promised. He broke the largest pimple and drained it of pus and dabbd it with first-aid cream. She stared at him, astonished, and she became very wet.

She will outgrow the acne and her skin will become smooth, he decided. He kissed her baby lips and her breath caught.

"When will you love me?" she asked.

"After I tell you about the guns . . . or maybe before."

He brushed her hair and she became wetter and more embarrassed because she was afraid that he could feel her wetness coming through her pajamas.

"I made the pillows," she said proudly.

"You do good work."

She picked up one of the pillows and traced the flower design with a finger, holding the design up for him to see. "I don't have any useful skills except I can sew very well."

He brushed her black hair, the dampness making the individual strands hang heavy and giving them a look of having been oiled.

"I'm going to rub your body with lotion now."

"I don't have any lotion," she said.

"I bought some at the shop. I will leave it for you when I go in the morning."

"Don't look at my leg when you rub me with the lotion."

"Your leg doesn't bother me."

He picked her up off his lap and stretched her out on the bed with her head on a pillow.

"I filled the pillows with small soft duck feathers."

"That's nice," he said and removed her pajama tops, massaging her small shoulders with cream. Her dry skin absorbed the lotion quickly.

She sighed down deep when his fingers worked down to her swollen breasts. "I got the duck feathers from

291

the restaurants."

He rubbed skin lotion into her breasts until she no longer could breathe and the fluid from her genitalia ran down the inside of her thighs and soaked her pajamas.

"Can . . . can you love me . . . now?" she whispered.

"Tomorrow you should go to the hospital and let a doctor look at the bump on your head and at your swollen lip. I would take you to the base hospital but I will be gone tomorrow. I won't be coming back."

"Talk to me about the guns while you love me. It will help take away the fear. Will you mind if I put my bad leg around you?"

"Do what you want." He rubbed her arms and fingers with cream. "I should have polished your fingernails; I will do it if I have time before I leave." He examined a finger and scraped at the old broken polish on the nail.

The rain was coming down harder and he could hear the water running down the slope to the bottoms. The pounding of the rain on the metal roof was loud, but reassuring.

Inside the girl's hovel there was little room to move around and the air smelled of mildew and mold. Chicken bones and cabbage leaves littered the dirt floor. The small, miserable dwelling was of no concern to him except that she was there and human contact was more important to him than smells and what things looked like.

He held her with one arm and placed her on his hip while he folded down the white sheets, and he thought how incredibly small she was.

"Are . . . we . . . going to . . . do . . . it now?" Her breasts were flushed and the tips had turned a bright pink; and they were twitching rapidly. Her arms were wrapped around his neck as though she was afraid of falling, and she straddled his hip, her crippled leg unable to hold to his waist and awkwardly hanging loose.

The sheets smelled of soap and he laid her on them.

"I washed them today," she said.

He knew she wanted his approval so he said, "They smell good; they will smell even better after your body has lain in them for a while."

The astonishment came into her eyes again.

He saw the spreading wetness between her legs and she turned her head from him. "Don't look," she said.

He pulled the pajamas down to her ankles and he touched her baby-smooth pubic area; she moaned and pulled the pajama leg up to cover her handicap. He undressed, kissed her bruised lip, and swelled inside her, and the little handicapped Da Nang street girl, Trang, took control of him and there was no more loneliness, no more fear, and he felt her strong leg holding him tight and her crippled leg quivering and grasping for him, and he was astonished at how marvelous and loving she was and it went on and on until she screamed and bit his arm and pulled his hair and she collapsed and lay still under him and he thought that he had killed her.

"Trang," he whispered. "Are you all right?"

The rain beat on the tin and the water dripped off and puddled around the hovel and ran off to join the river in the bottoms. The lantern hanging above the bed swayed a little from the wind blowing in under the roof and the shadows moved gently on the walls. The yellow light from the lantern and the swaying shadows and the sound of the rain softened the night.

"Trang." He patted her hand.

Her eyes opened halfway and her lips parted.

"Do you know where you are?" he said.

She nodded and her lips moved and the lids of her eyes opened and closed.

He put her pajamas on and pulled her close to him under the cool sheets and rubbed her hands and her crippled foot until she was breathing regular and she fell asleep with her head resting on his chest and her short leg

293

thrown over him. While she slept he held her hair tight in one hand and a warm breast in the other and he wasn't afraid or lonely and he was thankful that he was here with her in her miserable home. He said a silent prayer for her.

After a while she opened her eyes and looked at him as though something miraculous had taken place. "Are we in love?" she asked, childlike.

"No—we've become good friends." He kissed the knot on her forehead. "That's more important than love."

"I'm going to believe that you are my regular boyfriend."

"If you wish." He kissed her puffed lip.

"Yes . . . you're right; being good friends is better than being in love." Her crippled leg moved up higher on his thigh and she fell back to sleep, holding tight to him.

Her new pajamas were fluffy and felt good against his skin, and the dampness of her genitals on his thigh was warm and pleasant; and the musky smell of her young body, coming through the sheets was exciting and much different from the body odors of Nghia and Ruthie or the other women he had known.

An hour later she woke again and looked at him with sleepy eyes. "Do you want me again?" she said dutifully.

"Yes."

She crawled on top of him and pressed her bruised lip to his mouth. "Ouch!" she cried and readjusted her lips so that the pressure was not so painful.

Her breath had become stale during sleep, but he didn't mind; it bothered him no more than did the blackheads and pimples or her gimpy leg. She was loving and good to him and he was grateful for her warmth and there was no more beautiful woman to him. The chemistry from the beginning had been right and he was bonded to her; and he would defend her with his life, so right was the raw material of their union.

He held tight to her hair and she pulled the pajamas

down and he felt the beautiful hot wetness, and she laid her bruised mouth on his lips, and she took control over him once again while he watched her long slanted eyes— black and wet and so different—caress him into her world of euphoria.

She would allow him to do nothing but lay underneath her, shaking, while she performed her artful ministrations, stroking his hair, her mouth against his ear, whispering to him, attending to his need. Throughout, his eyes were glued to hers, fascinated by the depth of her sincerity and the immense pleasure that she was bringing him.

"Talk to me about the guns while I love you," she said.

"There is much to talk about."

"Talk about what you fear."

She loved him and he twisted her hair in his hand and told her about the high ridge he would have to come down and the drop into the narrow canyon with the ninety-degree turn and about the guns pointed at him because the gunners knew from what direction he must come.

She whispered love to him and her smell was like that of an Asian deer and her wetness was thick and hot and ran down his thighs, and she held him tight and he told her about the wall of flak he must fly through and that if he didn't take out the guns the attack planes couldn't deliver their bombs.

And he told her about Nghia and Ruthie, about Colonel Dasher and Bamburger and his bitterness in having to fight while the others remained at home. She held him tighter and flooded him with her wetness and cried with him when she felt his muscle stiffen and jerk inside her; and she sucked out his fear, his loneliness, and the hateful bitterness, and stored it in her womb to prize.

Throughout the night he kept her close to him, smelling her skin, holding fast to her hair, touching her

face and all parts of her body with his fingers, talking to
her as she fell in and out of sleep clasped to his hardness
with her small fist.

The rain stopped and he rose quietly from the bed so as
not to disturb her and got dressed. While she snored
lightly he brought the lantern close to her face and kissed
her scratches and bruises, and he smelled the wetness
between her apricot thighs and kissed her deformed leg.

He emptied all the money he had into the shoe box and
blew out the lantern.

Colonel Dasher stood on the platform, his bullet head
pointed at the ceiling of the briefing room like an artillery
shell ready to go off. "Men!" he roared. "This morning
you are going to make the most important strike of the
war. You Marines have been ordered by Washington to
destroy Ban Dau because of your proven tenacity to take
out difficult targets . . ."

Cleanhead went on with his pep talk, but Battaglia
wasn't listening after the first few words. When the
planning officer and strike leader began their briefing he
would tune back in.

He unfolded the telegram from Nghia and read it again:

PLEASE FORGIVE ME. I WILL LOVE YOU FOREVER.
CHILDREN FINE.

With the hurry and confusion of those last minutes in
her dressing room at the hotel, there had been no time for
a proper good-bye. He thought of leaving a letter for her,
but he could think of nothing to say that wouldn't reopen
old wounds. Better to let her remember him as he was,
happy and in love with her—and let her go on believing
that he was still alive.

". . . the weather has cleared and you should have a

296

clear run on the target," the planning officer was saying. "The A-7s will be loaded up with five-hundred-pounders and the A-6s with thousand-pounders." He went on to give takeoff times, tide and wind data, ingress and egress routes, pilot-RIO-aircraft assignments, and the other particulars given on all missions.

Bamburger then got on the platform. "I'm leading the strike and expect each pilot to maintain strict radio discipline. I want no stragglers this trip—we need every pair of eyes available. You RIOs cover each other's six-o'clocks."

He paused and looked around the room until he found Vince. Their eyes met and held like two steel magnets clashing; and Cleanhead, standing off to the side of the platform, saw the two personalities collide and decided that the competition was healthy.

"Battaglia will go in first to knock out the guns and he will be our FAC and MIGCAP coming off the target," Blackjack said, his eyes on Vince and his voice careful not to reveal his doubts about him. "Protect your six-o'clocks . . . the Migs will be up . . . and call out all SAM launches. When someone gets bagged call out the chutes and get accurate coordinates. We'll give the downed pilots protection, alternating off the tankers, until RESCAP gets them out."

The planning officer took over again. "Launches will be staggered so that flights will arrive over the target at intervals of fifteen minutes for maximum coverage. Six waves will hit Ban Dau beginning at sunrise, the last flight taking off from Da Nang when the first strikers are on their way home. Battaglia's two sections of F-4s will take off first, destroy the enemy's antiaircraft artillery and surface-to-air missiles, then become forward air controllers and direct the strike for the bombers coming in behind them. They will also have to take on any Migs coming to Ban Dau's defense."

Colonel Dasher was back on the platform, pacing back and forth, hands clasped behind his back, his bloused boots coming down hard on the wood. He stopped and squared his shoulders to the flyers. "I'm convinced that if we bust their balls at Ban Dau the NVA offensive will die and Ho Chi Minh will get serious at the peace talks and we'll be out of Vietnam within the year."

"The commies will never quit," Vince said under his breath.

Kruger gave him a puzzled look.

Dasher had a few more words to add with regard to strategy and how close they were to bringing the North Vietnamese high command to its knees. He concluded with, "Good luck, men, and Godspeed," and left the room to be alone before he took up his usual position on the flight line to begin his vigil throughout the morning until the last jet returned.

Outside the door he delayed and listened to Blackjack finish up the briefing with screen projections of Battaglia's reconnaissance photos. Blackjack detailed the targets for the pilots, and with authority and confidence gave an articulate and professional reiteration of the strike plan.

"Maybe I misjudged him," Dasher said quietly, and walked off into the darkness to await the dawn.

The experts had done a good job in identifying from the photos the camouflaged ammo dumps, truck parks, stockpiles of munitions, cave entrances, rail lines, roads, and communication installations. When the gun emplacements and SAM sites came on the screen, Battaglia's stomach twitched and the sweat beaded on his forehead, and he remembered the ugly rocks and steep walls and the depressing desolation of the ridges and canyons.

"How do you feel about going back?" Kruger said.

"Got to win the war—didn't you hear Cleanhead?"

"I've got a better answer."

"I know—it's our job," Vince said. "And we get to go home sooner."

Vince knew why he was going back, and it wasn't because it was his job or to win the war. He was going back for the reason Nghia had said: because he could never live with himself if he didn't go; the guilt would destroy him. He wasn't fighting against communism or to win this dirty, unpopular war. He was fighting to keep the guys he was flying with from getting killed and he was fighting to protect his self-esteem and to keep the respect of his friends. He was frightened and it was embarrassing that it showed.

After the briefing, Blackjack came up to him in the locker room. Vince was getting into his flight gear.

"I've been watching you dress," Blackjack said. "You look nervous."

"I'm okay."

"Everyone needs to be under control on this one—I can't afford a single mistake. I'm depending on you to take out the guns, and if you don't think you can hack it now's the time to tell me."

"I told you I'm okay," Vince said.

Bamburger put a boot up on the bench and lit a cigarette. "When Dasher asked me the other day if I thought you were up to leading the attack against the guns I withheld judgment and told him I thought you were the best man for the job. I knew he wanted you to be out front on this one."

Battaglia bristled. "What are you getting at?"

"Just this: I need a superior effort from you today, and I'm giving you an opportunity to ground yourself if you feel that your condition will impair the success of the mission."

Vince drew himself up and he remembered Nghia and the kids and the little street girl, Trang, he had left only a few hours ago and who lay asleep in her hovel.

"I'm flying this mission, Blackjack, and nothing you can say is going to talk me out of it. You'd like nothing better than to see me ground myself; that would set you up real pretty with Dasher, but I'm not about to give you that satisfaction." He tested the emergency radio pack and slipped it into its place in a zippered pocket on his G-suit. "You've been riding my butt ever since I came aboard the wing, and I've had a bellyful of Blackjack Bamburger. If we weren't so close to launch I'd take off these bars and step out behind the barracks and have it out with you. In fact, you better watch yourself up there today, because I may just decide to flame your arrogant ass."

Blackjack looked incredulously at him. "Do you realize what you've said?"

"Fully. And if you want to court-martial me, you go right ahead. Dasher is just waiting for you to pull a bootlicking stunt like that. He'll kick your teeth in."

The pilots and RIOs had stopped dressing and stood mute, listening to Vince and Bamburger go at it. Many favored Battaglia, but Bamburger had a good number of supporters too, mainly the career flyers who understood both how Blackjack thought and his need for a clean fitness report to be in line for promotions, and who disliked Battaglia for being Dasher's favorite.

For a moment Bamburger was speechless, his face red and his lips working mutely. Finally realizing that he had to say something to save face he blurted, "You're a lone wolf and not a team player, Battaglia; you don't give a damn about this war or anything connected with it. Civilians like you have no business being in the Marines—you're a hazard." With that he stormed out of the room, his survival vest and Mae West thrown over a shoulder. He stopped at the door and said, "We'll have this out when we return from the mission."

Vince looked at the men's sullen faces and turned back

to his preparations, frowning. *He's right and everyone in the room knows it.*

After the tension in the room dissipated, Kruger, who had been listening intently during the argument, walked up to Vince and stood beside him for a few seconds, fumbling awkwardly with his g-suit adjustments.

Battaglia looked up. "Something on your mind, Kruger?"

Speaking low so as not to be overheard by the other men, Kruger said, "This thing between you and Blackjack has me and the other guys worried. I can't speak for them, but I have to fly with you and . . . well . . . I just . . ."

Vince went back to lacing his boots. "I understand how you feel. If I could fly this mission without a back-seater I'd let you stay behind, but as it is you're stuck with me. I'll do the best I can to get you back safely and then you can put in for another pilot. That's the best I can do."

"It's nothing personal against you, Vince, and I don't know exactly how to put it, but I joined the Corps for the long haul, and I think it would be best for both of us if I flew with someone who had the same career objectives as me—if you know what I mean."

"Yeh—I know it's tough on you," Battaglia said. "You're married, aren't you?"

"My wife and I want to start a family and do all the square things that families do, and she's behind me a thousand percent about staying in the Corps."

Vince could never understand this kind of thinking when men were at war. "You're lucky," he said. He remembered the scene with Ruthie before he'd left for Vietnam.

"I think so." Kruger fumbled some more with the adjustments. "Bamburger is right, you know."

"How's that?"

301

"You're a lone wolf," Kruger said.

"Maybe so—I like it that way."

"It's all right if you want it that way—but it's wrong if you hurt others in the process."

"I haven't time to talk philosophy," Vince said to Kruger, looking at his watch. "Launch is in forty minutes. Coming?"

"I'll be along."

Vince checked to see if his survival vest was filled with all the required articles, donned the Mae West and .38 with ammo belt, and picked up his helmet, oxygen mask, parachute, map case, and photos of the target. The burden of his gear he had never gotten used to, and when he walked under its weight he felt like a pack mule disguised as a fighter pilot. When he settled into the cockpit, however, all the awkwardness disappeared along with the restlessness and worldly associations, and he became fitted to the airplane like a hand to a well-tailored glove and only one thought dominated his mind: get the job done.

Battaglia headed for the flight line and his Phantom, disturbed by what Kruger had said. Time was running out and there were only minutes left to find a solution.

Last night as he'd lain awake with Trang's gimpy leg wrapped around him and he listened to her baby snoring, he'd wrestled with being responsible for what might happen to Kruger. It was enough to be afraid just for himself, but the additional fear for Kruger—and the burden of guilt he would have to carry the rest of his life if he lived and Kruger died—was unthinkable. Kruger represented all the things that Vince wanted but knew he would never have. Especially, he had a loving wife, a fine woman who supported him in everything he had undertaken. If Kruger flew with him this morning, she would become a widow, and this Vince knew he would never be able to live with.

The fear that Battaglia had felt the morning he dashed down the barren ridges of Ban Dau the first time came back when he climbed into the seat. He stared down the dark flight line at the Phantoms lined up, their long noses and bodies giving them the look of prehistoric reptiles, and his stomach felt like a large stone had settled in it.

He was the first to arrive on the line except for a shadowy figure pacing back and forth beside the runway. To assuage his fear he started a letter to Nghia, writing on a blank page on his knee pad. He stopped writing and saw Blackjack again standing in front of the men in the briefing room: "Most of the flak is located at these three points," Bamburger said, pointing to a photo projection on the screen. He lit a cigarette and looked at the heads until he found Vince. "Battaglia and his guys are assigned flak suppression. They'll be going in low, coming in over the top of the ridge, hidden until the last minute. If they don't take out the guns on their first run they'll go back again. When they're finished *all guns will be down*," he said, his look firm at Battaglia. "The A-6s and A-7s and the rest of us loaded up in F-4s will have a clear run on the target. When the last attack plane egresses, I want Ban Dau to be nothing but a pile of rock and gravel." He dropped the cigarette on the platform and squashed it with his boot.

"First launch is at sunrise, 0600, that's Battaglia. Garcia's flight will take off fifteen minutes later, and so on with the rest as scheduled. . . ."

Vince's hands were fastened on the control stick, the blood drained from his fingers. The fear was at the back of his throat and he wanted to vomit it up. *I can't take Kruger and myself into that fiery hell—it's certain death. The guns will blow us to pieces; I can't go in there.* The hatred for those who had called him back to active duty swelled down deep and rose into his mouth with the fear and destroyed his confidence to face the danger, and he

303

shamefully admitted that bravery was reserved for men like Blackjack Bamburger, gallant men who he despised for petty and perverse reasons. He slammed his fist down hard on the knee pad, and he was ashamed and bitter and afraid. His mind darted here and there like a punch-drunk fighter in a dark room, seeking a way to avoid the dangerous blows.

He had one foot out of the cockpit and was about to pull the other one out when he thought of Nghia, Autumn Dove, Ly-boy, and himself walking in the garden at the Da Nang house, the tamarind flowers floating down into the courtyard and settling into the fish pond. He heard the frogs croaking and smelled the red mangos and orange papaya swollen and ripe on the trees. *What would they think if I grounded myself and didn't fly the strike against the guns? Could I ever face them?* He leaned his head on the top of the windscreen and pounded the plexiglass in frustration, fighting the fear of dying and confused by his fear that he would be branded a coward.

Then the thought came to him—the perfect way to justify not flying the mission. He would do it for Kruger. He would ground himself and save Kruger's life, and his wife would be eternally grateful to him for his unselfish act; he would heap disdain on his own head to save a friend.

Vince crumbled back into the seat and buried his head in his hands and began laughing uncontrollably. *What an ass I am to think that I can rationalize away this mission. What a stupid jerk.* He looked into the sky at the disappearing stars, and in the middle of his fear finally realized that there was no escape for him.

He had always been afraid that Blackjack was a better man than he was—that was clear now—and Colonel Dasher had secretly entertained the same thought. That's why Cleanhead had never interfered in their sparring, even encouraging competition between them in hopes that Vince would win out for himself and get his head screwed on straight in the process; and it was for this reason that Dasher had wanted Vince to take out the guns at Ban Dau.

He returned to his letter to Nghia and in the glow of the panel lights read what he had written. He wadded it up in disgust and threw it on the deck. It was filled with self-pity. *Snap out of it.*

Remembering the love they'd shared, her unselfishness and wisdom, the freshness of their relationship, and the joy and loyalty and companionship of Ly-boy and Autumn Dove, he wrote another, more hopeful letter. He spoke of the first time they had met (at the bus stop) and how he had thought her to be the greatest thing since ice cream, and never dreamed he would see her again. He wrote of their time together at the Khach-san Bong and the jealousy (not disgust) that he felt when she went with other men and the joy she brought him when she said that she wanted to be his and no one elses. He told her of the pleasure she'd brought him at the Da Nang house, how he was sorry for misjudging her (the late nights with her sick cousin) and that as sure as God was still on his throne in Heaven, she would be delivered from her bondage to Kai and be freed forever from prostitution.

Finally, he wrote of the happiness that Autumn Dove and Ly-boy had given him, and the fun and love they had all shared together, and how his greatest wish was that the four of them could have become a permanent family.

And then unexpectedly, he found that he was telling Nghia that he had found his reason for fighting the war and why he was facing the guns at Ban Dau.

He folded the letter and wrote Nghia's name and address, care of the Khach-san Bong Hotel. He heard his name called and looked over the nose of the jet at the shadowy figure that had been pacing along the edge of the runway.

Out of the darkness the shaven head of Colonel Dasher emerged, followed by the glowing embers of his cigar. He stopped at the port side of the aircraft, just ahead of the wing, and looked up at Vince leaning out of the cockpit.

"What are you doing out here so soon?" Cleanhead asked.

"I was nervous and wanted to be alone, Colonel." He handed the folded letter down to Dasher. "Would you mail this for me, sir?"

"Be glad to, but why don't you mail it yourself when you get back?" Dasher asked casually and looked at the name and address on the outside.

"Without putting too fine a point on it, Colonel, I don't think I'll be coming back."

Cleanhead looked at him for a few seconds without speaking, the glowing cigar tip pointed up at Vince. The sky was already paling over the rice paddies and it would soon be time to launch the mission. "It's that bad for you, is it? Think you've lost the edge?"

Vince sensed that the colonel was waiting for him to say the right words, words that would determine whether or not he would let Vince fly the mission. It was being left up to Battaglia to decide what to say—to decide his destiny.

Knowing that he was being evaluated, Vince chose his words carefully: "Writing to a woman has a way of settling your mind and getting your priorities straight."

The paternal feelings that Dasher had for Battaglia were never stronger then they were now, less than an hour before he would be sending the lieutenant on the most important and most dangerous raid of the war. For Vince to fly the mission and successfully attack the guns would mean a great deal to the colonel, settling questions he had concerning Battaglia's character and determining the course he would take in the Marines; for Dasher was convinced that if Vince flew against the guns and

306

successfully completed the strike, he would see the error of his bitterness and become one of the finest officers in the corps' history.

Nevertheless, his fears for Battaglia's safety were strong and he was reluctant to let him go on the strike. With all the seriousness he could muster to communicate the gravity of the decision that he was going to make, depending on the answer Vince gave, he said, "If you ask me to, I'll ground you this morning and put another pilot in your slot."

Here was Vince's reprieve, the way out he had been hoping for, but he knew that if Dasher had really wanted him to stay behind this morning he would have flat-out told him not to fly—not give him a choice. Battaglia felt that Cleanhead was testing him to see which way he would spring, inwardly wanting Vince to say no to his offer.

If Dasher had arrived a few minutes sooner and had made the offer, Battaglia would have probably accepted. Now, however, it was inconceivable that he would stay behind while the others went. How strange the influence of a woman and the bond between men.

"Nothing can keep me from making the strike, sir—I'm going."

Dasher was not persuaded by Vince's answer and gave the young man another chance to change his mind. "Are you absolutely sure, boy? Battle fatigue is a common occurrence out here and nothing to be ashamed of. You're flying every mission available and you have the right to pass one up."

"Not this one, Colonel—I have no choice but to make this one count; I've got to fly into Ban Dau and take my chances like the rest of the men."

Dasher liked what he heard and knew before any more was said that his doubts about Vince were no longer valid.

"I've been wrong about a good number of things, sir,

307

and it took the words of a good man to make me face up to myself," Vince said.

"Who's the good man?"

"Major Bamburger."

Vince would never forget Cleanhead's expression. His eyebrows arched and jaw dropped, the cigar fell from his mouth and he grabbed it, burning his hand.

"We had words in the ready room and I'm afraid we both were pretty hot. After I cooled down and had time to think about what Major Bamburger had said, I realized that everything he had alleged about me was true and that I have been behaving like a fool and jeopardizing the lives of the men I fly with."

"Well, I'd never have thought that I'd hear you say that about the major."

"He's a good man, sir—a true professional—totally committed to his job. The man's got courage and he puts the missions he flies ahead of everything else. He was right in wanting to ground me after the briefing. I was nervous and uncertain . . . I would have been a hazard to the mission. I'm okay now. See . . ." He held his two hands out over the canopy rails for Dasher to see that they were steady.

Cleanhead grunted. "So Blackjack was ready to ground you . . . in spite of everything, he was willing to prevent you from making the strike; the mission was more important than his fitness report after all," Cleanhead said quietly to himself, rubbing his chin. "I'm afraid I've been wrong about some things too, Lieutenant."

"There's one more thing, Colonel. I've now got a personal reason for fighting this war, something I've lacked before."

"The girl and the kids?" Dasher held up the letter.

"Roger that, sir. If I get back I'm going to somehow work it out so that she and the children can live a normal life."

"You can tell me about it after you clobber Ban Dau,"

the colonel said. "Here comes your backseater."

"Good morning, Colonel." Kruger saluted Cleanhead.

Dasher returned the salute. "You're navigating for the entire section of flak suppressors, Kruger; get 'em in and get 'em out; and when you come down the ridge of guns bring Vince down on the big ones first, those are the babies we want the most. Remember that you're the first aircraft into the canyon and the others will need as much help as you can give them. You boys bust them good first and the guys behind you will clean up behind you." He stuffed the stogie between his mule teeth and twisted the ends of his handlebar mustache. "See you bums when you get back," he said, and grinned and threw the men a salute. He walked down the line, hands clasped behind his waist, to give final words of encouragement to the other pilots and RIOs climbing into their planes for preflight checks, the sounds of the "Marine Corps Hymn" fading away with him.

"Wish he was leading the strike, Kraut," Vince said, using Kruger's call sign now that the mission had officially begun.

"Roger, Dogbone; some men are just born leaders."

"Let's get these systems up and working," Battaglia said. "Time to get airborne and start the show." He was feeling better about the mission, though the fear was still present. *If Blackjack has the guts to go this morning, so do I.*

The crew chief for his aircraft was already on the job and rushing around under the F-4 checking for leaks and loose rivets and supervising the loading of rockets and bombs that Battaglia would use to attack the guns. Air-to-air Sidewinder missiles were loaded on launch rails for the dogfights that would come against the Migs.

Battaglia donned the crash helmet that was resting on top of the windscreen and plugged in the oxygen hose and radio cord. A crewman standing with one foot in an outside foothold and a knee placed on the canopy rail strapped Vince into the shoulder harnesses and safety belts, and secured him to the ejection equipment. Then came engine start.

With the crew chief plugged into the intercom jack in the plane's belly, Vince and the sergeant went through the maze of checks on the flight controls and sensitive systems to assure that the jet was ready for flight. As the checks were called out, Battaglia would manipulate the numerous switches and controls and study the whirling and jumping gauges.

After a final check on the ordnance slung under the Phantom to assure that it was all secured tightly, the sergeant gave Battaglia the thumbs-up sign and ordered the wheel chocks pulled.

"Your radar and ECM up and functioning, Kraut?"

"Roger, all systems go, Dogbone."

"Let's go to button orange—time for roll call." Vince throttled up for a final surge check on the two General Electric engines, then pressed the mike button. "Dogbone to Ghost Flight . . . check in."

"Dash Two?"

"Dallas boy . . . all set?"

"Dash Three?"

"Billy Sunday . . . go."

"Dash Four?"

"Bronco . . . ready."

Vince preceeded down the line until all aircraft commanders had checked in, then called the tower: "Ghost Flight ready to roll."

"Roger, Dogbone—proceed to arming area."

With the rice paddies now visible in the shadowed light and the eastern sky turned the color of gunmetal, the crew chief unplugged his headset from the F-4 and used hand and arm signals to direct Vince and Kruger out of the parking area and onto the taxi strip to the arming pad.

Behind Battaglia, Ghost Flight trailed, each aircraft swinging into position, leader and wingman together.

Vince and his wingman pulled onto the hot pad,

ordnance pointed into the paddies so that in the event of an accident the rounds wouldn't hit another jet. The hot-pad crew quickly set the fuses and armed the bombs, shook the ordnance to be sure it was secure on racks and rails, and signaled the planes out of the arming area and onto the runway. Two more Phantoms rolled onto the hot pad, engines screaming.

Lined up on the runway with his wingman, Vince radioed the tower: "Dogbone to Home Plate; Ghost Flight ready for launch."

"Roger, Ghost Flight . . . you are cleared for launch. Good luck . . . and clobber them."

"Ready, Kraut?"

"Ready as I'll ever be."

"Dogbone on the roll—Ghosters form on me at angels ten and we'll hit the tankers above Vuon Di."

Battaglia pushed the throttles full forward to one hundred percent RPM and ignited the afterburners. The Phantom jumped and up they went in a fiery launch, the tailpipes burning a hole in dawn sky.

"Look at the sun, Dogbone," Kruger said as they broke over the horizon.

Vince wheeled the jet in a climbing turn east, into a magnificent rising sun, the top of which was chinning itself on the edge of the South China Sea.

"It's a good omen," Vince said. "The Japanese pilots in World War Two said that the first plane to see the rising sun would have the most success during the day's raid."

He rolled the F-4 hard over ninety degrees so that the jet's belly was against the sun, and he looked down and watched Ghost Flight leaving the runway in pairs and pulling around in a climbing turn, afterburners glowing in the morning air.

It was a reassuring sight and the fear went down into the deeps of his bowels and lay hidden, subdued, but always there, waiting.

Chapter 17

Each Phantom took its turn on the tankers to top off its fuel tanks, then formed on Vince. Battaglia slammed the throttles forward and wheeled his jets north and pointed his nose high to climb into the towering cloud columns.

The sky was becoming lighter each minute, and by the time they reached Ban Dau the morning ground fog would be burned away and the target would be washed in bright sun.

"Turn to two-nine-five," Kruger said.

"Roger." Battaglia gave the F-4 some left rudder and Ghost Flight made the correction.

Miles behind them Blackjack Bamburger and his first wave of strikers were climbing into their fighter-bombers. At 0615 he signaled his aircraft commanders and they began their takeoff rolls.

Following the same route as they had on the recce flight, Kruger directed Vince across the familiar checkpoints, making frequent course changes to confuse the North Vietnamese radar. They crossed into Laos on schedule, heading east at an altitude of thirty-five thousand feet.

The radios were silent and the tension built.

At the North Vietnamese fighter base at Kep near Hanoi, communist pilots started engines of their Mig-21s to begin routine patrolling of Ban Dau and the Ho Chi Minh Trail.

The verdant mountains of Laos were peaceful and gave no indication of the violent battles that had taken place there in the past months. For thirty-five thousand feet, war was remote and impersonal.

"Time to reverse course and begin descent for the long dash," Kruger said. "Turn to zero-eight-zero."

The Sunday drive had come to an end and the sightseeing was over. Vince pulled forward on the inertia reel and the fear that he had covered rose up into his stomach and his body stiffened against the straps.

"Roger, Kraut. Dogbone to Ghost Flight . . . coming around to zero-eight-zero and descending to the deck."

Down they came, falling like lightning bolts, thundering at Mach two, Vince leading the jets to treetop level and using the hills and valleys and ground clutter to mask the ingress into Ban Dau.

"Five degrees left," came Kruger's steady, reassuring professional command. "You will take it in sixty seconds."

Laos was left behind and the Phantoms thundered into North Vietnam—the jungle flashing by like the torrent of green water racing over the rapids in the river below them.

They turned up—north—and followed the course of the river, eight jets going into hell—rooster-tailing the river water behind them, the roar of their thrusting engines filling the valley so that there was no other sound.

"Turn four degrees left."

Suddenly the ridges and mountain spine filled the windscreen and Vince began the steep climb from the valley floor to the high desolate rocks and crevasses and spiny crags and ugliness. Down the ridge and into the canyons—thundering—thundering—thundering—

the radios silent, the men holding to the planes in a frenzy of speed, and always the thought: *Would the guns be waiting and would the flak be heavy and accurate?*

"You've got it now," Kruger said. "Cook 'em good."

All Vince's combat instincts sprang forward and he turned the airplane over to them, leading Ghost Flight into the great maw that was Ban Dau.

There it was again—the junction of canyons. *No thinking now. If I think, I'm dead.*

"Drop tanks and arm your ordnance," he ordered the aircraft commanders. "ETA two minutes." He selected BOMBS on the fire-control panel and jettisoned his external fuel tanks.

The turn was tighter than he remembered and the G forces tugged heavily at his face, pulling his lips and cheeks back, stretching them like rubber over the bone. All the terror of Ban Dau that he had collected now surged into his throat and he thought for an instant of Nghia and Ly-boy and Autumn Dove and more than ever he wanted to live; but it was only an instant. The barren ridge was before him and there was no more time. He was depending on surprise and if he had calculated correctly he would be bringing his jet over the top of the ridge onto the exact spot where the main 100mm batteries were dug in. *Stick back into the belly, now hard against my thigh.* "Dash One in!"

The F-4 bristling with bombs and rockets shot up over the ridge, climbing and upside down and Ban Dau spread below. Hanging in the straps, Battaglia centered the controls and looked hard, his eyes flashing across the canopy.

"Two o'clock," Kruger said.

"Got it."

He had popped up too far to the right. Kicking the jet a few degrees left he centered the bombsight on the long black barrels—muzzle flashes instantly erupted from the guns—and rolled the F-4 around on its axis. A five-hundred-pound bomb dropped from the rack under the jet and exploded into the muzzle flashes. The concussion of the blast rocked the plane and Vince came hard right, stick back and into his thigh.

"Eleven o'clock," Kruger shouted.

Reversing into a half roll, Battaglia selected ROCKETS and brought the sight onto a second set of 100mm guns. He pressed the switch on the stick and a pod of Zunis smoked into the guns. Rock and dirt erupted and before banking away he saw the bodies of gunners hanging over the parapet and the guns tilted forty-five degrees. A fire had broken out in the pit.

"Dash One off." Vince pointed the Phantom's nose high and he climbed up and away from the smoking ridge, the flak bursts chasing him.

"Dash Two in."

Battaglia swung around to the south, coming in behind the trailing section in Ghost Flight to take up his position at the end of the daisy chain to wait his turn for another run on the target.

"Dash Two off."

Kruger was bending and twisting in the backseat. He was a big man and muscular, able to fight the G forces and watch the vulnerable six-o'clock position where Mig attacks came from.

"Dash Three in."

The element of surprise now gone, Battaglia would be making the second run from a steep diving angle of fifty degrees. The wide orbit position in the daisy chain was shrinking and his turn would be coming up again in less then a minute. Dash Two, his wingman, was climbing in behind him.

Dash Four, the last flak suppressor in the first section, gave the damage report: "Two main batteries of one-hundreds down . . . third still firing."

"Bronco . . . this is Dogbone. Concentrate your fire on the last one-hundred-millimeter battery. I'll bring my section down on the seventy-fives and the SAM sites."

"Will do, Dogbone."

"We've got Migs at five o'clock." It was Kruger. "Ten thousand feet above us, ready to jump in."

"Okay, Ghosters . . . we've got company up here. Looks like ten Migs in two sections . . . one at the north end and one at the south . . . they won't bounce us while we're in the flak . . . they'll try to take us coming off our bomb runs, hitting the stragglers . . . so stack up and stay tight . . . wingmen and leaders together."

The last jet in the daisy chain was going in and Vince's turn was coming up. He selected BOMBS again and was preparing to push over when his radio crackled.

"Dogbone, this is Cobra." It was Blackjack. "I'm ten minutes from Bull's-eye with my strikers. How's it look?"

"Cobra . . . Dogbone . . . the big batteries are down and we're starting to work over the seventy-fives and SAMs. Migs are in the area. Come on down—the party is getting hot." He smiled and waited to see how Blackjack would react to his comment.

There was a long pause, then his headphones crackled again. "Take care of the Migs and get those seventy-fives and SAMs. When we get there I want the party busted up."

"Roger, Cobra—will do." He smiled. "Hear that, Kraut?"

"Yeh—just like that, work a miracle."

Far below, the Phantom ahead of him rippled its bomb load into the fire-spitting ridge. Vince lost sight of it in the heavy smoke, and when he saw it again pulling up on the far side of the mountain spine it caught a burst of flak and the plane went into the top of the ridge, exploding on impact.

316

"Who bought it?"

"Langlois and MacKay."

"See any chutes?"

"No chutes."

Vince went into his power dive, rolling the Phantom over on its back and slicing down hard at a steep angle, his stomach in his throat, hating the guns and holding the fear down where the hate was.

"A lot of goofballs coming up at us a hundred feet below the ridge crest at the north end," Kruger said. "That's what got Langlois and MacKay."

"That's where the seventy-fives are concentrated," Vince said. "I'm going after them."

The red goofballs slashed by the canopy, their smoke trails twisting in long strings behind. The flak came up in black bursts of twos and fours and the air sizzled hot.

The Phantom shook and rattled, making it difficult to track the target, though there was no doubt where Battaglia had to fly the jet to bring his bombs home.

"Ripple your load behind me, Bronco. They tried to hold back until the attack planes got here, but we forced them to open up. This is the jackpot—don't hold anything back."

"Gotcha, Dogbone—we've each got a rack left. We'll put it in where you dump yours."

Battaglia rolled a few degrees right, placed the nose lower—lower—lower and then slammed the stick into his leg. The ring of fire floated into the bombsight and he toggled the rest of his bombs.

Kicking in the afterburners and hauling the controls into his gut, the F-4 climbed straight up and away.

"Good show, Dogbone. Your ripple went right down the line—*perfect!*" Bronco said.

"Can you see the SAM sites, Kraut?"

Kruger twisted and looked down and backward. "Almost directly below us."

Battaglia came up over the top and rolled the jet inverted. As he went into the roll he snatched a look at two Mig-21s high above him, winging over and starting in on his Phantom. He completed the roll and arched down in a screaming dive. Two of the SAMs were spitting smoke and fire, rising from the launch pads.

"They're coming straight for us," Kruger said.

"Migs, SAMs, flak—we've got it all this morning, Kraut."

"Break off or we've had it."

Battaglia ignored Kruger and selected ROCKETS. "Ever seen a SAM shot down while it's tracking you?" He pulled the trigger and two Zunis streaked out from under the Phantom.

There was a second of fearful anticipation, followed by a terrific explosion—then another. The two Zunis scored a direct hit on the first SAM and the explosion set off the second SAM just leaving the launcher. The entire flaming cauldron of molten fuel and metal fell back into the launch pad and exploded the remaining SAMs and launch equipment.

"Good lord!" Kruger said.

Vince quickly twisted the jet away from the inferno and climbed for altitude. "Where are the Migs?"

"They broke off and are climbing away—three o'clock."

"I'm going after them." Battaglia said. "Dogbone is MIGCAP," he radioed to the other aircraft.

He rolled left, put the stick in his belly, and climbed after the Migs, the Phantom's afterburners cooking.

"Who's that straggling in the daisy chain?"

"Dallas Boy," Kruger said.

"The Migs are going after him . . . easy meat, they think. Give me a good setup, Kraut—I want those two."

"Rog, Dogbone . . . bring it around ten degrees." Kruger watched the two dots on his radar move to center scope.

"Do I have lock-on?"

"Steady . . . bring it over a bit more and back off or you're going to overshoot them."

Vince watched the two Migs start their turn into Dallas Boy's six-o'clock. All he needed was about thirty seconds and he would have the Migs locked up on Kruger's weapons system. If he alerted Dallas Boy now (who hadn't seen the attacking Migs) he was taking the risk that the Migs would break off and he would lose them.

A terrific burst of flak went off directly in front of the F-4, rocking the jet in violent gyrations. Vince could actually see the hot metal and flaming gases spew over the Phantom and past the canopy. He shut his eyes and tried to make himself smaller in the seat, listening to the sizzling metal pop and crackle around him.

Miraculously the F-4 didn't break up as he had expected, and when he opened his eyes there were no red flashing panel lights. All his senses had been shocked and oversensitized and were made extremely acute—everything had become super-real: the engines thrusting underneath him surged loudly and he could hear the combustion of gases deep inside the turbines. The inside of the cockpit was vivid with a clarity he had never experienced before—the numbers on the gauges, the scratched glass on the dials, the peeling olive-green paint, the hard black plastic rubbed smooth, the torn seat cushion, the sheen of the exposed aluminum handles . . . the details of which were all so lucid that he thought that he surely must be seeing the atoms and molecules, the very essence of the material.

His eyes were wide, the pupils dilated to the maximum diameter, and the sky in front of him, which a few seconds before had been only a pale wash of noncolor through the windscreen, was now a brilliant panorama of bright hues: the deep azure blue sky, sparkling in its

319

clarity; the billowing, pillow-white clouds, so intense in their whiteness that his eyes hurt; and the black puffs of flak flowers blooming around him in a daring display of deadly beauty.

The Migs, turning in slow motion in front of him in the crystal-still air, were like two silver fish swimming in a bright sea, their aluminum skins and the red stars painted on their fuselages and wings glaring in a scintillating blaze of sunlight.

"You've got lock-on . . . cleared to fire."

Kruger's voice in the helmet headphones was so transparent and distinct that it seemed to be echoing from the depths of a deep well; and the missile tone enunciating in the background was shrill and piercing.

"Pull the trigger, Dogbone, or you're going to lose lock-on."

Vince was mesmerized by the beauty of the enemy aircraft, sleek, bright, and fast, moving—no, floating—above the Phantom's nose in a slow, exaggerated ballet in vivid technicolor.

"Come on, Dogbone—fire."

The hard plastic grip in his oversensitized hand was so tactile and the controls so perceptive the the slightest touch brought instant response to the thundering Phantom.

"What's the problem, Dogbone?"

He squeezed the trigger (he seemed to only have touched it gently) and a Sidewinder missile streaked from the launch rail under the F-4's wing tip and smoked after the lead Mig. The white plume of exhaust from the rocket motor arched high and the missile gracefully turned with the Mig in a wide sweeping curve.

Kruger's voice from the deep well and the blazing sky and the beautiful towering clouds and the wheezing of the oxygen regulator filled Battaglia's head with a swelling so great that he thought he was going to lose consciousness.

The Mig exploded in a ball of fire. The wingman broke hard right and Battaglia quickly rolled inside his turn.

"Go for number two," came Kruger's icy order, detached and without a hint of emotion—the professional all the way. "He's locked up for you."

Again the pristine clarity, the exactness of detail, the shadow of the tailfin falling across the aft fuselage, the red star outlined in white, and the gleaming unpainted aluminum panels were all too real and he remembered the hot summer days on the farm when the air was so pure and his senses so keen that he could count from as far away as he could throw a stone the number of wheat kernels in the head of a single swaying stalk.

"I wonder what he's thinking?" Vince said.

Kruger made sounds between his teeth. "Shoot!"

"He knows he can't escape."

"His pants are filled and it doesn't matter what he's thinking," Kruger said. "Blow him away."

Nowhere in all eternity was there a moment so awesome, so terrorizing, as when you had an enemy plane on your tail and you knew you couldn't shake him; the seconds expanded into long spaces of time in which you desperately tried everything you could remember to throw off your adversary, fully aware that nothing was going to work because your time had arrived, and you sat there in the seat, the shoulder harness and seat belt and oxygen mask biting hard into your skin from the G forces and you waited helplessly for the explosion that would tear you apart.

Battaglia flew his F-4 through the turns, feeling the same dread the Mig pilot felt and hating the job he must do, nauseated by the killing.

"Don't push your luck, Dogbone . . . we can't stay behind this guy all day. The flak is getting heavy and my ECM is sputtering like crazy. We've got a SAM tracking us."

The Sidewinder came off the rail and flew up the Mig's

tailpipe and the resulting fireball tore off the tail. The pilot popped out like the top of a bad boil, but Vince didn't have time to see if his chute opened. He hoped that it would.

"Break hard left," Kruger said.

The Phantom made a hard break and Vince fought to look down and back, the great pressures pinning him against the seat. The SAM was breaking through the clouds and arcing over to follow his break. He rolled the jet over on its back and tore several panels off the wings in an attempt to outtwist the SAM.

He never got into the dive that would have eluded the Soviet missile. The impact wasn't violent, it only made the F-4 lurch slightly, and it sounded like the tap of a nickel on a tabletop. The inside of the cockpit looked like a glowing Christmas tree: every panel light was bright red—but surprisingly, the jet flew straight and level. Then all of a sudden it yawed to the right and the nose fell off into a steep dive.

"Punch out, Kraut—the party's over for us."

Kruger needed no second command (Vince heard him eject behind him), and just before Battaglia ejected he heard Bamburger talking to his strikers as they arrived over the target; and then came the assuring call from his wingman: "Dogbone and Kraut are hit and going down five miles east of Ban Dau . . . Mayday, Mayday . . . I've got one chute—"

The cannon shell exploded underneath him and he was shot out of the stricken jet. He got seat separation and a few seconds later he felt the jar of the chute opening and he looked up to see the bright orange panels blossomed above him.

Swinging in the chute harness he felt numb and wondered if he had been injured. He wiggled his toes and fingers and was relieved that he could feel them. Below and off to his right, Kruger was drifting in the direction of a small clearing. Vince worked the cords to steer his own chute in the same direction.

Ban Dau was covered with smoke. *Blackjack and his boys are hitting them good—I suppose I did the best I could to clear the way for him; at least he didn't have to worry about the one-hundreds, and most of the seventy-fives were down and one or more missile sites were destroyed. He can't complain about that.*

A strange peace came over Vince as he hung in the parachute straps and surveyed the battle of Ban Dau that he had dreaded so much. Now that the terror of Ban Dau's guns was behind him and he had lived through the strike, he experienced a great release and felt free from the heavy weight of responsibility that he had been carrying around with him from the time he first knew that he would have to face Ban Dau. He was so relieved that he began singing at the top of his voice, "The Drunken Sailor," an old English naval song he had learned during his days at officer candidate school at Quantico. He became animated and belted it out, waving at the F-4s that orbited above his chute, following him down. His spirits soared and he figured that he and Kruger would be rescued in no time at all. The Sandies would be coming in first to pave the way for the Jolly Green Giant, and there would be the Huey gunships, and before he knew it he would be aboard and whisked back to Da Nang and before noon he and Kruger would be slugging down some of Cleanhead's smooth amaretto.

The ground was coming up fast and he focused on his landing. Kruger had missed the clearing and was drifting into the trees. Vince pulled on his cords, collapsing one side of the chute so that his descent wouldn't be so severe, putting him in a drift angled away from Kruger and into the center of the clearing which now looked awfully small.

The more he tugged on the cords the faster he descended, though he was able to alter the drift. Finally, he was too close to the ground to continue steering the parachute and he was forced to take his chances.

Able to get his back to the direction of drift he hit the ground and rolled, getting balled up in the shrouds, only a few feet from the edge of the clearing. Even before he was cleared from the parachute, he had his emergency radio out and was talking to Bronco and Dallas Boy orbiting his position.

"Turn off your beeper," Bronco said. "You're telegraphing your position to every gooner in North Vietnam."

Battaglia switched off the radio distress signal that is built into every aviator's parachute and that lets his buddies know that he's out of his aircraft and falling.

"We'll fly RESCAP as long as the fuel lasts, and then take turns off the tanker so you have cover until Jolly Green gets here with the Sandies," Bronco said.

Two jets streaked low over the clearing. "This is Dallas Boy, Dogbone. Kraut is a thousand yards up the ravine north of you—caught in a tree. Think you can fetch him?"

"I'll give it a try," Vince said. "Any NVA troops in the area?"

"Can't see any from up here."

Battaglia moved cautiously into the trees and worked his way north until he found the ravine. "I'm in the ravine," he said on the hand-held radio. "Which way now?"

"Follow it west," Dallas Boy said.

Vince looked up into the sky but he couldn't see the jets. He followed the dry streambed, breathing hard and stumbling over the rocks and fallen trees. The brush was thick and he had to make detours, further delaying him. The stress of being shot down was beginning to tell on him and he sat down to rest; he held out his hand and couldn't steady it, so strong was the trembling; his legs were also shaking badly.

Forcing himself to continue, he walked until he

thought he had covered a thousand yards—but had not found Kruger.

The emergency radio crackled: "Jolly Green is on the way—ETA twenty minutes," Bronco said. "Can you get Kraut here by then?"

"Yeh—if I can find him. I'm about a thousand yards up the ravine now."

"Can you help Dogbone locate Kraut, Dallas Boy?" Bronco said.

"I don't see Kraut's chute in the trees anymore. I'll check it out," Dallas Boy said.

There was the scream of an F-4's engines far off, getting louder, and then Dallas Boy was overhead dipping his wings to Vince standing in the streambed.

"He's still there—another hundred yards up from you. He's limp in his chute straps."

Bronce was back on the radio. "Dogbone, our fuel is low and we can't stick around. The Sandies are coming in behind us to fly cover—we'll be back after we find Big Bird's gas station. Good luck."

"Roger, Bronco, and thanks."

Battaglia listened to the Phantoms form up, their engines fading away until there was only lonely silence left. The fear tried to come up but he shoved it back down into his bowels and he started to walk the ravine to find Kruger.

It took him another ten minutes to reach his RIO. The man was unconscious and his feet dangled five feet above the ground. He pulled on Kruger's legs and the branch upon which the chute was caught bent far enough so Vince could cut the cords with his Ka-Bar knife, the same knife his father had carried on Tarawa and Iwo Jima.

Kruger was tipping well off to the side, and when Vince cut the last of the parachute cords he dropped at an awkward angle and the two men fell heavily to the ground. Vince rolled Kruger off him and lay on the ground for a half minute to catch his breath. His radio was squawking.

"Dogbone, Dogbone . . . Tiger One on station with four Sandies to cover your rescue. Have clearing in sight and see your parachute. Jolly Green right behind us coming into the LZ. Where are you?"

"Tiger . . . Dogbone; I'm up the ravine north of the LZ, cutting down my backseater. He's unconscious and I'm going to need time to get him to the clearing."

"Is there an LZ near you were we can bring in Jolly Green?" the A-1 pilot said.

"Negative—too many trees and rocks. Can't get a chopper in here."

"We'll stay as long as we can."

The whine of the big propeller-driven engines on the A-1s gave Vince confidence and he quickly looked over Kruger for injuries. Both of his arms were broken and he was bleeding from cuts on his hands and face where he had come through the trees. He had removed Kruger's crash helmet and Mae West and was lifting him across his shoulders to carry him back down the ravine to the clearing when he heard the Sandies firing. He picked up his radio.

"Dogbone, there are gooners in the LZ; they've found your parachute; best you bug out. We'll stay in the area and look for another LZ or until you advise. Jolly Green has been diverted and will wait for our call."

Vince's hopes sank. He sat with Kruger in his arms, knowing that Cleanhead's amaretto would have to wait.

Colonel Dasher sluggishly pushed the tip of his cigar into the ashtray on his desk and twisted it as if he were hurting something. The armored lids over the gunmetal eyes were heavy and his voice was thick and he talked with forced effort. "Why didn't the rescue chopper and the Sandies get there sooner and why weren't you on the job directing the rescue and who the hell gave Ghost

326

Flight permission to leave Battaglia stranded?"

"Sir," Blackjack said, "I can only answer one question at a time."

"You will damn well answer all of them simultaneously if I say so, Major." He stormed around the room, cursing, hands waving in the air, red-faced. "I lose one of my best pilots and no one knows what the hell happened." He slammed his fist on the desk and the model airplane flew off and crashed on the floor. Dasher looked down at it broken into pieces and was quiet for a long time, his face drawn and he looked very tired. *What makes these men get into their planes and face such terrible odds . . . not just once, but day after day?*

Bamburger looked embarrassed and his gaze shifted to the floor. His crash helmet tucked under his arm and the oxygen hose was hung up in the Mae West. He shifted his feet nervously.

The unmailed letter stared up at Cleanhead. He turned it over and saw Nghia's name and the address of the Khach-san Bong, and he knew that Battaglia would want her to be the first to know that he had been shot down and was missing, presumably captured and imprisoned.

Colonel Dasher had remained in operations throughout the day, listening to the radio reports between the pilots and Home Plate, haunted by the memory of losing his first son on a bombing raid. Now he had lost a second boy the same way, and he was bitter and shaken and he stayed close to the radio, praying that a supernatural act of God would pluck Battaglia from the hands of the enemy and deliver him safely back to Da Nang.

Dasher turned to Bamburger, his eyes hard and his skin tight over the gleaming shaved head. "Tell me again as close as you can piece it together what happened."

Blackjack, fatigued by hours of bombing Ban Dau and flying search-and-rescue for Battaglia, looked at Dasher with his red-rimmed eyes and wearily explained once more what he could of Vince's last hour before all communication with him was lost. Dasher bent forward, hanging on every detail:

"I heard Battaglia's wingman call *Mayday*," Blackjack began, "and report his position. There was some confusion as to what kind of hit he took—flak or a SAM, but it was confirmed that he flamed two Mig-21s less than a minute before he had to bail out."

"Why didn't you go immediately to his aid?" Cleanhead thrust his jaw at the exhausted strike leader.

"Sir, with all due respect, my job was to bomb the munitions. My strike force had just begun the attack when Lieutenant Battaglia got into trouble."

"But if you had been there with your heavily armed jets you could have cleared the LZ of those friggin' gooners and saved Battaglia; the Jolly Green could have picked him up."

"Colonel . . . the lieutenant was a thousand yards away from the LZ attending to Kruger who was unconscious. It was impossible for him to get back to the clearing without leaving Kruger." Blackjack was sweating heavily and he had grown weary of the conversation.

Dasher, in his frustration of losing another son, pressed for someone to lay the blame on. "Nevertheless, if you had come to help the Sandies when Ghost Flight left their RESCAP to refuel, Battaglia could be standing right here giving his report firsthand instead of the two of us jawing about probabilities."

Blackjack, shaking with anger and exhaustion, had been pushed to his limit. "My job was to deliver the bombs and destroy Ban Dau. If I had left my primary mission and directed my jets to protect Battaglia, as you have suggested, I would have been defying orders and putting the entire mission in jeopardy." He paused for an instant to regain control of himself. "I'm sorry that we lost Battaglia, but it was a good strike and we did our job. We hit every objective and destroyed Ban Dau; Vince

Battaglia helped enormously in accomplishing that. Regardless of the friction between him and me, I feel a great personal loss. I was wrong about him . . . he was a courageous pilot."

Colonel Dasher's face loosened and the stiffness in his neck and jaw relaxed. He slowly lit another cigar and inhaled long and deep.

"Everyone in the wing knows how you felt about Battaglia, Colonel," Bamburger said. "It was no secret that he was your favorite—that couldn't be hidden; but it was a good mission and the loss of Battaglia shouldn't take away from the tremendous job accomplished by the rest of the men. They deserve better."

Bamburger was no longer concerned about his fitness report or promotion. He was fed up with accusations and criticism, and he was tired—dead tired. The war would go on without him or Battaglia and there were always good men to replace those that had fallen. Tomorrow he would climb into his jet and fly into the face of death again. Maybe it would be his turn tomorrow to be shot down, and so where would the fitness report and promotions be then?

The cigar smoke trailed over Dasher's shoulder and collected under the ceiling of the quonset hut. The colonel was staring out the window, down the runway.

Without a word, without even a salute, Blackjack walked out of the wing commander's office, awkwardly rolling from side to side in his Mae West, g-suit, and survival vest, the oxygen mask and hose dangling from the green-and-gold crash helmet under his arm.

Cleanhead Dasher was no longer concerned about Major Bamburger, and he didn't bother to look when the door slammed. He was concentrating on the small space of sky he could see through the window—looking north.

Chapter 18

The two spit-and-polish young Marines dressed in class A uniforms walked into the Khach-san Bong Hotel in Cho-Chan, carrying an official U.S. military mail pouch. They walked directly to the lobby desk and asked for the manager.

The hotel had become quiet and the tiger girls peeked out from behind the potted palms. Clusters of them walked out of the bar and dining room and stood together staring at the Marines. There were whispers, but no one talked, and when the manager came out of his office, a hush covered the lobby.

"Yes, what can I do for you?" the manager said. He stood stiffly, sensing the importance of the visit.

"We have been directed to personally deliver an official correspondence from the U.S. Marine Corps to a Miss Van Tran Nghia. Is she here please?"

"I am Nghia." She stepped out from the crowd, her face expressionless, and walked toward the men.

The Marines kept their official stolid faces, but inwardly smiled at the sugar-cane walk that approached them. The bold look of the penetrating phoenix eyes told them to hurry about their business and that she understood why they had come.

"May we see some identification, miss?"

From the small purse in her hand she took out her ID

card and gave it to the sergeant.

"Thank you," he said politely and compared the photo on the card with the face in front of him, his look lingering more than the acceptable time on the classic features and pouting lips.

None of the onlookers had yet spoken and the manager remained stiff, as if at attention, nervously adjusting his glasses on his nose, and looked back and forth at Nghia and the Marines.

The sergeant unlocked the chain attaching the pouch to the corporal's wrist and then used another key to open the pouch. He withdrew two sealed envelopes and handed them to her.

"Please sign here," he said.

Nghia patiently signed with a delicate, even signature and without noticing held the two letters to her breasts. "Thank you," she said and walked to the elevator, the crowd parting for her.

In her room (she had moved into Vince's old room on the fourth floor) she placed the letters on the table and sat down. One letter, the more official looking of the two with Colonel Dasher's name typed under the Marine Corps emblem on the envelope, had *open first* written in longhand on the outside.

She opened the envelope and slowly unfolded the letter, her heart beating rapidly, and read Colonel Dasher's paragraph stating that Vince had been shot down over Ban Dau and was officially missing in action.

At that point she stopped reading. "He is alive and my heart tells me that I will find him." She wiped the tears from her eyes with the meaty part of her palm and continued reading.

Dasher went on to explain the particulars of the shoot-down, how Vince had been in communication with the other pilots after he had bailed out and landed on the ground, that he seemed to be uninjured and had been

331

administering first aid to his RIO when North Vietnamese infantry found his parachute and equipment, and that shortly thereafter all communication with him had been lost, though rescue operations continued in search of the two men for two days. Up to this point the letter was straightforward and official.

In the letter's conclusion, Dasher expressed his personal condolences and ventured a personal opinion that Vince was alive and a prisoner of war. He also mentioned that though his only contact with Nghia had been brief, his impression was very favorable, and that he knew from his talks with Vince that he would want her to know what had happened to him.

He went on to mention the second letter and that Vince had given it to him to mail to her minutes before he had taken off to fly against the guns, knowing that he wouldn't return.

Nghia smiled, remembering Dasher's hard-bitten attitude toward her in Da Nang, but even then she had known that he secretly approved of her and thought her good for Battaglia.

The last thing the colonel wrote was to tell her not to hesitate to call on him if he could help her with regard to what Vince wanted for her and the two children, and if she had questions that had not been answered in the letters.

Before opening the envelope containing the letter from Vince, she brewed two cups of green tea and took them out to the balcony. She sat down and talked to Vince about the lovely potted peonies and told him that the wind chimes were playing a particularly enchanting tune this afternoon, and that the sky was the bluest she had ever seen it over the river.

She touched her cup to his and toasted his courage and success in attacking the guns, and for a few minutes watched the white clouds drifting north toward Ban Dau where she knew he was, waiting, and thinking of her.

Nghia's love for Vince was unselfish and required only that Battaglia be available for her to love, which he was, in her memory and sitting across the table, drinking afternoon tea with her. She was not sad.

She felt no loss, only gain; Vince had faced the most terrifying experience of his life and met it courageously (as she had known he would), and she had helped him meet it. She was happy for him.

When he had come to her in Cho-Chan and later when he had received her in Da Nang and she lived the happiest moments of her life, she had seen the new strength growing in his eyes and she had stopped worrying about him. Even if he had been killed at Ban Dau (which she had been prepared for) he would have been victorious, and that was something they both had known without expressing it to each other. Her return to the Khach-san Bong with Kai had been the only solution to free him.

No . . . she was not sad. She was happy for Vince . . . and proud. Her path was before her and she knew the direction she must now take. She had thought about it many times and the details were well formed in her mind. The only thing that remained was to begin—and that she would do as soon as she read Vince's letter.

Kai was alone as he always was on Saturday night. At 11:00 P.M. without fail he would spread his books out on the table of his cheap room above the Blue Orchid Casino and add up his fan-tan winnings and the profits from Nghia.

The week had been a good one, Nghia alone netting him ten thousand piasters. Next month he would take her to Cambodia and then to Malaysia, where he had made arrangements to bed down his tiger girl with several aging generals, each willing to pay a small fortune for exclusive

333

rights to her. She was worth all the trouble she had caused him with that Marine in Da Nang, and now that he was permanently out of the picture he could concentrate on plans for Nghia's international debut in the capitals of Southeast Asia and the Middle East.

Normally, Kai avoided drugs of any kind, for he was well aware of the weakening effect they had on the mind and body. Their degenerative characteristics did not mix with business, except when he wanted to turn a high-risk quick profit and smuggled a kilo of heroin to the U.S. or France. Tonight, however, he was in high spirits and in the mood to celebrate, so he lit the opium pipe after recording the entries in the ledgers and sat back in the wooden chair and placed his feet on the table and puffed and dreamed of the larger sphere of influence and the bags of gold Nghia would bring him.

Outside at the curb in front of the Blue Orchid, a shapely girl in a flowered ao dai stepped out of a cab and walked through the doors of the casino, past the noisy, packed gaming tables and walked up the stairs to the floor above. A large purse was slung over one shoulder and she walked with firmness and resolve.

In his opium-soaked brain, Kai heard a knocking at his door. He became irritated at the persistent knock and ignored it. The girl tried the doorknob but it was locked, so she continued to knock, knowing that he was in the room. She heard the chair scrape against the floor and the footsteps coming to the door. The long Manchu eyes looked up and down the hall and her pouting lips tightened as she opened the purse and drew out a .38 Smith & Wesson. She wrapped a towel around the barrel of the gun.

He opened the door and began laughing at the wrapped towel pointed at him, unable to see the gun buried inside, and said, "What do you want? If you need money you must wait like you always do, until I pay my bills. I told you not to come here." He laughed loudly and pointed at the towel. "What is that thing?"

She said nothing and pulled the trigger. The towel acted as a silencer, muffling the shot, and the cloth caught fire. Kai fell backward, eyes wide, mouth open and a red hole in the middle of his forehead.

Nghia let the towel fall to the floor, carefully put out the flames with her foot, and kicked it into the room. She closed the door on Kai and locked it. The next morning, she, Autumn Dove, and Ly-boy boarded an Air Vietnam flight to Da Nang.

Cleanhead carefully looked over the young woman standing in front of him. She was dressed in the black pajamas and conical straw hat of a country peasant, but her skin was honey-fresh and her hands smooth and delicate, the typical roughness of the rice farmer absent. The boy and girl standing beside her were dressed the same way.

"It's a long chance you're taking, and a dangerous one," Dasher said, "but it might work. In fact it is the only chance Vince has."

"If I find him, I free him from POW camp; but must find before communists take him Hanoi. Too many soldiers Hanoi—POW camp very strong Hanoi."

Dasher regarded her for a few seconds, thinking that this young woman possessed a rare love that he had never before seen. "Are you sure you don't want any supplies to take with you . . . weapons, food, medicine . . . anything at all that we can help you with? How about a map?"

"I want nothing, only dongs you give me. I born, live that area, near Ban Dau. I know how take care myself and children. Live off farms, jungle, buy food with dongs, find everything I need like when poor and live with family and relatives in North Vietnam before Ho Chi Minh shake hands with Russia."

"Makes sense," Dasher said. "Traveling light the way you are dressed, you blend in with the people and the countryside and won't draw suspicion . . . a peasant girl with her younger brother and sister."

Nghia smiled. "You fly us now to place where Vince shot down?"

"I'll take you out to the helicopter. The pilot and crew have been briefed on your mission and you will be in good hands. They will put you down in the same clearing where Vince was last seen."

The drive in the jeep out to the helicopter pad took about ten minutes. Nghia and the colonel didn't talk, the only conversation being reassuring comments to the children from Nghia that the trip would be a safe one and that there was nothing for Ly-boy and Autumn Dove to fear from the helicopter though it would be a noisy ride and they would not be able to see anything but the night sky.

The jeep stopped in front of the dark hulk of the Huey, and in the darkness Autumn and Ly-boy shivered, though the night was warm. The crew took the kids aboard and strapped them into the jumpseats, and they were dumb with fright and curiosity and anxious for the trip to be over with.

Nghia and Dasher stood outside the door for a few last words.

"It's a brave and unselfish thing that you are doing," Dasher said to Nghia. "Remember that the chopper will return for you in three days, at midnight." As a measure of courtesy he refrained from smoking one of his cigars. "I wish I was going with you."

"No can make you look Vietnamese," Nghia said. "You no have hair, nose too big, eyes too round, body too tall and thick." She patted his beer belly and laughed.

336

Cleanhead sucked in his stomach, embarrassed, and smiled with her.

The jet turbine began its start-up whine and the blades slowly lifted from their droop and rotated two full revolutions before they flattened out and the characteristic *chop-chop-chop-* began to cut the moonless night.

Dasher squeezed Nghia's hand. "Find him and bring him back," he shouted above the whipping blades. He handed her up to the waiting crewman and waved goodbye.

The Huey's engines reached for takeoff RPMs and the pitch rose to a scream and the children covered their ears and huddled together, leaning on each other in the jumpseats. The helicopter vibrated violently and oscillated up and down on the skids, then, with a jolt, jumped into the air, blades beating wildly, and shot forward and upward, Dasher standing below in the rotor wash, hands on hips, his thoughts going ahead of Nghia into North Vietnam.

The Huey banked hard and climbed to three thousand feet, pointed north and west, and flew toward Pleiku and the northern highlands, the *whump-whump-whump-whump* of the blades and vibration of the airframe too noisy to allow conversation below shouting in someone's ear.

The strange ghostlike glow of the red caution light inside the Huey distorted the features of the crewmen and made them look like creatures from a bad dream, further frightening Ly-boy and Autumn Dove. Nghia put her arms around the children and pulled them closer to her in a comforting embrace, and they felt more secure and able to endure—at least for a while longer—the shakes, the noise, the scary shadows, and the mysteries of a night being invaded by the weird contraption they were flying in.

Nghia trusted the men and technology, and above all

337

else, Colonel Dasher, to put her down where they had said they would, and she had no fear of the ride, though she was apprehensive of the effect it was having on Ly-boy and Autumn.

When the Marines put her down in North Vietnam, she would be guided by her instincts, her love, and she promised herself that she would find Vince Battaglia though she was without the benefit of a sophisticated plan or any kind of military support. Her instincts were well developed and she would remember the terrain, the villages, the directions, and she would think and act and talk convincingly, totally dependent upon her wits. It could be no other way. She dozed in the jumpseat.

The change of pitch in the rotor blades and the quick drop in her stomach alerted her to the helicopter's approach into the landing zone. She looked out into the blackness, and for a moment, as she watched the stars pass by the open door while the Huey banked, there was doubt and a frightening feeling of aloneness, a fleeting panic that held her tight; but when the skids touched down in the elephant grass and the door gunner jumped to the ground, and she heard the blades reduce speed to the whispering swish of idle, she quickly unbuckled the children and herself, and the next minute she was hurrying into the treeline to await the dawn, all her senses alert and her mind a squirrel cage of activity anxious to begin the search for Battaglia.

The dark form of the assault helicopter rose from the elephant grass, pivoted south and east, and Nghia watched—squatting at the edge of the clearing, holding to the children—the Huey disappearing over the trees, chuffing in the night to finally disappear into the void.

The night covered them like a heavy blanket and there was a bite in the air, a coldness that had not been evident in the Da Nang night much farther south along the humid seacoast. The three of them crouched close together for warmth and they listened to each other's shallow breathing and to the sounds of the night closing in on them.

"When will the sun come up?" Autumn Dove snuggled closer to Nghia. "It is cold and dark and there are things in the jungle that eat people."

"I had an aunt who got eaten by a tiger," Ly-boy said. Nghia pulled Ly-boy's hair. "Hush up and stop frightening Autumn."

They spoke Vietnamese and no English, and Nghia practiced using North Vietnamese idioms and accented her words in the north's manner of speaking. The stories she told the kids helped ease the strain of being so far from familiar things, and to hasten the coming of dawn.

Autumn fell asleep first, her head drooping an inch at a time, and finally her chin dropped heavily against her chest. Nghia, her back against the buttress of a large banyan tree, the ropy vines hanging down around her, adjusted the girl's head so that it rested on her own breast which served as a pillow, and cradled her with her right arm.

Ly-boy talked on about tigers and how he wasn't afraid of them (to build up his courage) and finally became fatigued by the effort of keeping up the conversation and fell asleep with his mouth open and holding to his crutch. Nghia held him with her other arm and in a few minutes she too was asleep. The small forest animals moved quietly around the little rescue party, their big nocturnal eyes wide and their noses curiously twitching at the unusual scent.

The earth turned throughout the night and soon a sun ray the diameter of a pencil broke through the jungle canopy and pressed on Nghia's face. She woke to the scolding of monkeys in the banyan, and her first thoughts were of her childhood home not far from this very spot where monkeys in banyan trees around her hooch also woke her in the morning.

"I'm thirsty," Autumn Dove stretched like a young cat waking.

"So am I," Ly-boy said, looking around at the strange trees and broad-leafed plants. "What is that terrible noise?"

Nghia pointed into the trees. "You had better get used to them because they will be with us wherever we go. Come—I will show you how I collected water when I was a child."

Using the hanging vines, the three of them climbed into the huge banyan tree and explored until Nghia found the right bole. She reached into a depression and pulled forth her cupped hand which dripped with fresh rain water. They all drank until their bellies were filled and then they splashed their faces with the cool water.

"How do you know where you are going?" Ly-boy said as he walked and munched on one of the bananas Nghia had picked from the rain forest.

"Trust me—we will be coming to a stream soon and it wil lead us to a village. There I will send you and Autumn to make inquiries about Vince."

"Won't people in the village be suspicious of us?"

"I don't think so, but it's a chance we will have to take," Nghia said. "Are you getting tired, Ly-boy?"

"I'm doing all right." He ate the last of the banana and bent his shoulder to the crutch.

Arriving at the stream, they had a drink of water, and in a few minutes they came upon the first hooch of the village. Nghia bought a chicken and some riceballs from a toothless grandmother, using North Vietnamese dongs that Colonel Dasher had given her, and proceeded to kill and clean the bird, then to roast it on an open fire.

They ate well and the leftovers she wrapped in a banana leaf.

"Go into the village and play with the children," Nghia said. "They should know something of Vince's capture. Find out where the soldiers have taken him, but don't act too curious. If anyone asks, just tell them you are brother and sister on your way to Xem Dai to help with the rice harvest and heard that an American was shot down. Stay away from the soldiers in the village."

Ly-boy and Autumn Dove left Nghia beside the stream, feeling uneasy and very much alone.

"We talk different than the North Vietnamese," Autumn said, walking into the center of the village and noticing a group of children playing a game with dried tamarind seeds.

"Not much different—the accent is a little strange, that's all. Just try to talk like Mrs. Minh the soup lady in Cho-Chan; she's from Hanoi."

Autumn looked at him doubtfully.

"Let me do most of the talking," he said.

"I'm older," she said, indignant.

"Do you want to argue or do you want to find Vince?"

Their attempt to join with the children of the village was a disaster. A boy made fun of Ly-boy's leg and Autumn Dove threw dirt in his face, and a big fight developed with Ly-boy getting knocked down and another kid stealing his crutch.

A young soldier of about seventeen pushed the children apart with the butt of his AK-47. "What's going on here?" he demanded.

Before any of the village children had a chance to say something, Autumn Dove boldly took charge and said, "My brother and I were on our way to Xem Dai to help with the rice harvest and we stopped here because we have never seen an American and we heard that one had been shot down and captured in your village; and then these

341

bad kids made fun of my brother's leg and stole his crutch which he can't walk without and they beat us up."

"She threw dirt in my face," the older boy said and grabbed Autumn's hair.

She gave him a stiff karate kick in the stomach and he folded over. "I want my brother's crutch."

The communist soldier recovered Ly-boy's crutch. "You are not welcome here, and it is better that you leave before there is more trouble."

"We want to see the American before we leave. We've never seen one."

"He's not here; he's been taken to Song Lau. Now get out of here before I turn you over to the commandant."

Tugging and pulling at Ly-boy to walk faster, Autumn Dove was so excited in discovering where the NVA had taken Vince that she lost her way and they stumbled around for a half hour until she found the stream again and followed it back to where they had left Nghia. "She's not here!" she screamed, and sat down in the middle of the water and began to howl.

"She can't be far," Ly-boy said. "Don't get upset."

"The soldiers have taken her away to prison and we are going to stay in this stinking little village for the rest of our lives," Autumn wailed.

"Calm down and let's think this out. I'm sure she can't be far away."

Vince lifted Kruger's head and fed him a spoonful of the thin cabbage soup.

"Thanks, old buddy," Kruger said. "Lucky for me they threw us together. Why didn't they put us in separate cages?"

"Who knows what makes a gooner tick? I'm surprised they even feed us." He spooned another mouthful of soup to Kruger. "This bamboo cage is too small to stand up in and barely wide enough to lie down."

"Save some soup for yourself." Kruger looked up at Vince. "I never thought I'd see the day when I was so helpless I couldn't feed myself."

"Maybe when the gooners transfer us to the Hanoi Hilton they'll have a doctor take a look at your broken arms. You need more than those crude splints they let me put on you. How's the pain?"

"Just keep talking partner; it keeps my mind off of it." He turned his head from the spoon. "You finish the soup."

Vince unzipped his flight suit and relieved himself through the spaces between the bamboo bars in the floor; the trench underneath received the waste and collected it with the rest, which gave off an unbelievable stench.

Finished, he squatted in a corner of the tiger cage and looked out between the bars. "Here they come again; our lunch and crap break is over so the guards are letting the citizens of Song Lau back into the zoo." He watched the people crowded at the gate pour into the compound, chattering and pointing at the Americans.

"Let 'em look," Kruger said. He was sitting at the back of the cage, his splinted arms hanging along his sides, and his intense blue eyes that looked out behind the mat of blond hair were fierce.

The Viets approached the cage a few at a time and looked in, curiosity expressed in their small eyes. Some squatted on their haunches and stared, and some picked their noses or talked quietly to each other and pointed at Vince and Kruger. A woman tossed a rock into the cage and laughed when it hit Battaglia's leg. Others also thought that was funny and amused themselves by throwing stones at the Americans. The guard stood by and laughed; they clapped each time a stone made it through the bars and hit the men.

"We'll be in good company in Hanoi," Vince said to take their minds off the stoning. "Over three hundred of us up there, I hear." A stone clattered off the bamboo and

343

glanced onto the side of his head.

"When do you think they'll move us?"

"Day or two, I expect; they don't keep downed flyers in the jungle camps very long."

Kruger was able to grin. "Be good to see Kutcher and Daniels and the other guys."

"Doubt if we'll see much of anyone . . . including each other. They'll separate us up there like the commies did in Korea; and they'll keep us isolated."

The barrage of stones suddenly stopped and the villagers moved back from the cage.

"Bolthead's coming," Vince said.

An NVA major, head stiff and inflexible on his fat shoulders (he had no neck), walked out of the hooch that served as his headquarters, and stood on the porch. When he wanted to look to the side he had to turn his whole body, and he was doing this now so he could see the cage. His narrow eyes were black and malevolent and the thin hairs on his upper lip curved down along the sides in a scraggly mustache. He gave an order and pointed to the cage.

In a few minutes a soldier pushed Battaglia up the steps with the barrel of his AK-47, and the bolt-headed major stood stiff on the veranda of the hooch, his tight lips pressed together.

"Sit down, Lieutenant. Smoke?" He offered Battaglia a Russian cigarette from his gold case and showed his uneven brown-stained teeth behind an evil smile. His tunic was open at the front and his fat belly hung over his trouser belt.

They had come into the hooch and in a flash Vince's eyes took in everything in the room—the picture of Ho Chi Minh on the wall, the crude table with a pitcher of water and a glass, the small desk with the paper and pencil facing him, the bag of rice in the corner, and the kerosene lamp.

Battaglia refused the cigarette and sat down. "You can skip the preliminaries—I know what you want from me." He was looking at the blank sheet of paper and the pencil on the desk.

"You are being impolite and I find your manners offensive," the major said. He lit a cigarette for himself and closed the case.

"That's your problem, not mine." Vince matched the major's stare. "I'm not writing any confession."

The major pushed the paper toward him. "Don't be foolish. All you have to write is what your countrymen are saying in your newspapers, on your television sets, and on your college campuses."

"And what is that?"

"That the war is wrong, that you are bombing innocent Vietnamese that want nothing more than to be left alone, and that the war is between the people of the south and doesn't involve the people of the north."

"That's a lie." North Vietnam is the perpetrator of the war and is directly supporting the war in the south with troops and supplies; and we only bomb selected military targets."

"You can either write the statement I want now, without further encouragement, or you will write it later after the encouragement is applied." He nodded to the soldiers standing along the wall.

The paper remained untouched on the desk, and Battaglia's wrists were tied to his ankles so that his back muscles and nerves were stretched and within a few minutes he experienced unbearable pain.

He lay on the floor in this twisted posture for five hours, and when he was thrown back into the cage it was another several hours before he could straighten his back. The major promised him that the "encouragement" would continue tomorrow.

Kruger shook his head. "Why don't you just write the

confession. They'll get it out of you one way or another."

"Maybe . . . maybe not."

"I thought you were the guy who was bitter against the war and without any loyalties. Wasn't it Blackjack that called you the civilian Marine?"

The people drifted back and resumed throwing rocks at the cages. They shouted curses at the Americans and smiled at each other. Once in a while a guard would stick the barrel of his rifle between the bamboo and make shooting noises and then turn to the crowd and laugh wildly.

The major sat on the veranda porch, hatred in his face, drank rice wine, and preened the long thin hairs of his mustache that hung limp from perspiration. He stared straight ahead, unable to twist his head, his flabby shoulders humped up to his ears and his chin resting on his chest.

"I wonder what he's thinking?" Vince said.

Kruger turned his head lethargically and looked at the major sitting on the porch. "Bolthead doesn't think. He only reacts."

A rock hit Battaglia in the shoulder and he brushed at it like he had been bitten by a mosquito. "I don't suppose my folks will be able to find Ruthie to tell her I've been shot down."

"From what you've told me I don't think you really care, or maybe you've changed your mind about her."

"She's a symbol . . . only a symbol. She represents the associations of a time when my life was predictable and ordered—and safe," he said, and laughed, though it gave him pain in his back.

"My wife will be worried sick for the first few weeks—she'll handle it after that. I don't suppose the gooners will let us send any letters home."

A man walked up to the tiger cage and urinated on Battaglia. The villagers laughed loudly.

Chapter 19

"Well, what did you find out?" Nghia walked out from the undergrowth and stood at the edge of the stream, looking down at Autumn Dove, who sat in the water, crying. She slipped the bundle off her arm and held her hand out to Autumn. "Come out of the water."

"I thought something terrible happened to you." Autumn clung to Nghia's waist.

"I wasn't afraid because I knew you were around here somewhere and would never go very far unless you told us first," Ly-boy said. "Autumn gets hysterical when something happens that she doesn't understand."

"You always think you're so smart, Ly-boy. You were afraid too, but just didn't say anything."

"I'm back now, so stop bickering," Nghia said. "I bought some food and a few things we will need, but first tell me what you heard in the village."

"The children were very mean," Autumn Dove said. "We got in a fight and a boy stole Ly-boy's crutch and a soldier told us to leave the village and—"

"Vince is in Song Lau," Ly-boy said.

"I was going to tell her—why didn't you let me tell her?"

"You are sure he's in Song Lau?" Nghia felt the hot tears fill her eyes; her voice caught and she looked away. "Is it possible that he is only a few miles from here, in the very hamlet I was born?"

"The soldier told us he was taken there," Ly-boy said.

"Come, Song Lau is a half-day's walk and we must get there before the communists take him to Hanoi." She slung the bundle over her arm.

The country road (more of a dirt trail that occasionally widened in the clearings) leading to Song Lau had little traffic, mostly peasants that drove oxcarts filled with rice bags or stalks of bananas, and no one said anything to Nghia and the children except for an old man, carrying a basket of dried chom-chom on the end of a bamboo pole, who asked if Xem Dai had received rain that morning.

By the time the trio reached the banks of the Phuong River, the sun had become a red marble and was resting on top of the largest of three hills overlooking the Song Lau valley. The marble began to roll off the backside of the hill and the tamarind trees lining the river cast their long shadows over the deep waters and darkness started its slow invasion of the valley.

Across the river and through the tamarinds and elephant grass, the pinpoint lights of cooking fires dotted the hamlet and created a tranquil scene of families gathered around steaming rice kettles that conjured up fond memories for Nghia. Surely she still had relatives living in Song Lau. She longed to find them and discover what happened to her mother and father, brothers and sisters; but the hurt was still close to the surface and it would be better not to unearth the family sins and spread the infection again. It would be less painful to leave the past buried. She was a stranger now, and she would be treated as a stranger, even as the enemy. There would be questions that she would be unable to answer and, after all, she knew the communist mentality only too well.

From her purchases of essential supplies that were wrapped in the bundle, Nghia and the children prepared a modest dinner of steamed rice and cabbage and dried fish. After dinner each got two dried plums and some crystallized ginger, and they fell asleep next to the dying embers of the fire, arms wrapped around each other.

Through the night Nghia dreamed of the weeks she had spent with Battaglia and the children in the Da Nang house with its flowering tamarind tree, the fruit trees and garden, the walled courtyard and its reflecting pool filled with bright-colored carp, and croaking frogs. Especially, she dreamed of Vince's tenderness, the way he held her hand and combed her hair, kissed the corners of her lips, and ran his palm the length of her legs from ankles up to the inside of her thighs, and how she had grown wet as if she were a young girl with her first lover.

The dawn streaked gray and the green, dark waters of the Phuong River flowed out to the mountains with the depressing silence of a new morning in communist North Vietnam.

Nghia shook the children awake and looked overhead into the teak trees, their reddish-brown branches barely visible in the smoky mists covering the jungle that dripped with hot wetness.

The dampness seeping from this heart of darkness had soaked through the clothing of Nghia and the children and left their skin feeling clammy. Nghia's hair hung straight and heavy as if coated with a thick film of oil.

"We will cross the river upstream and look for Vince before the village comes awake," Nghia said.

She raised the leg of her pajamas and untied the heavy-Ka-Bar knife from her calf, cut a hole in the top of the green coconut that she had collected the night before, and passed the coconut around for everyone to drink from. The clear milk and nutritious endosperm was cool on their lips and filled their stomachs.

"The forest is scary—I don't like it," Autumn said.

Ly-boy looked around, his eyebrows raised. "It's dark

349

and slimy and the noises are awful, like the animals hiding behind the trees waiting to eat you." He moved closer to Nghia.

"We have work to do," Nghia said. "The sooner we find Vince the sooner we will be out of this frightening place."

Song Lau was only a few kilometers from the Laotian border and was located in the thickest and most inhospitable jungle in all Southeast Asia. It was a dangerous and formidable environment where tigers roamed, poisonous snakes hung from trees, and leeches and sucking insects attached themselves to the skin and drained a person's blood.

The trio reached the bamboo footbridge spanning the river gorge and Autumn Dove looked down into the cruel rocks and white water fifty feet below. She froze with her hands gripped to the horizontal bamboo poles and refused to take another step, her eyes wide with terror and her face drained of blood.

"This is the only way across." Nghia tried without success to unclench Autumn Dove's fingers. "You must try to walk to the other side.

"I can't . . . I just can't."

"If I go first, will you follow behind me?" Ly-boy said. "Nghia can hold you from behind."

"I will not walk across this bridge."

"You must."

"I won't."

The bridge swayed on its ropes of vine and the spray and mist from the crashing water below rose up from the rocks and covered the span.

Nghia dropped the bundle from her shoulder and pulled Autumn Dove back off the bridge. "You stay here with Ly-boy. I will go across alone."

Ly-boy looked at Nghia doubtfully.

"I will be back in a few hours—you two take care of

each other. There is food in the bundle. Also, stay hidden . . . there are soldiers all around this area and they could become suspicious and ask questions." She thought for a few seconds. "Ly-boy, we are going to need weapons. You and Autumn learned how to obtain necessities while living in the streets of Cho-Chan. Follow the soldiers and see if you can steal two rifles with ammunition." She kissed them both and, with the fleetness of a rabbit, ran across the long bridge and disappeared into the thick undergrowth of ficus on the other side.

The dawning jungle was filled with an oppressiveness as heavy as lead. Nghia followed the forest path that wound through the wild rubber trees and stands of teak, their branches and trunks covered with ropy vines and hanging moss. Large orchids in a variety of colors grew in the crotches of the trees and the monkeys, only beginning to wake, stared down at her from their nests.

She skirted the main part of the hamlet and stayed on the periphery, coming out at the top of a slope that led down into a deep ravine where she remembered the French garrison at Song Lau had built a camp before the fall of Dien Bien Phu. It was here that she expected to find the North Vietnamese military post where Vince and Kruger were held prisoner.

The ravine was filled with ground fog and it covered her descent along the trail cut from the limestone walls. The path was wet with the decay of leaves and several times she slipped on the steep trail. The smell of rotting jungle was everywhere.

At the bottom of the ravine the trail widened, and through the trees she could see the perimeter wire of the communist compound. There was still very little light and the camp was covered in a blanket of gray mist.

Cautiously approaching the wire she heard women's laughter and she jumped into the ficus along the trail and

351

lay hidden. She looked out between the broad leaves and waited.

A group of young women dressed in ao dais emerged out of the mist and the two guards at the gate freely ran their hands over the girls, ostensibly to check that nothing was concealed under the ao dais, everyone laughing, and unlocked the gate, patting each girl on the behind before releasing them onto the path back to the village.

Nghia smiled behind the ficus and watched the Song Lau whores file past her. She knew how she was going to get into the compound.

The rest of the morning, before returning to Ly-boy and Autumn Dove, Nghia explored the hamlet. Little had changed in the years since she had been sold into prostitution. The storytelling tree where the elders used to spin yarns for the children still stood in the center of the village, as did the community well where she'd drawn the family's water. A freshly laundered ao dai hung drying near the well.

The old hooch where she had lived with her desperately poor family had burned down and in its place was a larger, sturdier home occupied by the communist cadre leader. Next to it was the communal center where political meetings were held.

A few people looked at her curiously, as if vaguely recognizing her, but she quickly moved on and acted as if she was busy and a normal part of the village's life, discouraging suspicion.

The sun was high overhead and hot when she finished her snooping and returned to the bridge. She had refreshed her memory to the layout of Song Lau and gathered information that would be valuable in getting Battaglia out of the NVA compound. The laundered ao dai was neatly folded and tucked under her arm.

From her side of the river she couldn't see the children, but she knew they were hidden in the foliage, waiting her return. Taking a few extra minutes to pick green bananas and breadfruit for roasting, she nimbly negotiated the bamboo bridge and melted into the jungle where the roar of the river was muffled by the ficus and ferns, the mahogany and teak.

The jungle sounds were normal—the usual calls of the parrots and the chattering of monkeys—but Nghia waited, quietly listening. Satisfied that there was nothing unusual about, she called for the children? "Autumn . . . Ly-boy . . . where are you?"

The rustling of branches turned her head into the massive ceiba tree spread overhead and she saw two peanut heads poke out from among the leaves.

"Come down—I have food to cook."

"Is it safe?" Autumn said.

"There were soldiers here earlier." Ly-boy pushed an AK-47 assault rifle through the branches. "They must be looking for this."

"And this." Autumn Dove showed her rifle.

"Good work," Nghia said. "Bring them down—we have plans to make."

Autumn slid down the great trunk first, the rifle and bandolier of ammunition slung around her small torso. Ly-boy was higher in the tree and followed her down a minute later with his rifle and magazines of ammo.

"Do you know how to use one of these?" Nghia asked Ly-boy.

He looked at one of the rifles a long time without saying anything.

"Don't try to be a big shot, Ly-boy," Autumn Dove said. "Tell the truth."

"I've seen rifles used by the ARVN soldiers, but I've never fired one. I think I can figure out how they work, though."

"Vince will know," Autumn Dove said.

"We may have to use the rifles before we find him." Nghia picked up a rifle and looked at it and frowned. "Heavy." She fitted it to her shoulder and aimed at a tree. "Find out how it works and teach me," she said to Ly-boy.

Nourishment was important to keep up their strength and to build up their reserves for the difficulties that lay ahead. Nghia started a small fire, and when the flames had burned down to a bed of coals she roasted the green bananas in their peel, and the breadfruit she cut into slices and placed next to the bananas.

"Where did you learn to do this?" Autumn said.

"You forget that I am a poor country girl. I lived in Song Lau until I was fifteen and many times I cooked just like this for the family. These things you never forget."

After their meal, Ly-boy went back to figuring out how to shoot the AK-47. "I think I know how it works," he said to Nghia.

"Show me," she said, squatting next to him.

"This metal case holds the bullets." He let her handle a magazine. "It goes in the bottom of the rifle, here." He shoved it up into the breech until there was a sharp *click*. He pressed the magazine release. "That's how it comes out when you run out of bullets and want to put in some more."

She went through the same motions on the rifle.

"When you want to shoot, you look through the back sight and line it up with the little post on the front sight that you point at the communist soldier you want to kill. Then you pull the trigger." He handed her the rifle.

They went upstream from the bridge where the roar of the river was very loud and the report of the rifle could not be heard. She sat on a rock and Ly-boy instructed her once again. She aimed the rifle at a breadfruit tree and

354

slowly pulled the trigger. Nothing happened.

"I forget to tell you," Ly-boy said. "You must pull this lever first to bring the first bullet up into position for firing."

Nghia pulled back the bolt on the AK-47 and released it with a *clank*. The top round in the magazine was shoved into the chamber and the rifle was charged.

"Good," Ly-boy said. "Now it's ready."

Autumn Dove closed her eyes and plugged her ears with her fingers.

A breadfruit the size of a man's head hung from a lower branch. Nghia carefully aimed while chanting: "Rear sight on, front sight on . . ."

She squeezed the trigger and the breadfruit splattered.

"Tot qua!" Very good! Ly-boy said.

"Did she shoot it?" Autumn Dove still had her fingers in her ears and her eyes closed.

Nghia fired several more shots with equally good results. "That's enough—I know how to use the rifle."

The three of them went back to the ceiba tree and had a long sleep under its branches in preparation for the longest night of their lives.

The sun had settled behind the forested hills, and Nghia rose from her nap and stood in the remaining light under the ceiba tree and wiggled into the tight ao dai she had taken from the village well. She lifted the leg of the pantaloons, retied the Marine Ka-Bar to her calf, and slipped the sling of one of the AK-47s over her shoulder.

Her hair was smooth down her back and she placed the wide conical straw hat on her head and said, "How do I look?"

"Like a jungle princess," Autumn Dove said. She smoothed out a wrinkle in the ao dai. "Be careful—please don't get killed." A tear dropped out from the corner of

355

her eye and she threw her arms around Nghia.

"I'll be back before the sun comes up."

"Will you have Vince with you?" Ly-boy said.

"If everything goes well." She turned toward the river and her breathing was quick. "Ly-boy, be ready to use the rifle."

Before he could ask how she meant that, she was gone, walking through the ficus and ferns, and disappeared across the swinging bamboo ridge to the other side of the river.

How will I get him out? Is he in the camp? What will I do when I get in? She was worried and afraid, and the concern on her face showed in the rosy twilight filtering through the trees.

The jungle trail, narrow and bumpy with tree roots, was not easy to follow in the darkened forest. The birds and monkeys had quieted with the coming of the gloaming, and Nghia felt lonely and not at all sure of the sensibility of what she was doing in North Vietnam. Her love for Battaglia pushed her on, however, and the odds against the success of the mission were forgotten.

She hid the AK-47 in the undergrowth and waited in the trees a hundred yards from the wire, and after the first whore arrived and went through the gate she hung back a few minutes and then approached the guards.

When she spoke, her Vietnamese was candy sweet and dripped with sensuality. "It's a beautiful evening; you handsome men must be lonely for a woman." She smiled prettily and moved up close to one of the soldiers. "Would you like to check closely under my ao dai to be sure I'm not bringing anything dangerous into the camp?"

The young man's face tightened and his eyes glazed over as Nghia took his hand in hers and guided it between her thighs, over her buttocks and across her breasts.

"Do I pass?" she murmured.

"It is a pity that you girls are reserved for the use of the officers only." He slapped her on the bottom and shooed her into the camp, locking the gate behind her.

The tiger cage was set at the back of the compound and guarded by a soldier armed with an AK-47. There was still enough light for Nghia to see that the cage was occupied by two men sitting on the floor. Her heart swelled.

As she approached the cage, swinging her hips sensually to distract the guard, her eyes were hard and focused on the dark-haired man inside the tiger cage.

Vince rolled his head upward when he heard the approach of steps in the still air of the camp, and at first thought nothing of the girl walking across the compound, for there had been girls every night since he had been brought here. Most stopped by the cage out of curiosity to look at him.

Something was different about this girl, however, and his jangled mind jumped around in confusion trying to put the illogical signals together. He watched her for a few seconds, unable to distinguish her features in the fading light, and then dropped his head to stare at the floor again, no longer interested. He heard the steps stop in front of the cage.

"Good evening," Nghia said politely to the guard.

"Hello, sister," He looked at her closely. "I haven't seen you before."

"I do not come often—there is work enough elsewhere that keeps me occupied—at the post in Lua Duong."

He frowned and tried to remember what kind of camp was at Lua Duong.

"How long will the American pigs remain here?" she asked.

"They will be taken by truck to Hanoi in the morning."

"They should be shot immediately for their crimes."

Vince understood little Vietnamese, but the girl's

357

words made his tired mind struggle to hear more clearly, for there was something recognizable in the sound of her voice that drew him. His head hurt from the effort.

He felt a bump against the cage and looked up. The girl was leaning against the bamboo bars, still talking to the guard. She had pulled the pantaloon up above her knee, away from the guard, and her exposed leg was right at Vince's eye level. He saw the Ka-Bar knife lashed to her calf only inches away, and he sat on the floor of the tiger cage staring at it, confused. Then it all came to him—the butter-smooth skin, the perfect curve of the leg, the dimpled knee, the honey-nut color; in a flash it was clear: the sugar-walk across the compound, the lyrical voice, the loose hand on the hip . . . He raised his head and looked into black bold eyes that stared through him and he thought he had gone mad.

Carefully he moved his hand up and pushed his fingers through the bamboo bars and pulled the tie string. The handle of the knife tilted into his hand and he pulled the blade into the cage with him. He couldn't resist leaving his hand on her leg for a few seconds, caressing the toned flesh with his fingers and remembering the pleasures that it had given him.

"I hate Americans," Nghia suddenly said to the guard. She kneeled down and spit on Vince, and whispered in English to him: "I watch for you at gate; I have rifle. Wait for dawn."

Nghia stood and looked across the compound to the major's hooch. "It is time for me to go," she said to the guard. "The commandant is waiting."

The guard spit on Battaglia and laughed. "Yes, you shouldn't keep him waiting for he becomes angry when his patience is tried."

Her walk to the hooch was slow and she felt Vince's eyes on every step she took. The tears were right at the surface.

What will I do when I reach the hooch? She stopped and looked in, a foot on the first step. The major with the fat shoulders and no neck lay on a cot, stripped and being fondled by one of the girls. The commandant was well oiled with sweat and looked like a seal lolling in the sand.

The light was fading fast, and when she looked back she wasn't sure if the guard was watching her, so she walked into the hooch and stood beside the girl.

"Hello, sister," Nghia said.

The girl looked up and frowned at Nghia's striking beauty. "Who are you? Where did you come from?" Her voice was edged with jealousy.

"I was invited by the commandant."

Nghia looked down at the major. An empty bottle of rice wine lay on the floor next to the cot and he snored loudly. He had enormous swollen testicles.

She talked with the girl until the last trace of sunlight was gone and then left the hooch and walked to the gate without being noticed by anyone.

"Leaving so soon?" the guard said.

"My officer is in a depressed mood tonight and is unable to perform. He dismissed me early."

"What a pity. With me you would not suffer such a disappointment."

She smiled sweetly. "Of that I have no doubt."

The guard took extra time to explore Nghia's body in the customary search, smiling at her healthy condition, and reluctantly opened the gate to let her out.

At the bend in the trail, Nghia recovered the rifle and hid in the ficus to wait the dawn. She sat with her back against a teak tree and stretched her legs out while she listened to the night sounds that closed in on her like a door closing on a dark room. The fright of being alone and not knowing if she would be dead or alive in the morning kept her awake for hours until she was overcome by mental and physical fatigue and she collapsed in sleep, the AK-47 wrapped in her arms and her head bent forward on her chest.

While Nghia slept in the undergrowth, Vince used the Ka-Bar to cut the lashing on the bamboo poles. "Keep a close eye on the gooner," he whispered to Kruger.

To Vince the sound of the blade slicing through the lashing was sweet music. Whenever the guard came within twenty yards of the tiger cage he stopped cutting.

The lashing was made from tough hemp stems, a coarse fiber that substituted for wire and defied the assault of the best blades. Battaglia worked feverishly, but not until the leaden light of daybreak paled the compound did he have two of the bamboo bars loose on the side of the cage.

Vince let the guard pass by the cage, then quickly squeezed through the opening and plunged the knife into the back of the man's neck, severing his spinal cord in an instant, not a noise coming from him. Battaglia stuffed him into the tiger cage and took his rifle and ammo pouches.

While the camp still slept, he and Kruger crouched in a bamboo grove near the gate and waited, just as Nghia had instructed.

"How are the arms?" He glanced at Kruger's splints and looked back at the guard pacing lethargically near the gate. The second guard leaned against the gate post, dozing.

"Getting better every minute," he said. "Where's Nghia?"

Vince looked up at the paling sky. "She'll make her move soon."

The Song Lau whores emptied from the hooches and gathered in the compound and walked to the gate, holding hands and laughing softly together. The guards came awake, felt them up, and dismissed them through the gate which they had unlocked and swung open.

As the last girl disappeared down the trail and the guard was pulling the gate shut, Battaglia jerked involuntarily and said, "Look—there's Nghia."

She walked out of the jungle, pointed the AK-47 at the guards, and waited. She had no evidence that Vince and Kruger had broken out of the tiger cage, but she knew that if they had, Vince would have followed her instructions and would be hiding close-by.

"What are you doing, woman?" the guard said.

She ignored his question and warned, "Don't try to stop me or I will kill you."

Fifty yards away, Battaglia walked out of the bamboo grove, helping Kruger, whose arms hung uselessly in makeshift slings around his neck. One of the guards, the quiet one who had said nothing when the girls came and went, swung his rifle down on Nghia. A wince of pain crossed Nghia's face and she shot the man dead. The other guard quickly stepped to the side and fired wildly, his bullets splintering the gatepost.

Nghia dove to the ground and rolled in a helpless attempt to escape the bullets stitching their way across the ground toward her. She looked up in desperation at Battaglia. The AK-47 was already bucking in his hands and she felt the guard's blood splatter over her. There was a heavy *thud* and the man, dead before he hit the ground, sprawled next to her, his eyes wide open and staring blankly up into the trees.

"Are you hit?" he said, kneeling beside her and pulling her into his arms.

"No . . . I okay."

"Thank God."

On his knees he cradled her. Nghia's long tresses hung straight to the ground and her long Manchu eyes, black and daring, looked deep into the back of his head. "I love you," she whispered.

"My God—how did you do it?" He could hear the

361

yelling and confusion behind him that meant that he had only seconds to act. "Let's go, Kruger," he said, and grabbed Nghia by the hand and the three of them plunged off the trail into the undergrowth.

Morning light had penetrated the thick forest canopy and the broad, deep green leaves of the ficus were now distinguishable against the hard reddish-brown bark of the mahogany and teak trees. A monkey looked down from a high branch and screamed at the intruders and swung away on a liana vine to another tree.

"How you doing, Kraut—need some help?"

"My legs aren't broken—it's my arms. Keep humping." Kruger would never speak of the pain that shot through every step.

Battaglia ran beside Nghia, slapped at the plants, and talked to her: "I have no idea where we're going, sweetheart; I hope you do. The entire garrison is after us and we don't have a prayer of getting away unless you have a plan to lose them."

Nghia, as well as Vince, knew their chances were slim that they could escape from Song Lau. The NVA were excellent jungle fighters and they knew the terrain and had an overwhelming force to run them down—and they were tenacious. With Kruger injured, the chances to evade their pursuers were further diminished. The intelligent choice—and the only real chance she had—was to reach the bridge. If she could get them to the bridge she knew they had a chance.

She took the lead and circled around to the trail that climbed out of the ravine. Vince saw the trail snaking through the mahogany and teak trees, and brought the group to a halt. Nghia looked at him, puzzled.

"We've got to slow them down," he said. "They're overtaking us and we won't last long at this pace. Up there in the outcropping of rocks where the trail cuts across the ledge we can set up an ambush."

They were all breathing hard and Battaglia felt the long wormy lines of sweat hot on his back, running down under his armpits and soaking into his filthy flight suit. "We stand a better chance if we can drop a few of them right away."

Kruger spit. His soil-caked face and brow were smeared black and encrusted with dried blood from the slashings he'd received when he crashed through the trees with his parachute. "Whatever you think Lieutenant—they never told me at Pensacola that it would be like this." His face pinched to hold back the pain.

They reached the rocks and Vince and Nghia quickly tore a number of ficus plants up by their roots and jammed them into the crevices for concealment. Down below in the ravine, the chattering Vietnamese stupidly bunched together and pecked about like a roost of barnyard chickens and searched the undergrowth for Nghia and their prisoners.

"We're in great position," Vince said. "They'll have to funnel up this draw to reach us and the cover is thin. We'll hold our fire until they're halfway up."

Rising out of the foliage, stripped to the waist and gleaming like a wet, lardy seal, the lock-necked major led his scattered troops to the bottom of the trail, pointed his pistol at the cliff, and shouted, "*Oug muon cac heo!*" I want the pigs! He charged up the trail, his troops running behind him.

Well hidden in the rocks, Vince and Nghia waited with their rifles charged, and when the commandant had gotten close enough so that Battaglia could hear his hoarse, whistling breaths, he shot him through the head.

They killed six and wounded four before the communists ran back into the cover at the bottom of the ravine.

"Let's get out of here, Battaglia said. "It'll take them a few minutes to recover, and by then we can have a good lead."

The relief was short-lived, however, and when they reached the top and looked back, the soldiers were running up the trail after them.

Nghia bolted down the backside of the slope, Vince right behind and helping Kruger. Within minutes, bullets were splattering into trees beside the trail and tearing through the undergrowth.

"They shout for us surrender," Nghia said, panting, the long hair flying about her head and shoulders, her strong, healthy legs taking long strides.

"How much farther?"

"Maybe one minute—two minute."

Vince could barely hear her voice over the roar of the river. The trail had curved down to run parallel to the gorge and the NVA bullets whined off the flinty rock in flat richochets. Kruger looked like he was going to pass out, but Vince kept him going, ready to heave him over his shoulder and carry him if he dropped.

Fifty yards ahead, the footbridge came into view, swinging in the gorge mist. The yellow bamboo, bleached white by the sun, stood like a span between life and death, and Vince instantly understood Nghia's plan.

"Help Kruger across, Nghia. I'll hold the gooners off until you get to the other side. Then you can cover me while I make a run for it."

An AK-47 firing on automatic opened up on the opposite side of the bridge, stopping the communists.

"Who's that?" Vince shouted.

"Ly-boy." Nghia was already at the bridge and had Kruger around the waist with one arm, holding to the suspension rope with the other.

They started across, the rifle slugs smashing into the bamboo and ripping the wood to pieces until it flew wildly around her and Kruger. Battaglia was crouched in front of the bridge, raking the trail with fire.

Halfway across the span, Nghia lost her grip on the

364

one-hundred-eighty-pound Kruger and screamed. Vince turned to see him fall into the bamboo poles and slowly begin to slip through, the bridge swinging in short arcs, his feet and legs searching for a purchase to stop his slide into the gorge.

The rifle slung over his shoulder, Battaglia leaped onto the bridge and caught Kruger by the foot and hauled him back through the bamboo and vine. Nghia was overcome with exhaustion from the long chase and slumped against Vince.

While Ly-boy continued his harassing fire, Battaglia carried Kruger over his shoulder and Nghia around the waist to the other side of the gorge and laid them behind the protection of the teak where Ly-boy was firing. He winked at Ly-boy and slapped him on the back. Autumn Dove had her head buried in the ferns, her hands over her ears and her little butt sticking in the air like a plucked chicken.

Ka-Bar in his fist, bullets whizzing over his head, Battaglia crawled back to the bridge and hacked away at the suspension ropes. The sky overhead seen through the tree branches had brightened and was streaked with the first blue of morning.

Working on his back and holding to the thick vine rope while he cut, he could feel the bridge sag with the weight of soldiers starting across. He picked up the rifle and shot the first man in line. The impact of the burst knocked him back into the soldiers behind him and he slumped into the raging water, taking another infantryman with him through the rickety bamboo.

Rounds from the NVA poured in on Battaglia and he had to flatten in the depression below the bridge. The knife was sharp and of excellent steel and cut well against the vine rope; he was more than halfway through and needed only another minute to cut the second rope in two. The first rope dangled above the water, one end still attached to the footbridge which now leaned at a precarious angle and swayed in greater and greater arcs.

The communists on the bridge, half of whom were struggling to turn back, the other half working forward to reach Battaglia, were unable to move faster than a few feet at a time due to the angle and unsteadiness of the collapsing bridge. The span suddenly dropped a foot and they grabbed the ropes.

Realizing that time had run out for them, and in a last burst of hate, the NVA rushed Vince at the same time the Ka-Bar sliced through the last strands of rope.

The bridge separated with a loud *pop* and splintering bamboo, collapsing in the middle and dumping the communist infantry into the gorge. The screams of the men and the breaking up of the bridge could be heard over the raging waters into which everything fell to be swept away and dashed against the cruel rocks.

Except for Autumn Dove, who remained with her head buried in the ferns, the rest of the party stood on the edge of the gorge and watched the grotesque spectacle of bodies and sections of bridge being torn apart by tons of white water. Not until the last arm and leg stopped thrashing and the bodies floated face down among the pieces of bamboo in the eddies and shallows did they turn away, pick up their weapons, and straggle into the jungle.

A few hundred yards into the rain forest, Vince stopped and pulled Nghia and Ly-boy and Autumn Dove into his arms. He had lost weight, he smelled bad, and he looked like hell, but none of them cared about that. They hugged him back and everyone had a good cry.

"You'll have to forgive us, Kraut."

Kruger smiled and leaned up against a tree, looking in the other direction, his own eyes growing wet.

"I was wrong about everything. I love all of you so very much."

366

"We love you too, Vince," Autumn Dove said. "I hope we'll never be separated again."

Ly-boy just smiled, leaning on his crutch with one arm and hugging Vince with the other.

Standing on tiptoes, Nghia's pouting lips were only a few inches from Vince's face, her two arms wrapped around his neck. She tied her arms there and tried to speak, her lips moving, but all she could do was cry and laugh.

They stood under the teak and mahogany trees, huddled together, surrounded by the ficus and ferns, and being scolded by the black monkeys, the first sun rays of morning breaking through the forest canopy in long pencil streams of light and casting a cathedral-like glow on their faces.

"Looks like we made it—good job, everybody," Battaglia said. "Which way now?—it's a long walk home."

Nghia pointed into the rain forest and, seeing Vince's worried face, laughed and then patted his cheek. "We be home Da Nang tonight. Chopper come midnight at place where you land with parachute."

Hand in hand they walked through the forest, noiseless and unmolested, putting Song Lau and all the war and suffering behind them, and they thought only of their future together. By nightfall they would reach the clearing. Nghia would cook them her good food and they would rest and talk about America. At midnight the Huey would come and take them back to Da Nang.

"You will like Wichita," Vince said to Autumn Dove and Ly-boy. "I'll take you to the secret hiding place and you can stand in the top of the old cottonwood tree and see miles of golden wheat waving in the breeze."

"What's wheat?" Ly-boy asked.

"Something like rice."

"Marines have base in Wichita for fly Phantom jets?"

Nghia said, her black marbles looking boldly at him the way they always did when something important was on her mind.

"The Corps has jet bases in El Toro, Cherry Point . . . and at Pensacola where new pilots are trained. Nothing in Wichita."

"Then we go Pensacola. You teach new pilots how bomb Ban Dau, kill Migs, and escape North Vietnam if shot down. Be big general soon."

"Stay in the Marines!" Vince said.

"We talk Colonel Dasher."

He smiled and squeezed her tight against him. "Maybe so . . . maybe so."

"Do they have kung-fu movies in Pensacola?" Autumn Dove said.